BLOODWISH

Book four

Tima Maria Lacoba

BOOKS BY TIMA MARIA LACOBA

Laura's Locket: A Dantonville Chronicle
BloodGifted: Book 1 of the Dantonville Legacy
BloodPledge: Book 2 of the Dantonville Legacy
BloodVault: Book 3 of the Dantonville Legacy

Published By
Tima Maria Lacoba

Editing by Dionne Lister
Book Cover by JC Clarke thegraphicsshed@gmail.com

Formatting By Paradox Book Covers & Formatting

License Notes

CONTENTS

CHAPTER 1 – PORTRAIT

Zoe Peterson's designer heels clicked on the parquetry flooring of her Surry Hills gallery as she prepared to lock up for the night. It had been a successful evening. She'd received several offers for one painting in particular. It was simply entitled, *My Laura*. The beautiful young woman in the painting had intrigued many.

One man had stood staring at it for, what seemed like, hours. That was one reason she'd noticed him: he'd barely glanced at the rest of the exhibition. The second reason was the fact he was also tall and attractive in a dishevelled kind of way. His mussed brown hair set off his ice-blue eyes, and he hadn't shaved in days, whether through laziness or an attempt to grow a beard, she couldn't tell. Then he'd abruptly left, without making an offer.

She shrugged, dismissed him from her thoughts, and continued to lock up. Zoe did a final patrol of the gallery before strolling past the other prize nominees to the portrait that had everyone talking.

The unknown artist had been a popular choice for the coveted prize. For the first time in years, the entire committee had voted unanimously. All had agreed the technical skill and the detailed approach to the subject was unsurpassed.

'Definitely should be entered in the Archibald Prize,' one of them had said.

She couldn't agree more.

Beneath the recessed floodlight, dark auburn hair, luminous porcelain complexion and unusual lavender eyes stared back at her. Who was she, this girl in the painting? The artist's lover perhaps? She wouldn't be surprised. If only they could find him, it would be the first thing she'd ask.

She craned her neck to view his signature in the bottom right of the painting – *John Phillip Reynold*. Why hadn't she heard of him before? Her secretary had scoured the Internet searching for any other works by him. He didn't have a website like most other artists. Mystery man.

David, her secretary and right-hand man, strode out from the office. 'I officially give up. Our man doesn't exist!'

'Any response to the notice in the papers?'

He shook his head. 'Not even a flea bite.'

'That's ridiculous! Nobody submits a portrait and then disappears.' Frustration laced her voice as she turned and faced him.

David crossed his arms. 'This guy did. I went everywhere online that was legal, and some that weren't. Even checked the hospitals in case the guy had an accident. And before you ask, I rang the morgue. They've got no one by that name.'

She rubbed her temples. Artists! Why did they have to make life difficult? According to the contest rules, they couldn't award the prize without the artist being present, and the official ceremony was only a few weeks away. Unless he showed up—and soon—first prize would go to the runner-up. Blasted shame.

'Maybe it's time we got the cops onto this.'

The front doorbell rang. She sighed. 'Doesn't the Closed sign mean anything anymore?'

'It's that bloke again, the one who keeps coming in here and staring at the portrait.' David nudged her.

Sure enough, peering through the dark glass and holding up—what looked like an ID—stood the same tall, attractive man. 'Open up. Police.'

The guy was a cop? Zoe's gaze panned to David.

'Don't look at me. I didn't call him.'

She hurried to the door, and cracked it open wide enough to examine his badge. 'Anything the matter?'

'Detective Inspector Matt Sommers. I need to ask you a few questions about one of your clients.' Steely grey-blue eyes gazed back at her. He pocketed his ID, unfolded the newspaper that had been tucked under his arm and showed it to her. 'The painter in your missing persons notice.'

Zoe recognised the advert she and David had just been speaking about. They had posted the first one a few months ago, doing a repeat, and final ad only yesterday. Her stomach gave a nasty little lurch as she worked through the reasons for the detective being here. There could only be one conclusion. 'The guy's dead, right? That's why you're here, isn't it?'

His lips thinned, and his gaze slid past her. David's footsteps echoed on the polished floor as he joined her. 'Is everything okay?'

'Somewhere we can talk?'

Her thoughts were a muddle as she ushered the detective into her office. Had his visits to the gallery been part of his investigation or something more? And probably more importantly, what to do with the painting if the artist really was dead? Then again, what could she or David tell the police? They'd never met the guy, only seen his photo, which he'd sent through with his application.

'Tell me everything you know about him.'

'Not much to tell. Never met him.' She retrieved a folder from her desk and handed it to him. 'All the paperwork's in there. The painting was delivered via courier.'

The detective's head bent over the mass of papers, his lips pulled taut as he stared at the artist's photo. She was sure he'd suppressed a sneer.

'Mind if I take these with me?'

'Go ahead. Everything's stored on here anyway.' She waved toward her laptop.

He placed the papers back into the folder, tucked the newspaper in as well, closed it and stood. 'Thanks. We'll keep you updated.'

'Something must've happened to him, right?' David, ever ready for any juicy piece of gossip, smiled and leaned forward in his seat.

The detective's eyes steeled. 'As I said, we'll keep you updated.'

'Wasn't he a mine of information,' David said as Zoe returned from seeing the detective out.

'Something's going on for sure.' She pivoted on her heel and strode back out into the dark gallery to stand in front of the painting of Laura.

'Now what? Keep it up or take it down?' David had followed her out.

Good question. There was nothing in the contest rules about withdrawing a deceased artist's work. That is, if he was dead. But, what if the guy was just a crazy recluse?

She stared into the unusual lavender eyes of the mysterious girl in the portrait and wondered if she knew.

CHAPTER 2 – NUMB

ALEC

I'd heard it said that the mantle passes from one generation to the next.

And Luc's was damned weighty.

Princeps for nearly a century, yet only now did it sit heavily on my shoulders. It had all been Luc's work—his machinations, his presence at my shoulder that ensured I had the respect of the Brethren.

But he was no more. Lord Luc Lebrettan, the man who had been my maker, my mentor and my friend was dead, leaving me as sole leader of the Brethren.

You wanted this, Munro—princeps without Luc's interference. Well, now you have it.

… But not like this! Not like this!

I stepped outside. Some of the staff were draping the sides of the chateau in black crepe. Blood tears smeared their faces. All wore black attire.

Three pairs of eyes turned in my direction, as I reached the crypt.

Blood, dirt and tears smeared Cal, Sam and Terens's faces. I dug my nails into my palms and clenched my jaw as I met their stares. None of us would ever forget Luc, but to our satisfaction, we'd dealt with their killers. Luc and Judith had been avenged.

I swallowed and glanced around the ruins. They'd cleared a lot— levelled the domes and filled in the massive cavity created by the explosions. Only a narrow opening remained. Some of the household staff helped, their green uniform jackets strewn on the ground. Using picks, shovels and some their bare hands, they brought down the remains of the chapel.

Nothing of the bloodvault would remain. Thankfully, we'd managed to collect most of the Ingenii blood vials, but some had still been destroyed. It was an inestimable loss. How would we keep its destruction secret? Should the Brethren find out, how would they respond? Each of the prefects had been given a few weeks worth of blood vials as reward for their loyalty to the Principate. At the time, it had been a good move as it had ended the rebellion. But how would they feel once the vials run out? Having tasted the daylight, would they demand more? I barely had enough left to cover the period of Laura's pregnancy. How much did each of the men have? I had no idea.

Cal spied me, dropped his shovel and brushed the dirt from his hair. 'You okay?'

I nodded. 'You?'

He shrugged and used his shirt to wipe away the dust and sweat from his chest. 'It'll take some getting used to. Good that Marcus is back.'

Marcus Antonius Pulcher had been their original commander, nearly two-thousand years ago. He'd passed command to his son, Luc, sometime after establishing the Brethren Principate.

'You are now Lord D'Antonville.' Cal's eyes bore into mine.

My throat dried. 'I know. Huge shoes to fill.' I looked around for Jake. With a flick of his head, he indicated the still-unfilled pit. 'Marcus and

Jake are down there. Went to get their bodies.'

A pit of another kind opened in my stomach. I swallowed hard, again. Would there be anything left to retrieve? The flames and heat from the massive explosions would have reduced everything to ash.

Cal must've read the expression on my face. 'Yeah, yeah, I know. Doubt there's anything left of them, but he had to go … you know….'

I nodded. Last chance to see his son, or at least his remains. That took guts.

Marcus appeared, springing from the narrow gap amidst the rubble— face ashen, jaw tightly clenched. His gaze met mine. 'Yours now. It belongs to the—' his voice raspy with unshed tears '-master of D'Antonville.'

Covered in black ash and grit, Luc's green ward ring lay in his open palm. It was responsible for the psychic shield guarding the princep's resident. For nearly two thousand years, it had been on Luc's finger. I glanced at Marcus. He was the first Lord D'Antonville before passing it to his son. He had as much right to wear that ring as I had. 'What about you?'

He shook his head. 'You've rightfully earned it. Take it.'

Over his shoulder, Jake emerged from the pit, dusted himself off and came towards us. Red rimmed his eyes. 'Luc explain how it works?'

'It's based on thought control. Imagine a shield around the estate as a door. See it opening and closing, allowing some to enter, some to leave.' Luc had explained to me how the ward ring worked early in my transformation.

Peeking above his shoulders, Terens's crossed swords caught the glint of moonlight as he and Sam approached. The thud of their boots on the frosty ground was reduced to a faint echo by the blood roaring in my ears. I shook my head to clear it.

I took a deep breath and slipped it on my finger. Unlike the serpent ring, there was no special warmth or tingling. Instead, as I looked into the night sky, the shimmering outline of the defensive shield appeared: a gossamer dome, through which I could see the stars, enveloping the estate in a protective bubble.

It was staggering.

My jaw dropped open. So this was what Luc had been able to see all these centuries! How would it look during the day? And this was what the now deceased Rebel prefect, Count Timur, saw around his fortress after stealing the ring from Luc. Much good it had done him. Acid burned in my stomach at the thought of the many lives he'd destroyed.

'Do you still believe you can replicate whatever it is in the Ingenii's blood that enables us to daywalk?' Marcus's voice jolted me from my musings. Bits of dirt and ash fell from him as he dusted himself down.

His question took me by surprise. Only the day before, he'd expressly forbidden me to attempt anything of the sort, fearful it could adversely affect the curse. Although I couldn't see how it could. 'Why this sudden change?'

His eyes held a dangerous glint as he shook specks of dust from his hair. 'I have nothing left that wretched witch can take from me. Luc was all I had, and he's gone.' The enlarged blue vein in his left temple throbbed. 'Deus! The curse is about to end, and he should've been here to see it! He did everything possible...'

In the short time I'd known Marcus, I'd witnessed a man with deep passions held in check with almost superhuman control. His many centuries secluded in a monastery no doubt contributed to that. But now, that control appeared to be at breaking point—and who could blame him.

'To prepare for this time. There was nothing left for him to do. Luc made his choice, old friend,' Jake said. He swiped Marcus's black coat from the ground and held it out to him. Night frost clung to the leather surface.

Their long years together, their shared suffering, had created a bond between them that transcended the normal military boundaries. Marcus had long ago ceased to be just his—or the others'—commander.

'He wouldn't have had to make such a choice if he'd been human. Or if Judith had been allowed to become Brethren.' Marcus's chest rose and fell rapidly as he threw on the coat and spun on his heel to face the ruined chapel. 'That damned witch ensured my pain would go on and on. But no more!' He unsheathed his sword and drove it into the ground, his other hand clutching the wooden crucifix at his chest. 'I swear on my son's remains that I will see this curse to its end, and then I will hunt down and destroy every last witch on this planet until not even a memory of them remains.'

The household staff stopped shovelling rocks and turned to stare at Marcus. Silence descended. No crickets. No night birds. The Earth's shadow passed across the surface of the moon staining it the colour of blood—a blood moon. It was only a lunar eclipse, yet a dreadful sense of foreboding chilled my bones. Was he serious? There could be hundreds, maybe thousands, of witches in the world, and only a few had true demonic powers.

Did he want to get himself cursed again?

Nor did I want to see a bloodbath with him slaughtering the innocent. I figured I had another six months to dissuade him from that course.

'Let it go, Marcus. Jake's right, Luc knew what he was doing. Revenge won't bring him back.'

A muscle ticked in the side of his jaw. 'All those years doing penance, and for what? To see my son die on the eve of freedom? It wasn't supposed to happen this way. He and Judith were meant to live … to hold their grandchild …' His voice broke and he turned his face from us.

Jake gripped Marcus's shoulder.

'Deus! Have you any idea how it feels to lose a son?' Marcus pointed towards the chateau. 'I won't find him sitting at his desk or striding through the grounds … sharing a laugh, remembering the past….' His hand shook as he leaned heavily on the hilt of the sword. 'God forgave me for what I did in that village, yet still the punishment goes on.' He sank to his knees in the dirt, head bowed low, his lips a taut line against the trembling of his chin.

I crouched until we were face-to-face. 'Marcus, I do know how you feel. I lost both my wife and son. But unlike you, I never had the joy of seeing him grow to manhood, to enjoy his company for more lifetimes than any human can imagine. You did. You had more than I could ever wish to have had. Mourn him, carry his memory in here—' I laid my palm on the crucifix next to his heart '–and see this through for him and Judith … and Laura.' I was seized by a great emptiness and forced back the tears that burned in my eyes.

He lifted his head and gazed at me as if seeing me for the first time. Scanning my face, and with a grim smile and nod, he rose and sheathed his sword then prised open the small red gem in the centre of the crucifix he wore. I hadn't noticed until now that it was a reliquary. Within sat three tiny glass vials filled with a dark substance, which gleamed dully in the moonlight. He touched one, voice barely above a whisper. 'Luc's ashes. I gathered as much as I could. So you see, I carry more than just his memory with me.' He closed the gem.

I guessed the other two were the ashes of his wife and daughter: Gallia and Julia, Luc's twin. 'Then you have more than me.'

In spite of his own loss, Marcus squeezed my shoulder in a gesture of understanding. The sadness in his eyes conveyed more than words. For a few moments we stood quietly, only the wind whistling in the topmost braches of the pine trees breaking the silence. He closed his eyes and turned his face heavenwards, his lips moving in silent prayer. The men stood at a respectful distance, heads bowed. They mourned Luc's loss, each in their own way. Soon our entire Brethren world would be in mourning. I was sure news of Luc's death was already spreading. Would it be greeted with sadness or rejoicing?

The king is dead. Long live the king.

We could expect visitors, and they would have questions. We needed to be prepared.

'No one must know about—' I glanced at the staff who'd resumed refilling the hole from which Jake and Marcus had emerged.

They dropped a large stone slab over the entrance, the thud reverberating through the ground and sending plumes of dust into the air. I stifled a cough.

The tomb of my friends was sealed forever.

They had no idea the bloodvault lay beneath their feet and I wanted to keep it that way. The Thierry's treachery had been a blow. The family had been trusted servants for as long as anyone could remember.

'Can't talk here. Luc's office.' I said it without thinking. A shadow crossed Marcus's face. When would we stop referring to that room in that way?

Jake raised an eyebrow and jerked his head in the direction of the staff. 'Don't trust 'em?'

Terens snorted. 'Fuck no! Not after what that bitch tried to do to us—locking us in the vault to die.'

'Exactly.' After the despicable disloyalty of Madame Thierry I doubted any of us would fully trust the household staff again.

We made our way to Luc's office. Adjoining the library, it was one of the few Brethren-soundproofed rooms in the chateau. Although the staff were all personally handpicked, our experience with the Thierrys had created a deep rift in that centuries-old trust.

I leaned back against the front of the malachite desk, somehow unwilling to sit in Luc's chair, the leather moulded to the outline of his shape. His scent—sandalwood and cinnamon—permeated the room coating everything in its lingering memory: paintings, framed photographs he'd taken and hung on the walls or perched on the shelves; books and scrolls, down to the Venetian glass paperweight my fingers brushed against.

I picked it up and rolled the cold, smooth polished object in my hands, letting my thoughts roam.

Marcus paced the room, occasionally glancing at Luc's chair, while Sam secured the hidden tunnel, the same one Madame Thierry had used to spy on us, disguising her scent to avoid detection. Cal and Terens took up position near the door and along one wall. Only Jake grabbed one of the guest chairs and straddled it.

I set the paperweight back on the desk, shut out the memories and focused on our next move. 'The Brethren mustn't know about the loss of the vault.'

'Could cause a few … problems,' Sam added as he swung the bookcase closed and clicked the lock in place.

Jake gave a derisive laugh. 'Understatement. They've tasted Ingenii blood. They'll want more, all right.' He glanced at his friends. 'We're older and stronger, yet it still took a hell of a lot of discipline to wait a whole year for our share.'

The others nodded. In the century I'd known them, not once had I heard them complain over Luc's exclusive control of the stored Ingenii blood vials. Collected over a two thousand year period, ever since the inception of the Bloodgifted, he'd kept them stored in a secret vault deep in the caverns beneath the chateau. One Christmas, he'd handed over several vials to each of them as reward for their faithfulness—a few days in the year in which they could daywalk—and it became tradition, a ritual almost, in which each man recounted what he'd do with his short time in the sun.

'That's the risk we took, so the sooner you and I can create a synthetic version the happier we'll all be.' I'd already sourced the lab equipment necessary. It was now a matter of ordering it and getting to work. We'd already managed to create an anti-white-oak serum so I was confident we could do this too.

'Deus, Alec! Please. Sit in that chair. I cannot see it empty, do you understand?' Marcus stopped pacing and turned to me with a pained expression.

Marcus needed the symbolic proof that his son had passed away.

Thoughtless of me—I should've thought of that. Perhaps meeting here was not such a good idea.

But there was no other room in the chateau where we would not be overheard. No, it was the right decision. Marcus would've had to enter eventually.

The leather creaked as I sat. I glanced up. Would Luc come marching through the door any minute and demand his rightful place? I almost smiled at the picture. Almost. No time for sentiment. We had more immediate concerns.

I leaned forward and rested my forearms on the desk. 'From now on, the tunnels are off limits to the staff. They're to use the stairs. Including the housekeeper.' Whoever the new housekeeper would be. Laura and Kari were interviewing for a new one, while I was responsible for sourcing a new estate manager.

Laura! I longed to hold her in my arms, ease her heartache, and her nightmares. She had grown close to Luc in the few weeks she'd come to know him. And Judith ... no words could describe her terrible loss.

The warmth of the ruby-red eyes of the serpent ring tingled my skin. Red eyes. All was well. Absent mindedly, I'd been twisting it round and round my finger.

'Damn tunnels.' Sam groaned, shook his head and stared at the ground. I remembered him warning Luc about them. Madame Thierry hadn't been the only one who'd made use of the old passageways. The chateau was a veritable rabbit warren—no doubt she'd ferreted them all out.

On more than one occasion Luc had complained about the constant beeping on his mobile alarm, due to movement in the passageways. Compliantly, Sam had switched off the beeper. Only the tunnels beneath the house remained alarmed.

Did Sam blame himself? But how could he have kept the alarms active without disobeying Luc? For all his precautions and meticulous planning, Luc had one fatal flaw—he had trusted his household staff, human and Brethren. Hell, we all did! They were extended family, descendants of the freed slaves who'd worked on Marcus's villa nearly two thousand years ago. He'd known each one from infancy. They were the First Families.

I cursed Constans Thierry for destroying that sacred trust. 'Re-alarm all the passageways. I'll inform the staff.'

Sam's hands trembled as he removed his mobile and punched a few buttons.

Terens came to stand next to him and flung an arm around his shoulders. 'Not your fault, bro. Get that in your head. Luc gave you an order and you followed it. He relied on the ward ring to give him warning. Nobody could have suspected her fucking housekeepership would turn bitch!'

'Who of us would've suspected such a thing?' Hands clasped behind his back, Marcus turned to the window. In the darkness beyond, his grim reflection stared back at him.

Daybreak was less than half an hour away. This was changeover time, when the human staff replaced the vampire. Both roamed the premises and with Sam's alarm system now reactivated, we could expect to hear the beeper at any moment. 'Best I let the staff know now.' Marcus grunted as I strode to the door and stood in the open doorway facing the library. The Brethren staff would catch my whisper anywhere on the estate, but not the humans. 'Hear me. All staff are to gather in the foyer. Inform your human colleagues.'

I glanced back. Jake gave me a nod and half-smile, but Marcus stood motionless. He was my sire's father and his blood flowed through my veins. We had a connection and I felt his pain.

Footfalls and muffled voices came from the foyer. The sweet scent of human blood tickled my nostrils; the human staff were gathering.

'Okay, let's do it then.' Terens slapped me lightly on the shoulder, no hint of a smile in his eyes. 'After you, Princeps.' He dipped his head in deference and stood aside to let me pass.

He rarely, if ever, called me princeps. For, compared to these ancient and powerful men, I was but a babe having been shunted into this office by Luc less than a century ago.

A new era, indeed, had begun.

The Rebels had been defeated, their leaders tried and executed, and the Principate had never been stronger. Soon, I hoped to manufacture a synthetic version of Ingenii blood, which would provide us with an unlimited supply.

Could I dare wish things would now go smoothly as the curse neared its end? Perhaps, if not for a deep gnawing in my gut. I ignored it and glanced back at the framed photos of Luc and Judy on the wall. *Rest in peace, my friends.* I strode through the library to the entrance hall where nearly a hundred pair of eyes turned toward me.

With a deep breath, I faced them determined to be as strong a princeps as Luc had been.

It was time to take the reins.

CHAPTER 3 - HOUSEKEEPING

LAURA

I once read somewhere that grief doesn't really end; it simply changes over time. It's not a place to linger. You move on and come out the other side, as spring follows winter. Sorrow passes, or maybe a part of it does. But like a virus, it lays dormant beneath the surface, out of view until a particular scent, a word, a name, or walking into a familiar room disturbs it and painfully brings it to the surface.

It'd only been a few days. I had to give it time. Although I'd known Judy, as my aunt, all my life, Luc had only entered it about a month ago. To avoid me being discovered by the Brethren world until I came of age, he'd kept his distance.

So little time with them. Now they were gone.

After a few deep steadying breaths, I slid my hands down the front of my lambs-wool dress and eyed myself in the mirror. My tummy was still flat, and would be for at least another month or so. None of the Brethren would guess I was pregnant, and that's the way I wanted to keep it.

I leaned into the mirror. My fingers traced pale skin and then dark shadows under my eyes. Every time I dozed off, I was trapped back in the vault, clawing at the stone walls, calling out for help as the fire roared around me, staring at Judy's lifeless body at my feet, Luc dragging the screaming Madam Thierry into the flames. I'd wake shivering, drenched in sweat and breathing as heavily as if I'd run a marathon. Sweet sleep evaded me.

The pregnancy-safe mild sedatives Alec had given me helped, but I now dreaded falling asleep. How long it would last, not even he knew. Pity mesmerisation didn't work on the Bloodgifted—Alec had tried. I would've welcomed a bit of hypnotherapy.

I sighed, leaning into the soft plushness of the sofa. Yet another resumé lay on the coffee table. I drew it onto my lap. 'Bring her in, Kari.'

Madame Sabine Gilbert came with great references. She would be the fifth prospective housekeeper Kari and I interviewed for the job. Although they all had come with impeccable references, I hadn't felt comfortable with any of them. After my experience with Constans Thierry, would I ever trust another? Again, the last few minutes of her life flashed through my mind. I forced away the horrific images by reciting a biblical mantra: *"The Lord turn his face toward you and give you peace."* As I stared at the beautiful landscape painting on the wall and recited, the images receded.

The door swung open. Kari ushered in a middle-aged woman, dressed in tweed skirt and jacket, with the whitest skin and hair I had ever seen. Albino? Her short bob bounced around the edges of her chin as she came toward me—hair that looked as soft as cotton wool. I resisted the urge to reach out and touch it. She extended her hand and, behind her glasses, sympathetic pale blue eyes gazed into mine. 'Milady Laura, may I convey my deepest condolence at your loss.'

Her voice as soft as her hair and was comforting. Her grip was firm, yet gentle. Capable hands, short nails, no polish. Solid and reliable sprang to mind. Was it gut feeling? Whatever it was, I felt at ease with her.

'Thank you. Please.' I indicated the other sofa.

Kari sat next to me, one booted foot crossed over the other. She wore black leggings and a double-breasted military-style jacket in honour of Luc—a style he'd favoured and which had been adopted by his men this week. The brass buttons caught the glint of light from the window as she leaned forward and picked up the pot of hot coffee from the table. 'Madame?'

The woman smiled and nodded.

'You're originally from the village. One of the First Families?' I asked. The previous applicants were not locals, having worked at other Brethren estates. Kari had sourced them from recommendations.

'Yes, Milady, on my mother's side. I've been away a long time. It's good to be home.' She smiled and sipped her coffee.

I glanced at her resumé. 'If you don't mind my asking, why did you leave Derbyshire?' The National Trust estate in England she and her husband had managed was a well-known, popular tourist spot. Anyone who could manage that should have no problems here.

She lowered the cup and saucer onto her lap. 'My mother still lives in the village here, in a house very kindly given to us by Lord Luc. With the recent death of my father, God rest his soul,' she crossed herself, 'she's all alone. And … her heart isn't sound.'

She said it matter-of-factly, though tears clouded her eyes. Madame Gilbert, too, had recently suffered the loss of a parent, and rather than uproot her ailing mother from her friends and familiar surroundings, the Gilberts had come home to take care of her. It showed a selfless spirit.

Kari beat me to the next question. 'You'd rather live in the village then, huh?'

Madame Gilbert's gaze darted from me to Kari. She blinked rapidly and set the cup and saucer back on the coffee table. 'If that's a problem–'

'Heck no. Isn't that right, Laura?'

When we first discussed hiring a new housekeeper and estate manager, we determined they wouldn't live on the premises. From our first meeting, Madam Thierry made me feel an intruder in my family's home. We would never again risk allowing the management staff to believe the chateau was their possession.

There was suitable accommodation on the estate grounds, and if the Gilberts preferred to live in the village, even better. It was within easy walking distance of the chateau.

'I understand if you'd prefer to stay in the village with your mother. It's not an issue.'

She clasped her hands together on her lap and smiled broadly.

'More coffee?' Kari asked.

Madam Sabine Gilbert ticked every box, even down to her sense of humour. She'd originally trained as a midwife, and explained, 'I married Valentin—he's an estate manager—so most of my deliveries were of the piglet and calf variety whenever the vet arrived late!' She laughed, and the fob watch attached to the lapel of her tweed jacket bounced on her chest.

I smiled. It seemed so long since anyone had laughed in this house that I didn't want her to stop. Just for a moment, the deep ache in my heart lessened. I craved more of that lightness.

Kari leaned toward me and whispered, 'She'll do.'

I agreed. 'When can you start?'

'Now, if you like.' She looked at us expectantly.

Kari and I exchanged glances. The memorial service for Luc and Judy was scheduled for two days time, and, once again, all the dignitaries of the Brethren were expected to attend. Many would be bringing their donsangs with them—their human blood partners. There was much to prepare. The sooner Madame Gilbert could begin, the better.

'Perfect. This couldn't be better timing.'

'I'm glad, Milady.' She smiled.

'Now, we need to show you around the house and grounds and introduce you to the staff, Madame Gilbert.'

'Do call me Sabine.' Her smile grew and she pushed her glasses back up the bridge of her nose.

She reminded me of the white rabbit from Alice in Wonderland.

'Magnificent,' she uttered, blinking up at the ceiling frescoes in the library. 'I remember playing hide and seek here as a child.' Her gaze travelled to the bookcases and the great globe in its stand in the centre of the room. It had been repaired since Alec had sent it careering across the floor. 'Every Christmas Eve, all the First Families were invited for the celebration in the great hall. Lord Luc used to hand out presents to each child.' Her eyes shone at the memory. 'And for that night only, all the children were allowed free run of the ground floor.'

Another unknown piece of my father's past slid into place. How little I knew of him. A wave of heat flushed through me at the short amount time I'd been given with him—all because of Madame Thierry. I'd never truly hated another human being before, but for her, I wished all the torments of hell.

I pushed my vengeful thoughts aside as, level-by-level, room by room, we reached the top—Luc and Judy's suite. It hadn't been opened since their deaths. Kari lingered on the top step. Crimson tears glistened in her eyes and she clutched the small perfume locket she always wore around her neck. It had been a present from Jake.

With heart racing and trying to ignore the cold, hollow pit that opened in my stomach, I grasped the doorknob only to see my hand was trembling.

'It's alright, Milady. We can always come back another time. When you're ready.' Her soft voice flowed over me like a warm blanket. Of course, but how long would that be— days, weeks, months?

'Fine by me.' Kari sniffed and dabbed at her eyes leaving red streaks on the backs of her hands. She wiped them down the side of her black leggings.

It was some comfort to share our grief. The shock of their deaths had hit Kari just as hard, just as wrenching, for she and my mother had been best friends.

I turned to Sabine and nodded, appreciating her sensitivity, yet unable to speak. It was all too raw, too soon.

'How 'bout you meet the staff now?' Kari called as she started back down the stairs.

'Capital idea.' Sabine tucked her hands into the pockets of her tweed jacket and followed Kari.

'Rest in Peace,' I whispered to the door, stroking the timber panel as if their essence was somehow infused into its grain. Then I followed them down.

CHAPTER 4 – RETURN OF THE LAMIA

A nightmarish shriek rang through the forest.

Crawling slowly from its cramped hiding place beneath the ruins of Timur's castle, the surviving lamia craned its leathery neck. It screamed again at the full moon. Those who heard its cry might mistake it for some night bird or an animal caught in a trap in the woods, gnawing off its foot in an effort to escape.

Burning desire for vengeance gave its mutilated limbs the strength to drag its mangled and pain-riddled body inch by inch through the rubble. 'The ssssoldier boys will pay. Yesss, they will,' it consoled itself as it tried to catch any warm-blooded creature that strayed within its reach, rats mostly, or the occasional mangy cat. But human, or better still, vampire blood, would work the magic to make it completely whole again, and stronger than before.

Somewhere beneath the blackened stones and charred timbers of the fortress lay the remains of its brothers. The blaze had spread rapidly, fuelled by rotting fabric and dry, wooden furnishings. Nothing had escaped its ravenous hunger. Its brothers had swung from beam to burning beam. As each one collapsed, the lamiae were trapped, caught in its fiery grasp.

They hadn't been in the fortress long enough to have learnt all its secret passageways, only the ones revealed by collapsing walls. It'd dived into one of them. Its brothers hadn't been so quick—a flaming beam had crashed on top of them.

Several thousand years they'd freely roamed the earth, survived wars and vampire hunters only to be imprisoned by one who claimed to be their brother, yet proved disloyal—Marcus Antonius Pulcher and his cursed band.

Its weakened muscles still managed to quiver with rage at the memory and fuelled its hatred. 'Hate isss good. It keepsss usss alive. I will avenge you, my brotherssss. Thissss I ssssswear,' it hissed.

It'd crawled through the exposed passageway, but not fast enough to escape the flames as they devoured its legs and licked up his back and along his precious wings. Its screams were lost in the maelstrom above him, as it painfully dragged itself below ground and to a place of safety.

Soon, soon, it promised himself, its ravaged body would regenerate and it'd be strong enough to take his revenge—destroy Marcus Antonius's house and all who carried his name.

A figure, dressed all in black, strode into view. The lamia hissed and slunk back into the shadows, rubbing ash over itself to mask its scent. By the moon's pale light, it recognised the insignia of a crowned black stag on a silver background emblazoned on the figure's coat.

Its body trembled. Those who'd burned down Timur's fortress wore that insignia. Whoever it belonged to was going to pay.

The man was alone. Its hunger gnawed. It needed only to enter its prey's mind, and its victim would willingly surrender to death. Vampire blood was richer, stronger, its healing powers surpassing even that of juvenile humans—although not as freely flowing. It took greater effort to coax it from a vein.

But in its weakened state, could it overcome one of the Brethren?

Excitement surged through its veins at the anticipated kill.

It began to inch forward. Then, another figure joined its intended prey. A growl of rage escaped its lips. *Not strong enough to take on two. Two too many.* Reluctantly, it slunk back into his hole, hissing in pain where splinters and the sharp edges of collapsed stonework dug into its body.

'Did you hear that?' Its prey asked his companion. 'A hiss?'

Brow furrowed, the other man looked about him then shook his head. 'Probably just a grass snake out hunting.'

Its prey sniffed the air again before giving up in disgust. 'Impossible to smell anything in this debris. How many bodies so far?'

'Two-hundred-and-ten Rebels, or what's left of them. And this.' He motioned to a tall Brethren member carrying a sack over his shoulder.

From the top, protruded the tip of a charred leathery wing.

The lamia snarled silently, its fangs extending well below its lower lip. It writhed on the spot, desperate to avenge its brothers.

'Patienccccce, patienccccce,' it consoled, envisioning the many ways it would suck the life-blood from its enemies.

The one carrying the sack dropped it on the ground and opened it. The first man covered his nose and peered in.

'Shit! Reek, don't they? First time I've actually laid eyes on one.'

The other two covered their noses with their sleeves as they leaned over the sack, grimaced and turned away.

'Never would've asked to be turned if knew I'd end up looking like that.'

The other two nodded.

'Weren't there supposed to be four?'

The lamia snarled and barred its fangs. How dare they! With its brothers dead, it was now the oldest of their kind and they owed it respect. Without it, the Brethren would not exist. Insolent fools!

Adrenaline coursed through it but the lamia remained utterly motionless, only its blazing eyes revealing the life within. One day, they would all bow down to it. It would come as surely as the Earth revolved.

One day.

Comforted by that thought, it coiled himself into as small a ball as possible… no sudden move or sound. It watched, mouth watering but it ignored the gnawing churning of its empty stomach.

'Take this back to Lord Karl. Tell him … we'll keep searching for the last one. The body's got to be round here somewhere.'

The tall Brethren heaved the sack onto his shoulder and hurried off.

The cloaked figure frowned. 'Search everywhere. I want that thing found. Two by two, understand?' He then hefted a massive fallen timber beam, threw it aside and peered at the ground beneath. 'Who knows how many hidden tunnels this place had. It's got to be in one of them.'

A satisfied smirk etched the lamia's scarred face at its ability to avoid their notice. They thought it dead. All the better. They would lower their guard.

'What if it's still alive?' The two exchanged glances. 'We can't take that thing on. Not even Lord Marcus was able to kill it,' the second man said.

'I didn't sense anything left alive …' its intended prey surveyed the area.

'Unless it's masking.'

The lamia sneered. A tinge of hope bloomed in its leathery chest, for the scent that now emanated from them was fear.

Not even the great Marcus and his soldier boys had been able to destroy it, and so it and its brothers had been imprisoned in separate fortresses, wings ripped from their backs. Even now, centuries later, the memory alone sent a searing pain along its spine.

Like an animal, it'd been kept in a cage at the bottom of a deep pit and fed a mix of animal blood and that of young humans, dropped down from above. It'd tried to catch every drop, licking it from its body, the moss-infested walls and putrid floor on which its cage sat before it sank through the cracks in the stone. Semi-starved, perpetual hunger clawed at its insides and weakened it into submission, but the fever of vengeance never abated.

As the centuries wore on, its immortality a curse, still it plotted and planned its revenge. Slowly its wings regenerated.

Then one day, the chain of its cage creaked, and it was pulled upwards.

Count Timur's face had grinned at it from the edge of the pit.

Hope renewed until one of its brothers was slain before its eyes—pierced through with one of the soldier-boys' swords smeared with Ingenii blood.

A shudder ran the length of its body as it recalled the scene, and then it remembered *her*. Timur had paraded her through his fortress—the Ingenii. How could it forget that enticing, yet deadly scent?

She too would face his wrath.

For now it was still too weak, and its beloved wings were damaged. Unless it could feed on something more substantial than cats, rats and mice, their regeneration would take longer, and it risked capture.

It sniffed deeply. No, no trace of Ingenii blood left on their swords. After slaughtering the Rebels, and its brothers, they'd wiped their swords clean.

Still it waited and ... watched.

Neither man moved. Its hunger grew. It found himself crawling toward them, all its concentration trained on the first man, boring through his skull and delving into his mind. *Find a weakness ...*

Its prey stopped speaking, his eyes glazed over, then, just as suddenly, he shook his head, unsheathed his sword and spun around. 'It's here. I felt it trying to get into my head.'

The lamia froze. It didn't dare even blink away the beads of sweat that broke out on its brow and trickled slowly down its gnarled face.

The other man whistled, and ten others joined them, the silver emblem on their badges glinting in the moonlight.

'Fan out, nets at the ready.'

With swords in one hand and nets dangling from the other, its enemies approached.

It was only a matter of time.

It could stay hidden and risk discovery, or it could make a run for its life.

Seconds ticked by.

CHAPTER 5 – IN MEMORIAM

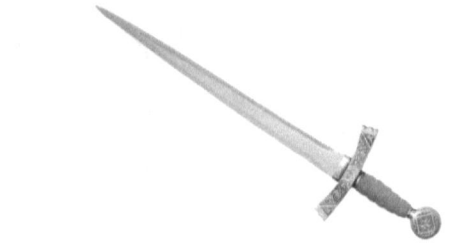

LAURA

A north wind ripped through the assembled crowd and tore at the lapels of my coat, digging its icy fingers into the tiniest exposed parts of my skin, and penetrating through my gloves to my fingers. I shivered and gripped the lifelike wax bust of Judy. I pressed the figure to my breast—the sculptor had captured her likeness, even down to the tiny dimple above her left eye.

How I longed to hug the real, living Judy to me. A swell of sadness filled me, the pressure building until hot tears stung my eyes. I bit down hard on my lip in an effort to contain my grief. If I started crying now I'd never stop.

Next to me, Alec carried a wax bust of Luc. He glanced at me, his expression grim, and whispered, 'Courage. We'll get through this.'

His quiet confidence gave me strength. The eyes of the serpent ring flared ruby red. As if in response, its twin on my finger did the same and spread its gentle warmth along my hand.

Marcus strode in front of us, his cloak flapping about his legs. With his hood thrown back and the wind whipping his collar-length black hair about his tear-stained face, he seemed impervious to the wintery blast. The crunch of hundreds of footsteps on the lightly fallen snow the only indication that Brethren and villagers followed behind in solemn silence.

From Marcus's lips broke the mournful dirge of a soul in pain, a cry from the heart of a loss so great, its anguish could not be contained. How could my pain compare to his—the loss of a beloved son with whom he'd shared countless human lifetimes. How much had they experienced together; how much had they endured?

Now he was alone.

At least I had Alec.

My heart ached for him.

An answering dirge rose from the throats of Jake, Cal, Sam and Terens, who marched on either side of us. Faces hidden within their hoods, they joined in the requiem, their voices blending with Marcus's, as our funerary procession wound its way from the great hall and through the woods to the stone monument, which had been erected over the site of the former chapel. A smooth, white marble block stood gleaming dully under the light of a full moon. Two niches carved into its surface, awaited their new occupants—the wax busts of my parents. And there, behind thick glass panels, would they remain, protected from the elements, forever together.

Announcement of Luc and Judy's death had caused a quake in the Brethren world. The secret Brethren website had nearly crashed beneath the influx of questions and messages of condolence. Luc, a formidable leader, had held the Principate together by sheer will alone. There'd been rumblings his passing could trigger a loss of confidence in Alec's leadership. It had been Luc who'd pressed him into the position while still a juvenile—an unheard of event in Brethren politics. And although Alec had gained many supporters over the years, there were those who still resented it.

But our allies were more powerful and numerous, and to see their faces among the mourners bolstered my confidence.

The scent of crushed pine leaves and newly dried mortar hung in the air as our procession stopped at the base of the monument. Marcus and the men ended their dirge. I looked up as the last note faded. The desolate cry of a raven—the bird of death—sounded.

As a former Roman military commander, Marcus chose to farewell his son following traditional Roman military practice. He climbed the three steps to the top of the platform and turned to face us. The scarlet trail of his tears seemed to leave permanent tracks on his ashen face. And once again my heart broke. How many more times would it do so? I lowered my head, resting my forehead on the small wax bust of Judy I clutched and swallowed down yet another deep sob.

'Brethren and friends,' Marcus's voice had me looking up again. He spread his arms. 'This night we come to mourn the greatest of our kind who had walked the earth. One I was privileged to call my son.' His voice wavered. 'Shall I recount his deeds?'

The crowd as one roared, 'Yes!'

He lowered his arms, tucked them in the folds of his cloak and gazed at the crowd.

'Lucius (Lucien) Antonius Pulcher Lebrettan, twin brother of Antonia, son of Gallia of the Allobrogii, Lord of D'Antonville, Prince of the Antonii, High Elder of the Brethren and Princeps Primus.'

His voice rang with pride as he recited a eulogy:

'In the dark days of our kind, order he brought, and the Principate he birthed.

At my side he cut down the savages who, in their bloodlust, brought the wrath of humans upon us.

He created the territories and appointed elders and prefects to govern them.

Where there was chaos he brought peace,

And in fairness and justice administered our laws by which all have prospered.

He was worthy of all honour.'

The assembled crowd repeated, 'He was worthy of all honour.'

Terens stepped up to the dais and lowered his hood. His voice rang out, almost in a chant.

'I, Tribune Sextus Terentius Varro, was there when Rome fell,

When the barbarians came,

Alamanni and Visigoth who harried the land.

Clovis, king of the Franks and friend of Rome, called upon Lord Lucien to protect the people.

At the Battle of Vouillé I saw him rout the enemy,

Slaughtered them in their thousands and sent them fleeing.

He was worthy of all honour.'

Again the crowd responded with, 'He was worthy of all honour.'

Jake now stepped up to the podium and took his place on Marcus's left.

'I Gaius Justinius, was there when one Jaroslav, proud Prefect of Moravia arose and sought the serpent ring,

Poisoned the hearts of the Brethren and warred against his own kind.

With courage and might, Lord Lucien threw him down and showed him mercy.

But in the blackness of his mind Jaroslav rebelled again and wrought destruction among his own kind.

Lord Lucien crushed the enemy and cleaved his head from off his shoulders.

Peace returned.

He was worthy of all honour.'

The crowd repeated the words.

Sam joined the others on the dais and recounted yet another heroic deed from Luc's past, as did Cal. Finally it was Alec's turn.

Vale Luc. May I do you justice. I caught his words in my mind.

For one maddening second, I was seized with the desire to run up to the dais and hug him. But I forced myself to remain where I stood even as every part of me rebelled at the physical distance between us.

'Brethren and friends, Lord Luc was my sire, my mentor and my friend.' He lowered his gaze to the marble slab on which he stood. 'And here beneath my feet he lies, at peace by the side of the one he loved— his sweet lady, prematurely cut down by a gang of Rebels.'

Hisses and loud cries emanated from many in the crowd.

'His heroic deeds have been recounted. Rather I will tell you something more of the man he was. Some thought him kingly, autocratic even. If that was the case, why did he willingly give up the office of Princeps? Surely those voices meant well?' Silence greeted his words. Several exchanged glances. 'Others said he'd hoarded the Ingenii blood for himself, yet every Elder and prefect here has walked in the daylight thanks to his generosity. Were those voices still well meaning?'

'They were wrong,' came O'Toole's strong Irish accent. The Prefect from Hibernia was one of the few from outside our immediate circle entrusted with our secrets.

'Aye,' many in the crowd called.

'Some thought him out of touch by outlawing white oak when the Rebels freely used it against us. Yet all Elders and prefects sitting here this night are immune to its deadly effects thanks to him.'

Alec was the one responsible for those last two positive changes, yet here he was giving Luc the credit. Was it loyalty, or was Alec subtly cementing support for the Principate? If it was the latter, it worked. Many were nodding and murmuring, 'True, true.'

'He did all this … to protect you.' He held out the bust of Luc and I almost expected the wax to come to life and speak. 'He was worthy of all honour.'

'He was worthy of all honour.' The solemn rumble of hundreds of voices swelled then dissipated into silence.

I shivered.

Alec remained standing as Marcus and the men sank to their knees. The gathering followed their lead, kneeling and bowing their heads. Only the lonely whistling of the wind in the topmost pine branches disturbed the silence.

Marcus rose, and as the gathering followed, Alec placed Luc's wax effigy within the niche. There was a click as he locked the glass panel in place.

The sound reverberated through me like a death knell. It was as the sealing of a coffin. The last farewell. Grief coiled around my heart and squeezed until the pain was almost physical.

Goodbye, Papa.

In spite of the cold, sweat coated my gloved hands and trickled down the back of my neck. Numb, I now stepped up to the dais and turned to face everyone.

I clutched Judy's wax bust to my chest and through blurry vision, surveyed the sad gathering. I blinked and cleared my throat.

'Here we gather to honour Judith Anne Dantonville. She was no warrior princess who fought with a sword or spear, but if the greatness of a person can be measured by their nobility of heart, by their kindness, compassion, loyalty, selflessness and courage, then she shone among the greatest. Of the line of Antonia, daughter of Marcus Antonius Pulcher, Ingenii, noble lady, wife, mother. Her gentle voice shall never again be heard—' I swallowed hard, my voice almost breaking '—and our loss cannot be consoled.'

In the crowd someone sobbed aloud. My heart lurched painfully. I swallowed and closed my eyes—had to get through this. Alec wrapped his arm around my shoulders, and it gave me strength.

I took a deep breath and continued. 'You all knew her ... her generosity of spirit, her gentleness. When Lord Luc made you quake, she calmed his storm.' Moonlight glistened on the bloodied cheeks of the Brethren and the clear tracks flowing down the cheeks of the villagers. Many knew her calming effect on Luc. 'And hidden from all were her own sorrows—that of a mother forced to hide her only child—me—in fear of her safety: my safety. Without her sacrifice I would not be standing among you here today.' Again, a painful lump rose in my throat. I did my best to squeeze out the words between sobs, and with my heart swelling, I cried, 'She was the best of woman and worthy of all honour.'

As one voice, the crowd repeated my final words until the ground beneath us shook.

My thoughts flew to my aunt Eilene and uncle John, the two beloved people who raised me, whom I had always believed to be my parents. Having lost their own baby daughter to Sudden Infant Death Syndrome at three months of age, Luc and Judy had entrusted me into their care—hiding me in plain sight for my safety.

To me they would always be Mum and Dad.

Dad's heart condition precluded their attendance here today.

I missed them.

But now, it was time to place the wax bust into its final resting place. With a kiss on her brow, I tucked my mother's effigy into the marble niche and clicked the panel closed.

Goodbye ... mother.

This was it. Judy was truly gone. My mind replayed every blessed memory I had of her, every moment from my earliest recollection of her, and I surrendered to the tears, letting them flow freely down my face, my shoulders heaving with the intensity of my grief.

Alec's arms encased me, his head resting on mine.

Through my clouded vision, two lifeless images peered at me from behind their glass confinement. The finality of it hit me hard, like a physical punch to the ribs, and I almost doubled over. I wanted to scream; to rage against those who'd caused their deaths and condemn them to an eternity of torment.

But none of that would bring Judy back.

I sobbed into Alec's shoulder until his voice whispered in my ear, 'Laura darling, John and Eilene sent a wreath. Can you hold on a bit longer?'

I gazed into his red rimmed eyes and nodded. His strength was my support.

Madame Gilbert stepped out from the crowd and handed me two large wreaths threaded through with black ribbon—one had been sent from Mum and Dad. Together, Alec and I placed them at the base of the monument.

The clear tones of a trumpet rang out. I held Alec's hand, and we descended the platform and, following Marcus's lead, marched three times around the monument in honour of the deceased.

The chilling cold numbed my cheeks mirroring that which gripped my heart. By the time we finished the frosty air had crawled up the glass panels obscuring the wax effigies behind them.

'Ninety days of mourning have begun,' Marcus announced.

Wails emanated from the crowd. Some beat their breasts; others even tore their hair. Another wave of grief crashed through me, and my breaths became shallow.

I can't sob again, I can't! It's tearing me apart.

So many people loved and respected my father, but now, no matter how much we desperately wished otherwise, he was gone. Forever.

Marcus's voice rose amid the clamour. 'There are to be no disputes among you for the courts of the prefects are closed. There are to be no festivities, nor feeding or sexual relations. Those in violation will be brought before me. I have spoken.'

Through the haze of grief, his proclamation stunned me. Ninety days without feeding! Could the Brethren last that long? What about the juveniles who still struggled to control their thirst?

Is that possible? I sent the thought to Alec.

No problem for the older Brethren. More of a struggle for the younger ones. We can drink any other liquids but not blood. Noble blood has been extinguished, so as a sign of mourning, no blood is to be taken.

I understood.

Both humans and Brethren wound their way through the crowd to lay their own wreaths.

Karl, the Prefect of Bohemia—and my friend—kissed my cheeks, after laying his wreath, and shook hands with Alec. 'If you ever have need of me, I can be here in a flash.'

'Thank you.' I pressed his hand.

He and Alec then moved some distance away to speak privately.

My friendship with Karl had grown since our time in Prague, while I was under his protection. If not for Karl, Alec may not have survived the lamiae attack Count Timur had unleashed. We owed him, but he wouldn't expect a return of that favour. As reward for his part in the downfall of the Rebel leader, the Principate had granted Karl all Count Timur's property and lands. This acquisition made him one of the most powerful prefects in the Brethren hierarchy. He was fortunate that Alec—as head of the Principate—had taken responsibility for the rebel's difficult juveniles. The Principate hadn't yet decided what to with all of them. From what I'd been told, it was standard practice to slaughter all a rebel's juveniles to ensure no future problems—a measure introduced after the Second Great Rebellion. But Count Timur's juveniles—mostly just kids—had not all been willing rebels. They had to obey their sire's commands because of the blood bond. Alec had given them a choice to join the Principate and promised them new sires, masters who would treat them well until they came of age.

Dominik was one of these juveniles. Only in his mid teens when Timur's henchmen kidnapped him and forced him into blood slavery, he'd been the first to pledge his allegiance to Alec if he were to take him on as his juvenile. He hero-worshipped Alec, following him around like a lost puppy. He stood in the front row next to Kari, wide-eyed, his gaze flicking between Alec, Marcus and the men.

On seeing me, he gave a faint smile and raised his hand to wave. Kari slapped it down. 'Inappropriate, kiddo!' she whispered.

The portly figure of a middle-aged man approached me. Next to him stood a tall blue-eyed man in the uniform of a French policeman. 'Our deepest sympathy, Milady.' Sad brown eyes regarded me through his spectacles.

Alec rejoined me, a deep crease wrinkling his brow.

What had Karl told him?

'Laura, may I introduce Monsieur Gilles Bouchard, Mayor of D'Antonville; and our local gendarmerie, Monsieur L'Agent Yves Morrell.' Alec shook hands with them.

'Thank you for being here tonight. You must be freezing.'

Bouchard shrugged. 'For Lord Luc, I would have come even if a blizzard blew. He was good to us.' He grasped both my hands and held them. 'A great loss, a great loss indeed. You will not be leaving, will you? D'Antonville needs its lord and lady.'

'I ... um...' I was newly pregnant, but for my last trimester we'd have to leave for Scotland. The curse stipulated my baby be born at the site of Roman massacre. As yet, only our inner circle—plus Karl and O'Toole—

knew I was expecting. Whether we'd return after that, I had no idea.

'We'll be here at least till the summer,' Alec said.

Bouchard released my hands and adjusted his bearskin hat. 'C'est bien. That is good.'

Morrel tucked his flat cap beneath his arm and raised my hand to his lips. 'Condolences, milady. We share your sorrow at such a sad time. Your good lady mother was much loved, her many kindnesses will never forgotten. I am at your service should you ever need it.'

I fought back the tears. 'Merci, monsieur.'

He placed the cap back on his head and grasped Bouchard's arm. 'Come Gilles. Let's toast our late lord and lady with your new bottle of Armagnac.' They trudged down the steps and disappeared into the crowd.

After the last wreath had been laid and condolences uttered, the crowd slowly dispersed. The temperature had fallen even further and the mist from my breath resembled tiny droplets of ice that drifted momentarily on the air before floating to the ground. I stamped my feet to keep the circulation going.

Alec wrapped his arms around me, but in spite of his warmth, the cold bit deep. 'My darling. You're freezing.'

With a long, last look at the monument, I turned away. Words floated around me, carried by the icy breeze. 'Don't mourn, ma petite. Live and be at peace, as I am.'

Only Luc ever called me "ma petite." Was it my imagination? Wishful thinking? Still, a weight lifted and an unworldly calmness settled over me. In the distance, the twinkling of the chateau's lights beckoned me into its comforting warmth.

I snuggled into Alec's side as we strode back: wherever my parents were, they were together. They had supported and nurtured Alec and myself to this point. The rest was now up to us. I determined not to let them down.

'I will, Papa,' I whispered to the night.

CHAPTER 6 – NOT DONE YET

MATT

Laura's portrait in the gallery haunted me. There, I'd said her name without my guts churning … entirely. Fuck! Why couldn't I get her out of my head? She dumped me for that bloodsucker, Munro, and that bastard had fucked with my mind.

My jaw clenched painfully at the memory.

Yeah, we'd broken up, but I wasn't done with her yet. She was a thirst I couldn't quench, a hunger I could never satisfy, a case that hadn't been closed. It gnawed at me, slowly consuming me, piece by piece. Every waking hour brought some fresh memory. Her face haunted my dreams. She got so deep under my skin that she was almost a part of me. If that wasn't bad enough, my work was suffering. Never had my private life interfered with my work before.

I hated the pitiful expressions of my work colleagues—yeah, I saw them—when they thought I wasn't looking. Or the whispered comments, or worse still, the derision of some who told me to "get over it."

I had enough.

I needed Laura back in my life, and the only way to do that was to remove Munro. Yeah, so okay, he'd saved my life. Lebrettan would've killed me for sure. Did that mean I owed Munro? Hell no! The fact was, he still wasn't human, and what's to say, he too wouldn't go rogue in the future? I wasn't taking that chance. He was a potential threat. They all were. Humanity wasn't safe with those creatures around.

And it was my responsibility to set it right.

I still had the newspaper with the missing persons notice I'd shown Laura. Yeah, I knew the truth, how that crazy, obsessed bloodsucker tried to rape and kill her because he couldn't have her. She hadn't lied about that. She couldn't. She'd break out in hiccups. Hell, I almost smiled at the memory, and for one insane moment, I knew exactly how that dead bloodsucking bastard felt.

With that, and the gallery files under my arm, I took a chance and strode into my Superintendent's office—Dave Delaney. My heart thumped hard enough to have a bloody heart attack at what I was about to spill to him.

'Be with you in a sec.' Dave shuffled a bunch of papers on his desk and stuffed a few of them into the top drawer.

'Take your time.' What the hell was I doing? Sense told me to keep him out of this. The guy had a wife and family and more opportunities for promotion. What I was about to tell him would either place him in danger or wreck our friendship. I could almost see him printing off an extended sick-leave form and handing it to me. But then again, he knew me; we'd worked together for years, and it was his encouragement and support that got me the promotion to DI. Could our friendship alone convince him that monsters really did exist?

Vampires are real, mate. If it sounded stupid saying that in my head, I could imagine what it'd be like coming out of my mouth. The air-con was going full blast, but that still didn't stop beads of sweat trickling down my lower back. *Bloody February humidity.*

Had to blame it on something.

Could I tackle this vampire vermin on my own? I could get try getting the necessary warrants, but Dave had better rapport with the judges than me, and he could obtain the warrants sooner, call a few favours in.

Either way, I had to set things right.

Dave slammed the desk drawer shut, looked up and gave me a grin. 'Right, what can I do for you, Matt?'

My throat stuck. I cleared it. He had no idea what I was about to hit him with. My hand shook as I laid my phone on his desk. 'Something on there you need to hear after I've finished.'

'Okay.' He leaned back in his chair, hands clasped on his stomach. 'I'm listening.'

'Before I start …' Voices came from outside his office. I didn't need anyone else hearing this. After closing the door, I grabbed a chair and perched on the edge of it. 'I'm telling you; I'm not having a nervous breakdown, and it's got nothing to do with my head injury. Doctors okayed me on that, so don't even think of suggesting I go to fucking Bali for a break, all right?'

His brows shot upwards. 'Glad we got that cleared.'

'Yeah, well, I had to say it coz you're going to have a hard time believing me. I didn't believe it at first either, till I … saw it.' I rubbed the damned sweat off my face.

'I've never seen you like this. What did you see?'

I told him everything I knew, including Munro's part and every particular of the meeting with him in the café, the day Laura introduced us. The day he'd taken her away from me. I clenched my teeth so hard that my jaw ached.

To give him credit, Dave didn't interrupt. Didn't throw me out of his office, either.

'What Munro didn't know was that I'd recorded it all.' I tilted my chin toward my phone on his desk. 'I'd pressed the Record button on my phone in my shirt pocket just as I'd reached the cafe. Nothing illegal about that,' I added when Dave frowned. Luckily, Munro hadn't seen the recording when he'd erased all references to Laura, including the few snaps of us together. All that I'd left of her. Bastard had even taken that away from me. 'After you hear the recording, you'll know why I wanted whatever I could get on him.'

I pressed Play and watched Dave's frown dissolve into a wide-eyed stare. His gaze flicked from the mobile to me and back again. I clenched the arms of the chair. His mouth slowly hardened accompanying the tightening under his eyes. He snapped the pencil he'd been doodling with and paused the recording.

'Lucien Lebrettan! Who would've thought. The guy was often seen out during the day.'

'The women's blood, remember? Enables them to come out in daylight. Anyway, he's dead now.' News of his death had even made it on the evening news here. To me, it was just one less vampire in the world. Pity it hadn't been Munro.

Dave shook his head and pressed Play again before he paused it a second time. '"Pernicious anemia"? Is that what he said?'

I gave a curt nod.

He replayed it. 'That's a threat. Send me that recording. I want it in my files,' Dave said after he'd listened to it for the second time.

'I couldn't make this shit up.'

'No, you couldn't. You don't have that kind of imagination.'

'Thanks, mate.' I'd take an backhanded compliment.

'I've got to rethink everything I thought I knew about the world.' Couldn't blame him for having a hard time believing it.

'I know. It hit me in the gut too.'

'This stays between us.'

'Hell, what do you think?'

Dave sneered. 'Munro played me good, didn't he.'

'At least he hadn't fucked with your mind as he did with mine.' My breath sawed in and out as I recalled how Munro had taken away six months of my life, to the time before I'd met Laura and before I'd learnt of their existence. 'My amnesia had nothing to do with my head injury. Munro wanted to be sure I couldn't remember anything about him and his bloodsucking lot.'

Dave slapped his thigh, stood and paced a few steps from where I sat. 'This changes everything.' He spun around to face me. 'I don't care if they're supernatural, ultranatural or bloody zombies. Nobody lives outside the law. With Lebrettan gone, Munro's in charge, right?' I nodded. 'What if he loses control again, and there's another killing spree?'

'Exactly.' Good old Dave. I wanted to give the old guy a hug.

'How do you want to handle this?'

'Use the law.' I pulled out the newspaper clipping and handed it to him. 'By starting here. Let me follow this up.'

He sucked in breath. 'Is that Laura?' Her stunning portrait in the Notices section stared up at him.

'Yeah.' I repeated what she'd told me. He scanned the notice. 'Munro may have killed Reynold to protect her, and it could've ended there, if not for the painting. It's public now and the gallery owner wants the painter found.' Okay, so they didn't exactly give me permission, but I reckoned the intent was there. 'Spoke to them last night.'

Dave laid the paper clipping on the desk. He remained silent as he resumed his seat, clicking his pen, his gaze flicking between me and the clipping. 'I'm behind you all the way in this, but are you sure part of it has nothing to do with Laura?'

I was expecting that. Still, it was a kick in the guts. 'It's got everything to do with her. She's only half human. What are the chances she won't turn into one of them?'

Dave shrugged. 'You'd know that better than me.'

His gaze cut through me like a knife. I knew what was behind those words. 'Laura and I are done. There's no conflict of interest, if that's what you're worried about.'

'Being done and letting go are two different things.'

'This is my way of letting go.' And protecting humanity—and Laura—at the same time. 'And dealing with the vampire menace in our city.'

His eyes bored into mine until my skin began to itch. 'I'll take your word for it.'

'You'll have to. Who else could you assign to this?' I pointed my thumb to the outer office. '*You* want to tell the team we're bringing in a vampire?'

He shook his head and rubbed his forehead. 'Can't believe it myself.'

I stood and leaned hard on his desk. 'If we can expose them, the whole world will know. Bringing in Munro is just the start. If we can detain him long enough for questioning—couple of days, maybe—he'll get hungry and the fangs'll slide out and those snake-like eyes of theirs: ugly, pale vertical slits.' I couldn't stop the cold wave that washed over me when I recalled seeing Lebrettan change right in front of me.

Bastard had enjoyed it!

Dave's eyes darted to my mobile. 'What was it Munro said about no cell being able to hold them? Something about a cornered blood drinker? I'm not risking my people, Matt.'

'Unless you know how to immobilise one.'

'Something tells me you've been doing your homework. Has it got to do with a certain type of wood?'

Munro had been careful not to mention which type of wood substance was their kryptonite, but it was easy enough to find if you knew where to look.

I pulled out a small plastic packet of powdered white oak from my pocket and held it out to him. 'It's white oak. As deadly to them as snake venom to us. They won't touch any human who has it in their bloodstream. If they can't feed, they weaken, and we can hold them.'

Dave opened the packet and sniffed it. 'Barely has a smell. Where'd you get it?'

'Bush is full of it. And in water, it's practically tasteless.'

He cracked a smile. 'Have you been drinking it.'

'Last few days. It's harmless.'

He grabbed his water bottle. 'How much?'

'Just a sprinkle.'

Dave added about a pinch to his water bottle and took a sip. 'Can't taste it all.'

'That's the beauty of it. It's non-allergenic, too. Won't hurt anyone … human, that is. Imagine dumping a load of it into the city's water supply.' I couldn't help grinning. In one swoop, we'd starve the entire vamp population; weaken them enough to eliminate them, and those who got desperate enough to risk feeding would die a nasty death.

Dave followed my train of thought. 'What about those who drink only bottled water? They'll still be vulnerable.'

I shrugged. 'Nothing we can do about that. At least the majority of the population will be protected.'

Dave clicked the hell out of his pen as he mulled it over. 'Can't hold a man just for questioning. We need reasonable grounds.'

'Laura mentioned Reynold having a studio at the Lebrettan house in Vaucluse. But if I go looking there, it'll only alert Munro, and he'll send his bloodsuckers after me.' I shook my head. 'This has got to be done without Munro suspecting a thing. If Reynold had an apartment somewhere else, I'll find it. Otherwise, Laura is my material witness. Pity I didn't record that.'

'As it's your word against hers.'

'I know, and that's why I need to get her to repeat it all, this time in front of another official, someone from Interpol coz she and Munro are in France right now, at the Dantonville estate, with no guarantee they'll be back anytime soon. Could you back me with the commissioner on this?'

Dave blew out a breath. 'Without a body, without being able to prove whether, in fact, Reynold is dead and how he died, it'll be very hard to mount a case of reasonable prospect of conviction against Munro solely with motive and the undefined existence of means and opportunity. All we know is that Reynold disappeared, and that really is as far as we can take it.'

'I know, I know—'

'Plus, you know how much that's going to cost the department even if we do get past that hurdle? We've had nothing but budget setbacks and staff cuts, and you want to use what little we've been allocated to fly halfway around the world without even a chance of a conviction let alone an arrest?' He lifted his hands and dropped them back onto his lap. 'No chance you're going to get it. You and I both know that without hard evidence, Interpol won't touch it.'

'What if I could get that evidence and guarantee an arrest?'

Dave's eyes narrowed. 'How?'

'Search Munro's apartment; look for signs of a struggle. He killed the guy. There should be blood, skin and even hair fibres. A forensics team should be able to find something.

'And what'll we compare it with? We need another sample, Matt. Otherwise it's a useless exercise.'

Dave was right. Where the hell could we get a comparison sample. I rubbed my face, searching for an answer, when, as they say, the proverbial bulb lit up. 'The painting … in the gallery. Get a forensics team to go over it. You never know; he may have touched it, left a hair somewhere on it, breathed on it…. I don't know, but there's got to be something.'

He grabbed a notepad. 'What's the name of that gallery?'

I told him. 'Once I get that positive DNA result, I need Munro to run. I reckon the last thing Munro'd want would be to be questioned in relation to Reynold's disappearance. And this time, he won't be able to fuck with my mind because the white-oak powder'll prevent it. Running would be his only option—an admission of guilt. I'd have him, and Interpol would have to issue a Blue Alert.'

'*If*, Matt. No guarantee he's going to do what you want.'

'Oh, I reckon he will, especially if he thinks he's protecting Laura. She's not just a material witness; but by covering it up, she's become an accessory. All I need to do is tell her I'm coming in an official capacity. It'll scare her enough to warn Munro.'

Dave chuckled. 'You've really thought this through. Remind me never to piss you off.'

I cracked a smile and sat back down. This was going to work … or not, depending on whether Dave could persuade the commissioner to extend our budget. Hell, I'd cash in my frequent flyer points if that's what it took. 'I'll get the paperwork started.'

'You know it can take anywhere between eight-to-twelve weeks to get all that together, and that's providing you can convince Interpol to cooperate.'

'I will.'

Knowing I had Dave's backing, I practically whistled as I left his office.

Munro's time was running out.

CHAPTER 7 – ANTIGEN

ALEC

'What are we missing, Jake? What am I not seeing?' I slammed my hand down on the bench top, setting everything rattling. 'Three months and we're still no closer. We should've identified and isolated that antigen by now.'

Jake grimaced as he stared at the platelets swimming across the imaging screen. It was one of a countless number of specimen slides we'd examined, and our blood sample was diminishing. 'I dunno. We've tried everything.' He increased the resolution and adjusted the excitation wavelength. Still nothing. 'And I've done that a hundred times, too. Still bloody invisible!'

His exasperation equalled my own. Unless we had a breakthrough, and soon, the Principate faced trouble. Word had already reached us that some prefects had broken the mourning rites and taken their blood vials. The fools had used up their meagre supplies, and were attacking those still in possession. Minor skirmishes had broken out into territorial raids, attracting the attention of local authorities.

Two breaches of decorum that had angered Marcus.

I threatened to confiscate the property of any Brethren found guilty stealing another's blood vials. How long that threat would hold, I could only guess. Among our kind, self-interest came second only to their blood thirst. As the weeks progressed, that situation would only worsen.

I'd taken a calculated risk in revealing the existence of the bloodvault. And sharing out a few vials in exchange for maintaining Brethren loyalty was, in my opinion, worth it. If not for the Rebel attack, the supply in the vault may have lasted years. None of us had factored in such unimaginable treachery.

We needed to find that antigen soon. I rubbed my jaw to loosen my tensed-up muscles. I yanked open the internal door. 'I need air.' And hopefully some inspiration.

Unbuttoning my lab coat, I strode out into the corridor and threw open the timber doors. The icy February wind hit my face, an invigorating blast after the stifling air in the lab. We'd been cooped up in there too long, desperately searching for that damned antigen.

I growled and kicked a loose pebble to loosen up my restless legs. The pebble shot across the courtyard with the speed of a bullet and embedded itself in a nearby tree.

'Cool.' Dominik's eager face smiled up at me.

I sighed. Since making him my juvenile, I had to get used to having him around. I understood that a fifteen-year-old needed a role model, but trailing me like a shadow was a bit much.

'You referring to the temperature or the rock in the tree?'

'Hey, the rock. Let me try.'

'Dom!' I grabbed his shoulder just as he attempted to whisk past me. Dominik's lack of co-ordination was a worry. He could miss entirely and land on his arse or he could send a tiny pebble sailing through one of the chateau's windows. I was in no mood to witness either. 'Get back inside and help Jake rinse out the slides.'

He made a face. 'Again? All I do is wash up stuff.'

'Consider it part of your science training until I decide which distance education program to enrol you in. You need to be in school.'

His face crumbled. 'I was hoping you'd forgotten about that.'

'Not at all. I'll look into it this week.'

'Do I have to? Since when do vampires go to school?' If he rolled his eyes any harder they'd end up in the back of his head.

'Fifteen-year-old ones, with centuries ahead of them, do. You've much to learn and practice. And no more argument,' I added, when he opened his mouth to, no doubt, protest.

He scuffed the toe of his shoe against the gravel, muttering in a mix of Czech and English. I overheard, "Not fair."

So was this what was awaiting me, this future taste of fatherhood?

Jake's chuckle drifted on the air.

Terrific. Still, perhaps it was time I trusted him with the blood samples. 'Want to help load the slides?'

Initially I'd wanted him exposed to the Ingenii samples to build up his resistance to its lure. To all Brethren, Ingenii blood was like catnip, especially to juveniles. And being around Laura, I wanted him extra resistant. His eyes widened, and the grin that accompanied it showed I was on the right track. 'No licking the samples, Dom.'

First day in the lab, I'd caught him bringing one of the smeared slides to his mouth. We were in mourning, and yes, I knew he was hungry, but the ninety days feeding abstinence wouldn't kill him. If anything, it would teach him discipline, something every juvenile needed.

Another reason I'd put him on wash-up duty was to keep him away from temptation. 'I've told you, Jake's told you: Ingenii blood is deadly to Brethren. Do something stupid and we won't be able to save you.'

'I won't, I won't. Promise. I do *not* want to die.' I almost laughed when he raced back into the lab as if the devil was on his heels. In spite of his unwillingness to return to school, the youngster had an aptitude for science and made a competent lab assistant.

The gravel crunched as I paced a few steps away from the small cottage that served as our makeshift lab. Across the drive, light streamed from the chateau's windows, but the one I was focused on was dark. It was after 2am. Laura was asleep. The steady thump, thump of her heartbeat reached me. Was she dreaming? I could almost see her molten-bronze hair splayed on the pillow, lips invitingly parted begging for me to taste her, the gentle rise and fall of her breasts ... and I felt myself hardening. Not one moment of the day passed when she wasn't somewhere in my thoughts, drawing me deeper and deeper into her. Laura owned me—body and soul.

The desire to sink my teeth into her soft, milky flesh and drink my fill grew. I thought of the last time I bit her, how she'd moaned with pleasure. I closed my eyes and tried to swallow my desire as my fangs slid down.

Damn! I inhaled, clamped my mouth shut and endured the burning pain until it passed. It wasn't just the period of mourning. Not until the babe was born could I partake of her blood again and feed from that silky throat. I needed to keep working, to keep my mind occupied lest my feet dragged me to her side to lay bare her throat ... Damn! I shook my head. In the last few days, the urge to bite her had been steadily growing, and it would only continue to rise after the period of mourning was over. Could we avoid each other, have no sex at all? I barked out a laugh. As if! I'd just have to suffer.

Any period of mourning was a dangerous time. From what I'd been told, there had been only two other occasions when our world had mourned the passing of a Great One. Each time, the period of enforced abstinence had led to many human deaths when the younger Brethren, particularly the juveniles, could no longer control their hunger. They'd fed until they'd made themselves sick. My chest tightened at the thought of that happening again.

Yet it wasn't the only thing bothering me. I hadn't told Laura about the lamia. One of the things had survived the destruction of Timur's fortress and somehow had eluded capture by Karl's men.

They'd managed to track it as far as the border of Karl's territory, and by his reckoning, the wretched thing was headed here.

Weren't we weak enough from the deprivation imposed by the period of mourning? How the hell could we possibly hope to kill it, let along resist the powers of the lamia in our present state?

Of all the lousy timing! I picked up another small stone and sent it careering into the sky, shooting through the hazy shimmer of the magical ward guarding the estate. At least the lamia had no chance getting through that.

Just then, a shooting star streaked across the sky before disintegrating in a puff of dust. The view of the stars here was without equal. Had I been in the city, with its glaring lights, the beauty of that passing meteor would have gone unnoticed.

I sucked in a breath. That was it! Why hadn't I thought of that before?

A surge of adrenaline shot through me and I raced back to the lab. Dominik was swapping slides and peering intently into the spare scope. Whatever Jake had given him to examine wasn't blood. They smelled like a collection of samples—cheese, saliva and … human urea?

'Wow! I never knew human shit looked like that?'

Jake glanced up, cracked a smile and shrugged. 'He's a teenager.'

As if that explained everything.

'Unless you've got a brilliant idea, I'm done for the night.'

'I just may have.' I flicked off the lights. We didn't need to use them anyway. Just another habit. 'We can't see it because there's too much light.'

He stared at me over the rim of his coffee mug. 'Fly that past me again.'

I grabbed the last sample of Laura's blood from the centrifuge and a couple of clean slides. 'We've been going around this the wrong way—relying on human methods. The antigen's there all right. We just need to coax it out. If we darken—'

'Dark field effect? We've tried that.' He emptied the mug and left it sitting on the bench.

'Nope, not dark field.' I smeared a drop of Laura's blood onto the slide and placed it under the 'scope. 'Our kind's nocturnal. So's the antigen. It'll only show up in the dark.' I hoped. It was a hunch and I'd learnt to go with them.

Jake's eyebrows shot upwards. 'How are you so sure?'

'I'm not, but it's the only thing that makes sense right now.'

He shrugged. 'Nothing to lose, eh.'

Exactly what I thought. I adjusted the lens, peered down the 'scope and waited. Five seconds ticked by, then ten. 'C'mon, I know you're there.' Light from the courtyard lampposts still filtered in through the windows. Perhaps that was the problem. 'Dom, close the shutters.'

Shutters protected the windows of all the estate cottages. Seconds after hearing the click of the final wooden shutter, total darkness engulfed the lab. Perfect. My pulse hitched up a notch when slowly, like a comet appearing in the night sky, tiny golden serpent-like filaments materialised from the black ooze on the slide—the antigen! It could be nothing else.

'Huh! Found you.' I grinned like a schoolboy who'd just been told the holidays were starting early.

'What's it like?' Jake's voice dropped to an almost reverent whisper.

'See for yourself.' I stood aside to let him take a look. There was no point in projecting the image onto the computer screen. The camera wasn't sensitive enough to capture anything in such darkness.

'Can I look, too?' Dominik hovered at my elbow, his own set of slides forgotten.

'In a minute. After Jake.'

Long seconds passed before Jake made any comment. 'Like nothing I've ever seen before. Didn't know what to expect, but seeing these things swimming around in here … Seems fitting they'd look like vipers.'

I glanced down at my hand. In the utter darkness of our blackened room, the eyes of the serpent ring glowed. Was it responding to the Ingenii blood?

Jake glanced up and gave me a smile before slapping me on the back. 'You should've gone for that fresh air weeks ago.' I chuckled as Jake returned to the 'scope. 'Sneaky little beggars! Hidden in plain sight like glow-worms in a cave.'

'My turn now?' Dominik practically hopped from foot to foot.

'C'mon quick look.' Jake rose and swapped places with him.

I tinkered with the camera settings on the desktop for a way to lighten the image, when Dominik tugged at my coat. 'Umm … something's happening. They're like, disappearing. Is it supposed to do that?'

The youngster squeaked when I yanked him from the chair. I peered down the scope. He was right. The serpent-like antigens were indeed disappearing—curling up and disintegrating. My stomach dropped. I increased the magnification, but it made no difference. It was gone. 'What the…?'

'I didn't do anything! I only looked,' Dominik wailed in my ear.

'It's okay, Dom. Not your fault.' I stepped aside for Jake as I tried to figure out what the hell was going on.

'Shit! We had them.' He banged the bench top and lifted his head from the scope. His eyes practically glowed in the dark as he gazed at me.

'Deliberate short lifespan outside its hosts medium so it can't be transferred?'

Made sense. 'Except via sex? Then how does it stay alive in the vials?'

'It's still in its hosts medium, but the moment you remove it—'

'—and it comes into contact with the air...'

He nodded.

There was our problem. The antigen could not be separated from the host's blood. Exposure to air triggered its self-destruct mechanism.

Our job just got a whole lot harder. 'Well, we've finally identified it. Stage one down. Now for stage two: identify its components for replication.'

'Got a feeling this thing's gonna fight us all the way.'

'Then we fight back ... and win.' We had no choice. I pushed away from the bench and retrieved the last blood sample. 'All that's left.'

With a grim smile, Jake snatched his discarded lab coat from the laundry basket. 'Easy peasy. Let's do it.'

'"Easy peasy?"' I laughed as I prepared the next slide. 'You sound just like—'

Jake elbowed me. 'Yeah, yeah I know. What do you expect after living with her for several centuries?'

'She rubs off on you.' Laura was convinced Kari was in love with Jake, but how he felt about her was not my concern. Still, it was interesting how he was copying her words.

'Yeah, she does. Ready to nick this thing?'

Infused with new energy, we set about mapping the antigen's DNA. Could we do it? Over the next few hours, we tried again and again with no success. The moment we came even close, the antigen would simply disintegrate.

I hated to admit it, but perhaps Marcus had been right. We were tampering with unknown forces. It wasn't that I feared some sort of retribution, but rather failure. The Principate was a direct consequence of the curse and its reliance on Ingenii blood. The Principate's demise would signal the end of the advantage enjoyed by the princeps. If we failed to replicate the effects of the antigen, my position as princeps—and Laura's guardian—would be in jeopardy. In vampire years, I was too young to enjoy the strength and speed I now rightfully claimed.

Once the curse was lifted, my power would fade, for there was every chance Laura's blood would revert to human.

So much at stake, and for all my scientific learning, I had to keep reminding myself that we weren't dealing with science, but magic. I had but to look at myself, and the rings I wore, to know the truth of that. But, from my understanding, magic worked only within natural forces.

This is what Jake and I focused on.

As it got close to sunrise, I sent Dominik back to the chateau for his day sleep.

Until he was out of his juvenile stage, Ingenii blood was off limits to him. At this early stage of his transformation, while his body was still adjusting, ingesting such powerful blood could even kill him. That I had been the only juvenile in Brethren history to feed from Ingenii blood attested to my lineage—a direct descendant of the witch Eithne, who had uttered the fateful curse condemning Marcus's family line.

For the next century, he would have to live in the dark. And unless we could create a synthetic version—once our own blood vials ran out—we would be joining him. But for the moment, and although there was still a day to go before the official end to the ninety days of mourning, Jake and I broke protocol and took our blood vials early.

We needed the daylight hours.

I gazed at the test tube I held. We were down to our last drop of Laura's blood. If pressed, we could resort to the Ingenii blood vials. More and more, it appeared we may have to—and that this whole endeavour may fail.

It was a prospect I dared not consider.

We slogged on until well after sunset when the phone in my back pocket buzzed—a message from Karl.

'Watch out. Heard from my contacts in Milan. Lamia's headed your way all right. It's killing our brethren and getting stronger. We're too weak to fight it.'

Holy mother of…. I tensed, closed my eyes and rubbed my brow. This was the last thing I needed. Damn lamia!

CHAPTER 8 – DIARIES

LAURA

The keys' sharp edges cut into my hand as I stood outside the door to Luc and Judy's suit, trying to suppress the rush of emotion. 'C'mon, Laura. It's been over three months. You can do this.' My voice sounded nervous, and unconvincing, in that empty hallway.

I could've asked either Alec or Kari along for moral support. But my heart told me I needed to face this on my own. Besides, Alec was busy in the lab with Jake trying to replicate the substance in my blood that allowed the Brethren to daywalk.

'You're not the only one who's lost loved ones in tragic circumstances. And, you know they're in heaven … happy.' I recalled Luc's whispered words on the wind, and my heart lightened.

I turned the key and pushed open the door. Pale crimson light seeped in through the partially draped window and crept along one wall, illuminating a portrait of Luc and Judy. Seated on a garden bench, she perched on his knees, both smiling, each captivated by the other.

Judy's perfume hung in the air—the sweet scent of tea rose and honeysuckle.

Breathing deep, I let it fill my lungs. Such power in the sense of smell. A stream of happy memories assailed me. I'd sought out that garden bench after I'd learned the truth about my parentage, and it was there Alec and I had first kissed. He'd even sat me on his knee the same way Luc had done with Judy.

Nothing in this suite had been disturbed since the day they'd died.

A sprinkle of dust swirled about me as I drew back the heavy red velvet drapes. It tickled my nose. Light flooded the room and glinted on the damask roses on Judy's chintz armchair, which gave a glorious view over the back garden. I ran my fingers along the firm cushioned seat, disbelieving that Judy would never sit here again. On the other sofa lay a paperback and Judy's afghan throw rug, half of which trailed on the floor. Had Judy even finished the book? Sadness weighed down on me.

My throat tightened. Her last hours in this room involved Madame Thierry knocking her unconscious and dragging her body down to the bloodvault. At least she hadn't suffered—it was all so quick. I thanked God for that.

I wandered into the bedroom. Her scent was stronger here, this time mingled with Luc's cinnamon and sandalwood. The bed was untouched, covers pulled back ready for the night, her dressing gown draped over on corner. Blinking back tears, I tore my gaze away. The last few months had drained me emotionally. I was tired of the grief.

I strode to the walk-in closet and opened it. 'What to do with all this?'

On one long side hung Judy's clothes. Her shoes, handbags and accessories were neatly arranged in drawers beneath. On the other side, were Luc's. His jackets and trousers brushed against piles of folded sweaters, T-shirts and boxes of shoes—never to be worn again. They would all have to be removed, to fit my and Alec's stuff.

Deep breaths, Laura.

I went in and trailed my fingers against the lines of fabric, brushing against soft satins, delicate silks and crisp cottons and linens. I tried to ignore the thousand little splinters of sorrow embedded between my shoulder blades as Judy's delicate scent mingled with the spicy masculinity of Luc's to waft from each piece of clothing I touched—each tiny molecule loaded with memories that flooded my mind.

A glimpse of green and blue sprigs on a white background peeked at me from among the hanging garments. I recognised the print as the dress Judy wore in the painting in the living room; fifties style, with square neckline and belted waist. So beautiful. How could I possibly store it out of sight?

I took it down and tried it against myself. Judy and I were—had been, I reminded myself – the same size. Several dresses of a similar style, each with a different print, hung along the same rack. Behind them, wrapped in a zipped plastic bag, hung a three-quarter length, creamy satin and spotted tulle gown with a heart-shaped neckline, a simple, white lace veil attached.

My heart stopped.

My mother's wedding dress. Couldn't be anything else. Directly below, in a long narrow carton, were a pair of silk elbow-length gloves. Instead of packing it away in a storage box, she'd kept it here, among her clothes. I couldn't begin to guess why.

Almost afraid to touch them, I hesitated then carefully slid the gloves on. Perfect fit. We even had the same size hands.

No storage wardrobe for these precious things. I slid the wedding dress and the fifties-style dresses to one side, separating them from the clothes that would have to be moved.

Now to find the matching accessories.

As I searched through various drawers, my foot kicked against something solid. A black metal-rimmed trunk sat wedged between several pieces of luggage. It was heavy, and as I eased it out layers of dust plumed around me. I sneezed. That was good, as it meant the previous housekeeper, whose name I couldn't bring myself to say, hadn't been snooping into it. She'd taken my mother's clothes before, so I wouldn't have put it past her to have pried into all of my mother's things.

The trunk was locked.

What was in there? What needed to be kept in a locked trunk?

I glanced around for the key.

Nothing.

Dumb idea anyway, Laura. If you want something hidden, you don't leave the key where everyone can find it! I'd carry it with me, with my set of house and car keys where they'd blend in with the rest.

The house keys I had didn't contain any extra keys—Kari and I had tested each one. That left only her handbag.

Judy had always kept it in the middle drawer of her bedside table. I hurried over to it and hovered my hand above the handle. Could I be so lucky? I held my breath as I slid the drawer open. It was still there. I hugged the black bag and inhaled its sweet leather scent as image after image paraded through my memory.

No more tears, Laura.

I began my search, shunting aside the thought that I was intruding.

For a relatively small bag, it contained so many compartments and pockets. Finally, my fingers grazed a small cold, metallic object.

That had to be it.

Attached was a black velvet ribbon, frayed at the edges. Traces of my mother's perfume clung to it. Again I inhaled and momentarily let the memories assail me.

Back in the closet, I knelt next to the trunk and inserted the key.

It fit.

Click. I shoved the lid open. Inside, lay a beautiful decoupage box.

Had my mother made it herself?

I lifted it out, grunting at the substantial weight. The sticky elastic band holding the lid in place snapping the moment I tried to prise it off.

Arrgghh! A cockroach scurried across my hand. I flicked the horrid thing off and shuddered, the box toppling from my grip, the contents spilling onto the floor. The beast disappeared into the dark recesses of the closet. I waited a few seconds for my heartbeat to return to normal.

Books ... journals ... diaries? Black, red, green leather bound notebooks of all sizes littered the floor. One had landed open, and I recognised Judy's handwriting.

... August 10 1940 Luc had to leave suddenly for 'D'Antonville. Chateau's in danger of Nazi occupation ...

My blood chilled—it was her diary.

Were all these her diaries? Should I, shouldn't I? It was such a private thing, yet there was so much about my parents' early lives together I knew nothing about. The time we should've had, had been stolen from us.

Heart hammering, I perused one after the other, flipping through the pages to see the inside dates ... this green one 1960; the black one was dated 1952; some of the brown ones—their covers frayed—were dated in the early 1930s.

June 2 1932 – Father spoke to me today. That doesn't happen often. Called me into his study. Informed me I'm to be married to his creditor – a man I've never met! If I don't consent he told me his life would be in danger. This man is a gangster who, he says, uses violence to retrieve his money, but he's willing to waive it if I consent to marry him. I WILL NEVER CONSENT! How did Father become involved with this man?

I'm only 20 and my father's selling me to pay his debts!

Oh my stars! This was about my grandfather, Owen Dantonville. I remembered him as a cold, distant man, but never in my wildest dreams could I have believed him capable of such cruelty.

The shaky handwriting and blotted words revealed my mother had cried when she wrote this.

My legs buckled. I slid to the floor and leant back against the closet's built-in drawers. Why had I never been told this? Was it referring to her first husband? A man, I recalled, my dad had disliked.

Like a moth to a flame, I was drawn back to the handwritten page in my lap.

I told him, pleaded with him, I could work to help him pay off whatever he owed. But he won't hear of it. Can I run away and teach music, support myself, live … live where? I could try. But he'd probably find me and bring me back. And father said this man's cronies would kill him, he owed so much money!

I'm too much of a coward to take my own life. God help me! I have no choice!

Beneath, she had drawn the image of a decayed rose, its petals falling and turning into tears as they reached the bottom of the page.

No amount of swallowing and blinking up at the ceiling kept my own tears from falling—my poor mother.

The next entry was dated a month later.

July 3 1932 – I'm a married woman.

No mention of her wedding. She probably couldn't bear to write about it, and that was borne out by the next entry.

July 4 1932 – I'm wed to a monster – a gangster. Begged him … but he took me roughly. Struck me because I was unwilling. My whole body hurts. His touch turns my stomach. I want to go home … as far away from this man as I can. Oh God!

I was queasy and had to cover my mouth as I read the next section.

July 6 1932 – Lied and said I'm in my monthly. Relieved he won't touch me for at least a week.

July 7 1932 – Father had the audacity to phone me, to ask me to drive him to a friend's place. I was sure his "friend" would be just another huckster or gangster like the beast he sold me to.

But he's not.

… His name is Lucien Lebrettan, a tall, strikingly handsome man – blond hair and the same lavender eyes as mine. Uncanny. I've never come across another individual with the same colour eyes as myself. He approached me in the garden of his house while I was waiting for father. Even now, all these hours later, I can't stop thinking about him.

… A note just arrived – from him. Can we meet? I must hide it from William.

If a heart could physically soar, mine did. It was like the thrill one gets when reading a fairy tale and you reach the part where the prince and princess meet. I leafed through a few more pages, skimming as I went, eager to see how their romance developed.

July 20 1932 – I let Luc kiss me, and how eagerly I kissed him back. How gentle, how patient he is – I'm overcoming my fear of a man's touch. We try and meet secretly every second day. Thank goodness for my work at the YWCA and the Ladies League. It's my excuse to escape. William suspects, and I catch him watching me closely but how can I help myself? Do I love Luc? Yes! If only we had met earlier. I know he would have saved me from this loathsome marriage and even paid off my father's debts. I feel no compunction to remain faithful. Luc is my love and my life.

My heart thrummed as I hastily turned more pages.

Aug 27 1932 – I'm struggling to believe what Luc told me is true. Tonight I learnt his true nature. Heaven's above, he is a vampire! He feeds from my father – my family! How can I accept this? I ran from him … can still hear his voice calling after me. If the phone rings I won't answer it. I can't.

Someone knocked on the door. I started, sending my pulse racing as I was wrenched back into the present.

'Laura, it's me. Package arrived for you.' Kari's melodic voice came from the living area.

A package? Who'd be sending me anything? Normally I would've heard her footfall on the stairs from the level below, but I'd been so engrossed in the journal entries, I hadn't registered a thing.

'Door's unlocked. In here … in the closet. Be out in a sec.' I swept up the scattered diaries, deposited them back into the box and then into the trunk, which I slammed shut and locked again. I pocketed the key and pushed the trunk back under the bottom shelf. I wasn't ready to share them with anyone … yet.

'How are you doing?' Her pixie face appeared in the doorway.

I shot to my feet. I waved my hand indicating the contents of the closet. 'Not sure. There's a lot to pack away. I haven't even started.'

The clothes would have to be moved to the storeroom. It was there that, over the centuries, Luc and his men stored all they had worn. It was a veritable costume designer's dream. Hundreds of years old, many were still in excellent condition.

'Let me know if you need a hand, okay? ' Her eyes gazed at me sympathetically as she pulled a large bulging yellow envelope from beneath her arm. She held it out to me. 'This came for you.'

'Thanks, Kari. Maybe later, after I've sorted everything out.' I took the package from her and examined it. 'It's from Mum. What could she be sending me?'

'Open it and find out.' In the blink of an eye, she'd made herself comfortable on the sofa and patted the spot beside her.

So much for privacy. Yet in a way I was glad she was here.

I drew the coffee table closer and spilled out the envelope's contents.

Photographs in a range of sizes, black and white and colour, stared back at me. I'd never seen any of them before, and since Judy appeared in only a few, she must have been the one taking the photos. Many were my baby photos where Luc held me. Others were taken at my school sporting events, and in each, Luc appeared clearly in the background, yet I didn't remember ever seeing him. There he was, smiling, leaning against a tree as a ten-year-old me kicked a ball around. And another where he sat in the bleachers near a bunch of boys as a teenage me made a home run for my high-school softball team's grand final.

He'd been at my softball game? My breath left me even as a tender warmth spread through my chest. 'I remember this.' I stroked Luc's face in the photo before I showed it to Kari. 'Only because part of the stand collapsed and some boys were hurt. It made the local papers.'

Kari chuckled. 'Luc caused that. I remember Judy telling me about it. She said the boys were making bets as to which of them would ... you know … get lucky with you.' She grinned and nudged me with her elbow. 'So he upended their seats. Several rows it was.'

My jaw dropped just as I burst out laughing. I could enjoy picturing Luc doing something like that now without fear of unleashing a flood of tears. I'd been grieving his and Judy's loss these last, nearly sixty days, and only now had the pain begun to lessen.

'I always liked him, except in his hairy-scary moments. Don't tell Jake I said that. He loved Luc like he was his own a son.' She shrugged, her mouth crinkling up into a sad grin.

That I could understand. Jake had known Luc since he was a baby, and the countless experiences they'd shared over the centuries could not have created anything but a strong emotional bond. What about the other men? Had they felt the same? I recalled the way Terens referred to himself as "Uncle Terens" the night he'd found me in Timur's fortress. 'It's all right. Uncle Terens is here,' he'd said as I'd broken down in his arms, having narrowly escaped a horrific torture at Rasputin's hands.

I shook off the memory as Kari dug into the package and withdrew a small faded-blue envelope. My name was written on the front. I recognised Judy's handwriting. She held it out to me.

Embracing the sadness, I lovingly traced the outline of my name because *she* had written it.

The envelope contained a gold bracelet in the form of a coiled serpent. It looked old, very old. A Latin inscription ran along on the surface: "Serpens Sanguinus."

Kari whistled. 'Will you look at that!'

' "Serpens" means serpent, but 'Sanguinus"?' I looked at her, hoping she knew.

'Mmmm … my Latin never was very good.' She tapped a finger against her chin. 'Sanguin? Something to do with blood? That would make sense.'

As I turned it around in my hand, there was no tingle, no hint of anything magic about it. Unlike the serpent ring, it was simply a piece of antique jewellery.

I opened the letter. The scent of sugar and rose water drifted on the air, bringing back memories of rainy afternoons, a warm kitchen and Mum's delicious chocolate croissants. My heart lurched. How I missed that simple time. It seemed an age away.

My dearest Laura,

Judy placed this bracelet into my safekeeping when you were brought to us as a baby. I'd forgotten all about it until I went through some old boxes and found it. It was around your wrist the day they brought you to us. You were sucking your tiny fingers and it looked so big on you. I know Judy was planning to give it to you herself, but you all left so suddenly that we both forgot about it. It had to be hidden, like they had to hide you, until the right time. From what I know, this bracelet can only be worn by the Bloodgifted and is passed down when the next one is born. I was told it once belonged to Luc's sister.

I checked the bracelet more closely. It was constructed such that the coils could be expanded as the wearer's wrist thickened. I slipped it on and tried to ignore the deep pang in my heart. I remembered the haunted look on Mum's face, her eyes glistening as she confirmed all Judy had told me the night I learnt my strange heritage.

'Wow! It's as old as the guys.' Kari rested her chin on my shoulder as her gaze scanned the letter.

'That would make it nearly two thousand years old!' Why did that vast stretch of time still surprise me? I should be used to vampire longevity by now. But it did explain the dents in the precious metal. Until Judy's birth, all the Ingenii had been men, armed with swords, engaging in battle.

I continued reading.

As you now know, they had to tell everyone you had died, and that the Ingenii bangle was buried with you. Like you, it had to be hidden to keep the pretense. Judy was worried one of the chateau staff might accidentally find it, so they thought it'd be safer all round if it was hidden in our house.

'Makes sense,' Kari muttered.

'Mmmm.' I nodded. 'They were right.'

My role and John's is over, but Lolly, we've loved you as our own and never regretted taking you into our home. You have been our joy, our life and our consolation. I hope you are happy, as you deserve to be. Write soon and let us know when you'll be coming home.

All my love,

Mum.

I swallowed back the tears.

'Lolly?' Kari glanced at me, eyes shining with mischief.

It'd been such a long time since anyone had called me that, and I had the feeling Kari was about to.

I sighed. 'When I was little, I couldn't pronounce "Laura." It came out as "Lolly." The name just stuck.' I shrugged. 'Mum occasionally calls me that at home.' I missed hearing her call me that—another time, another world.

'Lolly,' she repeated. 'I like it.'

I rolled my eyes and angled my wrist to get a better look at the inscription. 'I'll ask Alec about the inscription. He probably knows'. I was told the part he'd played in my protection, so he had to know the significance of the bangle.

I rubbed my chest at the now-familiar ache. My parents' faces materialised in my mind, and again I heard Luc's words so recently whispered to me in the dark, "Be happy, ma petite." The ache eased.

'Jake'd know. He's been there since the beginning.' Kari's eyes shone as she said it. Any excuse to see Jake and be near him, even if he didn't return her affection. Poor Kari. She was hopelessly in love with him.

'Maybe later. He's in the lab with Alec, and this isn't important enough to disturb them.'

She pursed her lips, crossed her arms and slunk back against the sofa, the very image of a petulant child.

I smiled and nudged her, my eyes briefly straying to the closet door and Judy's hidden diaries. What more of her life would I discover within their pages?

CHAPTER 9 - EXPLOSIVE LITTLE BOOK

LAURA

'Oh my stars!' I said loudly. The last of my mother's diaries sat open on my lap. It had taken several weeks, stealing time wherever possible, but I eventually got through them all.

I set the book aside, uncurled myself from the sofa and went to the window. It was good to stretch my legs. How many hours had I been lost in my mother's world? When I'd sat down to read, the welcome weak winter sunshine had flooded the room, its beams striking the crystal chandelier drops and scattering rainbows across the stucco ceiling. Now, the shadows had lengthened, and a damp chill permeated the air.

I shivered.

As I gazed out at the expansive lawn and the line of bare-branched trees that hugged the drive, images of what I'd read jostled for attention in my mind, the words screaming from the page.

I confronted father. He denied nothing Luc had told me! Heaven's above, not only did he know, but he'd married me off to that gangster to spite him! To continue the curse, to make Luc suffer!

Those lines, dated July 27th 1932, hit me the hardest. The more I learnt about my grandfather, the more I disliked him. Luc would have surely paid his gambling debts if he'd but asked. Who knows if all that had been a lie? How better to get back at Luc but to emotionally blackmail his daughter—the next Ingenii—into marrying a beast of a man, a criminal. And for what? For being one of the Bloodgifted?

Wicked man!

It explained why my grandfather had never been welcome in our home, and why I'd rarely been allowed to see him. Dad must have known.

My hands shook with rage, and I had to remind myself it was all now in the past, and my mother did have her revenge. Her written words were burned into my brain.

In anger, I did something a daughter should never do – I struck my father … He raised his hand as if to strike me back when Luc stormed into the room and threatened him. "Touch her and I'll kill you." That moment I realised who the true monster was, and it wasn't Luc.

That day, she'd left her husband and moved in with Luc. For days afterwards, the pages in her diary were filled with drawings of hearts and flowers, little snippets of poetry and the remnants of a dried rose.

My mother had found happiness.

Although they'd made personal vows to each other, I knew they weren't officially married until I was born—in a secret ceremony attended only by Luc's men. My parents had defied the moral conventions of the day by living openly with each other. I smiled as I remembered what she'd written:

Let society frown and censure. Nor do I care the Ladies League calls me an immoral, adulterous woman for leaving my husband. The real sin lies in society's hypocrisy.

Her courage filled me with pride. They would have moved back here at the time, if not for my grandfather, who refused to leave Sydney. Luc could have lived on the blood vials—as Judy had not yet reached her coming-of-age—but that would have revealed the existence of the bloodvault, for how could the Princeps daywalk and maintain his power without the Ingenii?

I glanced back at the brown leather diary on the sofa. It wasn't Judy's latest one, but it contained more than just her personal thoughts. In it, she'd recorded the names of her first husband's financial contacts—individuals and groups on his crooked payroll. Among them, names of prominent businessmen, companies, even policemen and local politicians. She'd threatened to reveal all unless he granted her a divorce, citing himself as the culpable party.

It had worked. Otherwise, as she wrote, Luc would've killed him, and she didn't want,

… that gangster's dirty blood on his hands.

But that wasn't all.

In one of her last entries, Judy had added an intriguing line mentioning the existence of another book, in which she'd recorded the names of all humans, including governments and well known politicians, who knew of the existence of Brethren throughout the world, and all the favours they owed Luc.

A black list!

My mind spun, imagining if this book fell into the wrong hands. Had she done it as it some kind of insurance to guard against a threat against Luc?

But where was it? Not here among the others, as I'd read them all, and the trunk was empty. Did it have a hidden compartment? I checked for a false bottom, tapped along its sides, back and front; pressed every button and indentation. Either it was incredibly cleverly concealed or it was just an ordinary old trunk with no secrets.

I sighed and gathering all the diaries, stacked them back in and closed the lid.

Only one diary I left out—the one mentioning this other mysterious book.

I re-read it, but there was no further information as I flicked the pages, except on the inside back cover where she'd drawn a symbol: the D'Antonville crest—of two serpents alongside a sword—above the image of an open book followed by the words, behind the precious pearl.

What the heck did that mean?

I copied the symbol onto a piece of scrap paper then locked away the diary with its other companions and pushed the trunk well back, against the closet wall. For extra protection, I covered it with a shawl and a pile of sweaters.

'That should do. Now to find that book.'

Since Alec would probably be stuck in the lab with Jake for a little longer, I figured I'd have the time to go hunting.

It was already early evening as I exited the closet. I switched on the lights and called Kari.

CHAPTER 10 – TOO LONG APART

LAURA

'I know this is the family crest, but what does this open book mean?' I handed Kari the slip of paper on which I'd hastily scribbled the image from my mother's diary.

She snuggled next to me on the sofa, her jean-clad legs tucked into green suede boots with heels I could only dream of wearing without toppling over.

'Library.' She handed back the note. 'Where'd you see it?'

I explained.

Her Nordic-blond brows shot skywards. 'Never knew she kept a diary. And all that's in it? Dynamite! I wonder if Luc knew and ...' she drew her teeth along her bottom lip, 'if Princi does.'

I shrugged. 'No idea. You're the first to know.' I'd even kept it from Alec all these weeks, not wanting to bother him with something that may not have been important.

Kari beamed. 'You mean, not even Princi knows?' When I shook my head, her eyes widened. 'It's hot stuff, Laura. You gotta tell him.'

'I know, but I was thinking, what if we find it first … check and see what exactly's written in it. Alec's got enough on his plate right now without adding more.'

I recalled the disappointed expression on Alec's face when Kari and I had wandered into the booby-trapped tunnels in search of him the last time we thought we'd had important information. It wasn't, and we'd nearly got ourselves killed.

'I'd rather hand him the physical proof, not just some lines from a diary saying the existence of a supposed black list.' And if it was in the library downstairs, then, hopefully, it wouldn't take us long to find. I tapped her on the boot and rose to go. 'C'mon, let's see where she's hidden it.'

'You're going to freeze like that.'

I looked down at my long-sleeved woollen tunic, velvet pants and black boots. Plus, the chateau had central heating. 'But it's only downstairs.'

Kari shook her head. 'Village library. Just about every building there has our crest … well, the older ones do.'

'Why would she hide it there?' Extra security in case the chateau's defences were ever breached? Possible.

She shot to her feet, eyes gleaming. 'Dunno. Let's find out. Wanna go? I'm sick of being cooped up and not being able to daywalk. Can't wait till the days of mourning are up.' When I hesitated, her eyes widened, and she slapped her forehead. 'Sorry, sorry, Laura. I didn't mean how that sounded. I can be so dumb sometimes.'

She thought she'd offended me. 'It's okay, Kari. Really. I understand.'

She grinned and flopped down on the sofa. 'It's only the village; it's not like we're going to Lyon or Avignon.'

It was so tempting. I'd gotten to know all the estate's housing, fields and woodlands in my daily walks, but in all this time, I hadn't gone beyond its boundary walls. Sabine did all the shopping and postal collection.

To see the village … get to meet the people, only a few of whom I'd met at the funeral. 'Okay, but I'll have to let Alec know.'

He was now the keeper of the green serpent ward ring, which shielded the chateau's grounds. Like an invisible force field, it kept out the Brethren. Being part human, I could travel through it, but not Kari: not any vampire. They needed Alec's permission to enter or leave.

Kari sprung from the sofa and clapped her hands.

'You going in those?' I pointed to her boots. They had the most incredible diamond stiletto heels. I was amazed that she could stand, let alone walk, in such high needle-pointed things. If it'd been me, I would've broken an ankle just trying them on.

She smiled and spun around on one of the heels. 'I can walk anywhere in these, even run if I have to. They're like slippers.'

I shook my head marveling at her, then strode to the window overlooking the courtyard and fixed my gaze on the whitewashed cottage Alec and Jake had turned into their lab. Apart from a sky full of stars, and a few shining lanterns in the courtyard, it was dark. Why on earth were their shutters closed? I knew they were in there. I could hear them. Since I had developed vampire hearing, we stopped using the telepathic powers of the serpent rings. There was no need. We could talk to each other anywhere on the estate within a two-kilometre radius.

'Alec, I need to go into the village. Kari'll come with me.'

The door of the cottage flew open. Before I turned around, Alec stood in the doorway of our suite, brows drawn, his lab coat flapping from the breeze of his speed. 'Why do you need to go into the village?'

That was quick. With his collar turned up and hands in his pockets, he managed to look sexy even in a lab coat. I refocused. 'Is there a problem?'

'Could be.' He closed the door, pulled out his mobile phone and showed me the screen. 'Karl's been keeping me updated.'

Kari peeked over my shoulder as I scrolled through several pics showing a wrecked pile with some of Karl's men, the crowned stag insignias on their jackets clearly visible, standing around a pile of debris. In a couple of images there were unrecognisable burnt remains. I could only tell they were the lamiae by what remained of their wings. There was no semblance left of the gargoyle-like creatures I'd seen in Timur's fortress. The first photo dated the day of the funeral. Three months ago.

So that was why he'd raced up here.

'There should've been four. Karl's men only found three.' He twirled the serpent ring on his finger, his gaze on my face but his thoughts, no doubt, on this problem, as well as on the fact he hadn't mentioned it to me.

I was about to open my mouth and ask why, when my conscience gave me a kick. Wasn't I keeping Judy's diary from him? I released a breath and handed the mobile back to him. 'So, the fourth one's survived and is out there somewhere.'

Alec glanced at Kari and motioned with his head toward the door.

'Okay, you two talky-talky. Holler when you're ready to go.' She grabbed a magazine from the coffee table and left the suite.

Alec shucked the lab coat, letting it drop to the floor, and helped himself to a glass of brandy. He downed it in one go.

It was then I saw the dark circles under his eyes, the worry lines around his mouth. He hadn't slept in several days, although technically he didn't need to. It was the burden of being princeps in his own right—no Luc hovering in the background influencing the Principate. He'd also accepted Luc's business responsibilities. As if that wasn't enough, he'd been stuck in the lab all this time.

Now this—a deadly monster on the loose.

He sighed. 'Sorry I didn't mention it sooner. Didn't want to worry you needlessly. You're grieving the loss of Luc and Judy, and now with the baby coming … Are we going to argue about this?' He poured himself another shot.

Am I some delicate daisy? 'Alec, I'm not …' The image of Judy's diaries flashed through my mind, again. I was keeping it from him for similar reasons. Guilt had me swallowing my retort. Perhaps now was not a good time to tell him, either.

Instead, I said, 'Okay, I get why you kept it from me. So … if I was to do something similar, you'd understand?'

He peered at me over the rim of the crystal glass at his lips. 'Like what?'

'Nothing really. Just saying.' Fingers crossed behind my back, I blocked any image of the diaries from my mind.

Alec's eyes narrowed.

Time to change tack. 'Those pics Karl sent you showed only three lamiae remains, right? Maybe they just haven't found the remains of the fourth one yet. It could be anywhere underneath all that mess, or even turned to ash, depending on how strong the fire was.'

He blinked, a slight crease between his brows as he set the glass down on the sideboard. 'It's alive, and it's killed several Brethren already. They've been tracking it. Last sighting was in Milan … just over the Alps. It's heading here.'

This was unexpected, but not disastrous and I was pretty confident as to what was going on in Alec's mind. 'And even if it does, it won't get past the ward ring, if that's what you're worried about.'

Alec cocked his head and gave me a smile. 'Read my mind.'

'And without the ring, either.' I wriggled my finger.

He sobered. 'You still have your dagger?'

'Never travel without it.' I patted the buckle of my jeans belt, which hid the jewelled knife Lucinda had so graciously given me. It had saved my life.

He poured himself another shot. 'Smear a bit of your blood on the blade. Do it fresh every day from now on.'

That idea didn't thrill me. I was no human pincushion. 'I'd rather keep a vial of my blood around for dip-and-stab-the-enemy occasions. Don't fancy pricking or slicing myself everyday.'

'We'll talk about that later. Now, why do you need to go to the village?'

Ice chinked in the glass as he dropped in a couple of cubes and refilled it. Was that his third or fourth shot? It was what Luc used to do in a crisis situation.

'Close your eyes.' I reached up and smoothed the hair from his brow then gently massaged his forehead and temples.

A light sigh escaped his lips, the tension visibly lifting from his features. 'Angel's touch.'

'Shhh.' I trailed my fingers along his ears and behind his head, letting my thumbs circle the base of his skull before twining his hair around my fingers. A tiny freckle at the base of his ear beckoned. 'Can vampires get drunk?' I whispered and kissed the delectable brown spot.

'No, but I wish we could,' he murmured into my hair.

His arms encircled me, the chill from the glass pressed against my back seeping through the woollen barrier of my dress.

We remained locked in each other's arms for several minutes, neither of us talking, simply enjoying the intimacy. We'd had little time for each other since the funeral, and with the restrictions imposed by the period of mourning, the time apart was affecting us both.

Alec lifted my chin. My pulse quickened as I gazed into the dark purple whorl of his eyes, my mouth drying as his thumb stroked my lower lip. 'Period of mourning's nearly over.'

'Actually, in twelve hours and thirty-four minutes.'

'Who's counting?' He smiled, and his lips grazed my waiting mouth. Although soft at first, his kiss grew hungry.

It ignited a fire between us. Our mouths meshed in a passionate tangle of lip and tongue, sending an intense ache of desire shooting from my belly to my groin that was almost painful.

Only he could only quench that ache. I needed him inside me.

Alec's own need pressed against my thigh, and I resented the barrier of our clothing. 'Damn the restrictions! I need you now.'

I tightened my hold around his neck as he lifted me into his arms, strode into the bedroom and kicked the door closed. Between feverish kisses, we shed our clothes and stumbled to the bed, which creaked beneath our weight.

I caressed the rock-hard muscles of his arms and chest, revelling in his strength. I uttered a deep moan as he sank fully into me, moving slowly at first then with greater urgency as my climax built.

This was no time for foreplay. This was a desperate thirst only he could quench.

'More. I need more,' I moaned into his mouth, the brandy on his tongue and lips making me heady. With my legs already crossed over this back, I pressed my heels into his buttocks in an attempt to push him deeper inside me. All the while my senses drank in his brandy-infused pine and musky scent, the softness of his hair beneath my fingers and the salty-sweetness of his skin.

Would I ever get enough?

'Whatever your pleasure.' He placed his hands under my backside and lifted me.

I threw my head back as he drove even further into me, the exquisite mix of pain and pleasure drawing a deep moan again.

Then he pulled almost completely out. No! A second later, I cried out as he surged into me, driving deeper and deeper until that sensual tingling spread from my feet, up my legs and into my core.

I sobbed in relief, the tears trickling down the side of my face and onto the pillow. Alec kissed them away, as he spilled into me and groaned his own release.

I floated on a blissful cloud, acutely aware of our panting breaths, the glistening droplets of sweat on our skin and the delicious fullness still nestled between my legs. Alec hadn't yet withdrawn. And I didn't want him to. How I'd missed his touch these last three months. How my body had ached for him.

If I had my way, no other Elder would be allowed to pass away for the next thousand years! I couldn't take another such long period of abstinence.

Alec lavished soft, feathery kisses over my face and down my neck, lingering at the spot where my pulse hammered. His slow intake of breath, the quick lick of his tongue and the sudden sharp pressure against my skin, meant only one thing—his incisors had slid down.

Alec had said he wouldn't feed from me during my pregnancy, preferring instead to live off the blood vials, but our prolonged separation had probably had an affect on his self-control. In a vampire's psyche, feeding and lovemaking were inexorably linked, and separating the two was unnatural. Would he be able to keep his resolution?

Would I?

I missed the heightened intimacy between us, the ecstasy caused by his bite. Would it really be so bad if he took a few sips?

Taking his face between my hands, I turned his head to face me. His struggle burned from the dark lavender depths of his eyes.

My heart lurched. 'A sip or two won't hurt, surely?'

The muscles in his neck corded, and he swallowed. Although his mouth was closed, the slight bulge above his lip betrayed the presence of hidden fangs. For a moment we simply gazed at each other.

A steely resolve appeared in his eyes. He shook his head. 'No, darling, it's not worth the risk.' He lifted himself onto his elbows, dropped a kiss on my belly and withdrew from inside me before loping off the bed.

Immediately my body resented his loss. 'Alec! Where're you going?'

He searched his pant's pockets and held up one of the blood vials. 'For this.' He then unstoppered the lid and gulped down its contents.

Looked like the period of mourning was over.

It was fascinating to see the dark circles beneath his eyes fade and his pale skin flush with renewed vitality. The corners of his mouth lifted into a sensuous smile, his eyes sparkling as they raked my body.

My stomach fluttered in delicious anticipation when he cast the vial aside and stalked toward me.

* * *

Beams of watery winter light trickled through the gaps in the drapes and settled on the peppermint-green checked comforter under which we lay entwined.

Hours of lovemaking had left us sated and languid. I ran my foot down Alec's leg, while my fingers traced the outline of the serpent tattoo on his chest.

'It's fading.'

'Mmmm … noticed. Little bit every day.' He curled an end of my hair around his finger and absently rubbed it against his lower lip.

The colours had become more muted, the edges less defined only since I'd fallen pregnant. A sign the curse was ending? The image of the serpent had first appeared on his chest the day my father changed him— a type of proof that he belonged to the House of D'Antonville, the clan of the cursed.

And now, after all these centuries, it had run its course. So too, it's visible reminder.

'I'm going to miss it. Looks kind of … sexy.'

His eyebrows shot skywards. 'Never knew you liked tattoos.'

'I don't normally. Just … it looks good on you.' This time I traced its outline with the tip of my tongue, stopping at the point above his heart, where two months earlier Jean-Philippe had rammed a stake.

That horrid day when I thought I'd lost him. Not even a scar marked his chest.

I pressed my lips to the spot and kissed it.

Alec's heart beat double-time, a rare occurrence considering how sluggishly his vampire blood usually flowed.

'Remind me to get a new one.' In an instant, he flipped me onto my back, pinning my hands above my head as his mouth teased my nipples until they stood taut, every nerve ending tingling all the way to my groin. His other hand massaged my core, round and round, flicking, pinching, rubbing, pushing me over the edge just as he plunged into me once more.

My stars! After the vigorous night we gave each other, how could my body still respond so readily to his touch?

A kaleidoscope of colours exploded behind my eyes and I released the breath I'd been holding in a blissful moan.

Seconds later, Alec threw his head back, the muscles in his neck bulged before he let out a long, drawn out sigh, and he relaxed, his hair dropping down over his forehead. He rolled to the side, taking me with him.

We lay there in exhausted silence for several minutes, the slow beat of his heart beneath my ear, our fingers interlocked with his thumb stroking the skin along my hand. He stared at the ceiling before his gaze panned to me. He drew our linked hands to his lips to kiss my pink-diamond engagement ring.

'What do you think about us getting married day after tomorrow?'

My heart jumped. 'Can't think of anything more wonderful … but it is short notice.' I glanced coyly up at him.

He chuckled and kissed the middle of my palm before he sobered. 'Call me old-fashioned, but I'd like us to be wed before our babe's born. Period of mourning's nearly over. Time to lift the gloom over this place. Get rid of all this black stuff—' he waved his hand at the wall where black cloth hid a beautiful gilt-framed mirror '—and bring back some joy.'

I glanced around our room, once Luc and Judy's. Even after all this time, the occasional hint of Judy's perfume floated on the air, as if she was still here. In a way it was comforting. And although it was now our suite, their portrait still hung in the living room above the fireplace. I couldn't bring myself to take it down.

Apart from shifting my parents' clothing out and moving ours in, Alec and I hadn't changed a thing. Not even the bed. It had been theirs. Perhaps I was even conceived here.

I stopped that thought before it could go any further.

'Glad you did that. I don't want to go there either,' Alec murmured.

Heat shot through my cheeks. 'You weren't supposed to hear that.'

He grinned and angled our linked hands exposing our brightly glowing serpent rings. 'No chance while we've got these.'

Those ever-telepathic little rings. How could I forget? 'And if I want to keep your birthday present a secret? How do I do that without you snooping into my head and spoiling it?'

Not that his birthday was coming up anytime soon, but he knew what I meant. I raised one eyebrow, just the way he occasionally did.

He gave me a slow grin. 'Mmmm … see the problem.'

'And…?'

Alec's eyes sparkled like he was enjoying a secret joke, the corners of his mouth twitching. Any moment a full-blown laugh would erupt from him. Oh, he knew how to mind-guard all right, but he didn't want to tell me.

Surely, some form of punishment was due. What could be better than to share all the activities that actually went into wedding preparations, no matter how small or intimate, especially as he'd sprung this so suddenly on me.

I straddled him, folded my arms over his chest, and nose to nose, conjured up images of wedding dresses I'd seen in magazines, cakes, flowers, decorated reception rooms and all the paraphernalia that went with it.

'Hey!' His eyes widened like saucers.

'Ha! Take that. We're sharing thoughts, remember? I can keep it up all day.' I hoped my grin was convincing.

He chuckled, and leaning up on his elbows, gave me a kiss. 'Don't picture my face when thinking. You've been doing it unconsciously. Not that I mind.'

His roguish smile would've slain a nun! 'Why didn't you tell me this before?'

He linked his hands behind his head and fell back against the pillow, the very picture of smug contentment. 'Must've forgot.'

Yeah, I just bet he did! I made sure his face was front and centre in my mind when I threw that thought at him.

Alec laughed. I hefted the nearest pillow, but he caught my wrists and rolled me beneath him, pinning my arms above my head. 'Just teasing. How can I can't resist when you take the bait so well.'

'You only do it coz you like wrestling in bed.'

'Can't think of a nicer pastime.' He interlaced our fingers and nuzzled my breasts sending tiny bolts of electricity shooting through me.

How could a girl concentrate? 'How long have you known?'

He lifted his head, his eyes serious as his gaze bored into me. 'Since your kidnapping. When I first tried to reach you, I was looking at the plane ... seeing that instead of you. It wasn't till I brought your face to mind, my thoughts got through to you.'

That awful, awful day. 'I kept your face before me the whole time. Your voice in my mind stopped me from breaking down.'

Images—both familiar and unfamiliar—flicked through my mind as Alec and I shared thoughts, and I saw the battle he'd engaged in after Karl had taken me to safety, how close he'd come to death: how close we had both come.

I threw my arms around his neck and hugged him to me, praying neither of us would ever be in such a situation again.

Alec held me just as tightly and whispered assurances in my ear as a cold shiver racked through me. 'You're home and in my arms ... safe. Leave it behind as a bad dream, my darling.'

Whether it was his words, the confident tone of his voice or the strength of his arms, but a sense of peace settled over me. My breathing evened and I snuggled into him, willing the world, and all its troubles, away.

Alec's lips sought mine in a kiss so lavish, so utterly consuming, he set my senses on fire. Then inch-by-excruciatingly-slow-inch, he entered me again, stretching, filling, until my body took all of him, and I heard him calling my name in my mind. I responded, and the serpent rings flared, their scarlet light blazing in the darkness and through the lids of my closed eyes.

Body, mind and spirit: Alec and I were joined in every possible way.

Nothing else existed but our own little world, cocooned in each other's arms riding the waves of pleasure we gave each other.

And as the afternoon shadows lengthened, our hunger for each other didn't abate. Over and over he pushed me into climax, until I thought I could take no more. But I did. Finally we lay sated and contented—at least for a while.

Fat, little cherubs, with their rounded, dimpled pink cheeks, smiled down at us from the ceiling cornices. They were a sweet reminder of the tiny cherub growing in my womb. *Not long now, and I'll be starting to show.*

'Perhaps we can leave the cake out.' But then again, what's a wedding without a cake?

'Come again?' His lips grazed my brow.

I turned more into his side to look up at him. 'You didn't hear my thoughts this time, did you?'

I'd been consciously picturing the cherubs.

He smiled. 'Only hear them when you want me too. Now you know how to do it. What's with the cake?'

'I was just thinking of the wedding cake, that maybe it's not such a good idea to have one. Besides me, and perhaps the housekeeper, who else would eat it? Mum, Dad and Jen are back in Sydney. Unless I send them each a huge piece so it won't go to waste I'll be stuck eating it all. I'll be showing enough soon.'

Alec gently placed his hand on my belly, leaned down and kissed it. 'Our babe's heartbeat's loud and clear.'

Our baby.

My heart fluttered at the words. 'First heard it two weeks ago. Got a shock as I thought my heart was doing something funny, until it hit me.'

He grinned and laid his head on my belly, his cheek warm against my skin, his dark hair contrasting with the fairness of my skin, like a raven with a dove. I ran my hand through his hair enjoying it silky smoothness between my fingers.

If we could have lain like that for the rest of eternity, I would've been content.

Alec rose and gazed tenderly at me, and smoothed the hair from back from my face. 'I'll talk to Pere Hubert later today. I'm sure he'd like to conduct the ceremony.'

Pere Hubert—Father Hubert—was the village priest, a kindly old man who'd visited a couple of times offering comfort and solace. His understanding and gentleness had touched me. 'I'd like that, too.'

Alec's lips brushed my belly. 'Would you be okay with a private ceremony, our circle only? I'd like to keep it from the Brethren for now. Not until our babe's born and we know for sure the Principate can function without the Bloodgifted.'

'Makes sense.'

Some time ago, I'd reconciled myself knowing my family and friends could not be at my vampire wedding—too tricky with a large Brethren presence. But that didn't mean— sometime in the near future—we couldn't retake our vows in Sydney for the benefit of the humans. We'd already discussed that, and Alec had promised.

'I intend keeping that promise.' He kissed me. 'But right now, you and our babe's safety is all I care about. Nothing else matters. You two are my life. I'm only sorry John and Eilene can't be here to celebrate with us. I know how much that would mean to you.' The vehement tone of his voice contrasted with the softness of his eyes as he gazed at me.

I swallowed down the lump in my throat. Was it possible to fall in love with a man more and more every day? Oh, yes, it was.

'It would ... and it wouldn't.' I sighed. 'Dad wouldn't enjoy seeing me married to you ... a vampire ... you know. If anything, it would hurt him, and I couldn't bear to see that.'

Alec rolled onto his back, taking me with him. His lips brushed the top of my hair. His other hand roamed my back and buttocks. 'I'm sorry, darling.'

'I hoped, in time, he'd get to know you ... see that some of his perceptions are wrong.' Now there appeared to be so little time, especially with me living on the other side of the world from Sydney. It would probably be at least a year until I saw him and Mum again, and his heart would have deteriorated further.

A dark cloud settled over my thoughts.

Alec kissed each of my fingertips. 'He knew Luc, and he'd met Marcus, who's the best of us. John chose to see what he wanted to see.'

There was no hint of bitterness or recrimination in his voice. It was simply a statement of fact as he'd observed it, and he'd known Dad far longer than I did. Although I didn't like to admit it, that much about Dad was true.

'Mum called him the stubbornest man in creation. You know she used to ply him with his favourite foods—sweets especially—whenever she wanted him to see things her way? It worked. She could whip up a dessert lovers dream cake in an afternoon, and by the evening, Dad was eating out of her hand.'

I wriggled my fingers under his nose.

'Yep, and....' An idea came to me. 'I'll bet Sabine could bake us a cake. Doesn't have to be elaborate. Get some flowers from the greenhouse, and the staff can decorate the great hall. And ... look—' My pulse raced as I bounced off the bed and ran into the closet. A moment later I stood before Alec, holding Judy's wedding dress against the front of my body, the plastic wrapping cool against my skin. 'It was Judy's. She'd kept it among her things all those years.'

Alec sat up, his jaw slack as he gazed at me. 'I remember her wearing it. Luc had asked me to be his best man.'

Time stood still as I stared at the beautiful man in my bed, the man who hadn't aged, and who drank my blood. The surreal moment that passed as quickly as it came.

I blinked. 'I keep forgetting you're a hundred something. Old man.'

He grinned, eyes twinkling, and tapped the empty spot next to him.

'Come here, and I'll show you exactly how *old* I am.'

I draped the dress carefully over the back of the sofa. Linking my hands behind my back, I sauntered casually back toward the bed. 'Don't want you to exhaust yourself.'

Alec gave a feral growl. His eyes darkened as his gaze raked my body before levelling with my eyes. 'Darling, after I'm finished with you, I'll have to carry you down the aisle.'

My breath left me as a delicious shiver sent my heart racing, and with trembling legs at the promised pleasure in his voice, I sank into his open arms.

Everything else could wait.

CHAPTER 11 - BEHIND THE PEARL

LAURA

A misty cloud of warm air hovered around my mouth, even as the icy night air chilled my cheeks. Kari and I stood outside the two-storey village library in D'Antonville, and I wrapped my arms around myself in an attempt to stave off shivering. Like the local primary school and the municipal hall, between which it was wedged, the library appeared to be a centuries-old building with inset columns, decorated stonework and a curved tiled roof.

Although no snow covered the ground, the frosty air had me longing to get inside. Our family crest—the sword and serpent insignia—stood proud and steadfast from the top of the façade. Directly below it, three arched windows spilled warm light onto the street.

The librarian was expecting us.

I still hadn't told Alec about Judy's diary, not until I was sure its information was as explosive as I suspected. He had enough to worry about. But, he hadn't been happy that only Kari would be with me.

'With that thing out there—'

'It's probably nowhere near us. And, besides, you know how feral Kari can get if I'm in danger. I remember the way she jumped on Rasputin's back.' And then he had mesmerised her and nearly killed her. Perhaps not a good illustration.

He'd then wanted one of the men to accompany us, but they were all busy, too. In the end, he'd come up with the sensible solution: extend the ward ring's shield to cover the main part of the village, but not as strongly as Luc had done in the nineteen forties who'd made it invisible to human eyes.

'Perfect.' I'd kissed him and, with Kari as my bodyguard, drove into the village.

Now, as we were about to enter, I sensed … something … as if I was being watched. I didn't know why, but my gaze was drawn toward the furthest end of the street, where the village church stood, an old medieval building, complete with spire, flying buttresses and its turrets adorned with grotesque-looking gargoyles.

Ech! Never understood the medieval penchant for those things.

My insides turned cold. 'Kari, is the church covered by the protective ward?'

'Aaah … not sure. Let me check.' Hand outstretched, she strode several metres down the street and stopped. 'It ends here,' she called over her shoulder. 'It's tingly. Why do you wanna know?'

'Had an odd feeling, that's all.'

Please, please let it not be the lamia. We were alone, and if it was, Kari'd be no match for the thing. Tentatively, I checked my serpent ring. Its eyes glowed right red. My pulse returned to normal—no danger.

Eyes narrowed, she turned back and surveyed the distant church. I heard her quietly counting, '… twenty-two, twenty-three, twenty-four…. Nah, all's good.' She scratched her head. 'I know what you were thinking. There are no extra gargoyles. But …' She did another pan of the street and sniffed deeply. 'I've never smelled the things, so I can't really tell.'

'Believe me, you'd remember if you did.' And since I couldn't detect anything foul either, I put my fears down to jittery nerves, and just knowing that thing was free and out there ... somewhere. Hopefully, not here.

She shrugged. 'No way it could get through the ward shield thingy anyway. C'mon, let's get inside.' The confident smile on her pretty pixie face allayed my fears, and linking arms, we hurried up the stone steps and through one set of three purple double doors above which busts of Voltaire, Rousseau and Thoreau gazed down at us from their carved niches.

I'm sure I must've purred when the warm air-conditioning hit my numb cheeks, along with the smell of freshly brewed coffee. Kari giggled and rubbed my face to get the circulation going. Her hands were toasty.

'Get ready to have your ears bleed. Adeline talks and talks and talks and—'

I slammed my hand over her mouth. 'Okay, I get it. Adeline doesn't get out much. Right?'

'You'll see,' Kari mumbled behind my hand.

A short, slim woman—in her early forties, perhaps—with a pert, upturned nose and rosy cheeks met us in the foyer. She looked vaguely familiar, as if I'd seen her somewhere, although we hadn't met. Or had we? And if she was as chatty as Kari had said, I was sure I would've remembered her.

'Milady and Mademoiselle Kari, come in, come in.' Her French accent fell softly on the ear. She beamed, revealing a gap-toothed smile. 'I've made some coffee. It should warm you up.'

'Sounds wonderful.'

Clear grey eyes regarded me with interest. 'How much like your father you look. What a loss, what a loss.'

I rubbed my chest at the wound her unexpected remark had opened. It had only just begun to close. Kari shot me a sympathetic look and I had to bite back the tears. *Deep breaths.*

She indicated the way to her office where a steaming pot of coffee and several mugs sat atop a bench. In a little sink nearby, I glimpsed a couple of food stained dishes. She must have only just finished her evening meal.

Atop a solid mahogany desk, arranged in military fashion and equidistant from each other, were pens, books and folders. Even the laptop sat at a perfect ninety-degree angle. And perfectly centred between all, an elegant wood and brass name plaque. I mentally translated it from the French: *Adeline Dalpuget, Head Librarian and Archivist.*

'We met, milady, briefly at the funeral, but I doubt you'd remember. So many people offered their condolences, and I was only one face among hundreds.'

As she spoke, I glimpsed an earring shaped like an ancient scroll, and I remembered seeing her at my parents' funeral. Why I should remember those particular earrings, I had no idea. Perhaps it was, unlike everyone else's dark sombre dress—some even had jewellery made from jet— those little silver dangly scrolls were like a cheerful light in a dark time.

'I do remember you. You sat with the First Families.'

Her grey eyes twinkled. 'Yes, yes I did. How kind of you to notice. I was with Monsieur Le Mayor and his wife, and our handsome chief of police ...' She rattled off a host of names, none of which I knew, adding little hints about their character traits. '... really shouldn't eat so much brioche. It gives him gas.'

Behind her, perched on the edge of the librarian's desk, Kari barely managed to disguise her snort with a cough as she downed her coffee. After which, she mimicked Adeline's chatter with finger movements and much head and eye rolling. It was all I could do to hold a straight face.

But we weren't here to socialise.

'The coffee was lovely, thank you, Madame Dal—'

She laid her hand on my arm. 'Just Adeline. I'm not one for formality. Lord Luc, God bless his soul—' she crossed herself '—called me Addy. It was so nice of him. He even let me—'

I cleared my throat. 'Adeline, did Lady Judith ever hand you a notebook for safekeeping?'

She shook her head. 'Not ever. Is that what you're looking for?'

'About this size.' I indicated with my hands. 'Black, red or brown leather. It's supposedly here in the library behind a precious pearl.'

Adeline's eyebrows soared upwards. 'Pearl? Obviously a mistake. The only pearls in this library are to be found in books. Which is natural, as books are pearls....'

Kari and I exchanged a glance. 'Hidden inside a book?'

Could that be what Judy's cryptic note meant? It made sense, but then again, wouldn't it create a bulge within the book it was hidden? Unless it was hollowed out.

'No, no, no. I know every book in this library. It's not possible.'

'You personally check every one? Open them up and see that pages haven't been removed?'

She stared at me, mouth opening and closing like a guppy. 'Ah, um … not … recently. There are thousands of books here, shelf upon shelf—'

'Then it's possible.' Could it be that simple? I couldn't wait to get started, sure the library would have something on pearls. 'Thanks for the coffee. Now, where're the books on pearls?'

I rinsed my cup in the sink and went to the door.

'Milady, wait. Let me show you.'

Adeline led us up a wide set of stairs into the main section of the library. Unlike the library in the chateau, there was no frescoed ceiling, marble columns or medieval globes. The interior was simple and modern, with a large central area filled with tables and chairs. I could see kids using the place during school hours, working on projects or sitting in nooks reading a picture book.

A small pang tugged at my heart. The Year 6 class I was meant to be teaching this year would have another teacher. Perhaps, when all this was over, one day, I could resume my teaching career.

'From here to here.' She pointed out two shelves with a range of books from the history of pearl diving to academic publications on oyster cultivation and the harvesting of cultured pearls.

'Kari, you take the this shelf.' I tapped the timber frame. 'I'll go through the bottom one.'

She nodded, and we set to work, opening every book, even checking the bindings in case the notebook had been hidden there. Adeline hovered at our elbows, reaching out then snatching her hand back as if worried we'd damage her beloved books. How did she deal with groups of school kids?

Compared to Kari's vampire speed, I must have seemed as slow as a snail. She was finished when I had barely completed half my assigned row. She pitched in to help.

'Nothing.' I threw my hands up when we were done and turned to Adeline. 'No special reserve?'

'I'm sorry, milady. This is it.'

'I don't understand. It must be here.' For good measure, I peeked behind the shelves in case I'd missed something.

Kari sat cross-legged on the floor and looked up at me expectantly. I joined her, resting my head in my hands while mulling over the possibility we might never solve the puzzle and find that notebook.

Although we had tried to be careful with the books, the military precision with which she realigned the shelves would have pleased any general.

Behind the precious pearl.

The words played over and over in my mind. It made sense to Judy, and I thought it had to me, too. Had I been wrong?

'Lolly, can I take a peeky at that note again?' Kari's cheeky wink at using my mum's pet name for me had me rolling my eyes. 'I reeeeaally like it. Please, can I use it?'

'Why fight it,' I said on a sigh. 'But not in public,' I stipulated as I reached into my pocket and handed her the slip of paper on which I'd copied Judy's sketch with the elusive words.

'Okey-dokey.' She hummed a little tune as she examined the note, and then her gaze roamed the library.

'Did I get it wrong, Kari?

'Don't know.'

Leaning my head back against the shelf, I spotted a dedicatory plaque on the wall opposite. My parents' names were on it. Luc had commissioned the building back in the early eighteen-hundreds, and Judy had sponsored recent extensions and renovations.

In all the years I had known her as my aunt, how little of her true life I had actually known; a whole other existence I'd been ignorant off.

As I stared at her name—Judith Dantonville—her initials stood out to me: JD. She'd often signed her name simply using her initials, with a small e after the D for the "ville" in Dantonville: JDe.

I sat bolt upright. 'Jude!'

'What?' Kari's nose crinkled as she turned to face me.

I shot to my feet, heart pounding. 'Judy's initials—JD with a small e added to it, stands for Jude, as in short for "Judy". Mum and dad always called her that.'

Kari and Adeline looked at me blankly.

'Don't you see? It's a play on her name: Jude for Judy, and Jude, a book in the New Testament, the Bible—"the pearl of great price." That's what she meant by precious pearl. It's hidden behind a bible!'

'Ha! I would never have gotten that.' Kari gave my arm a gentle punch.

I turned to Adeline. 'Where's your religious section?'

She pointed. 'Up there. Next level, next to philosophy.'

I all but ran, sure I was right, and scanned the titles. There, to my right, several Bibles sat together in a range of sizes, colours and languages. I chose the most non-descript looking one, pulled it out and peered behind.

Barely visible, it's dark brown leather cover blending with the timber hue of the shelf on which it lay, was Judy's diary.

I reached in and pulled it out.

Over my shoulder, I heard Kari suck in a breath.

* * *

'Laura, neptis mea delictissima, what are you doing here at night?'

'Arrgghh!' Like a jolt of electricity, Marcus's voice behind me made me jump, the diary dropping from my hands. My heart thumped triple time.

'Didn't mean to scare you.' He stooped to retrieve the fallen notebook and handed it back to me. A smile played around his mouth, but sadness lingered in his eyes.

He and Cal appeared from nowhere. I knew they'd been away quelling a dispute between prefects and were expected back any day, but I would never have imagined them suddenly showing up here.

'How come I didn't hear you, grandfather? Isn't my hearing like yours now?'

'Seems you were too engrossed in looking for that.' His gaze panned to the leather bound book in my hand.

True. Even from a young age, whenever I concentrated on a task, the world around me seemed to disappear. My friends had to tap me on the shoulder to get my attention for no matter how many times—or how loudly they called—I didn't hear them. It had been one of the banes of my life. I had hoped that with my newly developed hearing, I could wave goodbye to that problem.

Alas not.

'How'd you know I'd be here?'

'I didn't. We came through the village on our way home and were stopped by the barrier. It doesn't normally shield the village ... not in a long time.'

'Soon as Alec let us through, he told us you were in here. Said you were looking for something,' Cal added, his eyebrow raised.

Marcus clasped his hands behind his back and rocked slightly on his heels. 'Mea Neptis, ordinarily, I wouldn't ask—it's your business. But, by being here at night when our kind is active, with a vicious lamia on the loose—yes, I've heard—that requires the barrier to be expanded in order to protect you ... You do know that the wearer of the ward ring has to exert extra energy to extend its field?'

Alec hadn't told me that bit. If I'd known, I'd have waited until the morning ... and then what, drag him away from the lab where he and Jake were working?

I swallowed as the blood drained from my face at his disappointed expression.

'I ... uh ...'

Kari sprang to my defense. 'This couldn't wait till daylight coz someone else could accidently find it and my blood vials are running low so I don't want to use them all up and Laura can't really go anywhere without me—'

Marcus held up his hand for Kari to stop, but his gaze remained on me. 'Why, Laura?'

Well, there was no point in hiding it now. I sighed and held the notebook toward him. 'Came to find this. Judy mentioned it in her diary. If I'm right, it contains the names of all Brethren and all the humans, including governments, that know about us.'

Marcus's eyes widened. 'Deus!' He took it from me and flipped the pages, his eyes scanning the contents at superhuman speed. Cal and Kari peered over his shoulder, and at one point, she released a drawn out whistle.

Cal swore.

Everyone was getting a look-in except me. 'Will someone please tell me what's in there? After all, I was the one who found it.'

'You know, she worked out all the clues by herself?' Kari gave me a gentle punch in the arm.

Marcus smiled and extended his arm. 'My apologies. You were right not to have delayed. Come, look.' With his arm around my shoulder, Marcus drew me to his side and showed me the pages. 'Powerful names here. Were it ever released to the public, it could topple governments and expose our world.'

'See. Told ya.' Kari grinned at me.

One list alone contained well known businesses and the names of contemporary, as well as past, heads of states and even monarchs ... and what each owed Luc in terms of money, but, more importantly, favours rendered. Some CEOs owed their positions to him.

So many.

My head swam. 'This is incredible.' I glanced at Adeline, who stood to the side, hands on hips, shaking her head and glaring at the notebook as if it were some kind of intruder in her perfectly ordered domain. 'And you had no idea?'

'Milady ...' She shook her head then spun on her heel and walked away, muttering, 'Must check every shelf. Can't have people hiding their things in my library whenever they want.'

'Poor, Addy. I reckon we just ruined her night, but it hasn't stopped her chatty-chatty.' Kari chuckled.

Marcus closed the notebook and handed it back to me. 'Keep it safe. Tell no one outside the family about this ... I assume Alec...?'

I slipped it into my shoulder bag. 'Doesn't know. I didn't want to bother him with it until I was sure it was important. He's got so much going on.'

He crossed his arms over his chest and regarded me with the age-old expression a parent uses with an errant child. 'Commendable sentiment, mea neptis, but as princeps, Alec must be aware of everything, for his safety and yours. Even if you think it's inconsequential, tell him anyway.'

I sighed. 'Yes, grandfather.'

He laughed, a genuine booming laugh. 'I enjoy being called grandfather.'

We left the library and tramped outside. Marcus scanned the silent, empty street. His eyes narrowed as he gazed in the direction of the church, the hoot of an owl snagging his attention. A slight frown drew his brows together.

'Sensing it, again?' Cal stood by his side, his fingers stroking the smooth hilt of his sword.

'Mmm ... not sure...' He threw back his coat and unsheathed his sword. 'Get the girls into the car.'

My stomach sank. 'I had a feeling we were being watched when we got here earlier tonight.'

Marcus turned to me and cocked an eyebrow before addressing Cal. 'Drive them back to the house, fast as you can. Zigzag.'

'But there's no way it could've broken through the ward.'

'Unless it was already here when the shield was extended.'

The implications of that didn't need to be vocalised. Marcus's grave expression said it all: the thing—if it was here—was trapped inside the protective shield … with us.

'Shit!'

'Go. I'll join you back at the house soon as I'm satisfied that thing's not in the village.'

'And if it is?'

Marcus slapped a hand on Cal's shoulder. 'You have your orders, legionary.'

Cal sighed. 'Sir.'

Kari bustled me into the back seat of our car, as Cal slid into the driver's seat.

'Where's your car?' I asked. How had they gotten here from the airport?

'Didn't bother with one. We ran. Only takes a few minutes to get here from Avignon.' Cal adjusted the rear-view mirror, staring back at the direction Marcus had taken, before starting the motor.

I glanced back as we drove away. The lights in the library were still on. 'Is Adeline safe?'

'As long as she doesn't come out. Lamia hate bright lights—burns their miserable eyes.'

I thought back to Count Timur's poorly lit, dingy fortress, and the lamiae clinging to the rafters. It was for their benefit the place had been so dark. Yet still it must've been too bright for them if they chose to hide in the darkest corners of the ceiling.

'Cal, she can't stay in the library all night.'

'Ask Alec to keep the ward in place at least till sunrise.' He barely gave me a minute to do that before swerving the car wildly from one side of the road to the next.

The seatbelt strained painfully against my torso as Kari and I were thrown about like a couple of rag dolls.

'Sorry, ladies. This is the best way to stop a flying lamia from attaching itself to us.'

I was too nauseous to respond. Thankfully, at the speed Cal was doing, we were through the gates of the chateau within a minute.

Servants ran out up to us the moment we arrived. I glimpsed Alec as I exited the car then bent over and threw up.

CHAPTER 12 - NOTHING STAYS HIDDEN

ALEC

'And you let her go alone, with only Kari for protection? She's no match for a lamia.' Marcus's words kept coming back to me as I scrutinised data in the lab.

Earlier in the night, I'd extended my senses, searching for unauthorised Brethren—and lamia—who could possibly be lurking in the area ready to take advantage of the raised barrier when I'd let Marcus and Cal through.

All had been good. The only other presence I'd sensed out there had been my new charge, Dominik. I'd given him the night off, told him to hone his hunting skills by chasing down deer in the forest.

'Laura's safe, Marcus. Plus she's within the barrier. You think I'd let her go if I sensed any danger? I can't keep her cooped up here. She's not a prisoner.'

There was a long pause before he'd spoken again, his voice carrying clearly on the night air. 'I'll drop by the library to see what was so important for her to be there tonight.'

He was beginning to sound like Luc. Why didn't that surprise me? Too many years secluded in a monastery may have done wonders for his character, but it froze him in time in regards to modern women. Laura belonged to the twenty-first century. She was smart and independent, and I trusted her judgement.

I got back to work. The screech of tyres at the entrance gates caught my attention. 'Cal's driving, right?'

'Yep. Like an out-of-control chariot in the hippodrome.'

'Remind me to never allow him to drive Laura again.'

Jake's laugh was cut off by Cal's voice. 'Alec, Jake, come quick.'

The urgency in his tone was enough. I tore out of the lab. Kari was hunched over a vomiting Laura.

'Blast your driving, Cal!'

Laura raised her head, her face white as alabaster. 'Not Cal's fault.'

'Sorry, Alec, I had to. Lamia. Marcus is out there trying to catch a scent.' Cal inclined his head in the direction of the village.

My insides may as well have turned inside out. Lamia! 'How the hell did it get into the village? I would've sensed it!' Damn! This was my fault. 'I should've been with you.' I picked her up and carried her into Luc's old office in the library, gently laying her on the leather sofa. 'Kari, glass of water from the fridge.'

Laura drank. Colour soon returned to her cheeks. She pushed herself up on her elbows. 'Funny how water tastes so sweet after throwing up.'

My pulse steadied. 'Feeling better?'

'Yeah.' She smiled and placed her hand on my cheek. 'Sorry to have scared you like that. I don't normally get car sick. Baby's changing everything.'

I placed my hand over hers and kissed the base of her palm. 'Until that lamia's caught, you're not going anywhere without me. Understood, Laura? I can't begin to imagine….' My throat constricted.

She leaned forward and lightly kissed my lips. 'I'm all right. Nothing happened, and I was safe with Kari.' She glanced up and gave Kari a wink. 'Actually, we don't know if the lamia is here. Maybe I was just being over sensitive.'

Now the hairs on the back of my head did rise. 'You sensed something and didn't think to tell me?'

'It was probably nothing. Overactive hormones.'

'Marcus didn't think so.' Cal walked in to the room. 'He's on his way back and wants to see everyone.' He grabbed a chair, brought it close to the sofa and straddled it. 'You okay, angel?'

'Fine, Cal. But I'm not driving with you again.'

He chuckled.

Marcus strode in, acknowledged us and then stood facing the window that overlooked the garden beyond, hands clasped behind his back. In the reflection from the darkened glass, his face looked grim.

Looked like lab work was over for the night.

The other men nodded as they entered. Stony faced. Even Terens. He could usually find some amusement in almost any situation.

Not this time.

My scalp prickled.

Laura sat up, handed her empty glass to Kari and took hold of my hands, her face etched with concern. 'Sorry if I got you in trouble. I should've told you, but … I wanted to be sure first.'

My scalp didn't just prickle. It outright itched. 'Sure of what?'

Her anxious lavender eyes bored into mine. When she bit her bottom lip my gut tightened. 'Laura, what did you not tell me?'

'Close the door.' Marcus swung around as Jake shut the door and leaned back against it.

Kari left Laura's side to stand next to him.

I found Judy's diaries in the closet when cleaning out. She kept a hidden notebook, with names in it. All humans who know about us … the Brethren, that is. She hid it in the library. Her voice spoke in my mind.

The tightness in my gut spread to my chest. Luc never kept written records of his human contacts. Security. I had to memorise the list. What had possessed Judith to do that? Then hide it in a public place?

And you couldn't tell me…?

Her eyes flared. *Same reason you didn't tell me about the lamia! You were so busy. I thought to save you …* She released a curt breath. *What if it had all been nothing and I'd had dragged you from the lab, huh?*

I was caught. Damned if I agreed and damned if I didn't. *Promise me, if you think anything's important, let me in on it.*

That goes both ways.

How could I argue with that?

At least now we're even.

She kissed my cheek and sent me a mischievous smile that shot my blood straight to my groin. Little witch! I didn't know whether to laugh or smack her bottom. I stored the latter idea for later.

She sat on the sofa, while I took Luc's place in the deep leather chair behind the princeps desk. He may have passed over, but his presence still lingered. I picked up his favourite fountain pen and … set it down again. It didn't belong in my hands. Leaning back in the chair, I waited for Marcus to begin.

'As you all know, one of the lamiae escaped the destruction of the Rebels' hideout and is presumably on its way here. Tonight, both Laura and I had a sense of its presence. I scouted round the village and the perimeter of the ward but couldn't detect its scent anywhere.'

My fingers curled over the arms of the chair. 'You and I both know I would never have allowed Laura to enter the village had I sensed presence of a lamia.'

Marcus raised his hands. 'It's all right, Alec. I'm not accusing you. On the contrary, you were right to do so.' He glanced at Laura. 'But, we'll get to that shortly.'

I sat back down, somewhat confused, expecting Marcus to explain that *shortly*.

'I was wrong then?' Laura's gaze flitted between Marcus and me.

'No, not at all.' He glanced at each of his men. 'Those of us who've hunted this creature know that it homes in on its prey by entering their minds from even hundreds, perhaps thousands, of kilometres away.' He turned to me. 'It explains why you didn't sense its presence.'

'Small consolation.'

'Like any predator, it enjoys the hunt, loves the taste of fear in it's prey. Makes it all the more satisfying when it kills.'

A strange quiet descended. We all knew that feeling.

The lamia wasn't the only predator.

I recalled my early vampire days. The constant thirst was all consuming. Damned hard to control. I enjoyed the thrill of the hunt, the taste of fear in my prey. And when I fed … ecstasy. My groin hardened. I swallowed hard, my knuckles tight. The edges of the desk cracked beneath my grip. A couple of the men fidgeted, their eyes on the ground, while Terens's eyes paled dangerously.

You okay? Laura's voice whispered through my mind.

I gave her a nod, and hoped my smile was convincing even as I fought to control my inner beast. The dark urge to hunt and kill was alive and well.

'Laura, mea neptis, we're being hunted.' Marcus's eyes paled.

Laura's face blanched. Her hands strayed to the hidden dagger in her belt. Was it a conscious movement? If so, she'd come a long way in such a short while. Her knife skills impressed me. I released a satisfied breath.

'But isn't the protective ward meant to block stuff like this? When Timur had the ward ring, Alec and I couldn't speak mind to mind. How's the lamia doing it?' Her gaze darted from man to man, finally resting on me.

'It's different from us.' I leant forward and rested my elbows on the desk. 'Its mind control is way beyond anything we can do. When Luc had the ward ring made it was to guard against others of our kind, not theirs.'

'It wasn't an issue then. We'd already imprisoned them,' Jake added.

Marcus nodded.

'But say, theoretically, it could be possible for one to physically get through the ward if it wanted to?' she asked.

'No. Timur had the ward ring. They'd need his permission to get out. They were trapped.'

'Okay.' Laura appeared satisfied, a small smile lighting her face.

But something else bothered me. 'Marcus. The lamia saw me as well. We all tried to kill it. Why is only coming after you and Laura?' I did have a suspicion. What I wanted was confirmation.

'We're just the start. Don't worry; it'll come after you as well.' His eyes narrowed, a sneer punctuating his next words. 'It wants vengeance for the death of its brothers, and of course, for being locked away. What could be better than to kill me and my next of kin.' His gaze locked on Laura. 'End the family line of Antonius.'

Laura sighed. 'Brilliant.'

I spun the serpent ring round and round my finger. Marcus had confirmed my hunch. The beast within me roared. It was time to hunt us some lamia.

'We need to go after this thing. Capture it and destroy it using a smear of Laura's blood. It's the only thing that works.'

'Alec's right. Why wait for it to come after us? I could do with good hunt. My blood's really up now.' Terens pulled his dagger from his boot and flicked it point first into the floor. With a satisfying thud, it lodged into the narrow mortar between the stone tiles.

'Remember what happened last time?' Cal tapped the front of his head. 'It nearly got me, man. I'm not confronting that thing unless I've got aluminium foil wrapped round my head.'

Cal facetiousness brought a smile to my face. But Terens appeared to be taking it seriously. 'Reckon it could work?'

Sam snorted.

I hadn't seen much of him lately. He'd been down at the crypt, in the tunnels—or what remained of them—rewiring the crippled security system and shoring up the chateau's foundations. It had been designed to withstand any explosion. Still, it didn't hurt to be sure.

'Sam, how secure are we?'

He pulled out his phone, punched a few buttons and stared at the screen before pocketing it again. 'No way can it get through.' He pointed at me. 'With the ward ring, this place is secure.'

I took his word for it.

'We caught it once before; we can do it again. This time, get rid of it for good.' Marcus's face creased into a feral grin, his eyes shining at the thrill of the hunt.

It was infectious. 'When do you plan to leave?'

'Soon as I can. I must contact the Elders and get them to send out some hunting parties. I'll take Terentius and Calixtus with me.'

Cal touched his head in salute. Terens grinned.

Lucky bastards! But I couldn't do that to Laura. She was my responsibility. Plus, I'd miss being away from her, anyway.

'Don't forget the aluminium foil,' Sam added with a smirk.

Hand up to her mouth, Laura tried to hide her laugh.

'Now, the next thing you all need to know.' Marcus's gaze connected with mine. 'The Brethren don't want the curse to end.'

'No surprises there,' Terens drawled. He flicked his dagger between thumb and forefinger, balancing the sharp blade tip on the end of his finger without drawing blood. He was quite adept.

Laura flinched a few times watching him. I tried not to laugh.

'They've tasted daylight, and with no more blood vials to come, they're edgy.' Marcus moved away from the window and perched on the corner of my desk—guess it was my desk now—knuckles white as his hands gripped the green malachite edge.

Jake and I shared a glance. No results yet. We needed a breakthrough, and soon.

'Anyone said anything … any hint of threats…?' Sam leaned forward in his chair, hands clasped in front of him.

Cal took his cue from Marcus. 'Not in so many words. They were compliant enough, but we sensed … something going on. I smelled anger and duplicity. If they're not plotting something, I'll eat my sword.'

'Shit! Why don't they give it a break. We shared the vials with them. Ungrateful mongrels!' I rarely saw Jake lose his temper. No doubt our slow progress in the lab was behind his outburst.

Hell, that bugged me too. Not much we could do about it, though.

'Between this and the lamia' —he took a deep breathe— 'perhaps now's the time to move the household to Caledonia.' Marcus's sudden pronouncement took everyone by surprise, except for Cal.

Why couldn't he simply say Scotland?

Laura's hand flew to her belly. 'But there's still plenty of time. I'm not due for ages yet.'

Terens stopped flipping his dagger, head snapping up as he gaped open mouthed at Marcus. 'Commander … why so soon?'

I rose from my seat. 'Marcus, with all due respect—'

'We can't! Alec and I are still working on the antigen, and we've had a breakthrough. Got the damned thing identified and isolated. Next step is replication. We're so close.' Jake pushed away from the door and approached Marcus. 'Just a little more time; that's all we need.'

'How much more time?'

Jake and I exchanged glances.

'Couple of weeks—'

'Month.'

Jake turned to me with an expression that didn't fill me with confidence.

Marcus's eyes flared. It wasn't like Jake to question his commander's orders. I couldn't remember the last time anyone had.

Jake lowered his head. 'Forgive me, Marcus, I meant to say Alec and I are still working on the antigen, and we've had a breakthrough. We're so close. Just a little more time, that's all I ask.'

'I'm sorry, gentlemen, but I don't believe we have a week, let alone a month, especially with half of our company away hunting the lamia. Nor do I expect them to come here. It's pointless, no? The grave site, on the other hand, if they were to destroy that or prevent Laura from coming anywhere near it … I think you can all see the problem.'

I did. According to the witch's stipulations, our child had to be born on the site of the massacre.

Luc had originally built a house on the site with an enclosing wall screening it off from human eyes. To make doubly sure no one would encroach on it, he'd used the ward ring to make it virtually invisible. The house had stood for centuries, until he'd replaced it with an impregnable fortress.

In my mind's eye, a shimmering haze surrounded the site. Anyone straying into the area would see a clearing surrounded by woodland. Apart from wildlife, I sensed no humans, nor Brethren in the area.

'Except for us, no one knows the exact location of the gravesite. And even if they do somehow manage to work it out, the ward around it makes it invisible,' I said.

'The shield fools the eyes, but not the nose.' Marcus tapped the side of his. 'Our scents are all over the place, and so is … hers.' He grimaced. I guessed he was referring to the witch who'd created the curse. 'Any of our kind can follow the scent, home in on it, even if they can't see it, then surround the place and prevent us getting in.'

'They want a fight? I'm ready.' Terens snarled. With a flick of his wrist, he pinned a a passing moth to the wall near where Sam stood.

Laura's eyes widened. 'I really need to practice more,' she muttered, her fingers stroking the belt buckle at her waist.

Another thing I'd neglected, stuck in the lab with Jake. The men were always ready for a fight, but she wasn't. The last thing I wanted was to expose Laura to more danger, especially now.

'I'll contact Dougal to get him to send out an extra patrol. Perhaps even send Sam to update the security monitors.' Sam gave me a nod and a smile. 'If any Brethren come within sniffing distance, Dougal'll take care of them. Meanwhile, with you, Terens and Cal hunting down the lamia, the rest of us can remain secure here, and hopefully, by the time Laura's due, Jake and I will have replicated the antigen, and we can join you there.'

'I second that.' Jake looked expectantly at Marcus.

'Who's Dougal?' Laura asked.

'Caretaker of the site. I appointed him after the First Rebellion. A good man.' A fleeting smile crossed Marcus's face.

Laura's gaze flitted to me, one eyebrow raised in question.

He's one of us, Laura—our clan. Marcus sired him. He's faithfully guarded the site for the last thousand years.

He's Marcus's juvy? I don't why that should surprise me.

Tell you about it later.

'Sounds like a plan. What do you say, Commander?' Terens retrieved his dagger, cleaning off the remains of the moth on his pants.

Marcus's gaze darted from man to man—each of whom gave brief nods of approval —then, finally, back to me. A smile stole across his lips. 'I approve.'

Jake heaved a sigh of relief and slapped me on the back. Would he have defied Marcus had I not received his approval?

Laura gave me a wink.

'Next thing.' Marcus motioned to Laura. 'Did you bring the diary with you?'

Our eyes briefly connected before she extracted a brown leather notebook from her bag and held it out to him. I couldn't recall ever having seen it.

'I think it best if you explain,' he said then indicated for her to pass the notebook to me.

I flipped through its pages, scanning through the lists as all eyes turned to her. Several names had been crossed out, others added. Judy must've kept amending it over time, as some of the details were out of date—the human names listed were now Brethren, yet others were recent additions, names I believed only Luc and I knew. Had he shared this information with her?

'That's it.' She finished relating everything, and, like a schoolteacher, clasped her hands in front of her, ready to answer her students' questions.

Terens swore softly as he sat back down and dropped his head back over the edge of the chair.

Sam looked shell shocked—staring open-mouthed at Laura. 'Why the would Judith write all that down? It makes no sense.'

'It kind of does,' Laura said. 'She'd used a similar ploy successfully against her first husband, so I guess she thought why not do the same to protect the man she loved? That,' she pointed toward the diary in my hand, 'was her insurance policy. Maybe she thought if they knew their names were recorded somewhere it would be enough to deter anyone from betraying them.'

'Okay, I'll buy that, but why hide it in a public place? Rather defeats the purpose, don't you think?' He shrugged and held his hands out as he panned the room.

'It's been there all this time without being disturbed,' I added. 'Who'd think to look behind an old bible in a small village library?'

'But why not here … in our library?' Sam pointed with his thumb towards the door.

'Because Madame Thierry would probably snoop it out, as she did everything else. Judy never liked her. Now we all know why.' Laura's eyes flashed, but her voice wavered as she aired what each of us had come to know, too.

Sam dipped his head, stuck his hands into his pockets and nodded. It wasn't that Judy had lacked faith in his security system. It was rather she had misgivings in the integrity of her housekeeper. And, sadly, those came to fruition in the most tragic of ways.

'The question is, what do we do with the notebook? Hide it or destroy it?' Marcus asked, his gaze landing on each of us.

CHAPTER 13 - EASY SOLUTION

LAURA

Destroy it? No! Everything within me screamed against that suggestion.

'Do we have to destroy it? It's one of the few things left of Judy's. Can't we just hide it? I'm sure it's safe to keep here in the chateau now.' I scanned the men's faces.

Jake shook his head. 'Burn it,' and 'Destroy it,' coming simultaneously out of his and Cal's mouths.

Terens shrugged and rolled his head to the side toward Sam. 'Yeah, s'pose. What do you think, bro?'

Sam's brows creased as his glance strayed to a section of bookcase near the door. 'I've re-alarmed everything and changed the security codes. Should be okay.'

Yes. 'Doesn't Luc have a hidden safe somewhere in here?' His name came out of my mouth so naturally. This had been Luc's office. *How long before I stop referring to it as such?* 'I mean—'

'It's okay, darling. I know what you mean. It's still Luc's office to me too. As for the diary...' Alec exchanged glances with Marcus, who'd paled at the mention of Luc's name. 'Nothing much in here that I don't know. Most of it's redundant, but there are still a few relevant names we wouldn't want anyone but us to know.'

I nodded.

'But still, I had to memorise that list to avoid this very situation.' Alec's gaze bore through me. He knew what that notebook meant to me, and from the gentle yet reproving tone in his voice, he disapproved of what Judy had done.

The seconds ticked by.

Like a statue, Marcus remained perched on the edge of the desk, arms folded, staring at the ground. 'Regardless of Judy's intensions, my son never intended that knowledge to be recorded.'

'Exactly,' Jake added.

'I'm sorry, Laura, but the information in this notebook is too dangerous.'

My heart sank. 'Looks like I'm out voted.' And had to accept the inevitable. Perhaps I should've left that notebook where Judy had hidden it.

Alec dropped the diary into a lidded metal wastepaper basket on the floor, pulled open the top drawer of the desk and withdrew a lighter.

I held my breath as he flicked it and a small blue flame erupted.

'Alec, wait.' Being so focused on the flame, I jumped at Marcus's voice. 'Hand me that book.' He flicked through the notebook again.

What was he hoping to find?

'I have an idea,' he finally said.

My breath hitched as he ripped out page after page, scrunched them up and threw them in the waste paper basket.

'Come, look.' He beckoned to me.

The pages had been removed so cleanly that I could see no tear mark. The only page left untouched was near the beginning, where Judy had left a brief note identifying the notebook as hers and that all the information it contained was correct. It ended with her signature and the date.

'Now watch.' Marcus then jotted down a list of his own—mimicking Judy's handwriting. Some names I recognised, some I didn't.

Incredible! How did he do that?

Who would've guessed he was a master forger. If I hadn't been familiar with my mother's handwriting, I could've easily been fooled. 'Those names aren't...?'

Marcus shook his head and smiled. 'Deus no! They're heads of criminal organisations, so if this ever falls into the wrong hands, *they* will be the targets.' He gave a grim little laugh, closed the notebook and handed it to me. 'Now you can keep it and hide it wherever you like. Judy's words are still there but without that confidential list.'

I hugged his neck. 'Thank you, grandfather, and I'm not going to ask how you know those crims. But how'd you forge her writing like that?'

His eyes twinkled, and he tapped the side of his nose. 'My secret.' And for the second time tonight, he boomed out a laugh. For those few seconds, the sadness had left his eyes.

'So all those centuries cooped up with monks copying manuscripts paid off after all, eh Marcus?' Teens drawled, a wide grin on his face.

'Maybe.'

Alec stood and inclined his head to Marcus. 'I owe you.'

'Couldn't bear to see my granddaughter unhappy. This seemed the best solution.'

'It is.' I tucked the notebook into my pocket, mentally picturing where to hide it, although it was no longer necessary.

Alec lit the discarded pages. We watched as the flames reduced them to ash, plumes of dark smoke curling up to the ceiling. Jake opened the garden-side doors, the sudden icy in-draft swelling the flames just as Alec slammed the lid shut.

'Just as well you don't have a sprinkler system in here,' I said.

'Too difficult to install in these old houses. Believe me, I've thought about it.' Sam's gaze scanned the room, brows drawn, as if mentally picturing the possibility.

The thought of a real fire in this beautiful library, with its collection of rare and valuable manuscripts was enough to make me shiver. Surely, there had to be a way to install one.

I'll talk to Alec abut it later.

Terens motioned to rise. 'We done?'

'One more thing.' Alec glanced at me, his voice whispering through my mind, *'Wedding.'*

I nodded.

Jake closed the garden-side door and stood leaning against it, arms folded across his chest.

Alec cleared his throat. He'd never done that before. Was he nervous?

'Laura and I would like to be married—before the baby's born.'

'Before I begin to show.' I patted my belly.

'Hey, sounds good to me.' Terens gave me a wink.

'Preferably tomorrow morning, now that the period of mourning is over and we can officially take our blood vials. A small, private ceremony, and since there's no chapel on the grounds anymore, we'd like it in the village church.' He held out his hand to me, and I grasped it.

Morning was perfect. No unexpected Brethren showing up ... or lamia, for that matter.

It took a moment, but soon the handshakes, hugs and slaps on the back began.

Marcus beamed. It was a day for firsts. 'Wonderful. Deus! We need some rejoicing.' He took hold of my other hand. 'May I give the bride away?'

Tears stung my eyes as I hugged him once again. 'Of course.'

The others filed out, leaving Alec and I alone.

Over his right shoulder, on the wall, hung another photograph of me. One of a myriad decorating Luc's study. How much time had Alec spent in this room, and its counterpart in Sydney, seeing the same pictures over and over again. It triggered a memory, a comment Luc had made the day Alec had asked me to marry him. At the time I'd been too overwhelmed by events to have given it much thought.

'Luc said that you'd been in love with me for years. How's that possible when we'd never met before that night in the cathedral?'

Alec's brows shot upwards and a faint smile graced his lips. 'That's out of the blue.'

I waved at the photo-covered wall. 'Seeing all this somehow brought it back.'

His gaze briefly swept the room before beckoning to me onto his lap. 'Luc noticed something I didn't, and only afterwards it made sense. I couldn't stop looking at you in those pictures. I watched you grow up in them. He was so damn proud of you.'

My heart lurched, and I lay my head on his shoulder. 'I wish we'd had more time.'

Alec kissed the top of my head. 'He was a wily fox. Every time we had anything to discuss, he'd insist on meeting in his office when we could have just as easily gone elsewhere. Always managed to bring you up in conversations … what you were doing, things you'd said…. It didn't dawn on me what he was doing until it was too late—until I couldn't stop staring at you in those photos … slowly falling in love with you, without me realising.'

'And you were never curious to see me in the flesh, so to speak?' I flashed him a grin.

From the slow upturn of his mouth and the sudden blaze in his eyes, I didn't need to mind read to know what was going on in there. 'I can't get enough of seeing you in the flesh.'

I rolled my eyes, though secretly, his words excited me. 'That's not what I meant, and you know it.'

He chuckled. Moving his hand from my waist to my belly, he gently rubbed it in small rhythmic circles. 'Not long now and you'll be showing.'

'Another few weeks.'

His expression sobered. I placed my hand over his and felt a slight tremble. Was he thinking of his first child, the one who'd died in childbirth more than a hundred years ago? I gazed into his eyes and a collage of images flooded my mind. Through Alec's eyes, I saw a smiling young woman in an old-fashioned, high-collared dress, hands caressing her swollen belly, the anxious yet excited expression as she went into labour … and a dead woman lying on a blood-and-sweat-soaked bed, a lifeless baby by her side.

A deep weight of despair descended. Overwhelming grief coursed through me, and I gulped down the bitter lump that had risen in my throat.

It's what he had felt that terrible day: a miserable helplessness that all his years of medical training could not save the lives of those he loved.

It was what he feared now.

I caught his face in my hands. 'That's not going to happen to me. I'm an Ingenii; we *don't* die in childbirth. You and I are going to have a beautiful child that'll end this curse and we're going to live happily ever after. Do you hear me, Alec Munro?'

I was reassuring myself as much as Alec. Fiery determination seized me. I grasped the chain holding the blood vial Luc had given me and dangled it before his face. '*If* anything does go wrong—which I don't believe it will—you are to use this on me and the baby. There's enough for us both.'

Alec's eyes moistened and he swallowed hard. 'The blood vial bestows immortality, my darling. It cannot be used on an infant … they'd remain a babe forever.'

My mouth dried. Immortality froze one in time. I had but to look at Alec to know that. The thought of my baby never growing up, forever an infant chilled my bones.

His hand closed over mine holding the vial. 'Hide it back beneath your dress, and let's hope you'll never have to use it.'

'I might if I become human after the curse is lifted. I promised Luc …
so we can always be together, since you've decided to remain vampire.'

Alec enveloped me in his arms, a deep sigh escaping his lips. 'How
could I take the other option if it means leaving you and our babe? Tell
me, Laura?'

I shook my head. 'It's not fair. Once the blood vials run out, you'll be
stuck in the night, never again to see the day.' I thumped his chest with
my fist. 'It's not bloody fair!'

'I'm reconciled to it. As long as I have you, all's good.'

'I love you,' I whispered.

Alec's lips crashed down on mine with a fierceness that shook me,
excited and exhilarated me, setting every nerve ending on fire. He was my
world, my compass, my true north, and in his arms, I was home. If that
meant an eternity in the night, then I'd gladly embrace my destiny to be
with the man I loved.

For those few blissful moments, I shut the world, and all its concerns,
out.

Live for the moment, Laura. Tomorrow has its own troubles.

Who knew what the next day would bring.

CHAPTER 14 - IN DEI MANUS
(IN THE HANDS OF GOD)

LAURA

'I promised there'd be no secrets between us, so now it's my turn to show you everything.' With me still seated on his lap, Alec spun around to face the desk.

'Like what?'

He angled the laptop, so I could see a 3D map of the chateau. Highlighted were a series of hidden passageways that connected every room in the place, including our suite. Each of them had a name, depending on where they led to. Ours was labelled "L'Eglise" - the church.

I pointed to it. 'Escape route in case of disgruntled Brethren?'

'Them, plus vampire hunters, murderous revolutionaries, Nazis, tax agents … all the nasties.'

I wasn't sure whether to take the last one on that list seriously until I saw his lips twitch.

'Funny guy!'

His mouth split into a grin, and he flicked the screen onto another image, this time showing the subterranean caves and series of labyrinthine passages below the chateau. One of which I had already become acquainted with, that led from the behind the Alabaster Throne down to the bloodvault.

Which was no more. I shuddered at the memory.

That passageway appeared on screen as blocked, as was the emergency escape route that had once led to the family chapel.

Also no more.

'It's been updated,' Alec said.

I nodded, took a deep breath and focused on the other tunnels and where they led, in order to bury the sad scenes that skirted the edge of my memory. 'This place is honeycombed with tunnels.'

'And I want you familiar with each one.'

'So I don't set off any more booby traps?' I raised an eyebrow and jabbed him in the side while trying to suppress a chuckle. He knew what I meant.

'Something like that.' He chucked me under the chin and then leaned down to open the bottom drawer of his desk. 'Look here.

I leaned down to get a better view.

See this little lever?'

'Uh huh.'

He pulled it toward him. One of the bookcases near the back of the room slowly and silently, swung open to reveal a dark passageway. 'When we get back to our suite, I'll show you where to find the lever that leads to our escape route.'

'Why wasn't I shown all this before?'

Alec leaned back in the chair, ran his hands through his hair and interlaced them at the back of his neck. His eyes lost their amusing glint. 'With everything that's happened lately … I've been remiss. I apologise.'

Hidden behind those words were: he'd been desperately working on replicating the Ingenii antigen, keeping tabs on the lamia, running the estate and being there for me when my world crumbled. Would I have even cared if he'd had shown me all this two, three months ago? Probably not. The time wouldn't have been right. He could've said that, but he didn't.

I cupped his face in my hands. 'You've nothing to apologise for. I don't think I would've handled it.'

'You were grieving, darling.'

'Mm hmm.' My eyes welled up. Whether my heart was still in pain, or the result of my pregnancy, I couldn't tell, but I preferred to blame my fragile emotional state on the latter. 'Damn hormones!'

Alec's mouth turned up at the corners. He cradled me to him, his cool lips brushing my brow. 'Want to go exploring? I know how much you like that.'

'Do you have the time? If not, it can always wait.' I didn't want him neglecting other important work on account of me.

Our serpent rings flared.

'Never think like that, Laura. *You* are the most important thing in my life.'

My heart melted, and we gazed at each other for what seemed like ages until our mouths meshed in a kiss that sent coloured lights exploding behind my closed eyelids.

'Or we can stay here and make love on the desk,' he murmured against my mouth.

'Tempting.'

He lifted me onto the desk and spread my thighs. My pulse went into overdrive, and with my blood pounding in my ears, I only just heard the banging on the door.

'Alec?' It was Sam.

We both froze.

'Yeah, what is it?' Alec called out.

'You better come out here. There's been a killing.'

Those few words doused the fire between us. With a heavy sigh, Alec lifted me down from the desk and flicked the lever, closing the tunnel entrance before striding to the door.

Sam stood there with the local police chief, Morrel, and Adeline who I'd last seen at the village library. She was clutching Morrel's arm, and tears smeared her face.

'Adeline, what's wrong?' I asked.

Her chin wobbled, and although her lips moved, no sound came out.

This was serious.

'Milady.' Morrel dipped his head in greeting. 'More sad news, I'm afraid,'

Cap under his arm, Morrel saluted Alec. 'Milord, Pere Hubert has been found dead in the church. Throat slashed. Madame Dalpuget found him.'

My blood chilled, my hand flying to my mouth as I stared incredulously at Morrel. 'Oh no! Who'd want to kill him?'

A split second later, Adeline recovered. 'I only dropped by on my way home to check on something in the church archives, and … and I tripped over him. It was dark, you see. "Oh! Pere Hubert, I'm so sorry. I didn't see you there," I said. There he was, lying on the ground. I thought he was in prayer, but at this time of night, I ask you, and with all the lights off?' Eyes wild, she continued. 'But he's a priest, so I suppose they do that sort of thing … on the ground … late at night … like a penitent with arms out wide … except he didn't answer me, which was so unusual. So I bent down, and … and … He was so cold.' Adeline buried her head in Morrel's arm.

Morrel touched her hand, which appeared to soothe her. 'Calm now, madame.' He returned his attention to Alec. 'I wouldn't normally bother you with what seems like a straight-forward homicide, but something about it bothers me. If you were to examine the body, milord, there'd be no need to inform the coroner in Avignon.' He raised his eyebrows.

In other words, were it a Brethren killing, it was best kept in the family, so to speak. No need to include the outside world.

Alec nodded. 'Of course. Has Bouchard been informed?'

Morrel shook his head. 'I thought it best not to until I'd spoken to you first. He'd only fret.'

'I agree. Let him sleep, for now.'

'Couldn't be one of the staff. Doesn't make sense.' Sam's brow furrowed, and he jerked his head toward Alec's hand. 'Ward ring would've warned you.'

Alec lifted his hand and looked at his serpent ring. 'Normal. Unless they found a way to circumvent it … which I doubt. Only one way to find out. Whoever it is will have left their scent.'

'Exactly.' Morrel donned his cap and extricated Adeline's hands from his arm. 'No need for you to see it all again, Madame. Perhaps you could stay here with Milady Laura.'

My hackles rose. What did he mean stay here with me? Why did men always assume the women stay behind? Was it some kind of protective instinct, or did they simply see us as the weaker sex and therefore a burden? Okay, physically weaker, I'd concede to that, but that didn't mean we couldn't look out for ourselves. I hadn't learnt to use a sword and dagger for nothing.

Unfortunately, there wasn't time to debate the issue.

'Is the body still there?' Alec asked.

'Oui. I left two of my men on guard. They know to touch nothing until you've seen it, milord.'

'Sam, go with them back to the church. I'll meet you there.'

'*We'll* meet you there,' I corrected him. 'My senses are just as good as yours and Sam's, and amongst the three of us we can work out what's going on. I'm sure Kari wouldn't mind looking after Adeline.'

'Laura, I don't think—' Alec began.

'I've seen dead bodies before. Two burned, beheaded dead things only a few months ago. Remember? And I know how to use my dagger, which, by the way, I can quickly smear with my blood if need be.' Before he could counter that, I added, 'Don't leave me out of things. And being with you, I don't need Kari as a bodyguard right now, do I?'

Alec released a long drawn-out breath and gazed at me tight-lipped.

Sam smiled. 'Good luck arguing with Luc's offspring.'

Not a second later, and Kari's pixie face appeared behind Adeline, grimacing, her mouth forming the word, 'No!'

'No slight to you, milady, but I would prefer to go home.' Adeline's ashen, teary face cut at my heart. She'd had a rough night, one that would affect her for a long time.

I gave Kari my most imploring face. 'Kari, would you mind seeing Adeline safely home? She's had a terrible shock.'

'Oh, I suppose.' She sniffed and draped an arm around Adeline's shoulders as she led her away. 'Don't worry, Addy. I'll stay with you all night, so you won't be alone.'

In spite of her protestations, Kari had a sweet heart.

'We'll take the tunnel. If it was one of the staff, that's the route they would've taken. Their scent will be easy to detect,' Alec said.

'Okay, fine. We'll meet you there.' With Morrel in tow, Sam turned and left.

I closed the door as Alec strode over to a tall narrow cabinet near his desk. Inside was an array of swords, axes and daggers. He chose one and strapped it to his side. 'Laura, go get your coat.'

It took me a few minutes to fetch my coat, hat and gloves. By the time

I got back, Alec had already opened the hidden passageway behind the bookcase. An icy blast from the dark tunnel hit my face, pinching my cheeks.

'Let's go.' Alec grasped my hand, dropped a quick kiss on my lips and led the way into the tunnel.

* * *

Although dark, I could see as clearly as day. Still, the automatic lights installed along the tunnel walls lit up as we approached. For a split second, I couldn't move, remembering all that had happened in these very passageways. I broke out in sweat, and my breathe caught in my throat, as unbidden images arose in my mind and threatened to drag me down into a pit of inconsolable sorrow.

Alec stopped. 'You don't need to do this, darling.'

It'd been three months since I'd last been down here, and at the time, we'd barely escaped with our lives when the bloodvault had been destroyed ... and my mother had been murdered.

The memory came crashing back, and my stomach hollowed out.

No, I didn't need to do this, but I had to. I couldn't let the sad memories cripple me and keep me from entering places I needed to access. Yes, I'd tragically lost those I loved, but these tunnels weren't to blame. They were for our protection. They were good.

Deep breathe, Laura. I squeezed his hand. 'I must. I can't' —I gritted my teeth—'won't let bad memories rule me.'

He gave a brief nod.

Fighting nausea all the way, I gripped his hand and concentrated on placing one foot in front of the other.

Part of the way led down through the maze of limestone caves beneath the chateau. Slowly my roiling stomach calmed, as, once again, I was entranced by the beauty of these caverns. We stopped at a sheer stone wall. Alec pushed aside a great slab of rock, revealing another tunnel that sloped gently upwards. Amazing! It was so well camouflaged; there was nothing to indicate the tunnel entrance was here.

'Do you count steps or something to know where each entrance is?'

'No. Much easier than that. Let me show you.' He guided me by my elbow, and we backed up a few steps. 'Look at the wall, and follow the line of blue crystals. Tell me what you see.'

Focusing my gaze on where Alec indicated, a distinct shape became visible where before I'd seen nothing. I gasped. 'It's a serpent.'

'The entrance to each tunnel begins at the serpent's tail.'

'How clever!' I scanned the cavern walls looking for the distinctive blue crystals, which now seemed to jump out at me. 'There's one over there … and there,' —I pointed— 'and there. How could I have missed it?'

'Because you weren't looking.'

It was that simple. 'What about the door?'

'The rock slides to the side.' Alec demonstrated by sliding it closed. 'See here, where the rock juts out from the wall? Grab and slide.'

I did so. The ease with which the massive rock face slid open surprised me. As we entered, the automatic lights came on, and the door slid shut behind us.

Every so often, Alec stopped to take a deep breath—and so did I. Had my sense of smell developed along with my sight and hearing? An amazing plethora of scents crowded my nostrils, from the stink of the dank moss covering the tunnel walls, the sharp odour of formic acid from various insects, such as black ants, to the pure scent of spring water somewhere further ahead.

But nothing distinctly Brethren—not that I knew enough of the staff to distinguish their scents, anyway.

'Anything?' I asked Alec.

He shook his head. 'You?'

'Lots, but nothing unusual.'

The tunnel came to a dead end. Alec reached up and pushed on a section of the roof. A small square, roughly the width of a man's body, lifted, revealing a manhole. He hoisted himself up through it and looked around before pulling me up after him.

'We're in the crypt. Those lead up into the church.' He pointed at six stone steps, their centres dipping from the wear of thousands of footsteps over time. 'And those,' —he pointed to another three steps ending at a closed door— 'lead up into the spire.' '

'Can you sense anything here?'

Again, he shook his head. 'No.'

That was positive. I was glad to see he kept his sword sheathed when we climbed the steps. The gilded stars painted on the church's vaulted ceiling winked down at us as we reached the top.

'Smell that? Lamia!' Alec's eyes narrowed as he surveyed the area, his hand tightening around mine.

I tensed. 'It's faint, but I can smell it.' It was small consolation that I'd been right all along.

Quiet breathing and the thud of two separate heartbeats reached my ears—the policemen. They snapped to attention when they spied Alec and me. At their feet, partially covered by a sheet, lay the body of Pere Hubert.

I sucked in a breath as another ache ripped my heart. What had that poor old man done to deserve being killed?

'No one else came in?' Alec asked them as we approached.

'No, milord.' The young policemen exchanged glances. 'Not while—'

'The scent's a few hours old.' Alec crouched next to the body and pulled back the sheet. The putrid stench I'd first encountered when imprisoned in Timur's fortress assaulted me. I slammed my hand over my nose and gagged.

'Poor Pere Hubert.' He was laying face down, arms out to the sides. His hands had been pierced, and when Alec removed the sheet entirely, so had his feet. Oddly, there was very little blood.

Alec swore.

A car pulled up outside, the church doors swung open and Sam and Morrel marched in.

'I'd recognise that foul reek anywhere.' Sam crouched next to Alec who was turning the dead priest's head to examine the neck. 'Shit, what a mess!'

I dry retched at the sight of Pere Hubert's mangled throat and spun around to face the open doorway. So much for my bravado.

'How long has he been dead, milord?' Morrel grimaced and waved his policeman's cap beneath his nose.

'Four, perhaps five hours, I'd say.'

'That's just before Kari and I went to the library.' I shuddered, and turned back to see Alec covering the body again.

His gaze connected with mine. 'It must have arrived in the village just before I extended the barrier, blocking me so I couldn't sense it. Yet' — his gaze slid to Sam and Marcus— 'you two did.'

Sam stood, retrieved the mobile from his pocket and pressed a button. 'We were closer to wherever it was hiding. It saw Marcus and Laura and probably saw an opportunity and draw them in.' Sam turned to Laura. 'You must've made eye contact without being aware of it.'

'All I did was look around the area in the open square. Could I have seen it without actually seeing it ... if you know what I mean?

Sam nodded. 'Possibly. It's after you, Laura.' He walked a few paces away. 'Marcus, it was here. It's killed Hubert.'

I shook my head as the horror of it all struck me. 'While we were in the library, that thing was here murdering a harmless old priest.'

My face must have said it all, for Alec straightened and drew me into his embrace. 'Marcus was right. I shouldn't've let you go with only Kari for protection. What if it had found a way through the barrier?' His body tensed.

'Is that possible?' Morrel asked.

'It is. We found a way when trying to get into the rebel fortress.' Alec related how they'd used the bodies of dead rebels to get through.

'Then none of the Brethren staff in the chateau are safe.'

A shiver racked through me and I leaned into Alec for comfort.

The staff regularly hunted outside the village, mostly in Orange and Avignon, and some as far as Lyon. Anyone of them could be targeted by the lamia to get through the ward.

'Could we confine them to the estate grounds till the lamia's caught?' It may not have been feasible, but I thought I'd ask.

Sam shook his head. 'That could take a while, and the blood supply won't last. For something that drastic, we'll need donsangs.'

'I can arrange that.' Morrel lifted the edge of the sheet and peered at Pere Hubert's body again. 'Why the display ... the hands, the feet?' The disgust in his voice was clear.

'It's baiting Marcus, mocking his and the priest's faith. They were friends. Used to have some lively theological discussions.' Sam's gentle eyes turned sad as he gazed down at the body.

Like a gust of wind, the church doors flew open, and Marcus marched in followed by Terens and Cal, their long black coats flapping behind them like ravens wings.

'Sieur Marcus.' Morrel inclined his head, then stepped aside as Marcus strode past him to squat beside his friend's body.

He sucked in a breath as he pulled back the sheet. 'I'm so sorry, Jules.' He bowed his head, and his lips moved in, what could have been, silent prayer. Then he kissed two of his fingers and touched them to the dead priest's brow. 'I promise you will be avenged. Rest now, old friend, and be at peace. In Dei manus.'

He rose and faced us, nostrils flared, his mouth curved back grimly, eyes slit into pale luminescent orbs. Never had my grandfather looked more dangerous. 'How I wish it was only after me. Now that we have the means, I'd enjoy the hunt and kill; fell that foul creature for good.'

That means was my blood, the only substance that could burn through a lamia's thick hide. Just a smear of it on sword or dagger did the trick. And right now, none of the men's weapons had even a dried drop of it.

I removed my dagger, took a deep breath and, trying not to flinch, sliced—not too deeply—across my palm. Ouch! That stung. Thanks to my genes I healed fast and the sting receded quickly.

Alec grabbed my wrist. 'Laura, what are you doing?'

'There's a vicious monster out there, and my blood's the only thing that can kill it. I can spare a bit. C'mon, give me your swords.'

Without hesitation, each of them carefully touched the tips of their blades to my bleeding palm.

'Nothing like a weapon of mass destruction.' Terens grinned and blew on the blade to dry it before sliding it back in its scabbard.

Even dry, my blood was deadly. I felt a modicum of pride.

Alec dropped a kiss on my palm before wrapping a handkerchief tightly around it. 'I'm sorry we can't replicate the antigen. It would save you having to do this.'

'Nothing to be sorry about. You tried,' I said.

'The curse was simply stronger, as I knew it would be,' Marcus said. There was no hint of accusation in his voice. It was just as he saw it. 'Forget about it. There's a greater problem needs dealing with: protecting the innocents in our care.'

'Why not leave here and head for Drunvela—all of us.' Arms crossed over his chest, feet spread apart, twin swords peeking out over his shoulders, Terens looked ready for battle. He gazed pointedly at Alec. 'Sorry, bro, looks like your time to copy Laura's blood's run out. Getting rid of that smelly shit's priority now, and the only way to do that is to use Marcus and Laura as bait. Where they go, it's gonna follow.'

Sam and Cal voiced their agreement.

'That's a hell of a risk.' Alec's expression darkened.

'It's pretty isolated, humans can't see it, and Laura and Marcus would be protected by the ward,' Sam added.

The eyes of the serpent ring on my finger flared, as an image of grey stone walls, mist, trees and jagged cliffs appeared in my mind. Instantly I knew where that was—the massacre site, and where I was supposed to give birth to our child in order to end the curse. 'Is that the place? Looks gloomy.'

'Yeah. Drunvela.' Alec sighed. 'I hate the idea, but Terens has a point. Other problem is, there's no lab set up, no equipment, and the nearest maternity hospital is an hour's drive away.' He rubbed his face. 'I'd hoped we'd have the time to set all that up. Damn!'

Marcus placed a hand on Alec's shoulder. 'My boy, Laura will be fine. Ingenii are very resilient, and I don't for a second believe we've come this far for something to go wrong at the end. Deus! I swear we will destroy the last of the lamiae and my precious granddaughter will have a healthy child that will end this curse. Of that I have no doubt.'

The endearment and utter confidence Marcus exuded dispelled any anxiety I may have felt, and I even had to stifle a smile hearing him refer to Alec as "my boy", considering they both looked to be the same age.

From the deep frown on his face, and the way his chest rose and fell, it was clear Alec was struggling to agree to the immediate move, and I was sure it had more to do with my safety than replicating the antigen.

It was up to me to convince him.

'Alec, I'm not due for months yet. Look, I'm not even showing.' I took a step back and indicated my flat belly. 'You still have time to order everything online and set it up, just like you did here.'

'It's you as bait that worries me.'

'What's better, wait here for the lamia to strike and lose more innocent lives—and you can't keep the staff cooped up in the chateau forever—or move to Scotland and deal with it there, where we don't have to worry which of our friends or family it'll kill next?'

Alec swallowed and gazed long and hard at me.

'Got no choice but to leave. If we stick around here those we love are in peril. Old smelly'll pick them off one by one until only we're left. You want that?' Terens's penetrating gaze latched onto Alec. Never had I seen him look more serious.

I felt the blood drain from my face, yet my hands automatically strayed to the dagger in my belt as a mix of fear and anger warred within me. How dare that wretched lamia threaten my family and friends? Although I missed them that moment I thanked providence that Jenny, John and Eilene were back in Sydney, safe on the other side of the world, where the lamia couldn't touch them.

My heart broke at the thought of having to leave the chateau. I'd grown to love it. It had become my home. But how could I stay, knowing the lamia would go on killing until it finally got to me and Marcus?

Alec gave a curt nod. 'Okay, let's do it.'

I had to look on the positive side. 'We can come back home when this is all over. It'll be here waiting for us.'

'That it will.' Alec rubbed his thumb across my chin, his smile strengthening my tiny bud of confidence.

Marcus carefully lifted Pere Hubert's body. 'I'll take him back to the presbytery and prepare his body for burial.'

'The undertakers can do the rest, Sieur Marcus, and if Milord Alec can sign the death certificate ... natural causes?' —Alec nodded— 'we can keep this contained.' Morrel replaced his cap. With a sad smile, he allowed his gaze to linger on each of us in turn. 'God's speed.' He turned on his heel and left.

'He's a good man,' Marcus said. Then he too, with his precious cargo, disappeared out a side door near the altar.

Alec's phone buzzed. He put it on loudspeaker. Jake's voice echoed through the church. 'Lamia's got Kari. I'm going after it.'

My blood froze. 'Where is she Jake? Is she alive?' *Please, please let her be alive.*

'Jake, you can't go against it alone,' Alec said.

'It's got Kari!'

'How do you know?'

'She's on the other line. I can hear what's going on.'

Moonlight slanted in through the stained-glass windows, casting an eerie glow on the men's faces as they tuned into Alec and Jake's conversation.

Alec swore and ran his hand through his hair. 'Swing by here. A drop of Laura's blood—'

'No time.' He rung off, desperation in his voice.

I remembered the psychic bond between sire and juvy. Lucinda had known that Jean-Philippe had died. Was Jake experiencing the same? Dread, heavy and immovable, settling in my stomach. I'd sent my dear friend into the path of the lamia. How could I have been so unthinking? Her sweet pixie face materialised in my mind. She'd been reluctant to go.

Please, let Kari be okay, I prayed. How would I ever forgive myself if the lamia hurt her?

Terens reached over his shoulder and silently unsheathed both his swords. With a glance and nod to Alec, he sped out the door. Cal followed.

Alec's eyes darted between me and Sam. I knew he was caught between two decisions, and this was no time for a debate.

I swallowed the painful lump in my throat. 'You can't leave me behind, Alec. Don't you see? It's my fault she's in danger.' I thumped my chest. 'My fault. She didn't want to go. I pushed her.... I'll never forgive myself if anything's happened to her. Don't ask me to stay behind. I'll go crazy waiting.' Tears stung my eyes.

Alec cupped my face. 'I'd love to forbid you, but I know how much Kari means to you. Promise me you'll stay by my side the whole time, Laura.'

'Promise.'

I pulled my dagger from its hidden sheath in my belt, my mind clinging to what my gut told me was a false hope. The lamia was at least three thousand years old, its age making it swifter, stronger and more deadly than any other living creature.

And Kari was facing it alone.

I bit down hard on my lip.

'Kari's a tough nut.' Sam tried to reassure me, but the anxiety in his eyes did nothing to alleviate the guilt that twisted my insides into knots.

Alec scooped me up, and he and Sam ran at blurring speed through the medieval part of the village, past the modern shopping centre and into a newer looking suburban area with wide tree-lined streets and double-storey brick houses fenced by tall hedges.

My dread grew as I envisioned the worst. Icy tendrils that had nothing to do with the chilly night snaked through my veins numbing my fingers, in spite of the woollen gloves.

Stay alive, Kari. Please, please stay alive.

CHAPTER 15 - DEADLY ENCOUNTER

LAURA

We stopped at the top of one street where all the lights had been smashed. Glass fragments littered the pavement below. If not for my enhanced vision, it would have been pitch black.

I searched for signs of deliberate vandalism, but there was no graffiti, no markers to indicate the work of a local street gang. And the poles were at least four metres tall No gang would bother to climb that high. They'd have to be able to fly.

Cries, loud grunts and what sounded like metal striking on hard leather broke the quiet of the night. And then … the screech of the lamia.

A battle was taking place. Was Kari in the middle of it?

My heart racing, I tightened my grip on my dagger hilt and clung to Alec as we sped towards the sound.

Porch lights came on. People spilled from doorways, presumably looking for the source of the noise.

This was bad. Most of the inhabitants this end of the village were not descended from the First Families, and so had no knowledge of some if its darker residents.

'What an eventful night this is turning into!' Sam sheathed his sword as several heads turned in our direction.

Alec sighed, and he and Sam exchanged glances. 'One side each?'

Sam nodded and sprinted toward a group of people milling near one house.

I groaned at the delay, but I knew what had to be done.

Alec lowered me to the ground, and we approached another bunch on our side of the road. All were in dressing gowns and wiping the sleep from their eyes, voices raised as to why such late-night commotion on a work night.

We had their attention. I didn't have to look to know Alec's eyes had narrowed into vertical opalescent slits. He made eye contact with each person. 'Go back to bed. You've seen and heard nothing. It's all a dream … Goodnight everyone.'

They blinked, and without a word, re-entered their houses. Mesmerisation had its uses. At least we wouldn't have to worry about the safety of the villagers—for now.

Save for Alec, myself and Sam, the street was empty again. Alec unsheathed his sword. Sam did the same, his normally gentle lavender eyes dissolving into deadly pale reptilian slits.

The grunts and screams were closer now. With me riding piggyback again, Alec leapt over a tall hedge … and into battle.

A single whiff of that nauseating stench, and my worst fears were realised. Yellow snakelike eyes connected with mine. Were they smiling or grimacing? I wrenched my gaze away from the grotesque lamia to look at Kari. Pinned beneath one of the lamia's talons, she yelled abuse at the monster while struggling to escape.

Jake's feet dangled in the air as the creature held him aloft by the throat. A trickle of blood trailed down Jake's neck.

I sent her to this!

'Kari!'

She whipped her head to the side to face me. 'Lolly! Scoot out of here!'

'I'm so sorry.' Dagger in hand, I stumbled forward.

Alec caught my arm and pushed me behind him. 'Stay here!'

My heart stopped as he leapt to Jake's aid. I followed his every move. As if in slow motion, he sprang onto the creature's shoulders, wrenching back its head as it snapped at him. Sword at its throat, still he couldn't get the blade to slice through. The lamia snarled and twisted from side to side in an attempt to dislodge him.

Jake swung like a rag doll in its claw. In the hydrangea bush at the foot of the steps leading up to her front porch huddled a whimpering Adeline.

'Oi! You ugly, smelly lump of slime!' Terens taunted the creature, distracting it as Cal slid beneath Jake in an attempt to slice the lamia's belly, it's only vulnerable spot, but the monster was too quick.

It twisted to the side, narrowly missing Terens with one of its talons, then aimed its gaze at Cal. For a second his sword dipped, eyes glazing over as the lamia's barred fangs struck out for his neck. I sucked in a breath. Just before its teeth connected with his skin, Cal ducked, grit his teeth, shook his head and took another stab at the creature.

To no avail.

What kind of skin could resist the men's razor-sharp blades? As long as they couldn't penetrate the creature's hide, my blood on their swords was useless.

With a loud cry, Sam attacked, drawing the lamia's attention from Terens, who dove for Jake's sword.

The lamia swiped at Sam with all claws extended.

Have to do something! My blood thrummed in my ears, and with adrenaline pumping through my veins, I pricked my finger with my dagger and smeared the smooth blade with my blood. With a shaking hand, I took aim at the lamia's eye.

My throat dried. But what if I missed and hit Alec or Jake instead?

Another hand closed over mine. I froze.

'No, mea neptis. Your heart is braver than your aim.' Marcus gazed at me, his eyes glinting with the excitement of battle.

Just then, Terens came crashing into the hedge near Marcus and me. 'Shit!' He recovered and glanced at me. 'What the hell are you doing here, pet?'

'Now's not the time.' Marcus unrolled a length of fine mesh from around his lower arm. He shook it free and held part of it out to Terens. It was a net. 'Take this end. And don't make eye contact with it again. You know better than that.'

Terens's lips thinned, and he gave a curt nod.

Marcus's words prompted a memory: lamiae were sensitive to the light. That's why it had knocked out all the street lights.

Not willing to take my gaze from Kari nor Alec, who still clung tenaciously to the lamia's neck, I searched my pockets, found my phone, flicked on the torch and aimed it at the creature's eyes.

Yes!

Temporarily blinded, it shrieked, dropped Jake and shielded its eyes.

'Deus! Clever girl.' Marcus grinned. 'Keep doing that.'

'Try and stop me.'

Terens gave me a wink. Then he and Marcus raised the net and ran toward the lamia.

Alec dropped from the lamia's back and crouched beside Jake, who lay still and pale on the ground, blood oozing from his throat. One of the creature's talons must have pierced his jugular. Alec ripped off his dark blue shirt and pressed it against Jake's neck. 'He's bleeding out! I need to stitch the wound.'

Kari screamed, the sound of it piercing my heart. She remained trapped beneath the lamia's powerful foot, her sword arm held out from her body, immobile. Unable to help him, she looked on helplessly as the man she loved bled out.

Regardless of Alec's assurances, if not for me, Jake wouldn't have gone after her to confront the creature on his own.

Blinking away tears, I struggled to keep my hands from shaking as I continued to aim the torch at the lamia's eyes.

If Jake survived this, would he ever forgive me? Would Kari? Sam stabbed at the lamia's wing countless times as Cal attempted to drag her out.

'Oh, no, no, no!' To my horror, the light from the torch began to fade. I'd forgotten to recharge the battery.

Terens swore. He and Marcus threw the net over the lamia, the metal links glinting in the faint torchlight before it finally gave out.

'I'm sorry. I'm sorry.' Shaking the phone did nothing.

Darkness restored, the lamia roared and tore at the netting holding it captive.

'Catch this!' Alec threw me his phone and looked from me to Jake.

Save him, Alec. I'll be okay. Marcus is here.

He swallowed hard, gave me a nod. *Keep your dagger out, and don't do anything reckless.* Alec quickly dragged Jake's unconscious body onto the porch, reached down for Adeline, kicked in the door and carried them both inside.

All the house lights came on same time as I flicked on his phone torch, increased it to full capacity and shone it directly into the monster's eyes.

It shrieked, cringed and turned this way and that to avoid the blinding lights.

As Terens and Marcus attempted to secure it with ropes, it swung around and ripped through the net. With one wing shielding its eyes, it continually swiped at Sam and Cal with its claws, sending the men crashing into the hedge. I cried out when it grabbed Kari, stood to full height and held her in front of its vulnerable belly.

With a piercing screech, it unfolded its wings, bounded off the ground and flew into the air, the net dropping from it like a discarded skin.

My legs trembled, and the phone dropped from my hand. I stood helplessly as the monstrous creature disappeared into the distance, Kari in its claws.

The men swore and tried chasing after it before giving up.

Only Marcus remained, staring after the creature, alone in his thoughts.

'It can't go far, can it? The ward won't let it escape.' I had to believe that.

Alec had extended the ward to ensure we were within its protection. But it meant he'd had to remove it from another part of the estate so as not to be weakened. Marcus shook his head and turned from staring into the blackness to me. 'Alec didn't extend the ward this far.'

A hard lump lodged in my throat that for a moment I couldn't speak, and strained to follow the winged form as it disappeared into the night sky.

Kari!

Hot tears spilled down my face.

CHAPTER 16 - VENOM

ALEC

Stay safe, Laura, stay safe, I repeated over and over in my head even as I set Adeline down and lay Jake on the floor in her front hall. His blood soaked my shirt. He should've stopped bleeding by now. He should be healing. Why wasn't that happening?

'Needle and thread. Adeline, I need needle and thread.'

She gazed at me through glazed eyes, chest rising and falling rapidly in the early stages of hyperventilation. Outside, the lamia shrieked. Adeline's eyes slowly turned in its direction, mouth opening in a silent scream.

I had no time for this.

I slammed the door shut and grabbed her shoulders. 'Look at me, Adeline.' Her eyes connected with mine. 'Calm down. You're safe now. But Jake needs help. Get me some needle and thread.'

The panic receded from her expression. She bobbed her head, 'Of course, milord,' and turned to find the items.

Jake moaned, looked about and tried to rise. 'Where's Kari?'

'Take it easy.' I eased him back down. 'The others are out there trying to get to her.'

He collapsed. 'Blame … myself … split second eye … contact…'

'Don't talk.' The pressure I applied to the wound wasn't stopping the bleeding. Why? Blood pooled on the floor by his head. His pallor grew by the second, his heartbeat slowing down to a mere vibration. 'Why aren't you healing?'

'Lamia venom … it's claw.' His voice was barely above a whisper. 'Anti-vampire … coagulant. Easier to … suck us … dry.'

'Son of a bitch!' Why hadn't I been told about this?

We'd encountered these creatures before and risked being clawed or scratched. Was this another piece of information Luc had neglected to tell me? Had I known, I would've prepared an antivenin. Stitching the wound would be useless if I couldn't remove the venom from his system.

'Damn Luc. Why didn't tell me?' I lifted Jake's T-shirt to look for any signs of internal hemorrhaging while keeping the pressure on the wound with my other hand.

Faint purple-blue blotches marred his chest and abdomen.

'Jake, where's the antivenin?' There had to be one if Luc had known about the lamia venom.

His head rolled to the side.

My chest tightened, locking my breath within me. Although faint, I detected a pulse.

Adeline returned with a small box in her hands, her eyes straying to the pool of blood on the floor. She trembled, and the box fell from her grip, spilling its contents. She slapped over her mouth, turned and fled.

The door flew open. Cal stood there, gazing down at Jake, nostrils flared, breathing hard. 'Fucking lamia!'

'The antivenin. Where is it? I don't know how much time he has left.'

Cal dropped to his knees beside his friend. 'Ingenii blood. Only thing that works. He's had his blood vial hasn't he?'

'About twelve hours ago.'

'Then he should be healing. Fuck! What's going on?'

'You tell me?'

Terens and Sam ploughed in. Both swore on seeing Jake.

'Shit! He needs—'

'He's already had some!' My mind raced through all the possible reasons why the Ingenii blood wasn't doing the job. Had the lamia venom mutated over time? 'Does all Ingenii blood destroy it or just First Blood?'

'First Blood's best. Works quickest,' Cal said.

I had no idea which blood vial Jake had taken. But from the looks of things, it hadn't been First Blood. 'We need more. Got any on you?'

'Back in the house.' Terens jerked his head in the direction of the chateau.

Damn!

Being outside the ward, my voice wouldn't reach anyone inside. Iphone! I could ring Dom. He knew where I kept mine. I reached into the back pocket of my jeans but then I remembered I'd tossed the phone to Laura.

Hell! 'Where's Laura?'

Terens laid his hand on my shoulder. 'She's okay, bro. She's with Marcus.'

Jake groaned. Beads of perspiration trickled down his temples and brow. He turned ashen.

My throat constricted, and I had to swallow hard to keep my voice even. 'C'mon. Hold on, Jake. Fight it.'

'Fuck! I'm not gonna sit here and watch him die. It'll be faster if I run back and get some.' Cal dashed off.

'You're going to be okay,' I lied, as Jake's pulse weakened to a flutter. 'Why wasn't I told about the lamia venom?!' I glared up at my friends.

Sam and Terens exchanged glances. 'Something you oughta know first,' Terens said. My scalp prickled. 'Smelly bastard's escaped. It's got Kari.'

It took a moment for that to sink in. I glanced down at Jake, thankful he didn't know.

I bowed my head.

Outside, Laura wept.

A rush of adrenaline surged through me. 'If Jake and Kari die, it'll be on your heads! If I'd been told about the venom, I would've brought several vials with me, and Jake wouldn't be dying in front of me right now.'

'It's not their fault, Alec.' Laura strode in, Marcus by her side. Her eyes were red and swollen.

She rushed to me, wrapped her arms around my upper arm and buried her head in my shoulder. 'It's my fault. Blame me if you have to. I'm the one who sent Kari beyond the ward. I'm so, so sorry.'

Her eyes tore at my heart. 'No, darling. You were trying to protect Adeline. She wouldn't've stayed at the chateau, and she never felt comfortable with any of the men. Sending Kari made sense. You're not to blame, so get that out of your head. It's this clan's damn secrets that are, and I've had enough of it!'

Just then, the decision was made. After our child's birth, I was going to step down from the princiship. Marcus could have it.

I glanced down at Jake, his pulse now barely detectable.

Marcus sighed, crouched by Jake's head and placed his hands alongside mine. 'Let me. I've tended many wounded.'

Sad eyes met mine, and in those mournful depths were reflected the pain of many lifetimes, of untold regrets, of friends and loved ones lost, and now, just before the end, it seemed as if he would lose another.

My anger dissipated.

'Press hard.' I rose and cradled Laura as Marcus replaced me by Jake's side. The bleeding hadn't abated, and the discoloured blotches on his abdomen had spread.

What was taking Cal so long?

Sam bit into his wrist, coaxed the blood out and pressed it to Jake's lips. 'Take it.'

Jake remained unresponsive.

Marcus touched Sam's arm and shook his head. It was too late for that.

Sam slid to the floor, stretched his arms out over his bent knees and bowed his head.

Laura left my arms, knelt next to Jake and took his hand. 'If only I could, I'd give you my blood.'

'Where the fuck's Cal? Would've been quicker if I'd carried him back!' Terens bellowed and strode to the door, tearing it off what was left of it from its hinges and throwing it down the front steps. 'Shit!' He turned to look at Marcus. 'Why isn't the Ingenii blood working? He's dying. Look at him!'

'The lamia sunk its claw too deep into him … held him too long … too much venom even for the Ingenii blood.' Marcus's gaze connected with mine. 'Luc should've told you … I thought he had.'

I huffed and leaned back against the wall in that narrow hallway, watching my friend's life ebb away, and there wasn't a thing I could do about it. I was powerless, helpless. Like Terens, I had the urge to rip something apart.

But it wouldn't help Jake.

I closed my eyes and took several deep breaths as the silence between the beats of Jake's heart lengthened. Where would I have been without his mentoring after Luc had transformed me? Jake had been a physician himself, posted to Marcus's cavalry unit several months before the fateful day that changed his life forever. From what he'd told me, he shouldn't have been out that day, but he'd persuaded Marcus to let him tag along. It was supposed to have been only a routine patrol.

Over the centuries, he'd kept pace with modern medical advances, gaining degrees from many prominent universities, although he'd never maintained his own practice. He'd taught me how to use my enhanced hearing to identify the slightest murmur or odd rhythm in the beat of a human heart, how to pinpoint problematic valves or vessels in the body without the use of electronic monitors.

My newly heightened sense of smell, he'd trained until I could detect almost any disease in the human body without having to wait for biopsy results. Over the years, I'd used that skill to save more than one life. When asked, I always put it down to gut instinct. The eventual lab results simply acted as my confirmation.

Jake had done the same with my other senses.

How much did I owe him? Words could never encompass.

Cal tore into the room, Dominik on his heels carrying my medical bag.

Bless that boy!

'Get these down his throat.' Cal threw me and Marcus several vials.

Just as we unstoppered the lids, Jake's heart stopped beating.

CHAPTER 17 - BLOOD TRAIL

KARI

I looked down. Gorges, rocky cliffs, dry land. I knew where we were. Those cliffs had caves where a nasty old lamia could hide out during the day.

Don't want to go into those.

Calm. Keep calm. Deep breaths. In, out, in out.

Jake! He had to be okay. Couldn't cry. Not now. Please, let the Ingenii blood work. Let him not be dead. Shitty, shitty lamia! And even shittier venom!

Ugh! Why did the stupid thing have to take me? Holy moley! It stunk. Like a thousand dogs had pissed on the same lamppost.

Up ahead was the old oak forest. I had a chance.

A sound like dry twigs being rubbed together came from above me. Was Stinky laughing? 'You think you can esssscape me? Your mind isss sssso open.'

Hells bells. *Brick wall … brick wall*, I repeated over and over in my head while keeping my eyes locked on the ground below.

'Impressssive.'

I concentrated harder. It was trying to break through, making my head hurt. I doubled the brick wall, adding concrete and barbed wire. *Try and get through that!*

'Your mind wallsss will not keep me out for long, little one.'

I knew that too. I had to keep it occupied—talking—so it'd stay out of my head. 'What do you want with me? Why didn't you just kill me?'

'Can't you guessss?' It laughed again. I wanted to stab it.

'I hate stupid games. Just tell me.'

Stinky's wings flapped. 'Jussstiniussss! I ssssmell his blood in you.'

Okaaaay. That probably wasn't good. My heart squeezed into a tight knot. Jake! Justinius had been his old name. He only changed it a century or so ago to modernise it. He had to be alive. He just had to. No nasty stinky venom could kill my Jake. The Ingenii blood would save him. But Stinky had pumped so much venom into him. What if even Ingenii blood couldn't help? Tears burned in my eyes. Princi would help him. Yeah, Princi was smart. He'd save my Jake.

Horrid, horrid lamia!

'My enemy'ssss child before me. Mine to take.' It grabbed my chin and forced me to look at it. It licked its lips and slid its pointy tongue down one fang and then the other. 'Long time ssssince I've had a female, and what better than my enemy'ssss.'

No way.

Eewww. Stomach turning. I wanted to vomit and cut the wretched lamia up into a million pieces all at the same time. I pointed with my thumb toward the road. 'Zoo's that way.'

Stinky sneered. 'Do not inssssult me any further, little one.' It squeezed my cheeks together so hard I thought my face would cave in.

I scratched and clawed at its hands, trying to pry them off. 'Let go of me, you stinking piece of crap!'

'What could be better. Take what belongssss to my enemy and make it mine. Take, defile and dessssstroy.' It released my face to raise its slimy head and shriek into the sky.

Oh crap! My stomach flipped. I had to get away. Now.

I looked down. Treetops. Mountains up ahead. Where was Stinky taking me?

Heat flushed through me. I gritted my teeth to stop my lips from trembling and coiled my hands into fists. *It's not going to win, it's going to win,* I repeated over and over. Stinky probably thinks he's won. I'd show him!

Good thing my arms were free. I sniffed. The wind was blowing in the direction I wanted. It was now or never. Slowly, so as not to alert stinky, I lifted my arm and bit deeply into my wrist. *Ouch!* Now I knew how Laura felt. *Please, Mister Wind, don't change direction now.* Didn't want Big Stinky smelling my blood.

I lowered my bitten wrist to my side. *C'mon, flow down!* I pumped my hand harder. One drop, two, three then four trickled down and plopped on rocks, grass and on the olive groves over which the we flew. Unless an animal homed in on the scent and licked it up, it would be enough of a blood trail for the others to follow. And follow they would. I was sure of it.

My stomach lurched again as Stinky swerved through some narrow gorges. 'Fly more smoothly, will ya? I'm gonna be sick here.' I yelled up at the big bozo.

Why didn't it fly higher, above the tree line?

I wasn't that heavy! Maybe it couldn't.

I craned my neck to check out its wings. Weren't the bottom edges meant to be thicker? Instead, they were transparent. *Hello!* Stinky didn't have enough power in them to lift us both higher, because those transparent bits hadn't fully regenerated.

I nearly clapped.

The old oak forest was right below us. Forests were good—lots of lovely sharp twigs and branches that could damage those delicate wings.

Time to take a dive, Stinky!

Taking a deep breath, I felt for the tiny perfume bottle pendant around my neck. It had been a present from Jake, to celebrate the end of my juvenile stage. For just a moment, I saw his beautiful face and wanted to be with him so badly that my chest ached. I hugged the pendant.

Have to do this.

My hands shook as I unstoppered the lid inside my jacket. *Deep breath, Kari. You gotta do this.* One, two, three … I mouthed, then splashed the perfume into Stinky's eyes.

Whoa!

Stinky bucked and reared. It was like being on a rodeo ride. 'It burnsss! It burnsss!' He screeched and dropped me.

Ha! Served it right. *Ow! Ow!* Leaves and sharp twigs smacked me in the legs and arms as I grabbed at anything to slow my fall. We weren't that high, but high enough that I could break a leg or arm. It'd take too long to heal—at least a day. Stinky would find me.

Oomph! Aaargghh! A sharp pain in my arm as I hooked it around a branch to break my fall. *Deep breaths, Kari.* I swung there for a second waiting for the pain to recede before dropping to the ground.

Above me, Stinky screeched and circled the treetops.

Ooh, it was mad! *Tough nuts, Stinky!* I chuckled and cradled my sore arm.

I squat in the giant roots of a she-oak and scooped up a handful of decayed leaves, grasses and dirt and rubbed them all over me to disguise my scent.

Okay, now what? I could stay hidden in the woods till daylight, or make a run for it.

I bit my fingernails. Decisions, decisions. Once out of the woods, it was open landscape. It could easily swoop down on me. Could I outrun it? No way, Jose.

I would have to stay put.

I felt for my blood vial beneath my jacket pocket. What if I'd smashed it against a tree? My heart skipped a beat just thinking about it. I'd last taken it two days ago, which was enough to get me through the new day. I clutched it to me. *Thank you, Princi.*

Yep, I could wait it out.

Why wasn't Old Stinky shrieking anymore? I stuck my head out from behind a root and peered up. The sky was clear. Where was he? There was no way he would've given up. My skin prickled, as if thousands of cockroaches were crawling over me.

A funny whistling sound … a thump, the rustle of dried leaves … the smell of rotting meat.

Oh no! I froze.

Stinky!

My chest constricted, but I had to know how close it was. Peering through the exposed tree roots, there it was, wings folded tight against its body, clawed feet digging into the earth. It angled its ugly, pointy head in all directions and sniffed the air.

Hells bells! It must have dived down through the canopy. If my heart beat any faster, I'd be human. And if I could hear it…. His head snapped in my direction and sniffed. My throat went drier than an old spinster's tit.

It knew where I was. How?

I sucked in a breath. Jake's perfume bottle. Some of the drops had fallen back onto my jacket.

Kari, you dope!

I shoved my blood vial down my bra then peeled off the jacket. After I kissed my precious perfume pendant, I flung it high into the trees. It would give me a few seconds to find another hiding spot.

Then I ran.

CHAPTER 18 - COLLATERAL DAMAGE

LAURA

Alec pumped vial after vial directly into Jake's heart. Once or twice, aware of my gaze, he glanced up. The pain in his eyes made my stomach knot.

This was my fault.

Cal crouched next to him, one hand squeezing Jake's shoulder. Two blood red trails slid slowly down his face. 'Live, brother.'

The world around me shrunk into a narrow tunnel where all that existed was Alec frantically working to save his best friend's life.

Jake lay still, face pallid. Unresponsive.

'Please, please Jake, open your eyes. Live Jake!'

I swiped away my tears and shoved my sleeve against my mouth to prevent a sob escaping.

'Another one.' Alec held out his hand, and Dominik passed him yet another vial.

How many did he have left in his medical bag? What if he ran out and Jake still hadn't revived? There'd be no time to fetch more.

I wrapped my trembling arms around my middle, briefly closed my eyes and prayed.

How many minutes had it been? Or was it hours? Still Jake lay there, his skin ashen.

My mouth dried when Alec rummaged around in his medical bag, frowned, then licking his lips he thumped hard on Jake's chest with one fist.

No heartbeat.

No response.

He thumped it again. Harder this time.

From the edge of my tunnel vision, Sam, who'd been sitting still as a statue on the floor, arms extended over his knees, now moved and crawled to where Jake lay.

In the doorway, arms braced against its frame, stood Terens. 'Why didn't he wait for us? Fuck! I'm the one who charges off into danger. Not him. It shouldn't have been him.' He punched the wooden frame, cracking it.

Alec thumped Jake's sternum again, waited three seconds, then again … and again. 'Damn you, Jake!'

A sudden, deep inhalation pierced the deathly silence. Jake's eyes shot open. He sat up and looked around. 'What the hell …'

If Marcus hadn't had his arm tight around my shoulders, I would've sunk to my knees with relief.

'Welcome back.' Alec sat back on his haunches and wiped his brow, undisguised relief on his face.

One heavy rock lifted from my heart, but there was still another so I barely noticed the shouts and laughter, the backslapping.

'Deus! Deo gratia.' Blinking rapidly, Marcus turned his face toward the ceiling.

Jake shot to his feet. 'Where's Kari?'

'That smelly bastard's got her, bro. Flew off with her.' Terens remained standing in the doorway, his tall frame blocking all view to the outside.

Jake's face darkened. 'Why didn't you go after it?'

Terens pointed to his sword hilts, jutting out above his shoulders. 'Do these look like wings to you?'

'There was nothing they could do, and you were dying. I pumped nine blood vials into you.'

Jake faced Alec, swallowing hard as his gaze took in the syringe and the empty vials littering the floor. Alec had used up part of his own supply. Realisation dawned on Jake's face. 'Dammit, Alec.'

'What did you expect me to do? Let you die?' He retrieved his bloodied shirt, collected and dumped the empty blood vials into his medical bag and handed it to Dominik. 'Take these back to the chateau. We'll be along soon.'

'Did I do good?' Dom gazed up at him in awe.

'You did.' Alec slapped him on the back.

Dom's bony chest thrust out, and an ear-to-ear smile split his face. It was almost painful to see how eager he was to please Alec, like a boy looking to his father for approval. And in a way, that's what Alec had become to him, and that wasn't a bad thing.

Jake took in a shuddering breath, hands clenched as he stood there. 'I'll give you back each one, Alec, I swear.'

'You owe me nothing. Go find Kari.'

'Jake.' I pressed his arm. 'Forgive me, Jake, please.' I would thoroughly understand if he couldn't … at that moment. 'You were nearly killed because it was my stupid idea to send Kari to accompany Adeline outside the ward. I should've thought … I'm so sorry.'

Jake's brows creased, he let out a breath and shook his head. 'Come here.'

I left Marcus's side to be embraced by Jake. 'Thanks sunshine, but get that idea out of your head. You're not to blame. Get it? Adeline needed an escort home and Kari was there. If not her, then one of us would've done it. Same result. It's. Not. Your. Fault.'

'Would you have rushed out like that if it had been anyone else but Kari?'

'Do you know that for sure?' Jake gazed earnestly at me.

I darted a glance at Terens, recalling his words from earlier that he was the one who always charged into danger ahead of the others. Him, not Jake. 'Yes,' I said.

Behind me, Terens muttered, 'Gotta learn to keep my mouth shut.'

Jake held me out at arms length, dark lavender eyes gazing earnestly into mine. 'I'll take the blame for that. Not you. Repeat after me: It's not my fault. Let me hear you say it.'

'It's not my fault,' I whispered.

'Now believe it.'

I nodded, although it would take some time convincing myself.

Jake dropped his hands and looked at Marcus. 'Which way did it go?'

'East.'

Jake's eyes blazed, his knuckles white as he unsheathed his sword. 'Let's go.'

'Let me know as soon as you find her,' Alec said.

Jake gave him a curt nod, and he, Cal, Sam, Terens and Marcus sped out into the night.

'*You're not going with them?*' I sent my thought to Alec.

Our gazes connected. '*Not this time. Kari's Jake's responsibility.*'

I should've felt guilty that I was relieved. I then remembered I still had Alec's phone. 'Thanks for the loan.' I handed it back to him. 'Soon as we get back, I'll recharge mine.'

He pocketed it. 'What Jake said.'

'When I know Kari's safe.'

'That's not how it works. I don't want you carrying a false sense of guilt, darling.'

'I can't help it!'

169

From the top of the stairs, came a faint whimper. Adeline! I'd forgotten all about her. Large round eyes peered down at us through the railing at the top of the stairs, the horror of what she'd seen holding her in its grip from the rapid beat of her heart and her small sharp intakes of breath.

I raced up the steps and crouched down next to her. 'You're safe now. It's gone. You can come down.'

She shook her head and backed away from me. One hand gripped the bannister while the other clutched the folds of her jacket at her chest. 'Go away! GO AWAY!'

'Adeline, it's me, Laura. You're safe.' I took a step toward her and extended my hand. The terror on her face tugged at my heart.

Adeline's eyes widened further, her breath sawing in and out. She scooted till her back was against the wall. The word, 'Monsters,' tumbled from her lips.

I called down to Alec. 'Adeline's in shock.'

He bounded up the stairs just as I knelt near her. Her gaze shot to him. She shook her head, turned her face to the wall and clawed at the wallpaper as if she could gouge a hole through it.

Alec crouched down next to her. 'Adeline, look at me.' His low mesmerising voice stilled her frenzied scratching.

Slowly, she faced him and raised her eyes to meet his, chin trembling. In all the years she'd known my family, had she never seen any of them in vampire form? If not, I couldn't blame her for being in such a state. The first time Alec had transformed in front of me, I'd screamed and sunk to the floor in a trembling mess.

But, to be confronted by them all as they'd battled the grotesque-looking lamia to boot would've been too much for anyone.

Poor Addy. How was her mind going to cope with it?

Alec's eyes paled. He cupped her face in his hands and soothed her. 'Shhh … All is well. No one will hurt you. You're safe.' He waited—and

I held my breath—until Adeline's expression calmed. 'Take a deep breath for me.' Her nostrils flared, chest rising and falling at the in rush of air. 'Again.' As she did so, her breathing returned to normal.

'Will she be all right?' I whispered.

'I think so,' he whispered back, before speaking to her again. 'Adeline, nothing unusual happened tonight. Kari brought you home. You couldn't find your key, so she forced your door open.'

That was as good an explanation as any.

'Have no fear. Go to bed now and sleep. It's been a long day.'

Alec stood and hoisted her to her feet. Eyes glazed, Adeline nodded, and seemingly oblivious to our presence, walked down the hall to her bedroom and closed the door behind her.

'She won't remember we were here?'

Alec shook his head. 'It'll be like a dream.'

'Cheaper than therapy.'

He smiled and took my hand as we went down the stairs. Before we left the house, Alec braced the door then texted Morrel. 'He'll keep an eye on her and get someone to fix the door in the morning.'

'He's a good man, and I think Adeline likes him.' I couldn't help noticing the way she'd clung to the police chief when they'd come to tell us of Pere Hubert's tragic death. I clutched my stomach as that thought led to the rest of the events of this night … and Kari.

My dear friend in the clutches of the lamia.

Please, Lord, keep her safe.

CHAPTER 19 - NIGHTHUNTER

MATT

I released a deep breath after exiting Jenny's apartment. It was done. For sure she was on the phone to Laura right now, letting her know I was on my way—just as I'd planned. So I'd invented a witness. So what? I needed Laura to be scared … enough to persuade Munro to run. It was the only way to issue an Interpol Red Notice on them: location, arrest and extradition.

I raced down the stairs to my car. In less than five hours, I'd be on a flight to France, and I still hadn't packed. As I drove, all I could think about was *her*. Yeah, I wanted to see Laura again, but if she responded to Jenny's warning as I hoped she would she wouldn't be there when I arrived. A tinge of regret that I wouldn't be seeing her tore at me, and the feelings I'd been trying to quash the last three months just resurfaced.

Mate, give me a break! I punched the steering wheel. The horn went off. Fuck! Guy in the next car glared at me.

'Ah, shut up!' I drove off and turned left. My block of flats was just up ahead.

I checked my watch after parking the car.

Dave and I had worked hard the last three months to get to this point, gathering the necessary evidence to get Interpol involved. Pity the information I'd got from Laura about Reynolds death was inadmissible. I'd need her permission to use it as evidence, and that was as unlikely as a snowstorm in Sydney in January. Regardless, forensics had found traces of unknown DNA on the portrait that matched blood splatters in Munro's flat. It had to belong to Reynolds. The poor, sick bastard had kissed the portrait on the lips after he'd finished painting it.

We issued a Blue Alert with Interpol. 'But I'm not going further than that,' Dave had said. 'It was sheer dumb luck I got a sympathetic judge to okay that forensics search warrant on Munro's flat. You know how flimsy our evidence is. Until we have something more concrete that's as far as we can go. I'm not sticking my neck out any further, mate.'

I was grateful.

Checked my watch again. Four-and-a-half hours before I got on the plane.

Damn city traffic! I sprinted down the corridor to my apartment.

Who the hell were they?

A couple of young blokes—faces unfamiliar—lurked just outside my apartment door: one tall with a shock of blonde hair so pale it could've been white. Backpack over his shoulder. The other, back against the wall, playing with his mobile, was slightly shorter and stockier. Ring in his right nostril. Never understood how anyone could wear one of those things. How the hell did you blow your nose?

At least they were humans: no lavender eyes. Dammit, when had I begun to think like that?

The white-haired one spotted me. He was no more than twenty, if that. 'You Matthew Sommers?'

What the hell? 'Who's asking?'

The other young guy—no, kid, no more than seventeen … eighteen at the most — pushed away from the wall and faced me. Checking out my

T-shirt? So it was a little crumpled. So what?

'Hard day, mate?'

Cocky little bastard. I ignored him.

The older one extended his hand. 'Alistair Davis. You recently ordered a box of white-oak bullets from us.'

Nice manners. North Shore, private boys school. Probably lives in Woollahra or Double Bay and goes to Sydney uni. And who calls their kid "Alistair" anyway. What the hell was he doing this side of town?

Then it hit me. I'd bought anti-vampire bullets from a couple of kids.

I resisted the urge to slap my head.

Hell, you never knew who you were dealing with online. But they looked innocent enough.

'You're Nighthunter?' It was the website I'd bought the first box of white-oak bullets, the ones that bastard Munro had taken from me. My trigger finger itched at the thought of him.

'That's us.' The younger kid approached. 'I'm Brad.'

The older boy jerked his head toward his friend. 'My associate. Mind if we talk?'

His "associate" pulled out his mobile and started playing with it. Bloody hell! Last time I'd buy anything online. I'd need to get a post office box, too.

The entrance door downstairs opened and closed. Someone could overhear us. I looked over my shoulder. All clear.

'Show me some ID. I'm not letting any underage kids into my apartment.'

'I'm twenty! I'm studying law at Sydney University.'

'Yeah, well, you're not a lawyer yet. IDs, now!'

Both grimaced when producing their driver's licenses.

'Satisfied?' Davis looked at me smugly, like he'd proven some stupendous point.

The younger kid handed me his. Eighteen three weeks previously, and the license was legit.

I strode past them and unlocked the door. 'Okay, you've got exactly ten minutes to tell me why you're here.'

I'd forgotten about the mess of newspapers, research notes and papers I'd left on the sofa. I could always make then stand…. Nah. I dumped it all on the coffee table, on top of a pile of other stuff.

'Take a seat.'

Davis picked up one piece I dropped. I managed to snatch it back before he saw too much. 'I see you've been doing some research.'

None of your business, kid.

I sat in the armchair opposite. How much did they already know? Hell, I'd ordered vampire-killing bullets from them, so they weren't here on a social call. They were sussing me out. I'd bet my promotion on it.

Only one way to find out for sure.

'Been long in the vampire-killing business?' Nothing beats directness. I sat back and relaxed, waiting for the comeback.

Brad's eyes popped. 'How did you know? We didn't say any—'

Davis slapped his arm. 'Shut up! Can't you see he's baiting us?'

I couldn't help smiling. Smart kid. 'With a name like Nighthunter and a website dedicated to all things vampire, not to mention selling white-oak bullets, which, according to legend—again, on your website—are lethal to vampires…' I spread out my arms then dropped them on the arms of my chair. 'Need I say more?'

They exchanged glances before the older one—Davis—leaned forward, hands clasped over his knees. 'All right, we won't deny it. Which is why we came to see you personally. We'd like to know why you purchased those white-oak bullets. We always do a background check on our clients, so, let's just say, I was somewhat surprised to learn you're a policeman…. Detective Inspector Sommers.'

Fuck! I'd been careless. 'So?'

These kids have clients?

'Not our usual clientele, if you know what I mean,' the younger kid piped up. 'Cops aren't exactly believers. Kinda the opposite, you know.'

Fancy that. 'Who is your usual "clientele"? Got a lot?' More kids with zits?

Still, it got me thinking. How many others knew about the real vampire menace in the city, not just these kids, but the wannabe loonies in their weird Goth clubs. Couldn't be too many. The Nighthunter website—from what I remembered—had only recently been registered. 'You only created that website a few months ago. How long have you kids been around?'

'I told you; we're not kids.'

'Yeah, yeah, I know. You're twenty and studying law at Sydney University. Now answer the question before I boot you out of here.'

They exchanged glances again. 'Okay, yeah, a few months.' Brad shifted uncomfortably. 'But we're getting more joining us all the time. They've lost—'

The older kid slammed his hand on Brad's shoulder. 'There are vampires killing adolescents in this city, as I'm sure you know, since you're a homicide detective. You can't tell your superiors for fear of ridicule, so you've decided to go hunting on your own. No other reason for you to have bought white-oak bullets from us. Am I right?'

This kid was twenty going on sixty.

I released a curt breath. 'Maybe.'

The younger kid hopped to his feet, a fever of energy burning in his eyes. 'C'mon tell us, will ya? You guys have done nothin' but cover it up! A vampire killed my sister. Sucked the blood right out of her. Two bite marks here,' —he dug two fingers into the side of his neck— 'and more over the rest of her body, and some weirdo didn't suck it out of her with a syringe, as the cops told us. The doc doing the autopsy said they found saliva on her throat, and it wasn't hers. She was' —his eyes filled with tears— 'fed on by more than one.' He angrily swiped them away. 'She was only thirteen. I wanna kill them!'

So that was it.

I thought back three months, to the dead kids we'd found. Munro had said it had been rogue elements among his miserable kind who'd committed those murders. I'd hated it, but at the time, I'd had no choice but to share information with him. True to his word, he caught and executed those responsible. He'd left me information where to find the bodies—in the burnt wreckage of an old, abandoned theatre in Rozelle.

The killings had stopped after that. But the damage had been done, and it was standing right in front of me.

These weren't seasoned vampire hunters; they were barely adult vigilantes looking for revenge. The teen I could understand, but the twenty-year old would be lawyer? What was his excuse?

'I'm sorry, son.' I turned to Davis. 'What's your score in this?'

His eyes narrowed. 'Seems I underestimated you, detective. I came to question you, yet we're the ones giving the answers.'

I bit back a laugh. 'Fancy that. Still waiting on yours.'

Davis pointed to his backpack. 'Mind if I show you something? It'll explain my position better than I can.'

I tensed. 'Unzip it, then lift your hands and slide it over with your foot. I want to take a look first.'

He shrugged. 'Sure.'

Inside was an old wooden box, a drink bottle and a notebook. Nothing suspicious. 'What's in the box?'

'Stuff. It belonged to my great-grandfather before being passed down the line to me. It hasn't been used in all that time.'

'Open it—slowly.'

I leaned forward to get a closer look. What's in fuck's sake was all that? Inside a red-velvet-lined box was the most outlandish collection I'd ever seen: a small, weird male figurine with lion's head and a set of extended double wings, a small box with half-a-dozen thumb length darts (white oak?), a long, narrow wooden cylinder that looked suspiciously like a blow gun, and an old-fashioned pistol with white-oak bullets. *Yep, I know those.* There was also a large sharpened stake and hammer.

'What the hell is this?'

He looked me dead in the eyes. 'A vampire-hunter's kit. I ... ah, need to add a bulb of garlic. You have any in the kitchen?'

Now I've seen everything. Heaven give me patience! These kids had no idea what they were dealing with or that most of the stuff in that kit was useless, especially that grotesque figurine. What the hell was that? Now, the white-bullets on the other hand ...

'The boxes of bullets you sent me. They're from this kit?' I pointed to the box.

'Only one of them,' Davis replied. 'There's not enough here, so we got the other one from elsewhere.'

My radar went up. 'Where from?'

'Avi—uh—place in France.'

Now that was interesting. It explained the delay between deliveries of the same order: they'd been waiting for the second box to arrive from overseas.

Ha! I couldn't believe my luck. I hadn't had time to organise the special permit to take my gun overseas. Probably wouldn't have gotten it anyway. I was hoping to get hold of some white-oak bullets while over there. Yet these kids knew exactly where to get some. And the gun that fired them too, I'd bet. Perhaps a more experienced group of vampire hunters, too.

They could come in handy.

Just maybe ... 'You have a contact there? How did you find out about them?'

Again they exchanged a glance, and Brad gave the older kid a nod. 'Might as well. It's not like he's gonna go over there tomorrow and suss 'em out; is he?'

I nearly barked out a laugh. *Kid, if you only knew!*

Davis reached into his vampire kit. From a hidden compartment, he pulled out a worn-looking, faded red-leather-bound book stuck together with tape. He held it just out of my reach. 'Found this when checking through the box. It looked ready to fall apart, so I taped up the worst bits. No one but vampire hunters know about this secret book. Do I have your promise not to reveal this information to anyone?'

'Like who's going to believe me?' And that was a fact.

There were handwritten notes on the appearance and characteristics of vampires. Even pencil colour sketches of their lavender-hued eyes. Laura's face shot into my mind. I shook my head to clear it. One sheet of paper showed graphic descriptions on how to kill them. I memorized it, as I doubted they'd let me photocopy it.

What these kids had was a vampire-hunter's manual.

So that's where they got the info for their website.

Further in were lists of names and addresses scrawled in different hands. Couldn't read a lot of them. On some, the ink had faded. From the ones I could make out, the initials PZ stood out.

'What's the PZ stand for?'

'Um ....' He dropped his gaze. Definitely hiding something. 'It's my grandfather's kit. He's in a nursing home, recently diagnosed with dementia. He told me our family history; stuff my dad never mentioned. Gramps said he wanted me to know everything before he lost it all, including where to find the kit.' He tapped the box. 'He said that it now belonged to me and ... that if needed, I should carry on the family tradition. I tried to remember everything he said as he's regressing more and more each day.' Davis blinked a few times and ran his sleeve across his eyes. 'Frickin' unfair! He's only sixty-nine.'

'I'm sorry, kid.' I meant it.

'Life's really crap sometimes, especially to those who don't deserve it. He's a top bloke, really. Looked after me and mum after dad ran off to

Bali when I was nine, the loser.'

What else was there to say? Some men should never be fathers.

A second later, he perked up and gave me an embarrassed smile. 'Argh, I didn't come here to blub.'

'It's okay. You're allowed to be human.' Unlike other things out there.

He nodded and a grin split his face. 'And that's why we've formed Nighthunter, in honour of Gramps.' Davis turned to his younger mate, and they bumped fists.

Heaven help me!

Something else caught my eye—some of the names in the book had either the initial "V" or "VN" after them. No date anywhere. These papers could be a century old, maybe older. Definitely before the age of typewriters. 'I'm assuming the V stands for vampire?' The kids nodded. 'So what's the VN?'

'Vampire nest.'

Ah huh! Made sense. The addresses with those initials next to them had been crossed out. Presumably wiped out by the vampire hunters? Most of those were from overseas. I didn't recognise any Australian locations. Laura—hell, I wished my damn stomach wouldn't roll like that every time I thought of her—had mentioned that her father's side of the family had arrived here from France over a hundred-and-fifty years ago: the human and the bloodsucking sides.

Had the vampire hunters followed them here? If they had, why was there no mention of the Lebrettan house in Vaucluse? Or any other vampire nests if there were over a hundred bloodsuckers in this city alone? Or had Lebrettan and Munro kept such a tight rein on their lot that vampire hunters had been unnecessary before now?

I needed answers.

'Davis, how long has your family been in Australia?'

Davis's head flinched back slightly, brows creased. 'What's that got to do with anything?'

'Just humour me, okay?'

He shrugged. '1890s.'

'From the UK?'

'Yeah.'

'Same.' And that's all they needed to know. Perhaps finding some common ground would get these kids to open up more.

'We tried to contact the names from the ones we could make out,' the younger kid said. 'See how many were still around. Only one answered us, the French dude. We got the white-oak bullets from him.'

Things were slipping into place.

So Davis's family brought the case over from the UK when they emigrated. Before that, it hadn't been used for ages. It certainly hadn't been used since ... or had it?

'You inherited that, right?' I indicated the box.

'Well, yeah. I told you: I'm from a long line of vampire hunters—'

'Who hadn't been doing much hunting in a long time. What happened?'

Davis locked his hands behind his head and gazed up at the ceiling before panning back to me.

Take your time, kid! I resisted the urge to roll my eyes and looked at my watch instead. Shit! I didn't have much time left.

'Like I said, the box was my grandad's. His pa had been a vampire hunter but they'd used a different name. He didn't say what it was. Said his pa forbade him to mention it. Only said they'd come here to keep up the fight, like they'd given it up back in the old country or something. But soon after arriving here, they'd given it up too. That's all he'd said, and all I know.' He shrugged.

Although I would've preferred to swallow acid, I had to hand it Lebrettan and Munro. They'd kept a tight rein on their bloodsuckers in all that time if Davis's family had stopped hunting—until the murders during Laura's ritual induction into the "family."

If it happened once, it could happen again.

I had no time to waste. But there was one more thing.

I leafed through the book. Had to be an address somewhere in here I could use. There! Two French ones: one in Paris and the other …

'Can you read that?' I turned the book to Davis.

'Avi—' He glanced at me, sighed, and then read the rest. 'Avignon. He's the one who wrote back.'

My luck was definitely holding out. I'd booked a flight direct to Avignon, plus car hire. According to the newspaper article, the Lebrettan estate was located neat there. As far as I could tell, it was only a short drive to D'Antonville.

It couldn't be any better. 'He the one who sent the bullets?'

'Ahhh … no. That came from a guy in Paris.'

Other side of the country. Not ideal. Perhaps the guy in Avignon could help out there. I took a photo of the page—and the notebook— then stood and did the same with Davis's box before closing the lid. 'Thanks. Now it's time for you go.'

Brad stood, fists clenched. 'What! That's it? No! We came here hoping you'd join us.'

'Not tonight, fellas.'

'But you believe us, right? Otherwise you would've chucked us out sooner.' Davis tucked the box into his backpack.

'Not denying it.' I strode to the door and opened it.

Brad gawked at me, open-mouthed. 'Then … then … I don't get you, man. You could help us.'

'There's no "us." Believe me when I tell you; you're way out of your league.'

'I'm the great-great-grandson of a vampire hunter. My family's been killing them for centuries. It's in my blood, so don't tell me I'm out of my league.' Davis's chin could not have stuck out any further.

I sighed. 'Listen son, you're the only so-called vampire hunter around, yet there's more than a hundred vampires. Doesn't that tell you something?'

'You mean there's more than one?'

'A hundred and twenty to be precise.'

They paled and exchanged a glance. Obviously they couldn't make a decision without checking with each other.

'Shit! We need more white-oak bullets—'

Oh, for fuck's sake!

'And more guns—'

'That'll shoot more than one bullet.'

'Yeah! Think the priest can give us some more holy water?'

'And garlic. Mum's got stacks—'

I slammed the door shut. They jumped. 'All right, let me put this another way. If you kids attempt to stake anyone you suspect of being a vampire, I'll have you arrested. Understand?'

'You're kidding!' Davis gawked at me.

No, I wasn't. I crossed my arms over my chest and gave them my stoniest expression. 'You think? Try me.'

Brad's nostrils flared, his eyes turning cold, hard and flinty. 'They killed my sister! Now I'm going to get them. Besides, they're not human, so it doesn't count.'

'Let me make a few things clear. One,' I held up a finger. 'You're both too young and inexperienced to go up against vampires. You'd be dead before you opened your box. Two...' I held up another finger. 'Apart from white oak, there's nothing in there that will kill them. Three, they're powerful, lightening fast and can hypnotise your puny brains into doing exactly as they want. And fourthly, antique or not, you need a license for that pistol.'

For a moment, they just stared at me open-mouthed.

'We need a license for an old gun?' Brad finally asked.

Bloody hell! 'Didn't you hear any of those first points I made?'

'Course, we did. So, you going to help us?'

Heaven help me. I resisted the urge to throttle them and throw them out of my apartment. Didn't matter which order.

Hell! Eighteen and twenty. They were just kids, yet so determined to kill some vampires. And in Brad's case, avenge his murdered sister. I had a sinking feeling nothing would deter them: not threats of arrest, nor the terrible danger they'd be exposing themselves to.

I rubbed my face. Tiredness and frustration sparked an idea—a lesser crazy alternative but still risky nonetheless.

"After all, they're not human," the kid had said.

Did I have the balls to suggest it?

After all, they're not human, played over and over in my mind. What if they were caught, or worse, got hurt in the process?

Could I risk their lives?

I went to the glass cabinet, pulled out a bottle of whisky and took a swig. What kind of arsehole asks a couple of idiot kids to do that?

'With or without your help, we're going to find them and kill them,' Davis said, and the younger kid nodded.

Decision made.

I took another swig of the bottle, stuck it back in the cabinet and turned to face them. 'There's a way you can destroy a whole bunch of them in one go without having to go anywhere near one.' They stared at me like two eager puppies. I felt like shit, but if these kids were determined... 'How good are you at arson?'

'Um ... never really—'

Brad elbowed Davis. 'I knew you'd know where to find them! Where they hide out during the day. Want us to burn it down?'

'It'll probably be guarded. It's risky, and you might get caught, or worse, get hurt. Still want to do it?'

My palms began to sweat. I had no right asking them to do this.

Too late to back out now.

No, it isn't! my conscience screamed at me. *But they're not human,* I mentally yelled back.

'There's a bunch of us. We can suss the place out, get around the guards.' Brad looked to Davis for confirmation.

The twenty-year-old nodded. 'Where is this house? Are the vamps inside?'

I gave a slow nod. 'Many. The place you want is in ... Vaucluse.'

CHAPTER 20 - KARI'S RUN

KARI

C'mon, hurry up, daylight! Never thought I'd ever say that, but I needed the sun to rise, now! I wove from tree to tree. Branches here were thick and some were covered in blossoms. Even Old Stinky's talons would have trouble getting through them.

I crouched into the hollow of one tree. *Slow down, heart ... slow ... slow. Don't want him to hear.* I snuck a peek behind me and sniffed. The smell of a thousand rotting corpses mingled with wrath made me gag. *I can't shake him. He's so close.*

Stinky screeched, and my pulse went maverick again. I ran. Sweat dripped into my eyes. I swiped it away and dodged between the trees until I got to the edge of the woods. *Now what?* I stared at field after open field. *Oh man!* I'd be a sitting duck. There was another forest—a thicker one—on the other side. So close. I needed to get in there. *But how?*

Again, that piercing shrill. It was hunting me.

I slapped shaky hands over my ears. *It's not going to get me!* The other forest wasn't all that far away. *Deep breath.* I measured my chances of making it across the open field: my legs versus flying Stinky. *It didn't look good.*

What I needed was one of those three-pronged weapons, like the ones Jake told me the old gladiators used in the Roman arena. I could swipe Old Stinky away, or better still, stick it up his arse if he tried to grab me.

Pointy stick. Wood. I was surrounded by wood. *Oh girl, you're such a dope!* I grabbed the nearest branch and broke off a long piece. It had lots of nice sharp twigs at its tip and along its length. I sighed. Enough to tickle him with, but not get through Stinky's hide. Something sharper. *Sacrifices must be made, girl.* My heart breaking, I unlaced my favourite boots and snapped off the diamond stiletto heels. *Ah, they'd only sink into the soft earth in the fields and slow me down, anyway.* I used the laces to tie them to my stick.

Okey-dokey, so it wasn't a three-pronged, sharp pointy thing; it was a two-pointed stabby diamondy thing. Fine. I clutched my stick and peered up through the maze of branches. *Where are you, Stinky?*

Movement up to my right. My mouth dried. He was circling the air practically above me, neck outstretched, sniffing. Could I make it across the field before it caught me?

Now or never.

Pulse racing like a rabbit at a greyhound meet, I streaked barefoot across the open field. *You just try it, Stinky!* I held my makeshift spear high in the air, my gorgeous diamond stilettoes shiny in the moonlight.

The whoosh of leathery wings above me, another piercing shriek.

You're not going to get me. Sweat dripped down my neck and into my bra. Not far to go. Forest ahead. Oomph! I caught my foot on a rock and landed face first in dirt. My makeshift spear fell from my hand.

No! Where is it? Where is it? My stomach doing somersaults, I whipped around and scanned the sky while groping for my weapon. Stinky was right above me, claws outstretched, mouth curved—was that a sick smile?

It dove.

Stinking piece of ... 'I'm not finished yet!' I yelled at it, shot to my feet, gritted my teeth and stabbed upwards.

A glint of mesh. Then another and another. Several nets sailed across the sky. Like little glinting stars, they wrapped around Stinky trapping its wings.

'Bring it down!' Marcus's voice boomed out.

Yes! I pumped a fist.

'Kari!'

I spun around, my blood rushing so crazy I was sure I'd catch fire. 'Jake!' I jumped into his arms.

'Thank the gods you're alive, Cara Mia.' He held me so tight, my ribs were squished, but I didn't care. His arms around me were heaven. 'I thought I'd go crazy.'

"He thought he'd go crazy!" A lovely swarm of butterflies took off in my stomach. *He called me, Cara Mia—my darling. He loves me! It has to mean that.* Maybe he hadn't realised it till now.

'Did it bite you ... scratch you....'

I shook my head. 'It wanted me alive.'

'For what? As a hostage?'

'Umm ... You don't want to know.' It was gross just to think about it.

Jake's body tensed. He eased me back and looked me full in the face then down the rest of me. My breath went for a gallop. I'd forgotten I was only in bra and leggings, having chucked my jacket to throw Old Stinky off my scent. And, I was barefoot.

My cheeks heated.

Jake's eyes paled, nostrils flared. 'He tried to ... violate you?'

'Kind of, but not kind of.' I told Jake what had happened and how I'd escaped. 'Old Stinky wanted to get back at you by taking me. Uchhhh! But I wouldn't let him do it.' I pointed to my cool weapon. It still lay in the grass where I'd dropped it. 'Wrecked my fave boots to make a spear should he try dive-bombing me.'

Jake's head zipped to the side checking out the spear. Then he laughed and hugged me again. 'You're one in a million. I'll get you a new pair of boots.'

Keep hugging me. Don't let go.

But he didn't. Sigh.

He stared at me for ages. His eyes darkened, before he blinked, released me and whipped off his long-sleeved T-shirt. 'Put this on.' Was Jake jealous? My heart went pitter-patter. I threw it on, hugged it to me and inhaled his yummy scent. 'The others needn't see you half-naked.' The crease between his eyes and the other scent her gave off.... Why was he angry? It wasn't my fault I had to dump my jacket and the lovely perfume pendant he'd given me. 'Are you cheesed off because I chucked the pendant? I really, really didn't want to, but I couldn't think—'

'What are talking about? I'm not angry with you. I'm proud of you, kiddo. Not many could do what you did.' He grinned and ruffled my hair. 'I'll get you another one.'

Kiddo? Why was he calling me kiddo, again. I caught his hand. 'Call me that again.'

'What?'

'Cara mia. That's what you called me a minute ago.' He'd meant it. Jake never said anything he didn't mean.

He looked away from me and strode toward the others. 'You must've misheard.'

'No, I didn't.' He kept walking. 'Jaaake!' I ran to keep up with him. 'But—'

'Not now, Kari. I've got a beast to kill.' He kept going.

Maybe he was just bashful in front of the guys? Or maybe not. Could I have really misheard? Cara mia does sound a bit like Kari ... kind of. Maybe he'd only rescued me because he was my sire, because it was his responsibility.

My chest felt as empty as if my heart had been ripped out and flushed down the toilet. I sniffed and wiped my eyes with the sleeve of his shirt.

Stupid Jake!

'Catch it! Hook the wings!' Marcus bellowed again. But each time they threw their nets Old Stinky evaded them and flew higher. *Rotten wings must be regenerating.* It gave one wretched screech and took off, like a rock out of a slingshot, flying in the same direction it'd been taking me: toward the mountains.

'Shit!' Terens threw a rock after it, which hit one of its feet. Stinky yelped, but it didn't slow down.

'Terentius and Calixtus, with me. We're going after it.' Marcus collected one of the nets laying in a heap on the ground and coiled it around his forearm. 'Justinius and Sempronius, get back to the house and tell Alec to move the household to Drunvela immediately.'

Immediately? Like now? My heart sank into the bottom of my boots—if I'd still been wearing them. There were no shopping centres in Drunvela. Not even a village. The place was boring. *You're doing this for Lolly, remember?* I told myself. Heck, I knew this was coming, and it was sure going to be harder on her then on me. She carried the weight of the curse—literally. I squared my shoulders. Lolly needed me, and that was it.

Marcus and the guys sped off into the distance, following Old Stinky's scent.

'Stick to Laura like glue from now on, Kari. Until this is over, I don't want you outside the ward.' Jake's voice always got deeper when he was worried, and I'd never heard him this worried before.

'Fine with me.'

'Okay, then.' He smoothed his hand down my cheek and my legs almost turned to melted butter.

Jake had the most gorgeous dark lavender eyes, long lashes. I didn't want him to stop looking at me. Just as I raised my hand to his, he dropped his, cleared his throat—when did he start doing that?—and turned away to join Sam. It was another stab to my heart, another bleeding wound alongside the others that wouldn't heal. How much of this would I be able to take? Until I had no heart left?

I pulled his shirt closer around me, his yummy scent filling my senses and splintering my heart even more. *Can't go on like this.* My mouth dried at what I knew I had to do. I'd stay until the Curse's end and then, if he hadn't said anything to me, I'd tell him. It was a leap year after all, a girl's chance to tell her fella she loved him. Resolve made my blood rush. Yep, I'd tell him, and if he wouldn't say it back to me … I'd leave and never come back. An empty blackness filled my soul at that thought. I pressed the spot above my heart. Yet, that kind of pain was better than seeing him with someone else, especially if that someone else was Milena.

Please, Jake, don't marry Milena … don't marry Milena, I chanted in my head all the way back to D'Antonville, hoping my thoughts would carry into his head.

A girl could hope, right?

My breath caught in my throat at the sight of the chateau's windows sparkling in the sunrise. Home! And yet I would have to leave it if Jake didn't want me. I rubbed my stomach to get rid of that awful hollow feeling as if my insides had been scooped up and thrown away.

The protective ward tingled as I slipped through with Jake and Sam. They'd been chitty-chattying the whole time on the best way to get everyone to Scotland. We stopped at the sound of Lolly's raised voice.

'Who's she yelling at?' I asked, but I was afraid I wouldn't like the answer.

CHAPTER 21 - I DO, I DO, I DO

LAURA

Of the many varied combinations of words in the English language, few have the power to bring sweat to your hands and cause that deep sinking sensation in the pit of my stomach as "we need to talk," or "we have a problem." Two seemingly bland phrases that could leave a blot on an otherwise pleasant day.

Still clutching my mobile, after Jenny had rung off, I sank into the sofa and stared out through the window to the copse of trees in the distance. Their bare branches swayed in the early spring breeze. But the air was just as frigid as the cold that enveloped my heart.

Matt was on his way here.

My stomach lurched. Not the first time in the last month. Morning sickness had truly taken hold and rarely did I pass a day without a couple of trips to the bathroom. My tummy was still deceptively flat and I splayed my fingers where a little bump would soon develop. 'Whoa! Take it easy. Deep breaths.'

I dropped my head into my hands. Why did Philippe have to enter my portrait into an art competition? He was dead. Matt knew the story. I'd told him. So why was he coming here with Interpol? What was he trying to prove?

Or, was it petty retribution? His way of paying Alec and me back for me leaving him?

I balled my fists, forgetting I still held the mobile phone.

Could he be that possessive?

That's nuts!

It couldn't be that, surely. It had to be something else. But what? And why did he go to Jenny? He could've easily rung me. And then I remembered that Alec had erased my number from his phone. But then again, Matt was a cop. He could find any number.

I closed my eyes as a myriad of questions spun around in my head like an out of control whirlpool. Somewhere among them was the correct answer, and I needed to know which one it was before Matt got here. And I had roughly two days—the time it took to arrive in D'Antonville from Sydney.

Of all the timing!

I stared out at the gathering clouds and then at my mother's wedding dress draped on the edge of my bed. In a few hours, I was supposed to have been walking down the aisle at the village church wearing that lovely gown, saying I do to the man who rightfully claimed my heart, my soul and who was my true other half.

But that dream would have to wait for another day.

Pere Hubert was dead, and Marcus, with some of the men, was out hunting the lamia responsible for his murder. My heart still ached for that kindly old priest and at the evil that took pleasure in such a heinous act.

I tore my gaze from my wedding dress and glared at the phone.

Matt Sommers.

I scrolled through my contacts list and stared at his name. Should I …

shouldn't I? My fingers twitched with indecision, my mouth dry at the thought of seeing him again, not as an old flame but as a subject in an investigation.

My head began to throb and a cold clammy sweat coated my palms at the prospect of having to repeat to the French police that horrible night Philippe attacked me. I fought back a wave of nausea as the scene replayed in my mind. I threw the phone on the floor, grabbed a cushion and buried my head in it.

The door opened and closed. Padded footsteps on the carpet and a gentle hand swept my hair back over my shoulder. 'What's the matter, darling?'

I turned my head and gazed into lavender eyes tinged with a dark ring of purple, their corners creased with concern. There was no way I could keep this from him, especially as we'd promised each other no secrets. I sighed and lifted my head from the cushion. 'Jen just called. Matt's on his way here, with Interpol. They want to interview us about Philippe.' I repeated the gist of the conversation.

Alec's jaw dropped. 'He entered your portrait into an art competition?' He plonked on the sofa next to me, sighed and laid his head back against the cushions. 'Of all the stupid things to have done.'

'Yep.' What else could I say? Jean-Philippe's obsession with me just wouldn't go away, even though he was long gone. It hung around like the proverbial bad smell. And now this. I snuggled into him. 'Mat'll be here in two days.'

Alec's eyes paled and a muscle ticked in the side of his jaw. 'Luc was right. He said I'd live to regret keeping Sommers alive. Now here it is.'

'No, you did the right thing. You're not a murderer, Alec.' Yet just as I said it, deep inside, I knew I'd still love him even if he had killed Matt that day, rather than mesmerising him into forgetfulness. That jolted me.

'I have sentenced men to death.' His eyes took on a hard edge.

'Because you had to. They were the murderers, not you.'

He gave me a half smile and rose, and with hands in his trouser pockets, he paced the room. 'Two damn days! We can't delay this move. Lamia could double back here at any time. We're safe enough, but not the villagers.'

'I'll have a word with him.'

I tossed the cushion aside and rose from the sofa. My phone, which I'd thrown on the floor, now sat on the coffee table. Alec must've picked it up. Darling man.

'You sure?'

No reluctance this time, no frantic heart thumping, I found Matt's number in my contacts list and pressed the button. And waited. 'I'm sure.'

Alec sat back on the sofa, one leg resting on his thigh, brow furrowed.

Matt picked up. 'Long time no see, babe.'

Alec growled, and from the two bumps that appeared along the top of his closed mouth, his fangs had slid down. Matt had that affect on him.

Matt must've added my number back into his contacts list. Probably hacked into Telstra's files to get it. Jenny wouldn't've given it to him even if he threatened her with jail time. *Love you, Jen,* I sent the thought to her.

'You don't need to come here. Why are you doing this, Matt? You know what happened.'

'Nice to hear your voice, too. Been thinking of me?' I could hear the smile on his face. It was enough to make my blood pressure rise.

Alec's growl deepened and he leaned forward, the loud crack of his knuckles filling the silence.

'Don't be juvenile, Matt. You're the last person I'd think about.'

'Yet here you here, calling me.' His smug little chuckle had me biting my tongue at what I really wanted to say. But I wouldn't give in to it.

Bastard's taunting you, Alec's voice murmured in my mind, his tone charged with lethal menace.

'I told you the truth, about what happened that night with … Philippe. Why can't you just squash this investigation? It'd be so easy for you.'

'Why would I do that?'

I swallowed, my heart pounding. 'Because Alec's innocent! You know that!'

'I only have your word for it.'

My blood boiled, and I wanted to scream into the phone. *Calm.* I took a deep breath. 'You know I didn't lie about that. I can't lie. I hiccup.'

'You and I know that, but no one else would. Besides, nothing would give me greater pleasure than to see Munro arrested for murder.'

His words chilled my blood. 'It wasn't murder! How can you blame him for something he didn't do?'

'It's not my call. Up to a jury to decide.'

'You scumbag! What sick game are you playing?' My body began to tremble, and queasiness spread from my tummy into my throat.

'Justice, babe. And if he's there with you, you can pass that message on, unless he's listening in.' Another chuckle.

My breath hitched. My gaze connected with Alec's. 'Justice? You liar! You want revenge; that's all. How about you stick—'

Before I could blink, Alec had swiped the phone from my hand, pressed the End button and threw it on the coffee table. Placing his hands on my shoulders he turned me to face him. 'Bastard was deliberately riling you, maybe hoping I'd take the phone from you and threaten him. Probably recording it all for evidence.'

My breath sawed in and out, so I could barely string two words together. 'The ratbag! I never knew he could be so vindictive.'

'You weren't together long enough, but eventually he would've shown that side of himself.'

Something else Matt had said before Alec had snatched the phone away. 'How would he know you'd be nearby?'

'The hitch in your breath gave it away. For sure he heard it.'

He would've too. Matt's police instincts missed nothing. I groaned and pounded my fists on Alec's chest. He could take it. I was like a fly swatting a rock.

'Feel better?'

I nodded. 'Never told him, but I hated when he called me "babe".'

Alec's chest rose and fell in a huff. 'Why didn't you?'

I just shrugged. 'Got used to it, I s'pose.'

He lifted my chin. 'Let me deal with Sommers from now on?'

'Gladly. What are you going to do when he gets here?'

'Nothing. We'll be in Scotland. I'll instruct the staff not to speak to him nor let him through the front gate. He'll have no option but to return to Sydney.'

'What if he follows us?' I racked my brain trying to remember if I'd blabbed all the details about the Curse to him. Had I ever mentioned the massacre site, where it all began?

'How would he know where we've gone? And even if by some stretch of the imagination he did find out, I doubt his superiors will let him follow us to Drunvela. They've got no body and nothing to go on. It'd be a waste of police resources.' He placed a finger on my lips as I opened my mouth to protest. I knew Matt. He was as tenacious as a bulldog, and I had a gut feeling that he wasn't going to let this go. 'And,' he continued, 'even if they did, it'd take a lot of paperwork and as well as convincing the Scottish police to agree. It could take months.'

I huffed and eased his finger from my lips. 'You don't know him. He's like Inspector Fix from *Around the World in Eighty Days*. You know, the detective who literally chased Phineas Fog around the world to arrest him for a crime he hadn't committed.' It was the closest analogy I could think off.

Alec chuckled and stroked a finger down my cheek. 'In that case, I'll mesmerise into believing what we want him to believe. That should get him off our backs. And I'll get Sam to hack into the police files, find out who the witness is and let the Brethren in Sydney wipe his mind. Then Sam can erase all information relating to Jean-Philippe.'

I inhaled and exhaled a relieved breath. 'That simple?'

He shrugged.

A knock on the door. 'Yoo-hoo! Can I come in?'

Kari!

My heart leapt. I jumped out of Alec's embrace to fling open the door. Sam and, a shirtless, Jake stood there with Kari in-between. Grinning and wearing, what I assumed was, Jake's long-sleeved T-shirt; leggings and … barefoot, she held her arms out. 'I'm baaack!'

I pulled her into my embrace, doing my best to hold in a stream of tears. 'You're not hurt? You're okay?'

'Nah, all good.' She patted my back like I was the one needing comfort.

Well, maybe I was. 'I'm so sorry, Kari. It was all my fault. I should never have asked you to go outside the ward.'

'Oh, don't be a nutso. If anyone's to blame, it's that stinky lamia. You know I had to ditch my all-time fav boots and Jake's perfume pendant to get away from it?' Her exaggerated pout and eye roll brought a smile to my lips, and the weight of guilt I'd carried since her abduction finally lifted. 'Gotta tell you all about it but—' she lowered her head and took a sniff '—I so need to take a shower first. I smell like Old Stinky. See you in a tick.'

'You do a bit.' I laughed and fanned my nose. 'Old Stinky? Does that mean the lamia's de—?'

She sprinted down the corridor leaving me mid sentence, but I couldn't remove the smile from my face. Warmth radiated through my body at having Kari safely back. It had to mean the lamia was dead. Had Kari killed or wounded it and my grandfather and the men had finished the job? I wanted to know. Guess I'd have to wait till she got out of the shower. My heart feeling lighter than ever, I turned to where Alec sat, deep in conversation with Jake and Sam. I hadn't seen either of them enter.

'Let me download the paperwork, and we can get to it.' Sam shook Alec's hand, a broad grin on his face. He pecked me on the cheek as he strode out.

'What was that about?' I'm sure my eyes must have widened. Sam had never done that before. It was nice, but unusual.

Alec rose and took my hands, his thumbs caressing the sides of mine. His eyes glittered. 'Marcus sent word. We're to leave for Scotland as soon as possible. The lamia's escaped.'

My heart raced and I sucked in a breath. 'It's not dead?'

He shook his head. 'It evaded their nets. They're hunting it, but it could come back here anytime. The villagers aren't safe.' He didn't need to add that the village had grown beyond the ward's capacity to cover it for any extended period of time.

'Of course.' I sighed. I'd been preparing myself for this moment. I could cope. 'I'll go pack.'

I turned to leave when Alec caught my hand. 'Wait. I'm not finished yet.' His eyes glinted and the smile that lit his face had my insides turning somersaults. 'Today was meant to be our wedding day, and it still can be. I don't want to leave this house until I ... can call you my wife.'

Wife! Who would think that such an ordinary word could sound so wonderful? Wasn't he just the most amazing man? His eyes darkened to the deep purple shade I loved, and the tenderness in them caused a warm wave to spread from my chest all the way to my toes.

'What do you say, darling? We've got a few hours before the jet'll be ready to fly us out. In the meanwhile, we can get married. In the conservatory. Sam's a JP, so he'll—'

'Sam's a JP?' I snapped out of my daze, my bewilderment with just how much I didn't know about these guys was a becoming daily habit.

'He's our fixer. Anytime a passport needs updating, a legal document needs … doctoring' —Alec's lips drew up in a lazy curve at his obvious pun—'whatever requires a stat dec, he does it. Makes sense for him to be a registered JP. Easier all round.'

'I s'pose it saves you having to look for a new JP whenever the old human one dies.' The depressing price of immortality.

'Sadly, yes.'

'How many JPs had you known before Sam took the job?'

'A few.'

I wrapped my arms about his neck. 'I'm all for it then, but what about rings? Unless you plan on using soda tabs.' I had my lovely pink diamond engagement ring, but there simply hadn't been time to shop for our wedding rings.

'You two sort that out while I'll go inform the housekeeper.' Jake slapped Alec on the shoulder and left. It'd been months, and Jake still referred to Sabine as "the housekeeper." Would he and the others ever get used to not having the Thierry's managing the estate?

Alec tucked a lock of hair behind my ears. 'I have my parents'.' The excited glint in his eyes was temporarily extinguished by, what I could only guess, was a rush of memory. 'My father kept my mother's wedding ring on a chain around his neck after she died. He passed it to me on his deathbed.'

I curled some of his hair at the nape of his neck around my fingers, my heart aching for his loss. We had both lost our parents, although to be fair, I still had my mum and dad: John and Eileen. 'I'd love to wear your mother's wedding ring.' And just as I said it, my chest tightened in the knowledge that his first wife had worn it also. After all, I wasn't going to be the first Mrs Alec Munro.

'No, she hadn't. We'd used her deceased parents wedding rings, and I buried them with her when she died.'

A pang of guilt struck me that I'd even had that thought. 'I'm sorry, I … don't know where that thought came from. It was so insensitive of me.'

Alec brushed the back of his fingers down my cheek. 'I got over that pain a long time ago. And no, you have every right to think that.' He leaned in and gently placed a kiss on my lips. 'You, and only you, are meant to wear my mother's wedding ring.'

Oh! He knew just how to melt my heart. 'You planned all that in those few minutes with Jake and Sam?'

'Among other things.' He grinned and brought my hands to his lips. 'I know it's not the wedding you deserve but it's the best I can do for now.'

Could I love this man any more? I cupped his face, drew his head down to mine and kissed him till we were both breathless. 'Your best is amazing.'

His smile lit a fire between my thighs.

'Can you be ready in an hour?' Alec's thumb grazed my lower lip, his voice seductively low and flowing over me like hot caramel sauce, his pine and fresh earthy scent making me heady. I inhaled deeply, infusing him into every cell in my body, my mind, my soul.

In one hour, I'll be Mrs Munro. Alec will be my husband. My pulse went for a wild gallop.

'Laura?'

'Yes, I'm here,' I said, almost dreamily.

Alec chuckled and brushed his lips over mine again. 'I'll get my stuff and get changed in Jake's room. Meet you in the conservatory in an hour.'

'I'll be ready.' Dress? Tick. Accessories? Tick. Veil? Tick. 'Doable.' I'd need a bridesmaid—at the very least I needed help with my dress because it had a zip at the back I could barely reach. Kari. 'Think if I asked Kari she'd like to be my bridesmaid?'

'Would I ever!' Her voice reached me from the hallway. In a second, the door flew open, and Kari stood there, face glowing, her wet, Nordic-blonde cropped locks slicked back off her forehead, giving her the appearance of a mischievous pixie. 'Well, c'mon then. Not much time.' She grabbed my hand and, with us both laughing, dragged me away from Alec and into the bedroom.

* * *

'What do you think?' I studied myself in the full-length mirror. My mother's three-quarter length creamy satin and tulle wedding dress hugged my figure perfectly. No evidence of a little bump yet. The simple tulle veil floated wistfully over my shoulders, held in place at the back of my head with an ivory comb.

Kari's reflection grinned back, giving me a two-thumbs up. 'You look gorgeous. Judy would be so proud.'

My heart gave a little kick. I glanced at my parents' portrait through the bedroom door. How I would've loved to have had them here with me, in this special moment. I swallowed against the tightness in my throat. 'Ah! Not now, Kari. You'll make me cry.' I blinked away the moisture that had pooled in the corners of my eyes, took a deep breath and fluffed out my mother's veil. 'I'm sure they know, and they're happy.'

Kari gave me a hug from behind, crossing her arms across the front of my shoulders. 'Yup!'

We stood silent for a few seconds, both in our own thoughts, before

Kari's eyes widened, and a look of horror crossed her face.

My insides plummeted, and my breathing quickened. I spun round. 'What's wrong? You sense something wrong?' I checked my serpent ring. If there was any danger nearby, its eyes would turn black, but they glowed bright scarlet.

'You don't have a bouquet,' she said in all earnestness.

Oh for crying out loud! 'Kari!' I slapped her arm. 'I thought it was something serious. Don't give me a heart attack before my wedding!' I took a few deep breaths and waited for my erratic pulse to slow.

'Oopsy!' She shrugged. 'Didn't mean to scare you.'

'Can we pinch some flowers from a vase? Nobody would know … would they?' I glanced around the room. None in here, but there was some in the living room. Sabine had fresh flowers brought up every second day from the greenhouse. I hitched up my dress and sauntered into the living room.

'Nooooo.' Kari followed me out. 'Everybody'll know where you got them from. They scream "house flowers!"'

She was right. Most of them were bulbs—tulips and daffodils—and some pansies. I sighed. We had fifteen minutes before I was due to meet Alec down in the conservatory, and I was out of ideas. 'Do I really need a bouquet?'

Kari's face lit up. 'Got an idea. Back in a sec.' She raced out the door. In the time I tried on the long white gloves, decided against wearing them and took them off, she reappeared arms laden with bunches of late-season snowdrops, magnolias, and sprigs of cherry blossoms that grew on the estate. The delicate perfume of spring flowers filled the room. 'Here you are, your bouquet, my lady.'

I nearly squealed with delight. 'They're perfect!'

We both turned at a knock on the door. Kari skipped over and opened it a crack. 'Just making sure it isn't Alec. Bad luck for the groom to see the bride before the wedding.'

'It's only the best man. So you're safe.' Kari flung the door open wide. Jake stood there, a box tucked under his arm and a smile on his face. 'I have something for Laura.'

'Ooh, what is it?' Kari clapped her hands, her face lit with excitement.

'I said it's for Laura, not you, kiddo.'

'I can be excited for her. Right, Lolly?' Her grin was so infectious I found myself laughing and agreeing.

Jake placed the wooden box on the table and opened it. 'Marcus asked me to give you this since he can't be here to give it to you himself.'

Sadly, Marcus and some of the guys had to go after the lamia. I would've loved him to have been at my wedding, but the creature was simply too much of a threat. He, Terens and Cal had had no choice but to go after it.

Kari sidled up to Jake, curling both arms through one of his as he held aloft a shimmering golden net of ruby-coloured jewels that sparkled like fire between his fingers.

I caught my breath. 'It's exquisite!'

'This was Gallia's, Marcus's wife … and your grandmother. She wore it at their wedding beneath her veil.' He held it out to me.

My jaw dropped as I stared at the magnificent headpiece, itself a nearly two thousand year old rare piece of jewellery. 'Jake, this must be priceless.'

He shrugged. 'It's just an object.'

'Easy for you to say.' I was afraid to touch it let alone to try to figure out exactly how to wear it. Yet, I couldn't help but let my fingers graze the fine gold filigree surrounding the glittering stones and dangling teardrop-shaped pendants. 'It's so beautiful.'

'Go on, Lolly. Put it on. Let's see how it looks.'

Excitedly, I pulled out the comb holding the veil in my hair and lay both on the bed. Then, with a deep breath, I gently lifted the priceless object from Jake's fingers and turned to the mirror. But, there was no clip to know which end was front or back. 'Think I'm going to need help putting it on.'

'Oh yeah, Marcus said the hanging stones go to the front.' Jake wriggled a couple of fingers at his forehead.

'Okey-dokey, let's do this.' Kari grabbed a chair and sat me down in front of the mirror. Taking the headpiece from my hands, she carefully positioned the teardrop pendant over the top of my brow before draping the rest of the coronet around my head. Then, with her hands resting on my shoulders, she cocked her head and gave a satisfied smile as she viewed her handiwork. 'How's that? Like it was made for you.'

For a moment, I was lost for words. The headpiece sat comfortably, hugging my head like a bespoke piece of clothing and cascaded down the back of my head like a glistening fiery waterfall. From whichever angle I turned my head, the effect was stunning. In the light from the chandelier, the little jewels glowed as with an inner fire, their blood-red hues a striking foil against my lavender eyes and ivory dress.

Kari whistled. 'Who needs a veil.'

Decision made.

Jake was standing back, hands thrust into his pants pockets, a curious little smile on his face. 'I remember a little girl who liked to suck the ends of her pigtails. And here she is, a beautiful bride about to be married.'

The unexpected note of sadness in his voice reminded me how old he really was in spite of his eternally youthful looks. He'd seen every Ingenii from birth to death. Would he see me grow old and die too? Ugh! This was not a day for being maudlin.

'I never did that!' Honestly, I couldn't remember if I did or not, but it was enough to shake him out of his melancholy.

'Oh yes, you did.' He chuckled. 'You were only three … and cute as a button.'

'*Was?*' I winked at him.

That brought a hearty laugh to his lips. 'You're still cute, honey, but I'll leave that department to Alec. And on that note,' he spun on his heel and went toward the door, 'I'll go see how the bridegroom's getting on.'

Kari's gaze followed him all the way out the door, and beyond.

My heart ached for her even as my hands longed to shake some sense into Jake. But that would have to wait for another time.

I stood and did a little twirl, enjoying the swish of the fabric against my legs, and the delicate tinkle of the gold links and clashing garnets in my headdress. I stopped and gazed into the mirror. 'Goodbye Miss Dantonville. Next time I look at you you'll be Mrs Munro.' I couldn't stop the smile that crept across my face.

* * *

Moonlight streamed in through the glass panels of the conservatory, sending watery ribbons of rainbows rippling across the polished floor to converge where Alec and I stood, hand in hand. Was this really happening? Breathless, my heart fluttered wildly at just the touch of his skin on mine.

"Laura Anne Dantonville, will you have this man to be your husband, to live together with him in the covenant of marriage? Will you love him, comfort him, honor and keep him, in sickness and in health; and, forsaking all others, be faithful unto him as long as you both shall live?"

Lost in the dark purple depths of Alec's eyes, the world fell away so I barely registered Sam words. My hands trembled slightly as I answered, 'I will.'

Sam then repeated the question to Alec. He gently squeezed my hands, his expression intense, his gaze penetrating deep into my soul.

'I will,' he answered. 'With all my heart, soul and mind. I'm yours for eternity, my darling.'

Could a heart burst with love? Mine was threatening to do just that. The words from the Book of Ruth in the Bible came to me in that second. 'Where you go, I go, and where you stay, I will stay. Your people shall be my people and your God my God. Where you die I will die, and there will I be buried.'

Alec sucked in a breath, his Adam's apple bobbing as he swallowed hard.

We hadn't had time to write our own vows, yet these words came naturally from my lips, unprompted and unrehearsed.

Sabine sniffed and dabbed her eyes with a hanky. 'C'était charmant,' she whispered.

'Okay, since you just said your own vows, we can dispense with the standard one.' Sam scanned the sheets of paper he held and shuffled a few before continuing. 'Um … let's see. Yeah, here we are. With the power invested in me by the state, I now pronounce you husband and wife.' He beamed at us. 'You may kiss the bride.'

Alec swept me up and kissed me to the applause of those attending. I wished for the kiss to never end. He was mine, just as I was his, in the most sacred of bonds. And ours was for eternity. Such a feeling of lightness entered my soul that I could have soared into the heavens. Our serpent rings came to life in a blaze of ruby light that filled the room and set aglow the smiling faces of those around us. Joyful tears slid down my face.

'Hello wife.' Alec's thumbs traced my cheeks and gently wiped away my tears.

'Hello husband.' We stood there, almost shyly, grinning at each other like a couple of school kids out on a first date. Considering my belly would soon be swelling, there wasn't much left to be shy about.

'Congratulations.' Sam shook Alec's hand and pecked me on the cheek. 'You know that's the first one of these I've done.'

Alec laughed. 'Well I'm glad we gave you the opportunity.'

Besides Jake, Kari and our housekeeper, Sabine, most of the household staff had quietly gathered. Grinning, they'd congregated near the entrance. Some threw rice, others confetti.

I smiled and waved back. 'So much for keeping this a secret from the Brethren.' By tonight, the whole Brethren world would in all probability know Alec and I were, indeed, the Promised Ones. Why else would an Ingenii marry her Guardian unless, unlike the rest of his kind, he could procreate? And the only one who could do that was the One spoken of in the prophecy. Many already had their suspicions and had voiced them. They didn't want the curse to end, for as long as there was an Ingenii, there remained the chance to daywalk.

The ending of the curse meant the loss of that hope.

Beings without hope either succumbed to despair or they lashed out against it.

I feared the latter.

Alec acknowledged the staff and dipped his head in greeting. 'I knew it was only a matter of time. Marrying you is worth the risk.' I was lost for words—it wasn't the first time he did it to me. 'Don't think of it now. This is our day, Mrs Munro.'

'Mrs Munro.' It sounded so alien and yet so right. 'I'll have to say it a few times to get used to it.'

'You've got the rest of our lives.'

A swarm of butterflies danced in my stomach as I pictured the years—maybe centuries—before us. I still had no idea how the ending of the Curse would impact me. What if I became fully human, with a human lifespan? I touched the ruby-pendant vial Luc had given me that contained three drops of blood from his family's bloodline. It was immortality in a bottle. I only had to drink it, and my lifespan would equal Alec's.

It all hinged on the little word 'if'.

Annnnd .... Now was not the time to think about it. I let it go when the pop of a cork broke into my thoughts.

'Here you go.' Jake handed me a fluted glass filled with bubbly champagne. He handed one to Alec. Lifting his glass, Jake toasted us. 'I wish you both all the happiness in the world. Salut!'

We chinked, and Alec and I linked arms and drank from each other's glasses.

From somewhere, music began to play: a slow waltz. Alec took me into his arms, and we twirled to its hypnotic strains. This was, indeed, our time, and enveloped in my husband's arms, my heart soared. I let the future and whatever it held disappear into the recesses of my mind.

CHAPTER 22 - PAZUZIM

MATT

I hitched up the collar of my coat as I exited the car hire depot. Damn wind had a chilly bite. Wasn't April supposed to be warm in this part of the world?

I blew on my hands and rubbed them together to keep warm, and scanned the parking lot. Where was this hire car? If—as I hoped—all had gone to plan, my drive to Laura's family villa in D'Antonville would be a waste of time. She wouldn't be there. No need to rush. But for the sake of protocol, I had to prove I was there; record everything in a logbook. I had to have evidence that Munro and his bloodsucking lot changed their location in response to Jenny's call.

Still, I preferred not be surprised.

I'd never told Laura, but two months into our relationship, I'd had a tracer planted into her phone. Over the years, I'd made a lot of enemies: bastards I'd put away, some serving life sentences with friends on the outside, friends who could hurt Laura to get to me.

She needed protection, and as I saw it, this had been the best way.

I should've removed it after we'd split.

Images of us together rampaged through my mind. *Damn it! No time for sentiment,* and sucked in some of that chilly air to numb my brain—and my dick.

The tracer app on my phone showed she was in Scotland. My ruse had worked. Still it was a kick in the guts. I hated that she was running from me. *Because you're still in love with her, idiot!* I snapped the phone wallet shut, my insides burning like I'd swallowed boiling rocks. She'd made her choice. Let her now see the consequences of it. *Keep running, babe. I'll still find you and that bloodsucking lover of yours.* An odd sense of excitement shot through me, like some kind of primeval urge that revelled in the thrill of the hunt … and kill. My fingers curled into fists in expectation.

But none of that would happen if I couldn't find that damn car.

I scanned the parking lot again and pressed the Unlock button on the key looking for the familiar "beep" and flash of blinkers.

Nope. Nothing.

'Hey!' Guy in a beige mac bumped my shoulder as he rushed past. He headed straight for the third row of cars, and into a black Renault, unlocked it and threw himself in. Lucky bastard's found his car. Must've switched the heating on full blast from the way his car windows were demystifying.

Why the hell hadn't I brought gloves? I dropped my suitcase and blew on my hands again, and that's when I spotted it, right next to beige mac guy's car: steel-grey sedan with the right rego plate. Why hadn't I seen it before? But, just to be sure, I pressed the remote again. The sedan's blinkers flashed. I hefted my bag, and my frozen legs couldn't carry me fast enough. And, I nearly got in the wrong side. Damn, I'd forgotten that here they drove on the right-hand side.

Left door, mate, left door.

I scouted the dashboard. First thing, switch on the engine for the heating. On. It took a few seconds, but eventually the hot air blasted the numbness from my face. Next, GPS … and there it was. I switched the language to English and punched in my destination. There was someone I had to visit, a man by the name of Robert Junot. I'd copied his details from the Nighthunter kids' notebook. His address was about a ten-minute drive from here, in the old part of town. I'd checked on Google maps before leaving Sydney; had even downloaded a photo of the place—Rue Racine, above a shop.

Ten minutes later, I sat parked just outside a building with set of weathered brown timber doors accessed via a courtyard.

I'd considered the possibility that whoever this Robert Junot was, might not want to share information with a stranger. Well, that was too bloody bad.

I got out of the car and pressed the doorbell.

'Qu'est-ce que te veux?' An old guy's face appeared in the top window.

'You speak English?'

'Allez-vous en.' He waved me off and slammed the window shut.

Reckon that must've been the French for 'get lost.' Great start. *Let's try again.* 'Robert Junot?' I pulled out my badge and held it up for him to see. 'I'm a policeman, from Australia, and I need to speak to you.'

No answer.

I pulled out my French phrasebook, some of the pages already dog-eared. I'd tried memorising a few lines on the flight over, but I gave up. 'Je suis … un polic … ier d'Australie'. No idea whether I'd pronounced it correctly or not.

He appeared back at the window. 'Stop murdering my language. I ask again, what do you want?'

Could've said he knew English.

I glanced around. Several people walked past. 'Not here. Can I come up?'

The old guy huffed. 'First door on the right.' He moved away from the window, and the front door clicked open.

I pushed it and walked through. What the ...? I waved a hand beneath my nose. The smell of fried fish, stale cigarettes, rotting wood, damp and who knew what else, all rushed at me at once. Didn't they ever air these places out?

The stairs creaked with each step. First door on the right, he'd said. Guess he meant the one with the five or six layers of peeling paint.

I knocked.

'It's open.'

The old guy sat at a small table, newspaper spread out before him, a cup of coffee in hand. It smelled good. I'd had breakfast on the plane, but the coffee wasn't drinkable. Never was on airlines.

'So what do you want, policeman-from-Australia?' He looked up at me from the top rim of his glasses.

I'd rehearsed what I was going say almost from the moment I'd left Sydney, yet here I was, and only one word sprang to mind. 'Vampires.'

Bloody jetlag must be draining my brain.

He removed his glasses and checked me out through narrowed eyes. 'You could have saved yourself a trip and just looked that up online.' He jerked his head in the direction of his desktop computer. 'Australian police have nothing better to do than chase myths?' He barked out a laugh.

I scrubbed both hands down my face. Why had I thought this would be easy? 'Take a look at this.' I pulled out my phone and showed him the photos I'd taken of the kids' box and his name in the notebook. I pointed to it. 'Your name and address are in here.'

He grabbed the phone from my hand, his face paling as he scrolled through. 'How did you get this?'

'Recognise the box?'

'Never seen it before. Your business here is finished. Get out.' He practically flung the phone back at me. His hand shook as he brought the cup of coffee to his lips.

'What are you afraid of?'

'Show me your warrant. If you are here officially, there should be a gendarme with you.' His gaze slid past me to the door. 'But no, you are alone. This—' his eyes narrowed, and he waved his hand at me '—has nothing to do with police business, does it?'

I pulled the warrant from my coat pocket and dropped it on the table. The guy from Interpol who'd met me at the airport didn't think it necessary to accompany me. 'It's only routine questioning,' he'd said. 'You don't need me for that. Send me a report when it's done.'

Lazy bastard.

So, yeah, I was on my own.

The old guy hunched over that piece of paper like a crab guarding his meal, bony finger hovering over one line. His lips silently formed the word, "Dantonville." Oh, yeah, he recognised it, all right. He swallowed, lips turned down as if he'd eaten something bad, and slid the warrant back across the table to me. 'My name's not on this warrant. You have no business being here.'

I stabbed a finger at the same spot. 'The woman, Laura Dantonville, is an Ingenii, recently come of age.'

His eyes flared at my use of that word.

'This man,' I bit the words out, pointing to the other name on the warrant, 'is the princeps, and I need to bring him in for questioning regarding a murder I'm investigating.'

He gaped at me. 'How do you know this? Who gave you this information? Tell me!'

But before I could answer, he broke out into a fit of coughing.

'Hey, you okay?' I slapped him on the back as it looked like he was choking. 'Can I get you some water?'

He waved me off and pulled an inhaler from his pants pocket. A few puffs later, the coughing stopped.

'Asthma?'

'Emphy ... sema.' He took a couple of deep breaths, his face registering relief. 'Take my advice, and don't smoke. Fucking things will kill you.'

I pulled out the only other chair at the table and sat facing him. 'Look, I came here hoping you'd help me out. So stop pretending you know nothing about *The Brethren...*' There was a barely detectible flicker of one eye when I spat the word out. '...as they call themselves. I need a way to bring their leader in without actually killing him.' *Yet.* That wouldn't serve my purpose. 'I want to expose them and let the law deal with them.'

He ground out a few more gravelly laughs between puffs of the inhaler. 'You're crazy!'

'Maybe, but if the world knows about them, we can get rid of them.' That was the plan.

The old guy shook his head, took a long deep breath and turned to stare out the window. 'You still haven't told me how you know all this.'

I figured there'd be nothing to gain if I withheld that info from him. You scratch my back, and I'll scratch yours, as they say. It was my turn to scratch. 'I was briefly engaged to her.' I pointed to Laura's name on the warrant. 'I met the ... *family.*'

His gaze snapped to me, eyes bugging in his head, then they narrowed as he read through my words. 'The female protected you.'

I nodded.

'Then you're an even greater fool!' He stood on shaky legs, and when I went to give him a hand, he slapped it away. 'Why didn't they erase your memory?'

'You stopped playing games, then?'

'Answer my question. And I'll let you know.'

Fair enough. I explained how Munro had wiped my mind. Lebrettan would've killed me, for sure. But it hadn't stopped me investigating them. It was small satisfaction that I'd irritated Munro enough for him to restore my memory in return for my help in protecting Laura.

What an upside-down shit situation. More proof, if I'd needed any, just how much his bloodsucking lot were out of control. Another nail in his coffin—*funny joke, man!*—as far as I saw it.

'You want to get yourself killed? Go. Leave me out of it. I said as much in my letter to the fool from your country who wrote to me, asking me to join them.' The old guy shuffled to the door, shoulders hunched, head down.

Davis hadn't mentioned that, the sneaky kid. 'Your vampire hunting days may be over, old man, but mine are just beginning, and if you can't help me, I'll go elsewhere or do it on my own.' *And heaven help anyone who tries to stop me.*

He halted just short of the door, straightened his back and turned to face me, his mouth pulled back in a sneer. 'And you know so much about killing fangheads. The great expert from reading one old book. Ha! You know nothing. Nothing! I was never a vampire hunter. The name in that notebook is my great-grandfather's, and after his deal with Lord Lucien, the fraternity disbanded. My father swore to have nothing to do with it, and neither will I. Be smart and do the same. Leave it alone. Go home and forget about it.'

Anger burned up in my veins. He may as well have told me to quit my job and join the circus! Not. Going. To. Happen. I stood and pocketed my phone while planning my next step. 'Don't you care about human lives?'

'There haven't been any vampire killings in this country for centuries.

And I want to keep it that way.' His eyes darted sharply to the side. He pulled out a walking stick from the umbrella stand near the door, raised it and brought it crashing down on the floor. 'You go after them, and they will swat you like I just did that cockroach.'

He doubled over in another coughing fit, the walking stick clanging onto the tiled floor to join the cockroach remains.

Oh hell! In spite of his protests, I half-dragged the old guy—coughing and spluttering—back to his chair at the table where he'd left his puffer and put it into his hand. Spots of blood dotted his lips and the front of his sweater—and my wrist and my leather watchband. 'You should be in hospital. I'll ring the ambulance. What's the emergency number here?' I dug the phone from my pocket. I'd managed to get an EU SIM card at the airport.

Puffer at his lips, all he did was shake his head and dismissively wave his hand at me again. 'No … hospital. I'm dying … anyway. They … can do … nothing, except give me another of those—oxygen bottles.' He pointed to a metal cylinder and breathing mask near the sofa.

'Why aren't you using it, instead of the puffer? It's more effective.'

'I'm managing.'

Stubborn old coot. I waited until he sat back and wiped his mouth, breath wheezing in and out of him, eyes streaming from the effort. After a few moments, his breathing evened again. Reluctant to say anything in case the old guy went into another coughing spasm from which he mightn't recover, I removed my coat, went over to the sink to wash the blood from my wrist and watchband. Some had even splashed on my bracelet. Like the watch, it had been a gift from my grandmother on my graduation from the Police Academy. She'd had my name, date of graduation and shield engraved on the silver plate and framed it with a black leather band. I'd promised her I'd never take it off.

'While you're there, can you get me some water?'

I looked over my shoulder. 'Feeling better?'

He nodded and took a couple of deep breaths. 'For now.'

Sorry, Grandma. I left my watch and bracelet on the sink to dry, filled a clean glass I found sitting on the dish rack and handed it to him. He gulped it down but grabbed my wrist with his other hand and turned it upwards. He pushed his glasses further up his nose, leant forward to take a long, hard look. 'Not possible,' he muttered. 'You're alive?' Mouth open, eyes wide behind his spectacles, he gaped at me as if I'd just sprouted horns.

'Of course, I'm bloody alive—'

'No, no, stupid man! Your family. Your family is alive and well? And the other one too? Why didn't you let us know? We all thought you'd been killed after your clan had left.'

'What the hell are you talking about.'

His frown deepened. 'This!' He shook my wrist. 'This mark.'

'What? It's just a birthmark. Nothing more.' I snatched my wrist back. My father had the same small squiggle-and-hook mark on his wrist. It was a harmless genetic thing.

He rolled up his sleeve and showed me his wrist. 'No, you are Pazuzim. Like me. See? Why didn't you tell me?'

The exact same birthmark stared up a me. My skin tingled as the blood drained from my face leaving me numb. 'I don't know the hell you're talking about.' But I couldn't tear my eyes away from the identical mark on his wrist. This was no coincidence. As far as I knew, my family had no French connections, so there was no way we were related. Yet, the striking similarity of the birthmark … and something else deep down in my gut that convinced me the guy was telling the truth. A lump the size of a bloody rock lodged in my throat, but I managed to croak out: 'What the hell is a Pazu …?'

Then it hit me, "Pazu" the "p" and "z" —the initials that Nighthunter kid Davis spoke about—stood for Pazuzim! I'd have to tell the kid when I got back.

'You don't know?'

'What?'

The old guy's brow creased till their fleshy lines touched the top rim of his glasses. 'Are you listening to me?'

'Yeah, yeah, I'm listening. Just … never mind. This stuff's all new to me.' And I didn't like not knowing something this important. My teeth clenched so tight that my jaw began to ache. How could my dad have kept this from me? He'd had to have known, for sure. I thought back to find any hints, any clues that could explain why he hadn't told me. Hell, there was nothing.

The old guy muttered something in French, rose from the table and trudged to a cabinet that was probably as old as him. The chipped and scratched bottom timber drawer grated as he struggled to open it. Any moment and he'd start coughing again. And this time, he could keel over from it.

'Here, let me.'

The damn thing slowly slid out, and he bent to lift a decrepit-looking dark green wooden box. 'Ah!' He grimaced and slammed his hand to his back as he slowly straightened. 'Cursed arthritis!'

'Where do you want it?'

'Table.'

It was surprisingly heavy. What the hell did he have in it? From the top drawer, he extracted a key and tossed it to me. 'Unlock it.'

The musty smell of old paper hit my nose as I opened it. Sitting atop a pile of yellowing sheets was the same worn-looking, faded red-leather-bound-book that Davis had shown me back in Sydney, minus all the sticky tape.

Junot's bony hand snatched it up. Nicotine-stained fingers shakily leafed through it. 'What did you say your name was?'

'Sommers.'

He grimaced. 'English.'

'Australian,' I corrected him.

He shrugged. 'All the same. Your family came originally from England, no?'

'Yeah.'

'Humph! Sommers, Sommers … I don't remember a family by that name. Mother's maiden name?'

'Paisley.'

'No, that's not it.'

I baulked at the implication. 'You're kidding, right? My family name in there.' I jerked my head to indicate the notebook.

'You have the mark. Your name *will* be in here.' He stabbed the book with a gnarled finger. 'The head of every Pazuzim family had a register of all the others in case they tracked a fanghead into another family's territory. You had to ask permission.' He regarded me again over the rim of his glasses. 'You sure you've never heard this before?'

'How many times…!'

Fanghead? I liked it.

'Humph!' He shook his head, the corners of his mouth turned down as he leafed through the pages of the notebook. 'Then there is much to tell you. I need another coffee.' He glanced up. 'And from the looks of you, so do you.'

'You have no idea.'

He actually cracked a smile in that craggy face. 'You're closer. Put the water on.'

While I did that, he flipped over a few more pages, muttering to himself the whole time—in French. 'Up to your right,' he hollered after I'd opened a couple of cupboard doors looking for the blasted coffee jar or tin, or whatever he kept his coffee in. 'Biscuit tin's next to it.'

'What did you mean, if my family's still alive?'

'Just what I said. Many families were wiped out, others died out or … disappeared. You know, like yours.'

Fair enough. I got where he was coming from. We'd emigrated from Britain to Australia, and my great-grandparents hadn't bothered to remain in touch with the other Pazuzim families. The question was, why the hell not? Had there been a falling out? Guess I'd soon find out. For sure as hell, I wasn't leaving until I got answers.

'The ones who got wiped out? How?'

'Their Principate ordered our extermination.' He sighed, pulled his glasses off his face and turned to me. 'At first, their high elder, Marcus, was against it. He wanted us turned and made their slaves. But he didn't know that Pazuzim cannot be transformed into one of them. What he got instead, from the few he captured, were mindless killers with the strength and speed that matched their own. They rampaged through their fortress, slaughtering every fanghead in sight. Marcus and his son, Lucien, barely escaped with their lives.' He gave a grim smile. 'It's legendary among our people.'

Biscuit tin tucked under my arm, I carried over two steaming cups of coffee and handed him one. 'And I know bugger all about it.' The coffee turned bitter in my mouth as I swallowed it down.

He shrugged, shoved the glasses back on his nose and returned to the notebook. After turning another page, his eyes lit up, and he slapped his palm on the table. 'Aha! Here it is. Listen.' He read something out—in French. The only word I recognised was "Sommerset."

'English, please.'

'It says that two families left England to go to Australia. It's dated 1893. The Sommersets and'—he glanced back to the notebook '—the Davidoffs.'

Sommersets? Now my stomach really did take a dive and I swallowed a deep gulp of coffee to settle it. As a kid, I'd accidentally come across an old photo among my dad's things. It was Family Day at school, and I needed to bring something. The photo had looked perfect, especially as it had a date—1893. I recognised the face of my great-great-granddad who'd brought the family to Australia from the UK. His portrait once hung in the living room until Mum had it moved into the hallway. But the name was on the back of the photo was John Ernest Sommerset, which had confused me. We were "Sommers" not "Sommerset".

Yeah, dad had been really thrilled when I'd asked him about it. To this day, I could still see his angry face as he'd snatched it from my hand. 'What were you doing snooping through my box, Matt? How many times have I warned you?'

I'd gulped back angry tears. He'd then made me promise to forget about the damn thing and the name on it. I'd promised—fingers crossed behind my back. I'd hoped I would have the guts to ask him when I got older.

He died of cancer four years later, and that chance had died with him.

'You are a Sommerset. Your ancestor changed his name to protect his family.' Junot pointed at me.

And that little revelation had my insides roiling. Family secrets. I hated them. Look what Laura's dirty little family secret had done to us.

My fists clenched.

Yet, as I thought about it, had Lebrettan known who or what I was, I wouldn't be alive now. Which raised the question: Why had my family—and the Davidoffs, which I assumed were that Nighthunter kid's family—left Britain? Had it been to follow Lebrettan's clan or to get away from them? If it was the latter, it certainly made the name change understandable, and with it all the damn secrecy. My father, and grandfather, were simply protecting us from extermination. And it had worked. I was living proof.

'Does it say anything more, like why we left?'

The old guy pushed his glasses further up his nose. His eyes scanned down the page, and he turned back through a few before pushing the notebook aside. 'Nothing here. Maybe this one …'

He rifled through a few loose papers, quickly scanning through each, 'Not these,' before dumping them on the tabletop. 'Maybe … this one.' How many notebooks were in that drawer? 'Did I tell you about the peace pacts between our people and the fangheads?'

I speared the old man with a look. 'Not yet. Pacts? More than one?'

'That's what it usually means.'

I tried not to roll my eyes. Think I lost out on that one.

'You going to ask me why they failed?' The corners of his mouth curled up. Old guy was enjoying this.

'Why spoil your fun.'

He gave a close-mouthed chuckle, dropped one notebook he'd been scouring through to pick another one. 'They couldn't control their rogues, so we had to. End of peace treaty.'

'The rebellions. Yeah, heard about them.'

'Humph! You learned much from your time with the Ingenii girl.'

I nodded, and tried to make sense of what he'd just said, about some sort of deal between the vampire hunters and Lebrettan's bloodsuckers, or fangheads, as he called them. From what Laura—I tried to ignore the tightening in my gut—had told me, Lebrettan had faced two rebellions in his lifetime, and both had been dealt with. But it had obviously resulted in human deaths. So, if the old guy's ancestors had been doing their share of vamp killing, did that mean there had been another more recent rebellion or just a bunch of them going rogue that forced the hunters into action?

Whichever it was, it again proved that if Lebrettan had lost control of his fangheads, then so could Munro. And it could happen anytime again.

Not on my bloody patch! My teeth clenched so hard that my jaw throbbed. I rubbed it to ease the ache, as yet again, images of Laura flickered through my mind, her unearthly beauty setting my groin afire.

Damn it!

I had to keep her face out of my head. 'Why renew the peace pacts if the vamps kept breaking them?'

'Because there weren't enough of us left to keep fighting, yet we were still a threat to them.'

Then I asked the burning question. 'What happened that forced my family to leave Britain? Were they running away to protect themselves?' If that was indeed the case, then our name change and hiding who or what we were all made sense … and I couldn't blame them.

The old guy put the notebooks down, leaned back in his seat and clasped his hands over his stomach. 'From what I know, the head of your family voted against another peace with the fangheads. Some agreed with him, others didn't. There was much arguing and accusing the others of forsaking our role. But, as in the past, there were those who argued that the cursed fangheads were different—Marcus and his clan. Marcus punished those who killed humans, hunting them down, leaving them to fry in the sun.' He shrugged. 'He and his clan were doing our job. After six thousand years killing fangheads, our numbers were low. Some believed we were no longer needed. Entire families had stopped hunting even earlier when there were no more fanghead-related killings in their territories. Their urge to hunt went dormant. So, a new peace treaty was made.'

I guessed those who didn't agree left the country. 'So that's why my family left Britain. They didn't go along with the decision, did they?' Why did that not surprise me.

He pursed his lips and cocked his head to the side, and that gesture worried me. Something was coming that I probably wouldn't like. I swallowed and waited.

'Your family—along with a few others—were seen as a danger to the rest and expelled, thrown outside the Protection of the Pazuzim. They could not expect help from other families if attacked by fangheads. Many were wiped out and with the rest we lost contact.' He looked thoughtfully at me over the rim of his spectacles. 'I'm glad your family survived.'

Yeah, thanks. Small consolation, yet my dad's reaction when I found my grandfather's photo as a kid now made sense. He *had* known, and his anger had most probably hidden his fear for me, and for my sister.

I dropped my head into my hands, letting my nails dig into my scalp in the off chance I was actually only dreaming all this shit. But, nope, I was awake, and it was real.

Bloody fucking real.

The old guy grunted. He'd pulled out something else from the drawer—a large and thick hardcover tome with the name "Junot", and right beneath it the same squiggle-and-hook image as my birthmark.

Any last miniscule bit of doubt about my connection to this old guy, and the vampire hunters and my family, just took one hell of a nosedive.

I needed a stiff drink. 'Got anything stronger than coffee?'

A small smile appeared on those pale thin lips. 'It is hard discovering who you really are, is it not?'

He could've slugged me in the face, the effect would've been the same. I hated the implication. Hated that I suddenly understood how it must have hit Laura when she'd learned the truth about herself ... and how it had changed her. That it hadn't been all her fault. If only she'd been told sooner.... If only I'd been told as well. Would I still have asked her out ... that day we'd met?

I rubbed my chest at the sudden tightness, and with coffee in hand, went to open the window. Too bad if the old guy complained about the cold air. Right now, I needed it to clear my head, make sense of everything. If I hadn't met Laura and seen the truth with my own eyes, I wouldn't be here, right now. In another life, I would've dismissed the old guy's words as dementia-driven ravings.

In another life.

What a joke! I allowed myself an ironic laugh.

'Something funny out there?'

'The absurdity of life, mate.' I turned my wrist up, my eyes tracing the outline of my birthmark. 'I'm supposedly from a line of vampire hunters, and I go and fall for a vampire … or half vampire. Ever heard of that happening?'

The old guy snorted. 'You do not love her. It is the Pazuzim in you. It drew you to her to get close enough for a kill.'

I spun around, spilling the few drops of coffee left in my cup. 'Bullshit!'

He pursed his lips and lifted his hands, palm upwards. 'Eh bien! I tell you the truth, and you say it's bullshit. Of course, you know better than me.'

'No way! I *never* had some sick urge to hurt her let alone kill her. That's just crazy.' The whole idea was repulsive. This time, the old guy was way dead wrong. 'We were together three months, and in all that—'

'Did you always want to know where she'd been, what she'd been doing or who she was meeting? Did you ever follow her, convincing yourself it was for her safety? Like some crazy stalker?' His brows rose, dark brown eyes lasering into mine, but that wasn't what made my throat suddenly dry—so much so, I couldn't even swallow.

I dropped into a chair, my sweaty hands scrunching the stained tablecloth in my fists, as scene after scene of me doing just as the old guy had said replayed in my head. Hell, wouldn't any cop with enemies do the same to protect his loved ones? Sure, a small voice in my head said, but I never interrogated my mum or sister the way I did Laura. I didn't secretly place a GPS tracker in their phones. Did I? *It was for her safety*, I said back to it.

My throat tightened and I tugged roughly at my tie to loosen it.

Damn! My hand shook, too.

'Aha! See? I am right, am I not?' Eyes glinting with satisfaction, he wagged a gnarled finger at me. Took all my self-control not to reach out and snap the wretched thing.

'Whatever I did was for her safety!'

He barked out a laugh. 'Of course it was; if that's what you want to believe. And gritting your teeth at me won't change the truth.'

I slammed both hands flat on the table and glared at him. 'I love her, and that's the truth!' And it was killing me.

He removed his glasses, sighed and rubbed his eyes, then rose, came to my side and placed his hand on my shoulder. 'I know you don't want to believe me, so let me ask you one last question, and perhaps you may begin to see.'

I shrugged. 'Doubt it.'

'This Ingenii … you said you dated for three months, no?'

'Yeah.'

'I assume she wasn't your first woman. I say this because you look in your thirties, and most men have known several woman by that time.'

'Bit nosey much?'

He tapped my shoulder a few times, before sitting down again. 'Did you try to protect those other women the same way as this one?'

It took all of one second for the proverbial penny to drop, and with it the remnants of my gut. 'No.'

He spread his hands and let them drop on the tabletop. 'Now you begin to see.'

And what I saw I hated, and no matter which way I looked at it, I had to admit the old guy was right, except for the killing bit. Yeah, I could've happily killed Lebrettan and all the others, but not her. Never her. And the more deeply I analysed it, I knew why. 'She's different. Not entirely human nor vampire either. Somewhere in-between. Maybe that's why those Pazuzim killer instincts didn't fully kick in.'

Junot's wrinkled face took on a pensive expression; his mouth drooped and he gave me a slow nod. 'Mmm. It's possible, although I've never heard of it happening before. But then she is, as you said— 'his thin shoulders rose in a slight shrug '—in-between.'

The old guy sighed and slurped his coffee. Must be cold by now. It triggered a memory. Laura's faced scrunched up in a cute grimace downing the last drops of coffee she'd left sitting on her desk. I'd gotten off work early and picked her up. 'One day I'll actually get to finish my coffee while it's still hot.'

That was a month into our relationship. When everything had been good. Before it had all changed.

Bile rose in my throat. I had to think of something else. Anything.

I closed my eyes, rolled my shoulders and let my head drop back to ease some of the tension. 'What the hell does Pazuzim mean anyway?'

Pages rustled, then stopped.

'Come, look at this, and you will know.'

He'd angled the book toward me. I leaned forward to get a better view of the weird-looking image he pointed to, and which I immediately recognised. It was the same as the small figurine I'd seen in Davis's vampire-hunting kit.

'Pazuzu. Babylonian demon-god and father of the Pazuzim. We carry his mark.' He lifted his wrist, exposing the little hook-and-squiggle birthmark we had in common.

I think my brain shorted out since I just stared at the old guy not quite believing what I'd just heard. Ancient gods? He had to be kidding me?

Nah, nah, nah, there had to be another explanation. Had to be. Another part of my brain, the part that was still functioning, piped up and reminded me that I'd thought there was no such thing as vampires either.

The old guy chuckled. 'You should see the look on your face!'

'Making your day, am I?'

'Best one I've had in months.' His wide grin revealed nicotine-stained teeth against cracked lips.

Bastard! I stood and paced around his kitchen. As far as I was concerned, there was only one God. The idea of other gods and goddesses ... whatever ... had to have another explanation. Yeah, I believed in demons, but more as personifying the evil in mankind rather than actual living beings. But, the birthmark ... Nope, no way in hell was I going to believe that shit. It was more likely some canny witch doctor or priest, or whatever they were thousands of years ago, that went around killing vamps and spun some crap to convince everyone else. Passed off his birthmark as a sign as having been chosen by the gods ... passed it down his line. That definitely sounded more like it.

'You honestly believe that shit ... some god called Pazuzu? Know what I think?' I told him.

He pursed his lips and shrugged again. 'Maybe, maybe not. But the maybe explains much more.'

'What do you mean?'

'One.' He raised a finger. 'We cannot be turned into fangheads. Doesn't work on us, as I already told you. Two.' He raised another finger. 'We are drawn to them with the desire to kill. Why do you think I live here, in Avignon? Because it's far enough away from the D'Antonvilles that those urges don't dominate me, yet close enough to keep an eye on them.'

I wasn't convinced. 'Those things can be explained genetically.'

He waved a hand at me dismissively. 'Have it your way. Believe whatever you want, but you cannot change what you are, and that mark on your wrist proves it.'

I slammed my palms on the table and leaned my face close to his. 'All it proves is that my family were vamp hunters in the past, and it was passed down to us by some ancestor who hated them as much as I do. And if he also passed down a genetic trait that prevents us being changed into one of them, then even better. Nothing supernatural about that.'

He huffed, spun the book around and leafed to the front page before spinning it back to me. I followed where his finger pointed. I had no idea what I was looking at, but, whatever it was, it was the stuff of nightmares. Hand-drawn pictures showed a walled city filled with people, many lying dead. Others were crawling up the steps of a pyramid-like structure, hands in the air as if begging their gods for help. In a separate panel at the bottom of the page was one hell of an ugly female—I could tell by the massive boobs—with a the head of a lion, nasty claws holding snakes and the feet of a bird. The creature was kneeling on a donkey. It was hard to tell, but it looked like she—or it—was laughing while a bunch of smaller human figures were shown transitioning into monsters. Hands and feet into claws, long tails, bat-like wings and faces so misshapen that all semblance of humanity was lost. Gargoyles. That's what those things looked like. Pity I couldn't read the commentary. It had been written in an elaborate cursive hand, and all in French.

'What the hell is this?'

'The beginning of all things. This'—he pointed to the hideous female figure—'is the Babylonian goddess, Lamashtu. The first vampire. She created the lamiae, those creatures you see, after sending a plague on the people.'

'What was her problem?' I couldn't believe I'd just said that. Gods and goddesses, my arse! It was probably lack of personal hygiene that had caused the plague, as with all other epidemics in the past. But then again, no plague had ever left its victims so physically deformed.

'Not enough worshippers. Who knows.' Those skinny shoulders rose and fell, again. 'Anyway' —he flicked to the next page—'the god, Pazuzu.' The image his stubby finger pointed to was just as grotesque as the previous one, although it looked more humanoid but with a lion's head, claws instead of hands and feet, and four wings, plus a very prominent penis—in case anyone was in doubt. 'He chose ten of his priests and tasked them with destroying the lamiae and all their changelings. To help them do this, he blessed them with sensing the presence of the fangheads before seeing them, being immune to their venom and giving them each a sword made of daylight. Just being—'

'Wait. What sword?' There was no sword in the kit Davis had shown me. No way I would've missed something like that, plus the box was too small.

'The one pictured here. Look.' Yep, there was Pazuzu, larger-than-life handing ten bald guys each a sword. An enlarged version of it appeared at the bottom of the page. And, in case I still had any doubts about my bloody birthmark, there it was—hook-and-squiggle—engraved on the metal.

The old guy glanced at me, a wry grin on his craggy face.

'Okay, fine.' I raised my hands in mock surrender. 'I'm a believer. Happy?'

His grin widened. 'Good.'

The rest of the images on the opposite page showed the lamiae almost shying away from the Pazuzim, who approached with swords outstretched. The next scene showed monstrous heads cleaved clean from their bodies. And from the looks of the smaller fanged figures with them, those swords separated regular vampires' heads from bodies, as well.

Nice. I couldn't hold back a smile.

But one thing bothered me. 'How is it possible ... if these things are the ancestors of all vampires, then why don't they look like them?'

'That, my friend, no one knows the answer to ... except maybe Lamashtu. Maybe she wanted only her children, the lamiae, to be in her image.'

'Guess we should be thankful for small mercies.'

Junot laughed. 'That we should.'

'Those things don't exist anymore, right?' But just as I said it, somehow I knew I was wrong. The stone gargoyles I'd seen perched on the rooftops of cathedrals and other old buildings had to have been inspired by something. Which meant, they hadn't all been hunted down.

Junot sobered. 'Five of those monsters escaped our ancestors. But you know who got them? The cursed one—Marcus and his men. They trapped them in nets and flung each of them down deep holes in a few of their lairs.'

'Why the hell didn't they kill them?'

'Couldn't. Without the Pazuzim sword, they're virtually unkillable, not even by their own.'

'Where are these swords?'

'Marcus's son, Lucien, destroyed most of them.' He flicked over to the near centre of the book. More pictures, but from a different hand, with their accompanying commentary. This one showed a bunch of vamps, fangs extended. Among them, faces I recognised—Lucien Lebrettan and some of his men—those I'd met in another time, another place, forever seared into my brain. My hands curled into fists. The old guy's ancestor had captured their likenesses well. It showed them directing others to throw the swords into a furnace. The bodies of dead men lay at their feet. I assumed they were slain Pazuzim known to the artist, as he or she had drawn them with care, including the Pazuzim symbol on the inside of their wrists.

'No fanghead can touch our swords or even be within a few metres of them. It weakens them. See here?' His lip curled as he pointed to the scene I'd just noticed. 'They've got to get their dirty donsangs to do it for them.'

The donsangs. I remembered Laura mentioning them—human partners to vamps and their own personal blood donors. It was gross, but the thought struck me: had Laura and I remained together and she transitioned into a vamp, would I have let her feed from me? And the answer that came back struck me even more—hell yes! But the old guy didn't need to know that. It wasn't important. Something else was.

I wanted the sword.

'Did my family ever possess one of these?'

'Yes.'

That one simple word cut straight through me. My father had known. His father had known, and they had said nothing. Nothing! And where the hell had they hidden it? I knew every corner of my old family home. My great, great-grandad—John Ernest—had built the sprawling Victorian soon after arriving in Sydney from the old country, in 1890s. It'd been passed down from father to son. I moved out as soon as I graduated from the police academy. But mum and my sisters still lived there. The place had been renovated a few times: walls knocked down, staircases moved, floors replaced. But if Dad had known about it, he could've easily moved it.

But where?

Safety-deposit box, perhaps? Mum, my sisters and I had gone through all of Dad's stuff after he'd died, sorting everything out, and there'd been no reference to anything like that. Where would I even begin to look? Then I remembered Grandad's old shack up on Cradle Mountain in Tassie. That's all we ever called it, The Shack. Everyone wondered at the time why he'd bought a piece of land off the mainland. It wasn't like

Tasmania was a stone's throw from Sydney. You had to get on a plane to get there. Still, I loved the place. Our family holidayed there every summer. And if ever there was place to hide something, that was it. But the hell where? I'd pretty much explored that entire place when I was a kid. So, there still had to be …

My pulse raced triple time. 'I may know where it is.'

Junot's eyes lit up at first then narrowed when I explained. 'No. We would never hide it so far from our hand. The sword not only protects its bearer but his family. A fanghead cannot enter a house of a Pazuzim that contains a sword. It's unheard of that one would place his sword away from those he was trying to protect. No, no no.' He vehemently shook his head. 'It must be in your family house. You must find it.' He stabbed a pointed finger in my direction.

I rubbed my hands down my face. Okay, fine. 'What I don't get is, if my great, great-grandad was forced to leave the UK because he disagreed with the peace pact and came here to hunt Lucien, why the sudden about-face?'

He lifted his hands and dropped them back on the table. 'That you must discover.'

'You reckon Lucien found out about him and threatened the family … or something along those lines? If he hadn't been afraid back in the old country what terrified him when he got to Australia, enough for him to hide the sword and keep the Pazuzim a secret?'

'You are the policeman. Go find out.'

'I'll do that.' Still, this whole thing had me stumped. Hopefully finding that sword would answer some of my questions. Which led to another question—did Mum know anything? Would Dad have kept this a secret from her?

Possibly.

But going home at this stage wasn't possible. I still had a job to do, and that meant taking the next flight to Scotland. Which led to the real reason why I was here. I needed white-oak bullets and a gun that fired them. Getting permission to take mine would've raised too many eyebrows in the department.

'Look, I can't stay much longer. But I was hoping you could help me out with some white-oak bullets and gun. Couldn't bring mine with me. Too much paperwork.'

He closed the book and rested his hands on it. 'It will be useless to you now. I have heard that their princeps made some … serum, I think it is, that makes them immune to white-oak.'

Damn Munro! How the hell could I confront him—or any of his lot—without the protection of white-oak? I may as well just bare them my throat. 'Where did you hear this?'

'I have my connections, and they are reliable. I may not be a hunter, but I keep my ears open.'

I had no doubt of that. 'Shit!'

With a groan, the old guy heaved himself from his chair and came to where I sat. One bony hand clutched my shoulder. 'Go home and find that sword, young man. Without it, you are helpless.'

Yeah, that's exactly what I was, and it threw my plans out of whack. Following Laura and Munro to Scotland was now out of the question. I had to go back to Sydney. It could be weeks, even months, before I could wrangle permission to pursue this again.

I took a deep breath and mentally rearranged my next move. Because of the GPS tracker, at least I knew exactly where to get my secondment in Scotland. The paperwork for that alone could take up to six weeks, and in the meanwhile, Interpol would keep me updated while I hunted for that blasted sword. This was just a minor setback. If the old guy was right, it must be somewhere in our old family house, and this was the best time to search for it. The house was temporarily empty. Mum and my sister, Clare, and her family were away on a Pacific cruise.

I told Junot about the GPS tracker in Laura's phone. Said they'd left the country for Scotland.

His eyes narrowed. 'What part of Scotland?'

I showed him their present location: Stirling. But he already knew that. 'Humph! Something's going on.'

'They're running from the extradition warrant. That's what's going on.'

'Mmmm. Maybe, maybe not. It might have nothing to do with you.'

'Bullshit!' It had everything to do with me. I stood and went for my coat. 'I'm off to D'Antonville to serve the warrant. Since it's daylight and the family's not there, I should be safe.' Before I left, I asked the question that had been nagging me. 'Where's your family sword? Still have it?'

His eyes narrowed. 'Stirling, Stirling. I know that name.' He scratched his head. 'But … it's just …' He shrugged. 'It'll come to me later. As for my sword…' He grabbed hold of his walking stick dangling from the back of his chair. I'd noticed before but hadn't paid much attention to the unusual shape of the handle, a snarling lion's head with double outstretched wings.

Pazuzu.

He flipped the head to reveal the hilt of sword within.

'Nice.' It may have been common a century or so ago, but nobody today would expect a walking cane to be concealing a lethal weapon.

'And this is where it stays.' I didn't miss the warning gleam in his eyes as he slid the head cover back in place.

I couldn't pretend it hadn't crossed my mind—to take the sword from the old man and somehow smuggle it across to the UK. But the risk of getting caught wasn't worth it. My job meant too much to me. 'It's all yours, mate.'

I slipped my coat over my arm, retrieved my watch from the sink and headed for the door.

'Wait!' Junot opened one of the kitchen drawers, grabbed a sheet of paper, a pen and scribbled something down then handed it to me. 'You ring or text me if you find it. Send me a picture. And let me know what you will do.'

I nodded my thanks. 'What if I have no other choice but to kill their leader, Munro? That'll be breaking your peace pact, wouldn't it?'

He pursed his lips and angled his head from side to side. 'Mmmm … the way I see it, that peace was made with Lucien, Lord of D'Antonville. He's dead, and no one has bothered to renegotiate. The peace is over.'

Music to my ears.

I said my goodbyes and left. Downstairs, I flung my coat onto the backseat of the car. Perhaps it had been the coffee, but I didn't feel the chill as I had earlier. My mood had improved too. It had been a good move to see the old man first. In the long run, it would probably save my life, seeing as the white-oak poison was now useless. But, on the other hand, I'd have a more deadly weapon if I could only locate my family's Pazuzim sword.

No, not "if". There were no ifs here. I was determined to find it and carry on the family tradition and clean, at least, my corner of the world of a fanghead infestation.

That was becoming my favourite word.

Smiling, I started the engine. My phone beeped. I fished it out and checked my messages. It was Dave. Talking was faster than texting. I had global roaming, and my budget for this trip would cover the call.

'Hey, Dave.'

'How was the flight?'

'Bloody awful, but I'm here now. On my way to the house.'

'Checked the tracker yet?'

'They're running. It shows they're in Scotland.'

He let out a light chuckle. 'You're little trick paid off. Sure Munro's with her?'

'Oh yeah. If I were him, there's no way I'd let her out of my sight, let alone pack her off to another country. He's with her all right.'

'Fine. I trust your judgement on this one, Matt. I'll initiate the Blue Alert.'

'Good. On my way to the D'Antonville house now. She may not be there, but the housekeeper should be. I'll take their statement as proof the family's gone. That's all I need.'

'What about your Interpol contact?'

'Lazy bastard told me to send him the report.'

He sighed, and I could almost see him rubbing his forehead. 'Nothing you can do about it.'

'Look, as long as I get a signed statement from the housekeeper then all's good and going to plan.' I hung up and pocketed the phone.

D'Antonville five kilometres. Time to get the preliminaries over with, and after that I'd get the next plane home. There was a certain sword waiting for me to find.

Oddly enough, I wasn't as disturbed by the sudden image of me standing by Munro's decapitated body, a bloodied sword in my hand, as I should've been.

I wanted him alive, didn't I? To expose him and his fanghead kind to the world?

That's what the law enforcer in me wanted, but not the Pazuzim. *He* wanted total destruction of the enemy, and his arguments were convincing.

The dark angel in me eased the car into the traffic.

CHAPTER 23 - DRUNVELA

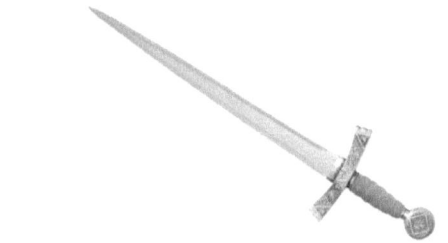

LAURA

It was just after sunset when our jet had landed in Edinburgh, and now were accelerating down the M9 in a four-car convoy of Range Rovers. In France, it had been black limousines.

The drive north-west, toward Drunvela, took less than forty minutes. As we approached Stirling, we veered off the highway into open countryside, past moonlit rolling hills, open fields and many trees still bare of leaves. Apart from the occasional whitewashed cottage, the area reminded me of the Southern Highlands back home in New South Wales.

Then the reason for being in a four-wheel-drive made sense. We took a turn off the road and onto a dirt track that skirted several fields. After a kilometer or so, we drove through a small woodland which then opened onto a wide meadow. There appeared to be nothing around for miles. A light mist rose from the ground partially obscuring the view beyond.

'Here we are,' Alec said.

'Where is it?' I peered through both front and side windows, but there was only grass and fog.

'On the other side of the mist. Now before we go through,' he turned to face me, 'the ward protecting this place is different from the one over the chateau. It's designed to keep everyone away—humans and Brethren. The Ingenii ring will protect you from its full effects, although the green serpent ring is more effective.'

'What effects?'

'Fear, terror, the urge to run away.' He twirled the ward ring round and round his finger, as if considering passing it temporarily on to me.

I didn't need to hear his thoughts to know that. No way would I let him do it.

I placed my hand on his. 'That's how I felt my first day of teaching. But I survived.'

He grinned, put his arm around my shoulders and pulled me close. 'Well, miss schoolma'am, this lasts mercifully less, around eight seconds.'

Eight seconds. I could handle that.

He turned to face the back window. 'Kari, prepare Dom.'

'Okey-dokey.' Kari's voice came to me as if she were sitting right next to me. She and Dominik travelled in the third car behind Jake and Sam, who were in the car behind us.

Alec then tapped the driver on the shoulder and urged him to go as fast as he could through the barrier. Just as we entered the ward, Alec lifted my chin. 'Look only at me, darling, and think happy thoughts.'

I could do that.

His eyes turned a dark shade of purple that I found irresistible, and then he kissed me, a long, deep, toe-curling kiss that was meant to override the sudden overwhelming sense of dread and foreboding, such I'd never experienced, that sank into my soul. A heavy darkness that seemed to suck all joy from me, as if all the world's sadness had been gathered into this one spot and I would be trapped in it forever.

I whimpered, and a shudder wracked me. Alec's grip on me tightened, and I clung to him even as the darkness threatened to devour me. My heart rate increased and beat painfully against my ribs. I panicked and clawed at Alec's arm.

Just another couple of seconds, his voice whispered against the darkness in my mind.

I couldn't think, couldn't fight against the nightmarish images my imagination conjured that even his kiss could not obliterate.

Almost there, darling.

I clung to him like a baby possum, trying desperately to savour his lips on mine, to inhale his scent until all my senses were overpowered enough to dispel the horror threatening to destroy me.

Alec! I can't take it anymore.

Then like a switch being turned off, the darkness that had settled inside me, dissipated like the mist we'd driven through.

We were on the other side.

I slumped against him, exhausted, breathing heavily.

'Here, take this. It'll help.' He unscrewed the cap from the thermos, poured out a cup of steaming hot chocolate and handed it to me.

I gulped it down. 'Wonderful.'

'You referring to my amazing kiss?' His mouth curled up into a mischievous smile.

'That too.' I ran my finger along the edge of the cup, scooping up the last remnants of the chocolate.

He shook his head in mock disappointment. 'Hard woman.'

I gave him a quick kiss. 'Seriously, if you hadn't done that, I would've been a screaming mess. It's horrible.'

'Brutal actually, but it's done the job keeping everyone out all these centuries. Luc brought me here in the first year after my transformation. I wore neither ring then, so I got it full force. It's something I'll never forget.'

'Neither will I.' I shuddered again as I handed the thermos cup back to him. 'At least we won't have to worry about unexpected guests. Nobody could get through that.'

'That's right. Safest place in the world for you, right now.' He leaned forward to look through the windscreen and pointed. 'There it is. Drunvela.'

I followed his gaze.

A lone monolith stood sentinel on a grassy plain. The moonlight's pale rays slanted off drab grey stone walls. The castle's turreted towers, crowned with conical tips, stabbed the sky like spearheads. In the distance loomed a jagged cliff as dark as the stones from which the building had been hewn. It had such a forbidding aspect, I almost expected to see Macbeth's witches huddled around a cauldron chanting, *Double, double, toil and trouble, fire burn and cauldron bubble ...*

My face must've reflected it.

'It's better on the inside.' Alec wrapped an arm around my shoulders and gave me a squeeze as we drove up a dusty road to the front entrance.

'I'll take your word for it.' I gave him a wan smile.

'It was never meant to be a place of residence. Just a fortress to make sure no one disturbed the site.'

I sighed. 'Fair enough, I s'pose.'

'Once our babe's born, we're out of here.'

'Rock on September.'

He kissed the top of my head. 'Amen to that.'

Gravel crunched beneath our tyres as we neared the front entrance. Carried on the night air, the delectable strains from a set of bagpipes drifted toward us. I rolled down the window to look for the source. A shock of frigid air blasted my face, numbing my cheeks, but that didn't deter me from shoving my head half out the window to get a better look.

'Oh joy! Guess we'll be hearing that for the next few months,' I heard Jake mutter in the car behind us.

'You bet we will,' I said back.

He groaned, but Sam chuckled.

A lone piper stood on one of the turrets, the tassles on his pipes waving in the breeze. The full moon's milky beams shrouded his figure, making him appear almost wraith-like, or a vision from the past that would dissolve once the last notes were played. I didn't dare blink in case the vision vanished, taking the sweet melody with it.

I'd never been to Scotland, yet as far back as I could remember, something about the country drew me. When my friends had listened to rock music, I'd preferred the melodic strains of a massed bagpipe band.

'I love the sound of bagpipes,' I breathed, lest I missed even one note.

'I know,' Alec whispered low in my ear.

I listened till the music ended and the piper lowered his pipes, the cold forgotten.

'Never did get the chance to show off my own piping skills, did I?'

Alec had his own set of bagpipes, yet the opportunity simply hadn't arisen for him to play. Maybe now? 'No excuses while we're here. You've got several months to get those cheeks puffing.'

He chuckled, leaned in close to me till his breath tickled my neck. In his deepest Scottish brogue whispered, 'Och! If I'd known how easily you can be seduced by a good set of pipes, I'da done so at our first meetin', lass.'

And he did it to me again. Although he'd been a lad of fifteen when he and his father had left Scotland for Australia more than a century ago, Alec had never completely lost his Scottish accent. Over time it'd been subsumed beneath the Aussie twang, yet occasionally, it would slip through. And right now, back in his native Scotland, it dripped from his tongue like the sweetest of honeys, and I wanted to lick up every delicious drop.

My mouth dried, and a swarm of butterflies played hopscotch in my belly. I turned from the window, his pine and fresh forest scent overwhelming my senses, his lips so close to mine that our breaths mingled. Staring into his dark purple eyes like a mesmerised monkey, I said the first thing that came into my drugged mind. 'Then I suppose I would've discovered what lies beneath a Scotsman's kilt sooner.'

He burst out laughing. 'Aye, that you would!'

Our car stopped and the door opened. I resented the sudden intrusion of icy air and an unfamiliar voice.

'Welcome home, Alec. Scotland hasna seen you in a long time.'

I assumed it to be the estate manager, Dougal. Alec had told me about him on the flight over.

'I first met him when Luc took me to Drunvela, soon after the war. Amiable bloke. I liked him. He was a carpenter and had been doing some work at the monastery at Iona, off Mull. Marcus was under-abbot there at the time. There was a Viking raid, and Dougal was fatally wounded trying to protect the monks. Marcus found him after he'd risen that night. He'd missed the whole thing. It had been a day raid.' He'd laughed and shaken his head at the memory. 'If only it had taken place at night. It would've been another story. Anyway, Dougal was dying, and Marcus gave him the choice of life.'

And, as they say, the rest is history.

'Dougal.' Alec helped me into my coat as we alighted the car, then shook the man's hand. 'Long time, all right. I only wish it could've been under pleasanter circumstances.'

'Aye, the passing of Lord Luc was sad news, indeed. My deepest condolences to you ... and to your lady.' A keen set of lavender eyes, framed by shoulder-length red hair landed on me. I had a feeling that nothing much would get past this man.

I nodded my thanks. Even though it'd been more than three months since Luc and Judy had gone, the gaping wound of their passing was still healing. It took only a word or even a particular scent to tear at its edges.

Dougal's sharp gaze darted from Alec's left hand to mine. 'I also hear congratulations are in order.' He lifted my hand to his fingertips. 'Can't say I blame you.'

It was silly, but a blush crept into my cheeks. 'Thank you.'

'I hope you enjoyed the piper. A certain someone—' his smiling gaze slid to Alec '—told me you're a Scot's lass at heart.'

'You ordered the piper?'

Alec merely winked at me—*darling man*—and tightened his grip around my waist. He then returned his attention to Dougal, and, with a tilt of his head, indicated the other cars from which Jake, Sam, Kari and Dominik alighted with some of our household staff. Poor Dominik. The drive through the ward must have hit him badly. After all, he was still only a kid at fifteen. Teary-eyed, he clung to Kari like a limpet. She rolled her eyes while trying to pry him off.

While Jake and Sam greeted Dougal, Alec checked on Dominik. He clamped a hand on his shoulder. 'You okay, Dom? Getting through the ward's rough.'

The boy gave a shaky nod. 'It's a bitch!'

Alec smiled. 'That it is.' He lifted his chin and examined his eyes. 'Mmm, good. Now, how about you help Jake set up the lab.'

The staff we brought with us unloaded box after box. Some held the medical equipment Alec and Jake had ordered—an ultrasound machine, various monitors as well as lab equipment. Alec hadn't given up trying to replicate the antigen.

'All's prepared, just as you asked.' Dougal snapped his fingers, and two men appeared from behind the front doors. They hefted a few of the larger boxes, then led Jake, Sam, Dominik and our staff inside. 'I've also set up some refreshments. It's in the high hall, or, if you prefer, I can have it sent up to your room.'

'The hall will be fine, thanks. I'm not in the least tired.' I may have been at the start of my second trimester, but I was certainly no delicate daisy. My energy levels were the same as they always had been, and especially since the morning sickness phase of my pregnancy seemed to be passing—I hoped—I hadn't been nauseous in days. That was definitely a plus.

Tucked into Alec's side, I stepped through the thick timber doors into the castle's main reception area. The scent of linseed oil and old oak tickled my nose. Amber light glowed from the fire in the great hearth, above which hung the serpent-and-sword D'Antonville clan crest. Dark wooden panelling covered the lower half of stone walls. Firelight flickered over the life-size mural that ran the entire length of the upper half of the wall. In bold colours and vivid detail was depicted the story of the curse.

I sucked in a breath.

Every face stood out of those I knew and those I didn't know. I recognised Marcus, but it was not the face of the man I knew. Where before had been arrogance and fury was now replaced with kindness mingled with sadness. And the witch herself? Somehow the medieval artist had managed to capture what she must have gone through—the anger, the fear and desperation to save her people. It was all reflected in her eyes.

The price of vengeance.

I sighed.

'This is the original on which the stained-glass windows in the chateau and Sydney house are based; aren't they?'

'They are,' Alec replied.

Sam sprinted in, downed a goblet of blood and wiped his mouth.

'Dougal, I'm off to do a perimeter run, see if we need to add a few more cameras. Let your men know.'

Dougal gave him a wave then he and Alec, each with goblet in hand, stood by the long table and spoke.

Kari joined me. 'That kid's like cling wrap. On the way back, he's sitting with you.'

I couldn't help smiling. Poor Dominik. He hadn't had anyone to smooth his passage through the ward, as I had. 'You know when we leave here, there'll be no more reason for the protective ward.'

Kari's face lit up. 'Oh yeah! I forgot. But he's still sitting with you.'

I shrugged. 'Don't tell me you held it all together your first time going through.' I assumed Jake must have brought her here during her juvy stage, so she had some experience of it. Otherwise, Alec wouldn't have asked her to look after Dom.

She snatched a look at Alec and Dougal, who were deep in conversation at the table, and leaned into my ear. 'I freaked out. Jake had to hold me all the way in.' Her mouth curled into a smile, eyes glazing over as she recalled the scene.

She really carried a torch for him. How I wanted to tell her to tell him, but it was none of my business, and besides, what did I know about matters of the heart. My first serious relationship was now turning into a nightmare, and my current one had been arranged by my parents. At least they'd chosen well.

'Alec did the same with me,' I whispered back.

Her eyes held a mischievous glint, and she nudged me with her elbow. 'Saw you two canoodling in the back seat.'

Why, or why did my cheeks have to flush? *Blame it on my pregnancy hormones.* But I couldn't keep the smile from my face.

'It worked.' I winked.

Kari laughed and linked her arm through mine. We strode over to the table where I helped myself to a delicious selection of little sandwiches and pasties. Kari picked up another goblet of warm, fresh blood. Strangely enough, the pungent coppery aroma didn't make me nauseous as it would have before my pregnancy. Was I becoming used to it, or was there another reason? With my sight, hearing and now my sense of smell heightened, was there a chance I was slowly … turning?

My stomach hollowed out.

Firelight glinted off the blood-laden goblets. I stared at them, imagining myself emptying their contents.

My stomach convulsed, and I nearly gagged.

Thank goodness! *Don't think about it again.* I drew a deep breath to steady myself.

'Laura?' Alec's voice startled me from my thoughts. 'You've gone very pale. Are you feeling unwell?'

'No, I'm fine, thanks. Passing thought.' I absently waved my hand and gave him a reassuring smile.

Alec's eyes remained on me, and I knew he was listening to my heartbeat and our baby's, satisfying himself that all was well. To dispel any concerns, I bit into one of the pasties on my plate and wandered over to him and Dougal, but the lingering taste of bile in my mouth made it feel like I was swallowing sawdust.

He drew me to his side, then scooped something from his pocket and handed it to Dougal. 'For you. Present from me and Marcus as reward for your faithful service. You've got eight days of daylight there.'

Dougal's mouth dropped open as he held the little glowing vials. Marcus and Alec had shared their own meagre Ingenii-blood supply. 'I don't know what to say, Alec, 'cept thank you.'

'That'll do.'

They clasped hands, Dougal grinning from ear to ear. 'Now to find a day when I can imbibe. Perhaps … at sunrise?'

'Why not? Go and enjoy it, man. Laura and I are safe within these walls, and we have Jake and Sam with us.' He slapped Dougal on the back.

Dougal's eyes shone. He opened his mouth to speak but shut it again, swallowed hard and simply gave Alec a nod.

'Oh, and one more thing. When all this is over, we'd like you to stand for the Eldership. By right of age, you're more than qualified, and more than deserving. Please consider it.'

He inhaled deeply and turned from us, bracing his arms on the table as he gazed in the direction of the tall arched windows. 'I've been here a long time, Alec, laddie, and I've never been out of Scotland. Ay, I've been to Dundee and Aberdeen and even Edinburgh, or wherever the hunt takes me, but' —he lowered his head and shook it— 'an Elder? Keep the peace and make decisions among Brethren? I can do it among my men, but I don't know if that's enough.'

It was odd hearing Alec referred to as "laddie" by someone who looked at least ten years younger. I had to remind myself that, although Dougal appeared no more than nineteen or twenty, he was probably well over a thousand years old, maybe more. To him, at only a hundred years old, Alec was a youngster.

That made me a veritable foetus! I bit down hard on my lip.

'Marcus thinks you can, and so do I. I'll leave it there.'

Dougal angled his head over his shoulder toward us. 'Isn't the Eldership filled? Where would I fit in?'

Good question, and I had a feeling I knew what Alec was about to say—his position as princeps. Would it bother me if he wasn't princeps? Not at all. I could think of nothing better than to live an ordinary life with my husband and child—or children—away from Brethren politics.

Alec caught my gaze before returning his attention to Dougal. 'There's a chance I may not be able to continue as princeps when all this is over.

With the curse lifted, I might be back to post-juvenile stage, and with Luc gone, I doubt I'll even be allowed to keep it. Marcus will probably step in and take up the princiship.'

'All supposition. You have a lot of supporters, Alec.'

Alec shrugged. 'I never wanted to be princeps. It'll be no loss for me. Laura and I can live a private life, and I can go back into medicine, where I belong.'

'Sounds good to me.' My thoughts strayed to the class I should have been teaching this year. My chest tightened at just how much I missed it … and an idea grew, one that would keep me occupied while we were here. My chest instantly lightened.

Alec shot me a quick grin, which sent a lovely tingle all the way to my toes.

'I'll see what happens first and then decide.'

'Fair enough. Let's drink to it.' Alec raised his goblet, and he and Dougal clinked and drained their contents.

'Now, on another matter,' Dougal wiped his mouth with the back of his hand, 'we've had whiff of Brethren sniffin' round. They can't sense or see us, of course, thanks to the ward.' He cocked his head and scratched the side of it. 'Except for that time when it did vanish for a wee bit. Pretty exposed, we were. I put on an extra guard, but nothing came of it, thank providence.'

That must've been the time our previous housekeeper stole Luc's ring to give to Timur in return for immortality. It had switched off the ward for a while.

'We rectified that situation, as you know.'

'Aye.' Dougal glanced in my direction, his gaze dropping to my belly. 'We don't want a repeat of that, especially now, so close to the end.'

Although I was barely showing—my baby being the size of an avocado—he could hear my baby's heartbeat as clearly as I. And being part of our clan, he knew the truth, for being Marcus's juvy, when the time came, he too, like Kari, would have to make a choice—death or an eternity as a blood drinker.

Alec's arm around me tightened. 'We're in your hands, Dougal.'

Dougal's gaze darted between the two of us. He dropped to one knee and bowed his head. 'If by my life or by my death I can serve and protect you, that I will.' His head shot up, his piercing lavender eyes connecting with mine. 'You and the wee bairn are safe here, m'lady Laura. This I swear.'

My eyes misted over at the ring of sincerity in his voice. I had no doubt he would be true to his word. 'Thank you.'

He rose and smiled, a lock of red hair flopping roguishly half-across one eye. He really looked no older than nineteen or twenty at the most. I pitied Scotland's females whenever he went out to feed. And he didn't have to worry about getting in and out of the ward since he wore a green serpent ring. 'I'm glad of the company. Been getting a bit bored with the lads. Your time here is promising to be interesting.'

Interesting was the last thing I had in mind. 'I just want this to be over with, and our child free of the curse.'

He sobered. 'Of course. I understand.'

Kari, who'd been leaning against the table sipping from her goblet, cocked her head to the side and quietly regarded Dougal. She seemed to be particularly interested in the subtle mass of rippling muscles barely concealed by his black T-shirt.

Could I dare hope that Jake was about to have some competition? Poor Kari had been mooning about him for months with seemingly no response from him. Dougal could be just the one to heal her broken heart. I only hoped he didn't already have a mate.

I sauntered over to her and lightly nudged her arm, letting my gaze slide to Dougal then back to her and I subtly cocked one eyebrow.

She smiled, almost sheepishly, and buried her nose in the goblet.

Yes! Goodbye Jake, hello Dougal.

'Good light tonight.' With a tilt of his chin, Alec indicated the arched windows through which a full moon shone. 'Perfect for viewing the gravesite and monument. You up for it?'

I sure was. 'Lead on.'

I'd have plenty of opportunities to see it during the day by myself, but Alec and the rest of the guys were trying to preserve their meagre stores of Ingenii blood. We'd become nocturnal again. And unless he and Jake could replicate the Ingenii gene, that's the way it would remain. But, I'd already reconciled myself to a nocturnal existence should Alec not succeed. As long as he was by my side, I could happily be a nightbird.

'Can I come too?' Dominik eagerly grinned at us. He'd been quietly circling the room, practically nose to wall, checking out the murals but never straying far from Kari.

I couldn't resist an inward chuckle at his teenage crush.

'Course you can, but stay close to Kari,' Alec replied.

Kari's mouth dropped, her eyes and head rolling so far back that I thought she'd fall backwards. 'Personal space, limpet,' she hissed when Dominik sidled up next to her.

I nearly chortled. Alec, my darling man, didn't have a clue!

'A moment.' Dougal raced out and returned seconds later holding a plaid hooded cloak. 'With your permission.' He glanced at Alec before draping it over my shoulders. 'April tends to be a wee bit nippy still. The wind's a blowin'. Tis a lovely coat you're wearin', but it won't keep out the Scottish chill.'

I thanked him and drew it around me. I didn't recognise the strange green plaid. 'Is it a particular tartan?'

'Aye, your family's. Tis the D'Antonville tartan. Lord Luc had it commissioned.'

'How much don't I still know?' Frustrated annoyance laced my tongue, yet my heart still lurched at how much time my father and I had been robbed off. Luc never got the chance to tell me everything. Everyday I seemed to learn something new.

I rubbed the soft wool against my cheek imagining him strolling through these grounds clad in our clan kilt … and that's a far as that thought went. I simply couldn't see him in a kilt.

'You got to know him, darling, and the things he considered important.' Alec pulled the hood of the cloak over my head.

'I s'pose.' A sigh escaped me.

'*If it's any comfort, Luc wouldn't've been seen dead in a kilt.*' Alec's voice whispered in my mind.

I slapped my hand over my mouth, as a laugh nearly burst from me.

Dougal wore the clan kilt.

Alec's choice of words could have been more sensitive, but if his intention was to stop me from sinking into another pit of sadness then it worked, as I preferred laughter to tears any day. My poor heart see-sawed from one extreme emotion to the next, even after all these months.

I blamed it on my raging pregnancy hormones.

'That's better.' His fingers skimmed the edge of my jaw. 'And now there's one last thing to for you see. Probably the most important of all.'

He grasped my hand, and we went out through a door at the other end of the great hall. It opened directly to an interior courtyard the size of a football field, its centre dominated by massive green mound. Not far from it stood what looked like a small colonnaded temple.

Two steps led inside.

This was no temple but a sepulchre.

Torches ensconced into the rough stone walls lit the interior, casting our shadows into unearthly, twisted shapes. There were no decorations, no statues, nothing to mark the person whose remains lay here. Only a simple inscribed white stone sarcophagus.

A strange awareness crept over me, like I was being watched, judged even. It was unnerving. I hung back.

'What's wrong?'

'Can't you feel it?'

Alec shook his head, furrows forming on his brow. 'Tell me.'

'Like … someone's watching me, weighing me in the balance. It's spooky, but it's the only way I can describe it.'

Dougal stepped up next to Alec. 'She knows you're finally here—a daughter of Rome. She's checking you out.'

The witch!

Deep in my veins, my blood turned into sharp slivers of ice. I shivered. An unknown voice whispered in my mind, *One who willingly bears a child to a son of Prythyn shall release the cursed ones.*

I sucked in a breath, knowing I had to respond. That everything depended on it. 'Alec, she spoke to me.'

He gripped my fingers more tightly. 'What did she say?'

I repeated the words. His eyes reflected such love and confidence in us, that it calmed my own turbulent emotions. 'Tell her the truth, darling.'

With hands clenched—one still holding Alec's—I searched my heart to find the answer the witch wanted to hear.

Then it came.

After a deep, calming breath, I placed Alec's hand on my belly. 'With all my heart, I willingly bear a child to a son of Prythyn, Alec Duncan Munro … because I love him.'

That was it. So simple, yet my entire being—spirit, mind, body—were tied up in those few words.

Alec leaned down and kissed me with a tender fervour that lit a fire down below. I felt his desire pressing into my thigh.

A sigh rose from the ground and reverberated through the chamber. As we pulled apart, the inscription on the stone sarcophagus glowed. Although I'd never studied Latin, the words and the meaning burned into my mind:

Here I lie, Eithne of the Prythyn, servant of the great goddess Melusine, whose dying lips cursed Marcus Antonius Pulcher and his men into beasts of blood and darkness. As long as the moon circles the earth, so shall this curse last until a Child of Light and Darkness willingly bears a baby to one of Prythyn blood, a descendant of my house. For the child shall carry the blood of Roman and Prythyn—one race, one blood. And the child must be born where I lie.

An intense humming filled the empty space, and the eyes of our serpent rings blazed to life bathing us with a radiant blood-red glow that swirled around us in a strange, luminous dance. The humming rose to a crescendo before slowly dying down, leaving us in silence once more, although my ears continued to ring from the magnitude of the sound. The light from the serpents' eyes also dimmed, leaving only the glow from the torches.

'Great gods, the serpents sang! She's accepted you.' Dougal's eyes burned brightly. He, Kari and Dominik stood just at the entrance. 'Of course I believed it when ye told me, but … but … what I just saw….' He waved his hand in our direction. 'There's no denying it now.'

Next to him, both Kari and Dominik's eyes were the size of saucers. Kari's normally short and spikey Nordic-blonde locks seemed to stick up more than usual. 'Whoa! That's what I call one out of this world light-and-sound show.'

Dominik merely nodded.

'Aye, and we were privileged to see it.' Dougal grinned and ran his arm around Kari's shoulders, giving her a comradely hug.

Alec remained pensive. What we'd witnessed was the beginning of the end of the curse, and its far reaching consequences for the Principate. And hopefully, if Alec was forced to step down as princeps, it would no longer be our problem.

'Before this year is over, everything's going to change, except for the Principate. That'll remain. Only we'll no longer be dependent on Ingenii blood.'

'You'll lose the advantage of daywalking and be like the rest of us.' Dougal gazed long and hard at Alec. 'Think you'll miss it?'

Alec gave me a sidelong glance and squeezed my hand. 'As long as this incredible lady is by my side, I can happily face an eternity of darkness.'

My heart melted. What woman's wouldn't? 'Always.' I wrapped my arms around his neck. 'If you have to live in the dark, then so will I.'

He kissed the tip of my nose. 'Might have to if the antigen keeps evading us.'

'Is that what all that equipment's for?' Dougal waved toward the castle.

'Among other things, yes. We're trying to replicate the Ingenii antigen, make an artificial daywalking serum.'

Dougal whistled. 'If you can do that, you're a wizard, man.'

'He's already created an anti-white-oak serum,' I proudly boasted.

'Which reminds me ...' Alec, still gripping my hand, turned and hurried down the steps and back across the courtyard. 'Dom, get me my medical bag.'

By the time we re-entered the great hall, Dominik was waiting for us. He'd perched himself on the edge of the table, legs swinging, one hand holding a blood-filled goblet the other Alec's black medical bag. 'Got it.' He held it up.

'Good lad.' Alec opened it and removed a syringe. 'C'mon, Dougal, your turn to be immunised. You're the last of us.'

Dougal didn't look too keen. 'You're gonna stick that thing into me?'

'You want to be protected from white oak?'

He gazed at the needle in Alec's hand and ran his tongue over his lower lip ... thinking. 'Sure, it's only ...'

'It's okey-dokey, Dougal.' Kari lightly punched his arm. 'I got it too. And look at me.' She did a little twirl. 'I'm super-okay.'

'Me too,' Dominik piped up.

Kari sent him a withering look.

'Och, I trust Alec, there's no question there. It's that thing.' He pointed to the syringe.

It never ceased to amaze me how some big, brawny guys who probably wouldn't flinch in the face of danger practically fainted at the sight of a needle. 'I hate them too, but this one's going to save your life.'

'A'right. Let's do it then.' He proceeded to walk toward the door.

'Dougal, where are you going?' Alec stood there, utterly bewildered, syringe at the ready.

'You want to do it here ... in front of the ladies?' Dougal looked horrified.

'Why not? Jake and other guys did,' Kari told him.

'They did?' His eyes grew wide, and he shook his head. 'Nah, I canna.'

Kari and I exchanged a glance. What was up?

He hesitated, then, on a sigh, 'Ladies, don't look. I'm not as progressive as the rest of you,' turned his back to us and raised his kilt exposing a portion of one smooth, white butt cheek. 'A'right, I'm ready.'

Kari snorted and spun around, her hand over her mouth, narrowly avoiding spurting the blood from her goblet halfway across the room.

Dominik just about fell from the table doubled over in laughter.

I'd bit down on my lip to stop that very thing, but it was bubbling out of me, and I was sure the image of Dougal's backside would stay with me forever.

'Dougal, what are doing, man!' Alec pulled his kilt back down. 'In the arm, in the arm. What were you thinking!'

He straightened up and held the kilt down, his knuckles white from the effort, face burning. 'But … but, isn't that where they stick those things? I was told—'

'Who told you?'

'A nurse, the other night, in Dundee. I don't know how our conversation got around to that, but I let her pratter on while I fed. She said that's the best place to administer a hypodermic.'

Alec roared with laughter. 'I'm sorry, Dougal, I'm not laughing at you, but you have to see the funny side.'

'Aye, I'm tryin', but not succeeding.' He glared at Alec. 'So, the nurse was wrong?'

'No, she wasn't. It isn't always necessary. A shot in the arm is just as effective.'

Dougal smoothed his palms down the sides of his kilt. 'Och! I'm so stupid. I should've asked. My deepest apologies, ladies.'

Poor Dougal. 'No, you're not stupid. It's an easy mistake to make. Besides—' I cheekily tapped Alec's backside '—you don't have anything I'm not already acquainted with.'

Alec grinned.

'Hey, I kinda like what I saw,' Kari quipped, a shy little smile on her face, totally at odds from the exuberant, in-your-face Kari I knew.

Things were looking interesting.

'Now, let's get this right, Dougal, shall we? Arm please, any one will do.' Regardless of the serious tone in his voice, Alec couldn't hide the twitch in his lips and the twinkle of laughter in his eyes. 'The only side-effect is temporary flu-like symptoms that last about thirty minutes. After that, you'll be safe from its effects.'

In less than second, it was over. Dougal paled and leaned back against the table. 'I've never had the flu. Is everything supposed to hurt?'

'Sadly, yes.' Alec slid one arm around Dougal's shoulders and eased him onto the floor. 'Dom, bring me one of those seat cushions.' Alec placed the cushion beneath Dougal's head. 'Lie here till it passes. You'll be fine.'

Dougal groaned.

Kari knelt next to him and took hold of his hand. 'I got it a few weeks ago, and see, I'm good.'

'Aye, lass. Tis a comfort.'

Alec sat at the table and drew me onto his lap. 'Now, what was that passing thought you had that frightened you?'

I was about to answer when my phone rang. It was Madame Gilbert. The first thing that ran through my mind was that something was wrong. Why else would she call? I steeled myself. 'Sabine, is everything okay?'

'Yes, all is fine here, my lady, not to worry. But the man you told us to expect was just here, Detective Inspector Matt Sommers. He had a warrant to question you and milord.'

A warrant? How pathetic, but still it didn't stop my stomach from turning into a bubbling cauldron.

Alec tensed, the smile vanishing.

I tried to rub the tension from my forehead. 'He's my ex-boyfriend, and he knows exactly what happened with Jean-Philippe. There's no need for any further questioning. He's just being a … nasty pain!'

She tsked, tsked. 'He cannot accept you choosing another.'

'In a nutshell.'

'So it was good I didn't let him through the front gates, as milord suggested. We spoke through the intercom. I told him you and milord are not here, and I don't know where you went or when you'll be back.'

'You're wonderful, Sabine. Thank you.'

She chuckled. 'I did nothing. All I said was the truth … except for one little bit, and that I don't regret. It was for your safety.'

She was a gem.

'But I must tell you; there is something that is strange to me. He didn't sound surprised when I said you were not here. He said, "Uh huh!" And that was it. As your housekeeper, I should be expected to know your whereabouts. But he wasn't interested. He asked me nothing, as if he already knew the answer. Then he went away without another word. Isn't that most odd? I thought it was best to tell you.'

Odd, all right, but nothing surprised me about Matt. 'I'm glad you did. Thank you, Sabine.'

'Then I'll be off, my lady. Keep well.'

She hung up, and I stowed the phone back into my jeans pocket.

'What the hell is he pursuing this for?' Alec's expression was dark. 'Doesn't he have anything better to do.'

'Obviously not.'

His expression softened as he brushed the hair from off my shoulder. 'Forget him. He can never find us here.'

'What about afterwards? How long does a warrant last?'

'Doesn't matter. Leave him to me.' The dangerous smile that curled his lips had me wishing Matt could just leave things alone … for his own safety.

* * *

It was a few days later that the dreadful news came. We were in the great hall, again. I'd just finished dinner. Kari and Dougal were playing a game of draughts. Alec was on his laptop ordering more pieces of medical equipment while Jake was setting up those that had already arrived, in our suite.

Alec's phone rang. Absently, he fetched it from his shirt pocket. Whoever it was from, had him drawing his brows together. He put it on loudspeaker. 'Richard, what's up?'

'Richard?' I mouthed.

'Amanda's donsang, Richard Weston,' Alec mouthed back. Amanda was head of the Bondi safe house and the newest Elder responsible for Australia and Oceania, the position my father, Luc, had created and then held after he'd relinquished the princiship to Alec.

'Terrible news. I'm so sorry.' Alec tensed—so did I. 'The Residence … has been burned down. It's gone. Everything … everyone.' His voice choked. 'I left a message on Amanda's phone, but you know she won't hear it till tonight.'

It was night here, but early morning in Sydney.

The blood drained from my cheeks.

Luc and Judy's Vaucluse home, had been burned to the ground.

No one spoke, shock and disbelief etched on every face.

A dry lump stuck in my throat as I tried to keep my emotions under control. But I knew I'd lose, especially when a sudden choking sob filled the great hall. Kari, arms folded over her stomach, doubled over and wailed. Drops of blood spilled from her eyes and splashed down onto the game board.

I jolted as the door crashed open, and Jake rushed to Kari's side. 'Kari? What's wrong?'

'They're dead! The Residence … in Sydney.' She ended on a strangled cry.

My vision swam, so I could barely make out Jake's unbelieving gaze pan to Alec and me.

Seated next to him at the table, I felt Alec tremble. 'Richard, do you know how it happened? An electrical fault, lightening strike …?'

'It was no accident … Humans … Daybreak attack, about an hour ago, and they used petrol. Even I can smell it.' Anger punctuated his voice.

Arson! My breath hitched. Alec uttered an oath.

'It can't be the Rebels. It can't!' My voice sounded hoarse. 'The rebellion is over.' It had been defeated, it's leaders executed. I'd personally removed their heads. The memory of it still made my stomach queasy.

Alec's brow furrowed, and the way he chewed his bottom lip told me otherwise. He looked up at Jake. 'Rebel donsangs? On a revenge attack? I know there's no known precedent, but it's not improbable, is it?'

Jake shook his head. 'I find it hard to believe.' He turned back to Richard. 'What about the security guys? Where were they?'

'Knocked out and dragged out of the house before it was set alight. Got a call from one of them when he regained consciousness. I drove straight over.'

'Are they harmed?' Alec asked. For a split second, he and Jake exchanged glances and I didn't need the ring's mind-reading abilities to guess what that was about, because at that moment, the same idea had occurred to me.

Were the security guards in any way involved in this? And if they were, then why? I had no doubt they were paid exceptionally well, so it made no sense to be disloyal. Besides, it would also have been too obvious. When I saw Jake subtly shake his head, I dismissed the thought too.

Richard spoke again. 'No, they're okay. Paramedics are checking them out now. Firemen are still here putting out the last embers. I've alerted all available donsangs to boost security around the other safe houses … just in case.'

'Good man. But whoever did this has already made their point. Couldn't make a bigger statement than hitting the Residence,' Alec said.

'Yeah, true. Just as long as they don't decide to make another one.' Besides Richard's voice coming down the line, men shouted instructions in the background—presumably the firemen. A police siren and the explosive crash of collapsing timbers and splintering glass had me shaking my head in denial. There was an intake of breath. Then Richard swore. 'Top floors just gave way. I'm switching to Facetime so you can see.'

Jake and Kari sprang to our side to view the screen. Dougal followed.

Something I thought I'd never see came to life on the screen, and I couldn't stifle the cry that came out of me. It couldn't be happening, yet it was. My eyes weren't lying to me.

Behind me, Kari quietly sniffed.

I could only imagine how Alec felt. His memories ran far deeper than mine in that house. When the phone cracked in his grip, I knew for sure. He quickly lay it down on the table. I ran my arms around his neck and rested my head on his shoulder as the horrid images continued on the screen.

My heart broke for the helpless and innocent sleeping Brethren staff who were trapped inside, who maintained the house while we were away, as the human staff had been given paid leave. And I grieved for my parents' once beautiful, historic home, now reduced to a blackened, and crumbling burned out shell. My mother's favourite sitting room, with its flower-shaped, vintage wrought-iron chandelier and walls lined with framed photos of her as a young woman, where we had bonded as mother and daughter, was irretrievably gone. My father's library, filled to the ceiling with priceless books and manuscripts, and where my life had been turned around after learning that Luc and Judy were my real parents, gone. And Alec's room, where we'd made love for the very first time, and the stunning ballroom where dear Kari and I had met and become fast friends, all now reduced to ash.

I swallowed the rock lodged in my throat and watched helplessly as smoke rose from the remaining pockets of flames the firemen were attempting to extinguish. I could almost smell the putrid air, its toxic fumes fanning my darker recollections of the ballroom where, as the new Ingenii, I'd been introduced to the Brethren Perfects and Elders, and where Jean-Philippe, my half-brother, had kept his secret studio.

I shuddered, not just at that last memory but at the sad certainty that all traces of Luc and Judy were being erased, almost as if the past were being wiped clean.

A grief so encompassing descended on me that I had to turn my gaze away from the screen. Somewhere deep within me came a stirring that frightened me: the desire to hunt down and destroy those who caused this, to suck the very last drop of blood from their veins and take pleasure in watching the life slowly recede from their eyes. The blackness threatened to engulf the last spark of light in my mind.

I was no vampire, but at that moment, I wanted to be.

I reached out to embrace the darkness.

'No, you don't. Don't give in to it, darling,' Alec's calm voice whispered through my mind. *'That beast only brings destruction. It uses vengeance as an excuse. It feeds on it.'*

Alec's arm tightened around my waist, his lips brushing my brow as I rested my head on his shoulder. *'It's so easy to give in.'* I sent back to him.

'Very easy. But the moment you let go of the struggle, you lose everything that's good in you. I know, I've been there. If I'd let it control me I'd be no better than the rogues I've hunted and executed.'

He sensed my pain. He understood it, and he eased it, and I loved him even more for it.

'At least they felt no pain,' Jake's voice broke into our mind talk.

Thanks to the death-like sleep of the Brethren that prevented waking, those poor people were cremated rather than immolated. Still, it was a terrible way to die, and it didn't change the fact that they were murdered.

'Aye, a small mercy, that.' Dougal leaned forward to see the screen, one hand on the table to steady himself.

'Attacking the Residence is a declaration of war, and we can't let it go any further,' Jake said.

Alec nodded. 'Agreed. We need to get the jet refueled and ready.'

I knew what that meant. He was leaving. A deep chasm opened in the pit of my stomach. Our eyes met.

'I'm princeps. It's my responsibility to protect the Brethren, and to do that, I've got to personally investigate this crime and find and punish those who did this. I can't do it from here.'

I took a deep breath and assembled my thoughts, my mouth drying at what I knew I had to do: let him go.

'I know.' I cupped his face and whispered, 'Go and find who did this.'

Alec kissed the inside of my palm and pressed it to his cheek, his Adam's apple working hard as he swallowed. He found this as hard as I did.

With his gaze still on me, Alec said, 'Richard, I'm on my way.'

'Was hoping you'd say that, coz there's something here you need to see. They left a calling card. Security guy found it on the ground next to him when he came round. Took a pic. Sending it through now. I—ah— didn't hand it over to the police. Thought it best not to.'

'You're withholding evidence. Is it worth the risk?'

'You tell me.'

Alec swiped to messages. A small card with the image of a four winged, claw footed creature appeared.

Jake leaned in for a closer look, as if not trusting what his eyes saw. He inhaled sharply. 'Blasted Pazu! Can't be. We dealt with them more than a century ago.'

Richard's voice came through. 'That's why the image rang a bell.

Amanda mentioned them once … ages ago. Can't recall everything but something about them being extinct.'

'That's what we thought.' Jake ran his hand along his face and scratched his short beard, a concerned frown puckering his brow.

I glanced at Jake. 'What's a Pazu?'

'I need a refresher, too,' Richard added.

Jake blew out a breath. 'They call themselves Pazuzim, sons of Pazuzu, families of vampire hunters. Been around for aeons. First hunted the lamiae, then the rest of us. That's their symbol.' Jake wagged a finger at the computer screen. 'Their god, Pazuzu.'

'Now, I remember,' Richard said.

'Eeewww … he's as ugly as Old Stinky.'

'Old Stinky?'

Kari came round Jake's other side and knelt on the floor, chin resting on her arms on the edge of the table. 'Long story, Richie. I'll tell you another time.'

'Sure, I can wait.'

She wrinkled her nose and angled her face up to Jake. 'How come you didn't show me this before?'

'I did, and their skin markings, how to identify them.'

'Yep to the last bit but nope to the first bit.'

'Uh! Never mind, you're seeing it now. *Anyway,* as I was saying, we'd kept tabs on the two families who'd followed us here from Europe—The Davidoffs and the Sommersets. When they came after us, Luc grabbed the Davidoff's elder son and held him for ransom in exchange for the sword. Davidoff refused to bargain. Said he still had the hammer and anvil on which to make a better one than him.'

Alec huffed and shook his head in disbelief. 'I couldn't believe it when Luc first told me. Some father! The boy was only six years old. That damn sword meant more to him than his own son.'

'Davidoff was a bastard, all right. It was his wife who got him to give in … eventually. She betrayed her husband to get the boy back. After that the family were essentially neutralised.' Jake smiled absently. 'He was a nice kid. I let him beat me at Chinese Checkers. Pity he was a Pazu.'

'What's so special about their sword?' Over the last few months, I'd seen a lot of magic, so it wouldn't have surprised me if there were some magical qualities about the Pazu sword as well. My father, Luc, wouldn't have demanded such a ransom price if it wasn't something extraordinary … or deadly to Brethren kind.

'It's the only weapon that can kill the lamiae and us. We can't go near the thing. It's like … the ward ring, creating a force field that weakens us the closer we get to it.'

'Nasty.'

'And very effective,' Jake replied. 'I've seen Brethren so weakened by it, they lay helpless while a Pazu relieved them of their heads.'

No wonder Luc wanted those things destroyed. 'Would it have the same effect on me? After all, I'm half vampire.'

Jake frowned and studied me awhile. 'I really don't know. It'd be interesting to find out.'

'It certainly wouldn't,' Alec said drew me closer, as if there was a Pazu sword nearby I needed protecting from.

'Still, I need to know these things,' I told him before turning back to Jake. There was something else I was curious about. 'What happened to the boy, the one you let beat you at checkers?'

'Grew up and got killed in the Great War.' Jake shrugged. 'Anyway, we destroyed the Pazu sword. The other family went into hiding. Changed their name, address … the whole thing. We hunted them till the war came and disrupted everything. After that, we heard nothing more from them. We assumed their males signed up and never came back from the war. Eventually Luc called off the watch. How they've remained underground all this time is beyond me.'

'Only their guys hunted you?' Why not the women, or was it some strange male-gene thing?

'Usually, although … I do remember some females being among them,' Jake replied.

'It's going to be hard tracking those families down after all this time,' Alec said.

'If they found us, we can find them. Marcus needs to know.' Jake pulled out his phone and strode to the other end of the hall.

Meanwhile, Alec picked the phone up and switched back to Facetime. 'Richard, have the medics finished with the guards? If they're able to talk, put them on. Preferably Elliott, if possible.' He then whispered to me, 'Head of security.'

'Hold on, let me check.' Richard's long, lean face appeared again.

I sensed something was bugging Alec. 'What is it?'

'Not sure. My scalp's prickling. There's something here I'm not seeing.'

'You will. You're a genius, didn't you know that?' I ran my fingers through his silky raven-black hair and massaged his scalp. 'Still prickling?'

He grinned and kissed the tip of my nose. 'Yes, but thanks for the vote of confidence.'

Richard approached one of the medics. There was a brief conversation. The paramedics insisted on taking them to the hospital to test for concussion since they had been knocked out.

'Give me a minute,' the team leader said to them, as Richard handed him the phone.

'Princeps, Lady Laura.' The man removed his cap and dipped his head in reverence. Dust and ash smeared his face, leaving a clear line on his brow above the cap line. 'I accept full responsibility and tend my immediate resignation.'

'We'll discuss that later. Just tell me what happened. I don't want to keep you too long. You need to get to the hospital.'

'Yes, Sir.' His voice took on a professional tone. 'Just after 0600 hours, the CT cameras went down. I sent out one of our guys to investigate. A minute later the lights went out. Then everything shut down. We thought it may have been a power surge and our backup system would've automatically kicked in. It didn't. Following protocol, I stayed in the surveillance room and sent the other two guys to check the backup generator and look over the grounds while I tried to get everything running again.' He grimaced and rubbed the back of his head. 'Communication went dead. I was about to ring the primary donsang when I got a bang to the head and woke up down by the pier, next to the others.'

It sounded like a professional hit to me, but something about the Pazu leaving a calling card was odd. 'Why on earth would they leave such evidence behind unless they want to be caught, which I hope they are.'

'Or maybe one of them was careless and accidentally dropped it,' the security guard added.

'It's possible.' Alec shrugged. 'Professionals don't make such a mistake, especially as almost everything can be digitally traced nowadays. It doesn't make sense.'

'That was my thought too. Took us completely unawares,' the security guard continued. 'We had a top-notch system set up here with a state-of-the-art firewall and warning system. How they got past it is beyond me.'

'No security system's completely immune from professional hackers. They always find a way.'

'Isn't that a fact!' I dug Alec in the side. He knew what I was referring to. His teenage protégé, Dominik, had recently hacked into the International Baccalaureate website to add gaming to the syllabus. I thought it had been underhandedly brilliant, but Alec hadn't been impressed. When I'd laughed, he threatened to hand the boys education over to me.

I took him up on the "offer". Well, I did have a Bachelor's degree in History and English before training as a primary school teacher. That's how I ended up as Dominik's tutor. It worked out to be the best way to keep me occupied over the coming months.

And that prompted another thought. Most hackers were like Dominik: young and super computer savvy. Could this have been done by teenaged humans who'd stumbled across the Pazu symbol or … Pazu descendants, perhaps? And, the only thing I could think off that would have brought our world—yep, it was my world now—to their attention would have been the murders at the time of the Ritual by Maris and her nasty gang.

It was a light-bulb moment because it made so much sense. Excitement shot through my veins like liquid fire, and I practically bounced in my seat.

'I think I've got it!' I shared my thoughts aloud. 'It so fits.'

'You clever cookie!' Kari grinned up at me and clapped her hand over mine giving it a gentle squeeze.

Alec smiled broadly, eyes glinting. 'It does fit.' Then his smile faded. 'So we have the rebels to thank for inadvertently resurrecting a dormant company of young and inexperienced Pazu. Wonderful!' He rubbed his brow.

'No matter which way I look at it, that's got to be it,' I said.

'It still doesn't answer the question how they had found out about The Residence.' Alec drummed his fingers against the side of the phone, his gaze fixed on Elliott, the security guard. 'Did you notice anything different on the street? Any suspicious cars or vans, the same people, possibly young ones … teens, early twenties, walking by more than once taking photos … anything?'

'Impossible to tell. People in cars stop all the time and take pics. The place is heritage. It's listed in books. We get busloads of tourists driving past the place all the time, getting out and taking snaps.'

My parents' home was well known. Judy once complained at the number of film companies pestering Luc to allow them to include the house in some movie or television series.

'True.' Alec let out a frustrated breath. 'Still, if they're undamaged, send me the recordings from the street-facing cameras over last forty-eight hours, street, lane and harbour views. You never know; we might spot something.'

Especially as vampire vision was far keener than any human's.

'Uh, might be a problem. The police will probably want to examine those.' Elliott glanced briefly back at Richard, whose voice could be heard in the background. 'Yep, the police are asking for the CCTV footage.'

'Forget it, then. Nothing we can do about it.'

'Yes, Sir.' He dropped his head for a moment. When he looked at us again, his face had hardened. 'Lives were lost on my watch.'

'Which is why you'll be making sure nothing like this ever happens again.'

'No, Sir.'

'Resignation declined. Review your protocols and see to the security of the safe houses—after you've been to the hospital.'

'Yes, Sir, and … thank you.' His face disappeared from the screen as he handed the phone back to Richard.

'Police are here, looking for the owner. What should I tell them?'

'The truth: that the owners are overseas and will get there as soon as we can. In the meantime, you and Amanda are our spokespeople. You know what to say.'

'Sure. Leave it to me.'

Alec rung off.

'Richard sounds like a good man,' Dougal said.

'He is. Got my full confidence. He's discreet and more than capable of dealing with the authorities, and he's one of the best lawyers in the city. Nice to have him on our side.'

'Marcus is on his way,' Jake said as he pocketed his phone and walked back over to us.

'Good. That gives us a few hours to get the plane ready.'

I was going to hate every minute that he was away from me, but no way would I hold him back. At least I'd have Dominik to keep me occupied. I'd already worked out an entire term's teaching program for him.

'Sam needs to know all this.' Just as Alec picked up the phone, Sam strode through the door. He'd been out hunting.

The grin on his face vanished and he stopped mid stride, gaze sliding from face to face. 'Okay, what did I miss?'

CHAPTER 24 - DELANEY'S DILEMMA

ALEC

Half a world away from her. My mouth dried as the thought kept bouncing around in my head. *Laura's in safe hands,* I kept telling myself. In the safest place possible. Jake, Terens, Cal and Dougal were with her, and our baby wasn't due for another five months. And Kari was devoted to Laura. Never left her side. Which was good, especially since I'd left Dominik's education in Laura's more than capable hands. The boy was okay but too early in his juvenile stage to be left alone with her.

Still, my gaze automatically went to the serpent ring. It's eyes glowed a safe scarlet, which only marginally lessened my anxiety. And just as I thought of using the ring's magical telepathic gift, her voice whispered through my mind.

'Miss you so much.'

We'd only been apart for twenty-two hours, and already, it seemed too long. Our parting kiss still lingered on my lips, her taste, her scent, like nectar to my senses. *My arms are empty without you in them.*

Aww ... that's so sweet.

My mouth twisted into a wry smile. *I can show you just how sweet I can be when I return.*

She laughed. *I'll hold you to that.*

The cabin vibrated with the lowering of the landing gear. From the window, the lights from Sydney's Kingsford Smith Airport winked up at us as we made our descent.

We're just about to land.

Take care, my love, and come back to me.

I will, darling. I promise. Reluctantly, I broke our connection when Marcus leaned across the aisle toward me.

'Don't linger with the customs officials.' In Marcus speak that meant mesmerise the officials to get through quickly. He'd terminated the lamia hunt right after Jake's call, and he, Cal and Terens had arrived at Drunvela within three hours. 'We were running out of blood vials anyway, chasing after that thing,' he'd said. 'There'll be time to catch it later.'

Compared to the situation we were facing now, the lamia was a lesser problem.

We taxied to a private terminal. Customs officials boarded and checked our papers, and we stepped off the plane in less than twenty minutes. Amanda and Richard were there to greet us. They bowed low. For a relatively young man, Richard already showed signs of early balding, his thin, dark brown hair barely covered a small bare patch near the crown of his head.

He strode forward, and we shook hands, his grey eyes deep with concern. 'Sorry you had to return under such tragic circumstances.'

I thanked him.

Amanda's lip quivered, her usual composure slipping. But it was more anger brought on by grief than from any sense of fear. Her strong protective nature toward those in her care fueled a Valkyrie spirit that few could match. With a sword in her hand, Amanda was a true nemesis.

'Condolences, my lords. Such a tragedy, and unbelievable that The Residence was attacked. It's unheard of. We're all in shock. It's Pazu, all right.' She and Richard exchanged a brief glance. 'We didn't want to cause a panic, so … apart from Wayne' —she indicated to a young man who stood by one of the cars, to come forward— 'we've shown it to no one else.' He looked familiar. 'Wayne's my juvy, so he can be trusted. He's been doing some digging, hoping to come up with something concrete before you landed.'

'Wise move.' I studied Wayne, and then it clicked. 'Didn't I see you at the Ritual?'

'Yes, Princeps.' He bowed low. 'We weren't actually introduced. It was my girl, Lora, who spoke with Lady Laura.'

'Ah, yes. She spells it L-O-R-A, as I recall.' His young donsang with the same name but different spelling. Laura had liked her.

'That's the one.' He smiled broadly. 'She'll be over the moon when I tell her you remembered her.'

How could I forget? She had revealed to Laura some of the more intimate methods of feeding. I'd enjoyed seeing her shocked reaction at the time and unsure whether she'd even choose me as Guardian. Yet, here we were, expecting our first child. Luc, the old fox, had been right. We had been meant for each other. Now he was gone, and so was The Residence. Which brought my thoughts full circle.

'Let's get going, and you can show me what you've got.'

Richard and Amanda led the way to our waiting limos. Marcus climbed in and took the seat near the window, facing the front. I took the one opposite, behind the driver. Sam joined Marcus and pulled out his iPad, while Richard and Amanda sat next to me. She indicated for Wayne to sit next to Sam.

Richard turned and tapped the driver on the shoulder. We sped off through the brightly lit city streets and into downtown evening traffic.

'No one's heard of any Pazu activity for ages. We thought they were finished … gone … dead.' Amanda turned to Richard. 'I'm now worried about Rich and all the other donsangs.'

'Don't be.' He clasped her hand and drew it onto his lap, his thumb drawing lazy circles over their linked fingers.

'We thought that too, lady' Marcus said. 'Our mistake.'

Wayne opened his own iPad and shared what information he had. 'I checked out every so-called vampire website there is. Look at this.' He turned the device around and pointed to the top of the screen. 'Same calling card they left on the guards. Is that dumb or what? Too easy.' He smiled broadly, eyes alight with excitement.

We too had scoured the net and found that same website in the brief time before flying out. It was the only site that carried that particular symbol. I was sure the police had the same results.

'Yep, found that one too. It's got to be them.' Sam showed Wayne his iPad screen. 'No other website uses that particular pic. I didn't have time to get the IP address. Did you?'

'Tried, but they've covered their tracks using a VPN.'

'VPN? Deus! I don't think I'll ever get used to this new abbreviated language.' Arms crossed over his knees, Marcus focused his gaze on both screens.

'You and me both, my lord. I leave it all to Rich.' Amanda gazed lovingly up at him.

Richard smiled and kissed her temple, and for one miniscule moment, I longed to have Laura just as near. But, I reminded myself for the umpteenth time, she was safer where she was, no matter how much I hated the separation.

'Virtual Private Network,' Wayne answered. 'It's like an alias that masks your actual IP address. A lot of hackers use it.'

'It's of limited use,' Sam chimed in. 'Even if we do manage to find the real IP, it won't tell us anything we don't already know: that they're based somewhere here in Sydney.'

Marcus pointed to Sam's screen. 'You can't locate a physical address?'

'Nope. We'd need permission from the server. Only the police can get that, and I doubt they'll be sharing that info with us.' Sam blew out a breath and slumped back against the seat. 'Unless Wayne here's better at hacking than I am, we're stuck.'

'Can you?' Marcus's gaze whipped to Wayne.

The young man's mouth slackened. 'Um … no, sir. It's too well encrypted.'

Marcus's eyes paled, his mouth tightening into a thin, pink slash. 'Are you telling me we can do nothing, and these men will go unpunished?'

Wayne swallowed, his panicked gaze flying to Amanda. She tapped his knee. 'It's all right. You did your best.'

Marcus grunted and turned his head to the window.

Damned if I was going to admit defeat. If we could only get a scent, even a tiny trace, we could track it back to them.

'Richard, what about the guards' uniforms?' The guards had been dragged out of the house, meaning the killers had gotten up close and personal, leaving behind unmistakable scent markers.

Both Marcus and Sam saw where I was going with this. Marcus turned from the window, his eyes bright, mouth creased in a faint smile. Sam sprang upright, and the two exchanged a knowing glance. 'All we need is a whiff.'

Being over eighteen hundred years old, he and Sam—and the other men—had the best-developed senses of all Brethren. No bloodhound could compete. They could detect and track even a tiny trace of scent to its source.

His gaze darting between them and me, Richard grinned. 'Aaaaahhh

277

... I get it.' He pulled out his phone and pressed speed dial. 'Hey, Richard here. You haven't washed your uniform yet, have you?'

I recognised the voice that answered: the head of security I'd spoken to the previous day. 'No. Why?'

'We might be able to get a scent off it and find the ones who did this.'

'You at the Bondi safehouse?'

'No. We're on our way to The Residence with the princeps, Lord Sam and Sieur Marcus.'

'Right. I'll get onto it. It'll give me time to collect the others' uniforms as well and drop it off to you.'

Richard hung up and pocketed his phone. I noted his concerned expression when he glanced my way: a slight crease between his brows, his keen eyes searching mine. 'What'll you do with the killers when you find them?'

Good question. I'd had a chance to think that through on the flight from Scotland. I knew what Luc's policy had been on the Pazu: total extermination, although they were humans. Luc had always had a gift for making exceptions to the rules.

But Luc was no longer here.

As far as I was concerned, the Pazu were human, and we didn't kill humans. Period. If I could, I'd hand them over to the police to face justice. And therein lay the problem: the Brethren would demand vengeance. Nothing less than their execution.

'I'm working on it.'

'If you hand them over to the police and the evidence isn't strong enough to convict them, they could get off lightly. No one's going to be happy with that.'

By "everyone" he meant my kind—Brethren. 'Don't I know it.'

Richard trod a fine line between justice for humans as well as Brethren. As a donsang, he saw both sides. But if push came to shove, as they say, which side would he choose? This situation could be the test. 'Something else you ought to know.' He cleared his throat. His usually laughing grey eyes were tight with tension—understandable, considering the tragedy that had occurred. Yet, I sensed something more. 'Something's off. The detective in charge, Delaney, is asking way too many questions about you, Alec. It's got my radar up.'

Mine just went up too. 'Dave Delaney?' There couldn't possibly be two officers with the same name in the local police.

'Yeah, that's the one. You know him?'

'We've met.' My scalp prickled. He was the interviewing officer when Laura had been abducted and injured by Maris's rebel group. It had been tricky going then. The man was sharp, and worse still, he was a close friend of Sommers. This was not a good sign.

All eyes turned to me. I explained the events.

'Oh, man!' Richard's eyes closed, and he dropped his head back against the seat. 'If Sommers told any of that to Delaney...' His eyes snapped open. 'I bet you he did. No wonder the man grilled me about you.'

If Richard was right, then I'd made a terrible mistake keeping Sommers alive. Once again, Luc had been right; I should've killed him that night in Laura's flat. The man had been carrying white-oak bullets. It was the only exception to the no-killing-humans rule, which meant he'd been fair game. I would've been justified if I'd ended him. Laura would never have known. But then, I wouldn't have been able to keep up the lie, and our relationship would've suffered. Maybe the way it played out was better.

Sam huffed. 'Nothing like a little complication to make life interesting.'

'I can do without that, thanks.'

'This detective's a human.' Marcus's eyes paled even further. 'Needs must.'

'I used that on him a few months ago.' I'd mesmerised Dave before, when he'd come too close to the truth. Doing it too often could cause brain damage, and the man didn't deserve that.

'One more time should be fine. If he has a strong will his mind will recover.'

I didn't want to prove Marcus wrong.

The drive to The Residence in Vaucluse took around forty minutes. I knew what to expect since the firemen had found the charred remains of several bodies in the burnt out rubble. And twenty-four hours later, they were still hauling out more bodies. But the scene that met us still took me by surprise.

A wave of nausea washed over me.

It was a full on police investigation, a crime scene and all that came with it: the police flashing lights, ambulances, and groups of reporters milling near the entrance. A black and yellow Crime Scene tape blocked our way.

This was a disaster. Never had we faced such danger of exposure. How we handled this situation would determine our future existence in this country.

Sam swore and cursed under his breath, threatening to hunt down and destroy all Pazu. Marcus's eyes dangerously narrowed, a pale gleam in the dark. What memories of this place would he be reliving?

Police approached our car. I wound down the window. One leant in. 'Sorry, sir, but this street is closed. Unless you're a resident, you'll have to turn back.'

I pulled out my ID. 'I'm Dr Munro, and that's'—I was about to say Luc Lebrettan's residence—'my house.' I pointed to the remains of Luc's old home, which now belonged to Laura and me, and I still wasn't used to it.

He scrutinised my ID. 'You'll find Detective Delaney at the end of your driveway.'

He lifted the tape and waved us on.

Our vehicle drove on to the end of the street toward the house. An ambulance passed us. Within it, I sensed the remains of two of our Brethren. Their essence was gone, yet still something touched my consciousness. An icy lump formed in my gut. They'd never had a chance, killed by the humans they were sworn to protect. My fists clenched.

Sam growled.

Richard and Amanda, hands tightly clasped in each other's, her head on his shoulder, quietly took in the scene. A single bloody tear slid down her cheek. Only young Wayne seemed animated, head down clicking away at his iPad keyboard. If I had to take a guess, I'd say he was trying to redeem himself in Marcus's eyes by locating the Pazu. I wished him the best of luck.

Once through the gates, the full magnitude of the tragedy struck me. Where once stood Luc's home-away-from-home—a unique, grand Victorian neo-Gothic mansion he'd tried to model on D'Antonville—there now laid a smouldering, blackened shell, the smell of its ruin leeching into my nostrils.

I wanted to gag.

The upper story had collapsed, and one of the walls of the lower half leaned dangerously outwards. A crane had been brought in to brace it. Police forensic teams, in their distinctive white overalls, clambered amidst the wreckage. Others carried covered stretches to waiting ambulances amidst more flashing police car lights.

Never in my life had I thought to see something like this. My throat constricted as another, more recent, scene rushed through my consciousness: another inferno in an underground vault and two precious lives lost.

As if having read my mind, Marcus whispered, 'Deus! I've seen too many fires.'

'Me too.' And I'd had enough. First it was from the Rebels and now vampire hunters. A fire of another sort spread through my gut, and had me clenching my fists. I longer to inflict the same sort of misery on those who'd caused this. Unless we destroyed them, this would happen again and again and again.

Now, I finally understood Luc's position, his uncompromising stance against the Pazu. It was the only way to deal with those who sought your utter destruction.

Repay in kind.

Amanda started. She dug into her bag, whipped out a handkerchief and wiped away the blood-red streaks on her cheeks. Then she reached back into her bag to produce a small box. 'Quick, put these in so we don't get any funny looks.' She snapped open the lid to reveal an assortment of coloured contact lenses, which she held out to us. Having the same lavender-coloured eyes would only arouse unwanted suspicion.

Except for me. Delaney already knew me.

Our driver stopped at the front entrance. And there, near where the front porch used to be but was now sealed off with police tape, stood Dave Delaney. Tie askew, hands in his pockets, he had the same deep bags under his eyes and tired expression as last time.

Richard leaned toward me. 'The guy knows me as the family solicitor, so it shouldn't raise eyebrows if I'm with you. That okay with you?' He was one of a long line of lawyers Luc had hired over the years, but unlike Richard, the others hadn't been donsangs. Having one in the family, so to speak, made things a lot easier.

'Fine with me.'

Amanda instructed Wayne to remain in the car, then she, Richard,

Sam, Marcus and finally me, alighted.

Delaney watched us with wary eyes. It wasn't that warm a night, yet a fine sheen of sweat covered his brow. He took a swig of water and wiped his mouth. There was no mistaking the scent of white oak.

This time my scalp didn't just prickle: it practically itched. This couldn't be just coincidence. Sommers must have told him everything he knew about us.

Marcus's nostrils flared, and a low growl vibrated in his throat. He and Sam encircled Delaney, taking position on either side. Any human knowingly found in possession of white oak was considered a threat. Prefects could order their execution. Maybe Sommers should've told him that, too, the fool. He'd inadvertently placed his friend in danger.

Sommers and I had a score to settle.

Delaney's head swiveled from Marcus to Sam; then his eyes connected with mine. He took another longer swig of water, unaware that the powdered white oak he was drinking no longer posed any serious threat to us. He may as well have been drinking cordial.

This was going to be interesting. I tried not to smile.

'Dr Munro.' He didn't extend his hand. 'I was surprised to learn that you are now the owner.' He jerked his head at the house behind him. 'What a fortuitous inheritance. Bet the insurance on it is good.'

'What the hell is that supposed to mean? That I killed Luc and married Laura to get my hands on it, then had it burnt down with people in it, all to collect the insurance money? You can't be serious!' It was laughable. In fact, I did laugh. It was so ludicrous.

On a few occasions I'd asked Luc to sell the old place and move into something more modern. This old place had been a money pit. He'd been forever repairing it. He'd held onto it for sentimental reasons because it had reminded him of D'Antonville. Lord knew how.

'You tell me.'

'I thought you to be a good detective, Delaney. Seems I was wrong if that's the best you can come up with.'

Oddly, his smug expression didn't disappear. All he did was raise an eyebrow, then looked down at his scuffed shoes.

What was he playing at? 'My people died in that fire. What are you doing to find them?'

'We're conducting our enquiries.'

'And? Any progress?'

His gaze shot up to me. 'You know something, Dr Munro? You're full of surprises.'

Marcus and I exchanged a glance. Where was this human heading with this?

'Care to explain?'

'I was hoping you would.' He took another swig of the white-oak-laced water while gazing straight at me.

Understanding hit. Delaney wanted me to reveal what I was. 'You're full of surprises, too.' I shot a look at his water bottle, then back to him, one eyebrow cocked. He got my meaning.

'Ah ... now we get to the crux of the matter.'

I thrust both hands into my pants pockets, too. Why not call his bluff. Let's see how much he really knew. 'You tell me.'

Delaney's eyes narrowed. 'All right, I'll start then: shall I? From a ... more convenient distance.' He moved away from Marcus and Sam, strode past me and went a few paces down the drive before turning to face us. 'I know what you are. Got it from a reliable source. Personally, I don't care about your dietary habits until people—humans, to be precise—start dying in my jurisdiction.'

My throat dried.

He indicated his eyes. 'Coloured contacts? Don't you ... people ... have purplish eyes?'

Next to me, Richard sucked in a quick breath.

Delaney's gaze shot to him, and he smiled. 'That seems like an admission to me.'

'An admission of what?' I asked.

He let out a deep breath, his stomach rising and falling with the effort. 'I'm not into games, Dr Munro. Drop the pretense. If you want me to say the word, I will.' He lowered his voice to a level only we could hear. 'You're vampires, blood drinkers, nosferatu or whatever you call yourselves. And you,' He pinned Richard his stare. 'I've yet to figure out what you are.'

'Keep figuring.' Richard crossed his arms over his chest and stared right back.

Wonderful! Another law enforcement officer knew about us, and now we had a standoff. Just what we needed. We may as well announce ourselves on national television!

'I see you're not denying it, Mr Weston.'

Richard tensed, although his facial expression gave nothing away. I figured years of court appearances as a defense lawyer had honed that skill.

'Oh, and in case you're thinking of wiping my mind, Dr Munro, or even killing me, I have my insurance policy right here.' He lifted up his water bottle. 'It contains a tablespoon of powdered white oak. I heard it can be quite nasty to you people.'

Delaney believed he had us cornered. Couldn't blame the man for being cautious.

Of course, I could deny everything. Who'd believe him? Everyone knew vampires didn't exist. He'd have a hard time convincing his colleagues and superiors ... if he was the lone voice. But he wasn't. He had Sommers to back him up: two-high-level-law-enforcement officers, who could make their colleagues listen.

As far as I could see, we had little choice but to level with him. Having him as our enemy or, worse still, to order his elimination was not an option I wanted to consider.

Marcus stood a few paces behind me. I angled my head toward him. 'What do you think?'

'We could do with his cooperation. Might even be useful as an ally. I'll stand by your decision.' I didn't need Marcus's approval, but I welcomed it nevertheless.

I turned to Sam, on my left. He gave me a curt nod. But it was Amanda and Richard who'd be the most affected. While the Principate was abroad, they were responsible for the humans in this city. And they didn't need someone like Delaney offside.

I turned to them.

They exchanged a glance and a few murmured words. Then Amanda gave me a nod. She took a step toward Delaney and removed her contacts. 'You're in no danger from us. We protect the people of this city. In fact, our laws prevent us from killing, and those who do are punished.

Meanwhile, Richard had pulled up his sleeve to reveal two tiny bite marks. 'I'm her human donor. She doesn't need to feed off anyone else, so you can stop figuring out what I am.'

Delaney's breath hitched. He pulled out a handkerchief and wiped his brow. His gaze darted back to me, Marcus and Sam. 'Bloody hell! That the same with all of you? You use donors?'

'That's right. You know who mine is,' I answered. That's how it worked for most of my kind, most of the time, at least. Some preferred to hunt but Delaney didn't need to know that. It would only complicate things.

'We don't need much to keep us alive. No reason to drain an entire body.' Amanda gave him a gentle smile. If it reassured Delaney, he didn't show it.

'What about those killings last December? How do you explain those? Kids. Just kids they were. Entirely drained.' He sneered in disgust.

'I'm so sorry. We caught those responsible. They'll never hurt anyone ever again,' Amanda replied. 'Unlike your world, we have capital punishment for murderers.'

It never ceased to amaze me how humans could fail in so many areas yet expect others, even among their own kind, to be perfect. 'You of all people should know that not everyone obeys the law. If they did, you'd be out of a job. You humans have your criminals as we have ours. And like you, we do our best to enforce our laws and deal with those who don't … to protect both our worlds.'

Delaney cleared his throat and briefly gazed down at his shoes, brow deeply furrowed. 'You the enforcer?'

'One of them.'

'Mmmm…' Whatever was going through his mind caused a subtle shift in his scent. His fear faded, and when his eyes connected with mine once again, I knew he was reassessing us. It wasn't exactly respect, but it was close enough. I'd take it. He tapped his forehead. 'The … uh … hypno-mind thing.'

'It saves lives. Keeps humans unaware of us.'

He took another swig of water then rocked back on his heels, eyes lowered, his mind sifting through all this. No doubt Sommers had told him about being mesmerised. Perhaps he was wondering if I'd done the same to him. I had, but this wasn't the time to tell him. Delaney's eyes shot back to me, narrowed and glittering like a hawk's. 'Can Laura be mesmerised?'

What the…?

Behind me, Marcus snorted. 'No Ingenii can be mesmerised. Their blood prevents it.'

Delaney studied him. 'And you are?'

'Commander Marcus Antonius Pulcher D'Antonville, Arch Elder of the Brethren … and law enforcer.' He stepped forward till he stood by my side, and, with a little smile, dipped his head in greeting. 'I'm Laura's grandfather. Lucien Lebrettan was my son.'

Delaney's eyes popped. 'Bloody hell!'

'In further answer to your question regarding my granddaughter, I believe she chose the better man.' Marcus placed his hand on my shoulder.

Ah! Marcus had caught the veiled insinuation quicker than I. In other words, did I mesmerise Laura into leaving Sommers for me? I would've laughed except it would have been an insult to the clever, witty and amazing women I was privileged to have as my wife. She left Sommers after recognising what kind of monster he really was, one capable of cold-bloodedly murdering her family in some misguided view that he was saving her.

My fists clenched so hard that pain shot up my forearms and into my shoulders. I took a deep breath and relaxed before answering him. 'If your source is so reliable, he would've told you that Laura is immune to any form of mesmerisation. She has her own mind.'

Delaney cleared his throat again.

The truth was hitting home, and as important as that was, I was here for another reason.

As the last ambulance drove away with the charred remains of my brethren, I reminded Delaney why we were here. With my thumb, I indicated the burnt out wreck of the house behind me. 'Our people died in that fire. I want their killers caught. You know this was no accident. The security guards were knocked out and dragged out of the way before the fire was lit.'

He had interviewed Richard earlier, so he knew I'd been informed about the events even before the police had been called.

'We have an idea who may be responsible,' Marcus said.

'Who?' Delaney's gaze latched onto him.

'A particular enemy who's been hunting us for centuries,' Marcus said. 'No one else would have reason for murdering our people.'

Delaney pulled out his phone, then turned the screen toward us. 'You recognise this? Forensics found it among the remains of one of the bodies.'

Looked like the Pazu had left more than one calling card behind. There was not much left of the card except for a charred fragment showing the left lower claw of Pazuzu.

'It's them,' I said.

'What do you know?'

There was no point in withholding anything. If we could cooperate in finding the Pazu killers, then the better for us all. I shared our information … and explained our history with the Pazu. A gust of wind blew ash into our faces. Another crushing reminder of the devastation we'd come back to. Would it have happened if Luc had still been alive?

Delaney coughed, swiped it away and took a swig of water, this time I believed, to get rid of the foul taste. He wiped his mouth with the back of his hand, his face impassive as he absorbed all I'd told him. Finally, he shook his head, closed his eyes and rubbed his forehead. 'Never thought I'd ever have to deal with a turf war between … vampires and vampire hunters.' After a second, a chuckle broke from him, the kind of mirthless laugh brought on by disbelief mingled with a grudging acknowledgement that this was reality and there was nothing he could do about it.

A moment later, he sobered and looked straight at me. 'All right, this is how it's going to work. These Pazu, as you call them, are humans, so they're under Australian law and its protection until they're caught and convicted. You'—he stabbed a finger in my direction, then swept it around to the rest—'are not to touch them.'

'Only if we have your promise they'll be duly punished, or our people will exact their own justice, as we have always done.' Marcus's voice was low and controlled but there was no mistaking the subtle menace in his tone.

Delaney ignored it. Instead, his eyes held a steely resolve. 'I don't care who or what you are and what you've always done. This isn't the Middle Ages, mate. We're a civilized twenty-first century nation, and we do things by the law here. And I represent that law, not you.'

Marcus growled. I don't believe anyone had ever called him "mate." 'Take care how you speak to me, human.'

Delaney paled and swallowed hard, but to his credit, he didn't take even one step back. Bravery, stubbornness or plain foolhardiness? I guessed I'd soon find out.

'It's your turn, Delaney. I told you what we found, now tell us what you've got. We have a right to know.'

Delaney cleared his throat again and tore his gaze away from Marcus. 'We identified two suspects from the CCTV footage your security guard provided. And when our computer forensics team matched that fragment to this—' He swiped the previous image on his phone for another. It was the identical website we'd found and whose IP address was locked to us. 'The same two perps are involved. My team's collecting them now.'

'That was quick. You're better than I thought.' Sam's half compliment didn't sit too well with Delaney, whose reply was a sneer.

Then his phone rang. He answered, his gaze never leaving us. 'Good work. Keep them separated till I get there.'

Did he know we could hear the voice on the other end of the line? They'd apprehended two young men, an eighteen-year-old and a twenty-year-old who admitted they ran the Pazu website. They were taken into custody and placed in separate interview rooms. One of them was a law student who insisted on being his own counsel.

Arms folded over his chest, Sam leant toward me and spoke too low for Delaney to catch. 'Juvenile Pazu. Typical self-righteous, cocky arrogance.'

'I've never met one.' All my information about them had come from Luc, and Marcus's chronicles.

'You're lucky.'

'We need to know if they're from both of the Pazu families who followed us here from Europe, or just one family in particular.' Marcus's concerns were justified. One of those families still was in possession of the Pazuzim Sword. That alone was a threat.

Delaney ended the call and slipped the phone back into his pocket. 'Don't plan on leaving the country anytime soon. I might want you for further questioning.' He turned away from us toward a dark blue sedan parked a few metres down the driveway.

Just leaving us standing there annoyed me. 'Wait!' I held up my hand for him to give me a minute as Marcus, Sam, Amanda, Richard and I gathered in a huddle.

'At least one of us needs to be there, see these Pazu for ourselves,' I suggested.

Marcus, hands on hips and with one eye on Delaney nodded. 'Absolutely, and that has to be you, Alec. The human knows you, and we all sense he feels more comfortable with you than with us.'

'He's right. You're the logical choice.' Sam slapped me on the back. 'Besides, we've got to be here when Elliott arrives with the uniforms. Then we can sniff out the rest of the bastards for ourselves. I'm itching to go hunting.'

I sensed Richard's disapproval. 'As your counsel, I should be there with you. Just in case, you know…. I don't trust that man.' He jerked his head in Delaney's direction.

'Not necessary. I'm not the one being questioned. At least, not yet. But thanks for the offer.'

'Fine.' But he wasn't happy.

'Well, that's settled.' I turned back to Delaney. 'I want to be there, to see them, see if they have a mark here.' I tapped my inner wrist. 'A tattoo. Hook and a squiggle. Looks like a birthmark. All Pazu have them.'

'I can check for that.'

Damn difficult man. 'You know I have a right by law, as the victim, to confront those responsible for this crime. You can't deny me that.'

Delaney deliberated. After a moment, he gave me a nod before climbing into his car. He rolled the window down. 'I'll meet you there. Waverley.' He drove off.

'Here, take this.' I handed Marcus the spare key to my Pitt Street apartment. 'I'll meet you back there.'

Amanda, Richard and I rejoined Wayne in the limo. He packed away his iPad and scooted across the seat toward the window, his face crestfallen. 'They got 'em. S'pose it's pointless trying to hack into Telstra to get the IP now.'

'For now, Wayne. Let's see first if they've got the right people.' I tapped our driver on the shoulder. 'Drop me off at Waverley Police Station.'

We drove to the Eastern Suburbs police station and stopped outside the red brick entrance. Just before I got out, Amanda caught my arm. 'I'll inform our Brethren that the police are handling it, and they've got two in custody. That should be enough to settle them … I hope.'

'Remind them: *no* reprisals. This doesn't change the law.'

'Understood.'

They drove off, and I stepped through the door to the front reception desk. It was unattended. A sign said, Ring the Bell for Assistance. So I did. A young uniformed policeman appeared.

'I'm Dr Munro. Superintendent Delaney is expecting me.'

'You have some ID?' I pulled out my driver's license. 'Thanks. Put this on.' He pulled out a visitor's badge before pressing a button beneath the bench top. A door to my right clicked open. 'Follow me.'

He led me through an open plan room scattered with desks and work spaces separated by partitions. Some were occupied. One or two officers briefly looked up as we passed. Through another doorway and down a corridor, he stopped outside one of four grey doors. Each had a small viewing window. He looked through and knocked. The door opened a crack and he spoke to those inside. I recognised Delaney's voice.

'He can watch from outside.'

Fair enough.

The young policeman closed the door. 'He said—'

'I know. I heard.'

He turned and left. I made myself comfortable by leaning my left shoulder against the door and peering through the viewing window. A young man with straight white-blonde hair sat with his back to the door. Delaney and another plain-clothes detective took the chairs on either side of him. Three empty glasses and a jug of water sat in a round tray in the middle of the table while a small camera at the far end of the table recorded everything.

The young man's head was turned toward Delaney. Although I couldn't see his face, I sensed no fear, not even a hint of tension or concern coming from him. He lounged back in the chair, one arm draped over the back, completely at ease. Was this the Pazu arrogance Sam had mentioned?

They had already started the interview.

I listened in and just caught his name and physical appearance being repeated for the benefit of the recording. Alistair Davis. The name was close enough to Davidoff that it was just possible he could be our Pazu.

Or not.

Proof, Delaney. I need proof. I winged that thought to him. Not that I expected a response, but he knew what to look for.

'Is that information correct, Mr Davis?' The other detective asked.

Davis shrugged. 'That's correct.'

Delaney motioned with his finger and his partner slid the information sheet across the table to him. 'We like to make sure all your details are correct, so there's no case of mistaken identity. I'm sure, as a student of the law, you understand that.'

'Of course.'

Delaney took his time perusing the sheet while his thumb mechanically clicked the spring lid of his pen. 'Seems in order ... wait. Seems there's no record of any distinguishing marks such as moles, scars, birthmarks and the like.' He slid the sheet back to the other detective. 'Would you mind correcting that omission so my sergeant can record it?'

Delaney's partner darted him a quick glance and turned the sheet over, pen at the ready. But before he did so, I'd managed to scan the sheet of paper looking for an address, and those physical details had already been jotted down.

I made a mental note not to underestimate Delaney.

'Um, yeah okay.' Davis drawled out a couple of things: scar on his knee from a boyhood accident, mole on his right shoulder. He then hesitated and slowly slid his left hand beneath the table but not before I saw a thick watchband covering his left wrist.

My pulse quickened.

Only a Pazu would hide his mark.

'Is that all, Mr Davis?' Delaney asked.

'Um—yes—no. A ... birthmark ... on my wrist.' The young man straightened in his seat.

Pulse racing now, I pressed my face against the glass to see the mark for myself.

Davis removed his watch, but his arm was clutched close to his body, so I couldn't get a decent view.

Damn!

'Would you mind showing it to my sergeant so he can record it?'

'Yeah, sure.'

I had to admire Delaney's interrogation methods.

Davis rested his hand on the table, wrist turned up.

And there it was: the reddish hook-and-squiggle of a Pazu. I needed no other proof.

As Davis described the mark, Delaney pivoted in his seat to face the door, swung one leg over the other and nonchalantly looked directly at me.

I nodded.

We understood each other.

As the questions continued, Davis became nervous. Not only could I sense it, but I could smell it from behind the door. He fidgeted in his seat, his head swiveling more and more often toward the camera.

'I ... um ... choose my right to remain silent. And ... to have legal representation.'

'I think that's a very good idea, Mr Davis.' Delaney terminated the interview. He stood and joined me outside. 'Let's see what the other one has to say.'

'Lead on.'

Delaney strode across the hall to Interview Room 2. 'Don't let him see you.'

I stood out of sight as he opened the door and closed it behind him. It was set up the same Spartan way as the previous one. At the head of the table, again facing away from the door, sat another young man. I briefly glimpsed his face when he turned to see who came in. This youngster was no more than in his late teens. Another juvenile Pazu?

Delaney used the same line of questioning as he had with Davis, beginning with the birthmark.

This youngster didn't have one. So what was he doing with a Pazu? And unlike his friend, he exuded fear. He stumbled over his words, and when he was shown the actual burnt card fragment sealed in a clear plastic evidence bag, he paled and dropped his head, shoulders bunched as if trying to hide.

'Do you recognise it?' The youngster shook his head. 'Try again.'

The boy raised his head, blinked at it and dropped his head again. 'No.'

Delaney sat back in the chair, hands clasped over his stomach. 'You know that card could still have some DNA on it. If it matches with yours, then you may be facing twenty to twenty-five years in jail for murder. On the other hand, if you tell us everything, it'll go more favourably for you.'

I had no idea if that was a normal line of questioning, but whatever Delaney was doing seemed to be working.

The youngster's head shot upwards, eyes wide as saucers, mouth trembling. His shoulders began to shake, and the tears followed. He sniffed and was passed a box of tissues.

'You have anything to say, son?' Delaney's calm demeanor got results. The boy cracked, and everything came spilling out.

'Okay, okay. It's mine. No ... um, actually it's Al's. I took a couple of his cards. I ... only did it because ... they killed my sister. I wanted them to know that we weren't taking it. They're the—'

Delaney stopped him. 'Son, are you confessing?'

The youngster bobbed his head. 'I wanted them dead. They're ... vampires. They're not ... human.'

'Did you say *vampires?*' The other detective asked. He and Delaney exchanged a glance.

The youngster nodded. 'I know you don't believe me. But it's true. They've been killing people in the city—my sister—since before Christmas. Al's family are vampire hunters. We didn't know where to find them, though, till he told us.'

Delaney's brow furrowed. He leaned forward. 'He? Who? Who told you where to find them?'

The youngster swallowed, grabbed another tissue and wiped his eyes. 'He's a cop, like you. Knows all about them. He bought white-oak bullets from us. That's how you kill them, you know. He told us where they lived. Gave us the address ... the place we burned down. He told us to do that.' The youngster became even more agitated. He shot from his seat, the chair clanging to the ground. 'We didn't hurt the security guys. We pulled them out of the way. We don't kill humans, only the vampires, so it's not really murder coz they're already dead!'

I tensed. There was only one person I knew who fit that description. The son of a bitch! My vision narrowed until I saw through a haze of red.

Delaney's face went ashen, and for a moment I thought he'd terminate the interview because we both knew who that cop was. To his credit, Delaney carried on, his face set like rock as he stared at the youngster, who now paced from one end of the small box-like room to the other.

Delaney rose and righted the fallen chair. 'Sit down, son. Here, take this.' He handed him a glass of water, then sat down again and waited for the boy to calm.

'Now, can you tell me this person's name?'

The youngster shook his head, fear written all over his face. 'He's a cop. You're cops....'

The implication was obvious: the police stuck together and didn't expose their own. I sincerely hoped Delaney would prove that wrong.

Delaney leant further toward him. 'I don't care if this man is our bloody PM. If he broke the law, he faces justice, just like anyone else.'

The other detective nodded.

For a few moments, the youngster studied them both. 'Um … Matt Sommers. He's a detective, an inspector. We checked him out before going to his place.'

The other detective terminated the interview. Both then sat in stunned silence until Delaney abruptly rose. 'Wait here,' he told his partner.

He left the room and stormed down the corridor. I was about to go after him, demanding to know where Sommers was, when my serpent ring flared and Laura's sweet voice whispered through my mind.

Alec, tell me you're safe. The ring's eyes are … darkish.

It's probably reading my murderous thoughts!

Can it do that? And why are you having murderous thoughts?

I rubbed my brow as I thought how to tell Laura that Sommers was responsible for the destruction of her family's home. Laura liked direct. Direct it was. *Somehow Sommers got in contact with the Pazu. He told them to burn down The Residence. Even gave them the location.*

She inhaled sharply. *He what? How? Are you absolutely sure?*

I told her what I knew.

How could he do such a thing?! The rotten piece of self-righteous … I hate him, and I never thought I could ever feel that way about anyone.

Don't feel bad about it. He's earned it.

I never want to hear the name Sommers again.

Which reminded me. *Laura, did he ever tell you about his family background? He knew yours was French, so did he—*

Oh, for sure. His sister was really into Ancestry dot com. She found out they're originally from Somerset in England. Why?

Then, just like that, things clicked into place. Sommerset. Sommers. The names were too similar to be a coincidence, and I didn't believe in coincidences, even though, just for a moment there, I was willing to give him the benefit of the doubt. Was it possible he belonged to the missing Pazu family? And that somehow, he'd reconnected with the other one? My head was buzzing.

The names of the two Pazu families who followed our clan to Australia were Davidoff and Sommerset.

Her breath hitched. *That's right, Jake mentioned it. I never made the connection.*

Neither did I … till now. Did you ever notice a strange birthmark on his left wrist? A reddish squiggly hook-like thing, about four-to-five centimetres long?

No. Come to think of it, he never took off his watch and that personalised black bracelet set he always wears. Not even in the shower. Oops, maybe I shouldn't've told you that last bit.

I smiled. *You had your own life before I met you, darling.*

Delaney returned carrying a large framed photograph, the type that mostly hung on walls, under his arm. We made split-second eye contact before he re-entered the room.

'*Darling, I have to go.*'

'*Love you.*'

'*Love you, too.*' Hearing her lovely voice calmed some of the rage flowing through me, enough for me to concentrate as the interview was resumed.

Delaney placed the framed photograph on the table and spun it round to face the youngster. It appeared to be a group photo, like one from a yearbook, with the names of the individuals at the bottom. He'd masked over the names.

'Look carefully at this photograph. Take your time. Do you recognise the man you know as Matt Sommers anywhere there?'

The youngster's eyes roved over the group photo. He pointed to one smiling individual.

It was Sommers.

No further confirmation was needed.

'Are you absolutely sure?' the other detective asked.

The youngster bobbed his head. 'That's him.'

A uniformed figure hurried down the corridor. He glanced at me, knocked on the door and handed Delaney a sheet of paper. He perused it and passed it to the other detective who slumped back in his chair, hands gripping the sides, his gaze glued on Delaney. 'You know what this means.'

'Interview terminated....' Delaney gave the time and date, then switched off the recording. He rested his elbows on the table and dropped his head into his hands. When he eventually raised his head, his face was white. The lines around his mouth and eyes had also deepened.

He stood, took the paper with him and pasted it, written side up, to the viewing window so I could read it. It was the transcript of an email from Davis to Sommers:

"Thanks for the tip-off. Successful raid and one less vampire nest in the city. Only four inside. Wished there were more. We could've killed them all. If you find the whereabouts of any other bloodsuckers let me know and we'll clean them out too."

Son of a bitch! Double confirmation he was behind it all.

One glance at Delaney and I didn't need to imagine the turmoil he was going through. Laura had mentioned how close he and Sommers were, almost like father and son. This news had hit him hard. It was all there in his face. The man had aged at least ten years.

He sat back down, the transcript curled in his fist. 'Issue an arrest warrant for DI Matthew Sommers.'

CHAPTER 25 - NOT AT MY HANDS

ALEC

I needed to escape that building. A blood rage so great descended on me, and I feared losing self-control. Sommers had much to answer for. But those two young humans weren't guiltless either.

Barely able to keep my fangs sheathed, I tightened my mouth and ran into the city. To its rotten underbelly: King's Cross. Where the homeless and desperate shivered in dark alleys that were filled with the stench of urine: where gangs roamed the streets in search of victims. Where mobsters, the gangsters, the criminals plied their soul-sucking trade in illicit drugs and prostitutes behind the facade of popular nightclubs. Dregs of humanity who thrived on the misery they inflicted on others.

They would not be missed.

My bloodlust grew.

A deep rhythmic thud boomed from the loudspeakers of one nightclub, its pink and yellow neon lights enticing passersby to enter.

'Oops, sorry maaaate.' Speech slurred and breath smelling of a mix of alcohol and vomit, one young human bumped into me. Eyes so bloodshot he could barely see, he and his group laughed and staggered past me, dodging traffic to get to the other side of the street. One of them pointed to a garishly lit club.

I lifted the back collar of my jacket and followed them in.

The blare of the lights, music and loud conversation assaulted my senses until I tuned most of it out and followed my nose. Unbidden, my fangs slipped low in my mouth at the intoxicating mix of scents from the sweat of gyrating bodies, alcohol and heated blood that hung in the air like a pheromone-laden mist.

It didn't help that I hadn't fed in more than forty-eight hours. Having lived on Ingenii blood for nigh on fifty years, ordinary human blood barely satisfied. But it would have to do as my Ingenii blood vials were running dangerously low.

I stalked the room, my nostrils dilating, searching for a particular scent, one that reeked of adrenaline fuelled by anger, aggression and evil intentions.

'Hello, gorgeous!' Voice low and filled with seduction—and wearing enough perfume to knock out a bull—the female who sidled up to me smiled and linked her arm through mine.

'Sorry, not shopping.' Not ever.

I unhooked her arm and wove through the crowded tables. I scanned the room, inhaling deeply. Among the intermingled scents, one stood out. It was unmistakable. At the far end of the room, clos to the corridor leading to the toilets, stood my quarry. He leant heavily against one of the high cocktail tables, breathing heavily, eyes fixated on a laughing group of young women seated nearby.

When one of them rose and headed for the corridor, he followed.

So did I.

He corned her outside the ladies restroom. Hand over her mouth, he slurred, 'I been watchin' you. Regular little cock-tease, aren't you?'

And that was the last thing he said. I tore him off her.

'Miss, next time, don't go to the restroom alone. Take a friend with you.'

Eyes wide, she swallowed hard, she nodded. A trembling 'Thank you,' left her lips as she ran back to her table.

The man swore and struggled in my grip, so I allowed him a glimpse of my inner beast. And damn me if I didn't enjoy it. Surprise, anger and terror washed off him in waves, which only fuelled my hunger.

With my hand around his throat, I dragged him through the exit, down the fire-escape stairs and into the dark alley below. Crouched low behind a dumpster, I forced his booze-filled gaze to lock onto mine.

'You will never hurt anyone again. When I'm done, you will go to the police and confess every crime you've committed.' I had no doubt what he was guilty of. It reeked from him like a foul stench.

I ignored the smell and turned his head to the side, exposing his throat. Beneath the skin, his pulse throbbed invitingly, the blood calling to me with its heady scent of terror-driven adrenaline. I bit down, hard. No vampire-numbing saliva for this piece of scum.

His struggles grew less the more I drank, deeper and deeper draughts, until he laid still in my arms. He wasn't dead. I'd left enough blood for him to survive, but he'd have a killer headache when he woke.

I dumped his unconscious body on the ground, covered it with part of a tarpaulin dangling from the dumpster, and left the alley. Filled with renewed energy, I ran through the back-city streets all the way to my penthouse. To anyone along the way, I would simply have been a slight blur at the edge of their gaze as I sped past.

By the time I reached my apartment building, had walked through reception and turned my key into my private elevator, some of my rage had dissipated. I could think more clearly on what to do about Sommers.

As my elevator approached my penthouse suite, I sensed Marcus and

Sam within. They must've had a successful hunt. Marcus stood facing the window, one hand behind his back, the other holding a bottle of freshly warmed blood.

'How'd it go?' I shucked my coat and dropped it on the sofa as I headed for the drinks cabinet. I had a full bottle of brandy in there, somewhere.

'Easy trail to follow.' The microwave pinged. Sam reached in to remove his own sustenance. 'Two youths, neither Pazu. They're confessing to the police right now.' He saluted with bottle in hand and brought it to his lips.

I loved mesmerisation, especially in situations like this. I was sure Delaney would be getting a call soon enough that they had two more culprits in custody.

Sam angled his head in my direction, sniffed and grinned. 'You've been hunting.'

'Had to. I know who's behind it all. Matt Sommers. I think he may be Pazu.' I found the brandy and poured myself a glass.

Sam stared at me as if I'd just become human.

Marcus spun around. 'You saw him? Saw the mark?'

'No, but it fits.' I told them my suspicions—the similarity between the surnames Sommerset and Sommers—and gave a brief report on what went down at the police station. 'The older boy had the mark. Has to be a Davidoff if Sommers is a Sommerset. But it was the younger one who picked out Sommers in a photograph. Sommers was the one who told them about The Residence and to go burn it down. Delaney issued a warrant for his arrest.' I downed two shots in quick succession.

'My estimation of Detective Delaney is somewhat improved.' Marcus's dry comment almost had me smiling.

Must be the brandy.

'There's something else,' I added. 'Madame Gilbert rang Laura.

Sommers showed up there with a warrant to question us about Jean-Philippe.'

Sam sank onto the sofa and knocked back the rest of his bottle. 'He's becoming a right royal pain in the arse.'

He didn't need to say it, and there was no accusation in his voice, but I felt it just the same: I should've killed Sommers when I had the chance.

I downed another shot.

'You're blaming yourself. Don't do that.' Marcus grabbed one of the chess-set stools and sat down, his back against the window.

'This could have been avoided.'

'My boy, you did what you believed was right. You showed him mercy. That he was unworthy of it is not your fault. Don't blame yourself. Had you known he was Pazu, you would've acted differently, and Laura would've understood … in time.'

'I should've seen it sooner.'

'Deus! That's so easy to say in hindsight. You'd never met a Pazu, had no experience with them. How were you to know? Even the most experienced of us who've fought them through the ages can be fooled. They're very adept at hiding.' He drank the last drops of blood in his bottle, placed it on the floor next to him, then moved a piece on the chessboard.

'That, and they can't let their target get away either. They study them, follow their movements, even ingratiate themselves with their kill before they strike. And once they do, they enter some kind of killing frenzy. They can't seem to stop.' Sam sat forward and twirled the empty bottle in his hands. 'You know, you're right, Alec. It should've clicked sooner.' He waved the bottle at me. 'Not you. I mean me. Actually, me and Jake. Come to think of it, Jake did notice. He hated the way Sommers kept tabs on Laura.' He huffed. 'It was right there, and we didn't see it. Ugh!' He knocked the bottle lightly against his head.

'There's still time to rectify it.' Marcus moved another piece on the chessboard.

Sam shifted further forward till he sat on the edge of the sofa. He blew a lock of his light-brown hair off his brow. 'If he's still in France, we can send a few of our men—'

'No. I believe Alec would like the pleasure.' Marcus gave me a half-smile, and, for a split second, I saw a glimpse of Luc in those features, before he returned his attention to the chessboard.

I swallowed down the knot in my throat. Damn, I still missed the old fox. He would've approved of his father's suggestion.

I shot Marcus a feral grin. 'He's mine, all right. Doubt he's still in France, though. He would've returned by now.'

I sank into the other end of the sofa from Sam and threw back another shot of brandy. Madame Gilbert's unease with Sommers's lack of surprise haunted me. 'Another thing. According to Madame Gilbert, Sommers sounded like he wasn't expecting to find us there.'

'When did she say that?' Sam placed the empty bottle on the side table and angled around to face me.

'When Sommers showed up at D'Antonville with a warrant to question us about Jean-Philippe. You were out hunting at the time.'

'All right, okay. Crazy Pazu! They don't know when to quit.'

'Especially this one.' Still, there was something else I couldn't quite put my finger on. 'What I want to know is: why did he bother travelling all that way? And if he did know we weren't going to be there, how the hell did he find out? We only made the decision at the last moment.' Brandy in one hand and crystal glass in the other, I stopped mid-pour, hit by a particularly troubling thought prompted by what Sam had said earlier. I put the bottle down. Pazu tracked their victim. Was Laura Sommers's prey? Is that why he'd been dating her? Had she been his intended victim? Had he been stalking her? There was no way he could have possibly known about our move to Scotland otherwise. He'd have to be tracking us. But how?

My stomach bottomed out as question after question crowded my mind, and, like the pieces of a puzzle, a horrifying image came together.

'He's tracking her. I'm convinced of it. Through her phone, I'll bet.' I shot to my feet. The serpent ring flared to life as I pictured Laura's face in my mind and called her name.

Her sweet voice answered.

Darling, get your phone. I have a feeling Sommers may have added a tracking device … some sort of spyware on there. I sent her a mental picture of her app page and what to look for.

What?!! No way. He couldn't have. Why would he do that? Her distress was palpable.

Because he's a Pazu, and that's what they do. I hadn't meant for that to rhyme.

I married a poet, and I didn't know it! She always knew how to make me smile.

'You, um….' Sam tapped his temple.

'Yeah, it's quite handy.'

'You think her phone's been jailbroken? Ask her if it's been running hot all the time or taking too long to switch off. Does the battery run down much faster than normal, or does the screen light up for nothing?' Sam said. 'Tell her to check her apps for any she doesn't recognise. Things like….' He named a few.

'Whoa, slow down a bit, Sam. I'll try and relay as much of that as I can. *Laura, here's what you have to do….* Sam walked us through it, and roughly ten minutes later, she'd found the spyware. 'Son of a bitch!'

Laura was silent at first before she let loose a string of cuss words I never thought she knew. I would have laughed if the situation hadn't been so serious. *How could he do this to me? Isn't it illegal? He's a cop for Pete's sakes! Of all the rotten, despicable…!*

I agree on all those counts, darling. I glanced at Sam. *Now let's get rid of it.* How do we get rid of it?' I asked Sam.

'Tell her to check her upgrades and download the latest one. That should reverse the intrusion. But to be really sure, tell her to reset her phone back to factory settings. I know it's a hassle to reinstall everything, but at least her phone'll be safe to use again.'

I relayed it all back to her.

She sighed. *Doing it…. To think, I'd trusted him. What a fool I was!* I couldn't mistake the hurt in her voice.

No, you weren't. You're no fool, Laura. He's a cunning bastard who took advantage of your goodness. He fooled us all, and now it's time to end it.

What do you mean, end it?

'Has she done it?' Sam asked.

I gave him a thumbs up.

Delaney's got an arrest warrant out for him for his part in the in the fire and deaths of our people.

Only a slight hesitation, then, *Good!*

'It's so weird seeing you staring off into space like that. If I didn't know you were mind talking, I'd think you were having a seizure.' Sam waved his hand in front of my face, then chuckled as I slapped it away. 'Saw Luc use it a few times, and he had that same faraway look. But unlike you, his lips moved, so I knew he was using the ring.'

'Well, now you know.'

Now I know what? Laura asked.

No, sorry, darling. That was meant for Sam. Seems my lips don't move when we mind talk. He was worried I may be having a seizure!

Her sweet laughter flowed through my mind, and the image of us intertwined in the most intimate of ways had me longing to end this business and be with her once again.

Hurry back. Miss you like crazy.

Miss you too. The serpent ring's eyes flared a moment, then died down, and Laura's beautiful face faded from my mind. It was an effort to let her go. Deep breath. I refocused. 'Laura's glad about Sommers's arrest warrant.'

Marcus turned his attention from his chess game and gave me a told-you-so smile, then moved another piece on the board. 'If this Sommers is a Sommerset, then he has the Pazu sword.'

Luc had told me that only one Pazu sword had been destroyed here: the Davidoff's. The other family had changed their name and gone into hiding. Who knew where they'd hidden the sword? Did Sommers know of it, or even where it was hidden? There was only one way to find out.

I glanced out the window. We still had around four hours of darkness before dawn. With Sommers's scent still fresh in my nostrils, it wouldn't be hard to locate his residence. The police were probably already on their way to arrest him. If the sword was there, we'd sense its presence at once. But what if it wasn't?

'There's no guarantee he's got it. It could be hidden anywhere.'

'No Pazu is ever far from their wretched sword. It protects them. Protects their families,' Sam said.

'Check.' Marcus moved another piece on the board.

From what I knew, none of our kind could come near, let alone touch, a Pazu sword. Within their houses, it acted like a protective guard, keeping us out. 'So if Sommers's great-grandfather wanted to protect his family, it'd be with the family rather than the individual.' It clicked. 'It must be at his mother's house.' I knew where it was. Laura had been there once or twice.

Marcus moved another piece on the chessboard. 'Checkmate.'

Could it be that easy? But it posed another problem. 'If the sword is there, we'll need Richard's help to get it out and destroy it. We can't touch the thing.'

'Get him to meet us there.' Marcus laid the king down at the foot of his queen and stood. 'We don't have much time. I do not want to see an armed Pazu.'

'Neither do I, but we just might if Sommers is there. What then?' I had no intention of going there unprepared. 'Do we have a Plan B?'

'Only this.' Marcus retrieved a silver dagger from inside his boot. 'I keep it dipped in a tiny vial of pure opium in the sheath. In the past it's been the only thing to have any effect on a Pazu. It knocks them out for a few minutes.'

'Sounds like a plan.' Hopefully, we wouldn't have to resort to it.

Both Sam and I knew Sommers's scent, so it didn't take us long to pick it up and track him to his apartment building. He wasn't there. Nor was the sword. Not unexpected, but it was better to be sure. He'd been there recently as his scent was fresh. We were then able to follow it to his family home in Glebe, in the inner west of the city.

At that time of the night, the suburban streets were empty. Shops were closed, apart from the Seven Eleven, whose sleepy cashier yawned behind the counter as we sped past. We rounded a corner, and Sommers's scent strengthened. This was the street. Only one house still had its lights on, and he was inside.

We approached. The presence of the Pazu sword was unmistakable. The closer I stepped toward the front gate, the weaker I became, until I could barely stand.

On either side of me, Marcus and Sam were also struggling to remain upright. They dragged their feet just to reach the front fence. From there, we could go no further.

'He was a damned Pazu all the time!' I said between clenched teeth and dropped to my knees.

The porch light flicked on, the door opened and Sommers stood there, a gleaming sword gripped tightly in his hand. His eyes had always been light, but now they appeared almost deathly pale as if life had receded from them.

'He's gone full on Pazu,' Sam uttered as he sank to his haunches beside me.

Only Marcus remained upright.

He threw his dagger. It embedded in Sommers's right shoulder. Sommers staggered back but recovered, pulled the dagger out and dropped it to the ground. His expression remained unchanged, as if he was impervious to the pain. He hadn't even bled. The wound instantly sealed.

'Is that normal?'

Marcus nodded. 'Only the strongest Pazu feel no pain and heal like us. It's the sword. It bonds with them. The Matthew Sommers you knew is no longer there.'

Sommers lifted the sword high and came down the stairs toward us.

'How long before the opiate works?'

'Deus! It should have by now.'

Wonderful. So much for Plan B.

Sam groaned and doubled over yet he still managed to whip out his own dagger and throw it. It never reached its mark. Sommers deflected it with the flat of the sword and it landed somewhere in the neighbour's bushes.

That blasted sword put us at his mercy. We couldn't touch it, let alone take it away from him. We were weak: he was strong, and he had the vampire-killing sword.

We were in trouble.

A cold wave spread from my toes up to my head. It turned the blood in my veins to ice. I could die this night, and Laura and our babe would be left alone to face this monster. The chill deepened and settled in my stomach.

We needed help: human help.

I glanced up at the dark houses around us. Time to wake up people.

'Sommers, put the weapon down,' I shouted at the top of my voice as I slowly crept back to create more of a distance between us. The further away from the sword, the stronger I felt.

Sommers was now on the bottom step, eyes glazed, both hands gripping the deadly Pazu weapon. 'I was coming to look for you, and here you are. Count the seconds, Munro.'

He jumped the fence and swung the sword straight at my head.

I ducked as the blade sliced close to my scalp. It thudded into the tree behind me.

Alec! Laura's voice screamed in my mind. *The serpent's eyes are black! You're in danger. I know it.*

Sommers has the Pazu sword. He's trying to kill us.

Weak as he was, Marcus tackled him, grunting as they hit the ground and rolled. Sam and I yelled out and tried to help, but weakness forced me to my knees.

One or two houses lit up. Not enough.

What can I do? What can I do? her panicked voice screamed.

'Unnatural bastards! Kill the lot of you.' Sommers stood over us. He brought the sword toward Marcus's head.

My limbs trembling with weakness, and the sweat pouring off me, I rose and kicked Sommers's legs out from beneath him. Then I collapsed. He went down, missing Marcus's head by millimetres.

Pray! I completely opened my mind, so Laura could see through my eyes. I heard her sharp intake of breath.

Doors were opening. Voices around us.

'Look ... look what that guy's got. Is that a ... sword?' one said, as he leaned over his fence to get a better view.

'Someone call the police.'

It was echoed around, and soon more than half the street, some in dressing gowns and various states of dress, congregated near the Sommers's house. Many were filming the scene on their phones.

Thank you!

Sommers sprang to his feet. He gazed around at the gathering crowd, and smiled. 'Nothing like an audience to get the juices going.' He lifted his hands, sword gripped tightly in one. 'Who wants to see a vampire die?'

'You're crazy, man,' someone called out.

Sommers's smile widened. He brandished the wretched blade and brought it down, stopping it a hair's breadth from my neck.

Laura screamed.

'I want to enjoy every minute of this.' He brought his face down to mine. 'You're not going to die quick. I want to see the fear, the terror in your eyes as I take you apart, piece by piece.'

Beads of sweat trickled into my eyes and my body trembled from weakness as Sommers laid the flat blade of the sword against my cheek.

Don't you touch him!' Laura screamed.

I couldn't move. My thoughts were with Laura and our babe, who I would probably never see. I swallowed hard and closed my eyes awaiting his blow.

Stay alive! Stay alive and come back to me.

Laura.

'Nah, I'm keeping you for last. You're my dessert. Your fanghead friends can go first.'

'Aarghh!' He kicked me hard then strode to where Marcus knelt, his head bowed low to the ground.

Alec! I love you! Please … try to move, crawl away. Anything. Stay alive!

Just to see her face again, to hold her in my arms…. I grit my teeth, dug my nails into the ground and clawed my way along the grass, away from Sommers.

Sirens!

Yes! The police are coming. The relief in Laura's voice reflected my own. But they weren't here yet.

'Ready to meet your maker?' Sommers stood poised above Marcus, sword held high.

No! Grandfather!

I held my breath, anger coursing through me at my utter helplessness.

People screamed. Some threw rocks and stones at him. Many met their mark but he appeared impervious, the rocks bouncing off him without leaving a mark.

More sirens. Flashing lights. Uniformed police spilled from cars and paddy wagons, tasers and guns aimed. They surrounded Sommers as he stood over Marcus, shouting at him to drop the weapon. From their talk, they were reluctant to take down one of their own.

'C'mon DI, put the thing down. Everything's going to be okay. Just drop it.'

He didn't.

Ignoring them, his gaze flew to me. 'Looks like you'll be first after all.' He kicked Marcus aside, strode over to me and planted his foot on my chest. The tip of the sword was aimed directly over my throat.

No! Leave him alone!

'Put the weapon down! Now!' police voices yelled.

'Just … shoot him!' I croaked out. Drained of nearly all strength, I relied on the police to do their job and hoped Sommers didn't plunge his sword into me before they did.

His features twisted in a semblance of a smile. 'I want to savour this moment.'

'Nooooo! Matt! Don't do it! Please, please, please …'

'Take all ... the time ... you need.' I turned my head toward the police. 'Shoot ... him!'

'Taser! Taser! Taser!' Police fired and Sommers cried out, his body contorting and jerking with electrical shocks.

The sword dropped from Sommers's hand, nicking my throat as it fell to stick in the grass. My neck stung. That was close. Any nearer to the middle of my throat, and I would've been skewered. Within an instant, the wound began to heal.

Two police grabbed me and dragged me to safety as others pinned Sommers to the ground. 'You hurt, mate?' one asked me.

'I'm fine. He missed.' Her voice echoing in my mind, Laura cried with relief. I sent to her, *I'm all right, darling. It's all right.*

'Not from what I saw.' The cop's gaze focused on my neck and down the length of the cut on my coat, brows drawing together when he saw no corresponding injuries.

'Good leather.' Far enough away from the Pazu blade, some of my strength returned, and I was able to stand and watch the evolving scene.

Marcus and Sam joined me. 'Deus! Glad to see you alive, my boy.' Marcus thumped me on the back.

'That makes two of us.'

Little did the police know they were doing our job for us. Soon Sommers would be arrested, and that damn sword confiscated. With any luck, I'd arrange for Richard to obtain it for us sometime later so it could be destroyed. I couldn't have planned it better.

A smile stole across my face.

Amidst all the shouting, and pinned to the ground, Sommers turned his head toward me.

'You fucking fanghead!' He threw off the men holding him down like they were made of paper and shot to his feet. He grabbed the sword. Holding it high, he came straight for me.

Oh! Laura sucked in a breath.

'Drop it! Drop it or I'll shoot!'

'Taser him again!'

Three tasers hit their target. He should've been completely incapacitated. There was enough power in those Tasers to floor an elephant, yet he still managed to stagger to his feet before finally collapsing.

It was unnerving to see a Pazu in all its strength.

Another police car swerved to a stop near us. The door swung open, and Delaney charged out. He squatted next to Sommers, who lay writhing on the ground. 'Matt! Look at me.'

'Kill the ... fangheads!' Sommers stopped twitching. He studied Delaney a moment, then tried to rise.

More police closed in, Tasers at the ready, some with guns.

'Stay where you are, Matt. Don't move.' Delaney placed a hand on his shoulder and kept him on the ground while he fished out handcuffs. 'You have to come with me. We have the youths who burnt down the Lebrettan place. They confessed everything. We know you're involved. I'm sorry to do this, but' —he took on an official tone—'Matthew Sommers, you're under arrest for complicity in arson with intent to murder.'

Sommers snarled, pushed him aside and sprang to his feet, sword in hand. 'I thought you were on my side. You understood. They're vampires ... fangheads. They're not human!'

Delaney paled and took a step back. 'Put the weapon down, Matt.'

'If you don't get out of my way, I'll have to kill you too.' He pointed the sword at Delaney's chest.

Shots rang out. Sommers fell to the ground, his body riddled with bullets. Not even a Pazu could survive that. Yet, in spite of our enmity, I automatically surged forward to give what medical aid I could. But the power of the sword held me back.

His heartbeat stuttered then fell silent, and I sensed the withdrawal of his essence.

Sommers was dead.

Laura's breath hitched. Since we were still psychically connected, the same tremor of shock that ran through her hit me. I hadn't expected this.

Oh Matt! She cried.

I'm sorry you had to see that. I did not wish that for him. I had more like several years in jail for him in mind or a complete mind wipe with no chance of reversal.

Neither did I. I ... feel sick..... Her presence retreated from my mind.

After the initial shock passed, I couldn't but thank whatever providence arranged it this way. His death did not come at my hands. I could look Laura in the eye with a clear conscience.

The police seized the Pazu sword and bagged it. Marcus, Sam and I stood at a distance and watched as the ambulance arrived and took Sommers's body away. I told them to head back to Bondi, to let Amanda and our Brethren know the danger was over.

Delaney came to me. For a few moments neither of us spoke.

'Off the record,' he began, voice strained with emotion. 'Tell me how this started.'

I did.

When I ended, he turned to me with red-rimmed eyes. 'I don't hold you responsible for what happened. The Matt Sommers I knew was not the same man I saw tonight. He was ready to kill me, and he nearly killed you.'

What could I say? I simply nodded.

'I've seen the work you do in the hospital, the lives you've saved and the glowing testimonials. You strike me as a good man, considering what you are. But I've arrested many killers who came across as good men.'

So why should I be any different? He didn't have to say the words. The implication was there all the same. At least he was being candid.

'John Philip Reynold. Portrait artist. Painting of his is hanging in a gallery in Double Bay. It's of Laura. The artist seems to be missing. Tell me what you know about it.'

My stomach took a deep dive. Damn Jean-Philippe! 'I believe you know the answer to that already.'

'I'd prefer to hear it from you.'

Two choices faced me: either mesmerise him or tell him the truth and hope for the best. If I resorted to the former, then it wouldn't be too hard to destroy the evidence by breaking into the gallery, stealing the portrait and wiping the minds of the staff.

It was a definite option.

But I thought I'd try the second option first. Delaney had been fair with me all this time. The least I could do was return the favour. I told him my side of the story.

Delaney listened, nodded once or twice, sharp but desperately sad eyes locked on mine. 'I see,' he finally said. 'I'm dropping the inquiry against you. Go away, Dr Munro. Don't let our paths cross again.'

Two nights later, and we were back on the jet, flying out to Scotland. The Brethren had been placated knowing the Pazu killers had been caught and would be spending a long time in jail. They weren't demanding a new princeps, which was the main thing.

Before we left, I'd arranged for the Pazu sword to mysteriously disappear from the police evidence room in a few months' time—after everything had died down. Amanda and Richard would see to its destruction. As far as I was concerned, the Pazu threat was over.

I sat back and closed my eyes, letting my thoughts wander to Drunvela ... to Laura.

Peace for now ... I hoped.

CHAPTER 26 - CURSE'S END

Five Months Later

LAURA

'Ooh!' I think I just had a contraction.

Alec and I had been sitting on the sofa in our suite, oohing and aahing over our baby's ultrasound pictures. She looked so perfect with a sweetly rounded head and button nose. So adorable. I was recalling the day, just having gone twenty weeks and squirming as Alec squirted the cold gel across my skin.

'Sorry, darling. I'd warm it up if I could.'

He and Jake had turned one of the guest rooms into a makeshift maternity ward. Every conceivable device for monitoring the baby's growth and my health had been purchased, including a state-of-the-art ultrasound machine. They'd even set up a mini ward in the tomb itself, in case there was a complication.

I prayed there wouldn't be.

I'd linked my arms behind my head. 'Pity summer's so short here. She'll be born when it's already freezing. Out there.' I jerked my thumb in the direction of the witch's tomb.

'That's Scotland,' he said with a grin, gliding the scanner thing across my swelling belly. 'Perfect.' His grin grew and lit his face as a clear image of our baby appeared on the ultrasound. 'It's a …' Mouth still open, he studied me, one eyebrow raised. 'Want to know what the sex of our baby is?'

Excitement rushed through me, and I raised myself up. 'Show me and let me guess.'

He moved the curser thing around to give me a clearer view.

'It's a girl, right?'

'And she's sucking her thumb.' His grin couldn't have been wider.

Such a rush of love washed over me as I'd never experienced before. If not for the icky gel, I would've run my arms over my belly to give her a mummy hug.

Our baby.

I couldn't take my eyes from the screen. A little girl. My heart leapt, and I remembered a scene, a thought Alec had shared with me—so long ago now, it seemed—of a raven-haired, blue-eyed baby girl giggling while being bounced on her father's lap. And here, on the screen, was that precious little girl. Had he had a premonition?

'Did you know we'd have a girl?'

He shook his head. 'It'd just popped in from nowhere.'

We'd exchanged glances, wondering if it was a coincidence. I tucked that thought away for later.

As we lovingly gazed at our baby's first photos, Alec became silent, and his smile faded. He angled his body to face me fully. 'Laura, do you remember when we discussed what could happen when the curse is lifted?'

'Sure.' I waved my hand with the serpent ring. 'These little beauties will probably give up the ghost.' I wondered if they'd uncoil and fall off or just turn into an ordinary piece of jewellery I could slip on and off at will. 'Will the telepathy thing go as well? I'm going to miss it if it does.'

He shrugged. 'We'll soon find out.' He gave me a wicked grin. 'It was fun getting into your head.'

'Until I knew how to block you out.'

He chuckled, for sure recalling the many times he knew what I was thinking before reluctantly sharing with me how he did it.

Sneaky vampire.

He became serious again. 'There's something else. There's … a possibility the ward will fail too. Luc's rings are connected to the witch's magic. When one fades, so will the other.'

'Makes sense, I suppose. We haven't really needed the ward since we arrived. It's been quiet. And afterwards, it won't really matter. Will it? There'll be nothing left to hide.'

'True too.' He sounded convinced, but the way his brows were drawn down and that faraway look in his eyes meant he had doubts.

'So, what are you planning?' Or rather, what had he already planned.

'I've asked Dougal to post extra armed sentries at the ward's edge and along the route back here. Traps have been set, too.'

I was about to ask if there was something he should tell me, like, was there another rebellion brewing, when 'Aaaahhh!' The film dropped from my hand as my first cramp hit. If I didn't know better, I'd say the muscles in my lower back and abdomen were doing their best to form a pretzel. 'I think … I've just had a contraction.'

For a second, Alec just gawked at me like a deer caught in headlights. 'But you're not due for anther two weeks.'

'Sorry. I've got no control over this,' I shrugged. 'It's early stages, anyway.'

For the next few hours, my contractions increased until they were about every twenty minutes apart. Alec paced our suite when he was not following me around, timing each one. Then they reached less than five minutes apart. He helped ease me into the sofa as my back ached too much to stand.

'Let's see how far you're dilated,' he said after the last forty-five seconds contraction.

I lay back and let him examine me.

Someone banged on the door. 'Laura? You 'kay?'

'Not to worry, Kari. I'm fine. Just early stages of labour.'

Despite my assurances, the door burst open, and a cyclone in hot pink burst in. 'Labour? That means it's coming now, right?' Kari's eyes could've doubled for dinner plates, they were that wide. She had a front-row view of my fanny.

'Kari, shut the door!'

'You're about eight centimetres dilated and'—his eyes widened—'and ninety percent effaced.' His gaze panned to mine. 'Honey, I think we need to get you down to the sepulchre.'

Whenever Alec called me honey, he was worried. More than a century earlier, he had lost his first wife and baby in childbirth. It haunted him. I could see it in his eyes.

He pulled down my dress and helped me sit up. 'It's time, Laura.'

It was late autumn, and although it hadn't yet snowed, the ground was frosty, the air icy. Sam and Dougal had spent the previous months setting up a temporary generator for the medical equipment and lighting they'd installed inside. Everything to make me as safe and comfortable as possible. But it was still a tomb, a cold mausoleum stinking of death. I had no intention of lying on a stone sarcophagus until absolutely necessary, when I knew the baby was definitely coming.

The door burst open, and Jake and Dougal rushed in. Behind them, others stood looking in.

'Laura—' Jake began.

I held up my hand. 'I'm fine. Really. No need to be worried.'

'Och, lass.' Dougal knelt by my side and took my hand. 'We couldn't help listening. We can feel it's time.' His gaze darted to my belly. 'Birthing's a serious matter. We ... I want you and the wee bairn safe.' His eyes were filled with concern. That was Dougal. Over the time I'd spent in Drunvela, I'd come to love him as a brother.

Touched, I kissed his cheek, and while Alec and Jake conferred, I asked him to help me up. I needed to go to the bathroom. As he did, the effort caused a strange popping sensation. A trickle of fluid flowed down my thighs and my legs, creating a small puddle on the carpet.

'Oh no!' I glanced from the floor to Alec. 'My waters just broke.'

Kari's mouth dropped open, and conversation stopped as all eyes turned to me. Then everything happened at once.

'Kari, get Laura's wrap.' At Alec's command, she dashed into the bedroom, and within the space of a heartbeat, she was back, wrapping it round me like I was a parcel.

'Ready?' Alec's concerned eyes bored into mine. I didn't need the mind-reading abilities of the ring to know what was going on in his head—the fear that history was repeating itself.

'As I'll ever be.' I smoothed back the hair from his brow. 'I'm going to be fine. Our baby's going to be fine. Everything's going to be okay. Do you hear me, Alec Munro?' I believed that with every fibre of my being.

A tight smile graced his lips, and with the slightest of nods, he scooped me up and ran, putting into action the procedure we'd been rehearsing for months.

'Breathe, Lolly, breathe.' Kari ran alongside us, actually doing the motions. She'd been watching more pre-natal videos than I had.

'I'm okay, Kari. Really.' Until the next contraction.

Alec's jaw was set hard. Something else was bothering him. Had it to do with what he and Jake had been talking about? 'What did Jake tell you?'

Alec darted me a look then gazed ahead again as he sped down the corridor, the stairs, and through the great hall. 'Dougal's men sighted the lamia on the edge of the ward.'

No, no. Not now. My heart plummeted. 'How did it know we were here? It can't get in, can it?'

'Not as long as the ward's functioning. Wretched thing must've followed our scent.'

'And if it fails? We'll be unprotected.'

'Dougal's men are monitoring it.'

'Get the generator going!' Alec called to the sentries as we sprang out into the courtyard.

Cold air hit my cheeks.

All was pitch-black until the generator whirred to life. Inside the sepulchre, lights came on. Various pieces of medical equipment were assembled on tables along the walls. There was even a clock.

I wondered what the witch, Eithne, thought of these recent additions.

A layer of thick blankets covered the stone sarcophagus. Alec gently laid me on it and placed a pillow under my head. Other blankets sat folded nearby. I didn't need them as Kari placed hot water bottles under my feet.

Alec donned his scrubs.

Jake came in and did the same. 'How you doing, kid?'

'Fine, I guess.'

'Zero hour.'

Wish he didn't put it quite that way. It was like waiting for a bomb to go off. 'Baby hour, which could be still a few hours away.' Mum—my aunt Eilene—said her baby had come roughly five hours after her waters broke. But my mother, Judy, gave birth to me less than forty minutes after hers broke. I hoped my experience would be like Judy's. Who wanted a long labour?

Jake gave me a nod, then went around checking the equipment.

Alec took my pulse and checked my blood pressure and temperature. He then placed a monitor on my belly. 'Baby's doing fine.' He sat at my side and held my hand. I smoothed the crease from between his brows. 'Stop worrying. We've rehearsed this so many times and for every possible contingency. You've got everything down pat.'

'I don't take anything for granted.'

'I know you don't.' I kissed my fingertip and pressed it to his lips. He clasped my hand and kept it there, kissing it back.

'Good to go.' Jake came to my side. 'How are the contractions going? How far apart?'

I was about to answer when the next one hit, and I nearly bit through my lower lip.

Alec held my hands in both of his as I crushed his fingers in my grip.

Jake drew a curtain over the sepulchre's entrance, giving me privacy from all those who'd gathered.

'Lolly, I'm out here if you need me.' Dear Kari. How could she possibly help? But I was glad she was near.

'All's good, Kari,' I was able to say when the last contraction ended.

'You're at least 9cm dilated, honey.' Alec got me prepped.

'Hopefully it won't take too long.' I caressed my belly, crooning to my baby within. 'C'mon, sweetheart. Mummy wants to see you.'

For the next four hours, I went through every relaxation and breathing technique I'd read about. Then the real pain began, like someone had taken hold of my insides and was twisting them into a massive knot. Mamma! Insides contorting, like a washcloth being wrung out, squeezed dry till there was nothing left in it to squeeze. Why hadn't I asked for an epidural sooner? Now it was too late. I always thought I had a high pain threshold. 'Aarrggh!'

Until now.

The urge to push was unbelievable. 'Baby's coming!'

The cycle of contractions increased until I couldn't tell when they began and ended. It was one long pull downwards, tearing my insides apart.

My eyes squeezed shut against the pain. I imagined myself reclining in a hammock on a tropical beach, the waves gently lapping at the sand beneath me.

But that did bugger all for me!

'C'mon, honey. One more push.'

Gritting my teeth, I took a deep breath and pushed until I thought my body would break. 'Puuussshing! Aaarrgghh!' Then blessed relief as my baby slid free of my body. 'Ah!' I lay back, breathing hard and utterly exhausted.

My baby's cries rent the air and echoed around that stony chamber. A great cheer arose outside.

Alec's eyes filled with tears. He cupped my face and kissed me. 'She's perfect!'

I wept.

Jake came to my other side, cradling our baby. He'd cleaned her and wrapped her in a blanket. He handed her to me. She opened her eyes and smiled.

I sucked in a breath, seeing my baby girl for the first time. Grey eyes. Stunning storm-grey eyes locked onto me. And she was smiling. No baby, as far as I knew, smiled at birth. My heart filled to overflowing with love for this tiny new human being, and a deep warmth spread though my soul.

'She knows her mother.' Jake stood proudly by, arms crossed over his chest, grinning from ear to ear. He then went to the entrance and popped his head through the curtain to those outside. 'It's a girl. Grey eyes. The curse is over!'

More cheering.

Tears trickled down the sides of my face. How I would've loved for Luc and Judy to be here to witness this moment. For Luc to hold his baby granddaughter and see the fulfillment of all his work. He should've been here. It wasn't fair. And just then, someone whispered in my mind, *Well done, ma petite*. Gentle peace, like a comforting blanket, enveloped me, and I knew then that all was well. That somewhere, he and Judy knew and they were happy.

I looked at my husband, who gazed at his tiny daughter with such love and wonder, and I thought my heart would burst with too much joy.

'Welcome to the world, my wee darling,' Alec crooned. He leaned down and kissed her tiny head.

'Say hello to you father,' I said.

'She's beautiful.'

'Like her mother.' Alec's own eyes swam. He stroked the length of my face, leaned down and kissed me. 'You were marvelous.'

'You helped.' We both grinned.

'She has grey eyes. Yours were lavender when you were born.'

I had been born under the curse, its sign being my eye colour. But the curse had no hold on our child. She had broken it.

Briefly, I closed my eyes and thanked providence. No more Ingeniie. No more Ritual. No more fear of being abducted to serve as blood slave to rival vampire clans.

She was free.

Alec sat next to me, one hand cradling our baby's head the other next to my shoulder. 'She's free to choose her own destiny.'

'My one wish for her is that she may be as happy as her mother.'

Alec swallowed hard, his eyes filled with such love as he looked from our daughter to me and back again. He leaned down and kissed her, the backs of his fingers tenderly caressing her plump little cheek. As his gaze panned back to me, an expression of utter astonishment crossed his face. 'Your eyes are changing. They're ... green.'

Jake came to us. 'Laura, you need to push one last time. Get rid of the afterbirth.'

With my baby on my breast, I did as Jake asked, my brain processing what Alec had just said. My eyes were no longer lavender. 'Do you have a mirror?'

Alec looked around. 'Ah, no. Maybe this will do.' He handed me an empty metal tray. The back of it was polished enough to see my reflection.

Emerald-green eyes stared back at me. It was surreal. Would I ever get used to it? 'It's definitely over then. I'm no longer Ingenii.' And with that came the understanding that, like my daughter, my blood was free of the Ingenii mutation. 'Does that mean I'm completely human?'

'I don't know.' Alec studied me. 'Do you feel any different?'

I peered around to read the tiny labels on some of the instruments ... and couldn't. Too small. Nor could I hear any of the conversations taking place outside the sepulchre. The hubbub of voices and murmurs, yes, but no distinct speech. And most of all, I couldn't hear my child's tiny beating heart. My heart sank. Those vampire gifts had been handy, even if for a fleeting while. Now, they were gone.

I cuddled my baby to me and sighed. Here today, gone tomorrow. 'The extra hearing ... sight' —I shook my head— 'gone. I'm human.'

'That's not a bad thing, darling.'

'No, it's not.' On impulse I reached out to pull aside Alec's shirt. 'Your tattoo.' Would that disappear? It, too, was a symbol of the curse he'd inherited through Luc. As we watched, the sword-and-serpent tattoo slowly faded until nothing remained to mar Alec's skin. I sucked in a breath. 'It's gone.'

Jake did the same, ripping off his scrubs and the T-shirt beneath. Both he and Alec grinned at each other ... and laughed. Full-bellied laughs that ripped through the chamber and beyond. They shook hands and slapped arms. 'Think Marcus has noticed?' Jake asked.

'Go ask him.'

I didn't know what I expected, but everything seemed so ... normal. No eerie lights or phantom voices, no humming or ringing bells. Apart from the excited voices outside, all was quiet.

The curse passed without even a whimper, except for my baby's cries. She started to wail. Her little face puckered up and her screams filled the chamber.

Healthy lungs.

I put her to my breast and her sweet little mouth latched on immediately.

A tickling on my finger. As I looked, the serpent ring uncoiled and slipped off onto the blanket. Alec's ring did the same, dropping to the ground and bouncing on the stony tiles.

'It's really over,' I said.

His smile said it all.

'I can't stand it anymore! Lolly, are you decent? I wanna come in.' Kari's voice rang out.

I was still exposed ... the soiled sheets ... and feeding my baby.

'Wait!' Alec called out. He strode to the entrance and popped his head through the curtain. 'She's feeding the baby, right now. Give us an hour.'

Contentment flowed through me. I played with her tiny fingers as she fed, enjoying the feel of her velvety skin and the weight of her body in my arms.

Alec and Jake cleared everything up and covered me and the baby with a clean blanket.

'It's been an hour. Can I come in now?' Kari's excited voice came from outside.

I nodded, and Jake pulled back the curtain.

Kari burst in, her pretty pixie face alight with excitement and curiosity. Smiling faces behind her peered in, Dominik among them.

'Can I come in too?'

Alec grinned and, with a jerk of his head, invited him in. Wherever Alec went, Dom was never too far away.

Hands behind his back, he shyly came to the foot of the stone sarcophagus on which I lay and craned his neck to get a good view of my baby. 'Are they always that small?'

I laughed. He'd obviously never seen a newborn before. 'Yep.'

'Aww … she's soooo cute!' Kari clasped her hands beneath her chin, rocking from side to side as she gazed, all starry-eyed, at my baby. Her arms shot out, fingers wiggling. 'Can I hold her?'

My baby was comfortably curled up in my arms; her eyes wide open, seemingly checking out her mother. She looked so content that I didn't want to disturb the moment. 'Wait a bit, Kari. I don't want her to cry and she might if I move her.'

She sighed and flopped on the end of the stone sarcophagus that served as my makeshift bed. 'I always wanted a baby. But …' She shrugged.

My heart ached for her. Being a vampire, Kari would never have a child. Her womb was dead. Just as quickly, her mood changed when she took a long, hard look at me, and her mouth dropped. 'Your eyes are green.'

'It's the new non-Ingenii me.'

'It's freaky.'

'You'll get used it, Kari,' Alec said.

'What's her name?'

'Yeah, what's her name,' Dominik echoed.

Kari slapped his upper arm.

Alec and I exchanged a glance. We had and yet we hadn't exactly decided on a name, although we'd played around with one—Sophie. It had been Alec's mother's name, and we both liked it. It meant "wisdom."

'Sophie,' I murmured and hugged her to me, savoring her sweet newborn scent. I could've happily sniffed her all night.

'Sophie, Sophie,' Kari crooned as she gently stroked her tiny head.

'Kari, check your tattoo. Bet it's gone,' I winked at her. Being Jake's juvy, she'd inherited the tattoo just as Alec had from Luc, and Dougal from Marcus.

She sneaked a peek beneath her flower-print cropped gym top. I tried not to giggle when she caught Dominik trying to have a look too and elbowed him roughly out of the way.

'Dom, get over here.' Alec grabbed him and pulled him over to his side.

'Ohhhh! It's all gone.' Kari let the top snap back to her chest when she was done. 'I kinda liked it. Made me look bad arse, you know?'

Alec laughed. 'Kari, nobody could be bored with you.'

I snuck a look at Jake, who'd just walked back in. He must've heard what Alec had said, for he looked right at Kari and smiled, then seemed to check himself and began packing up the equipment.

I did not get that man. What was going on in his head?

Just then, the crowd at the entrance parted, and Marcus, Sam, Cal and Terens strode in. They'd removed their shirts. Not a single serpent tattoo was in sight, but each had their sword strapped to their sides, except for Terens. His two were strapped to his back.

I sent up a silent prayer for the ward to hold so they wouldn't have to use them.

A strange shimmer filled the chamber, and a hushed female voice uttered the word "Choose."

The witch.

This time, I'm sure everyone heard it. For Dominik wasn't the only one with mouth agape, trying to locate the source of the voice.

Kari and Dougal together with Alec, Marcus and the rest of the men sank to their knees and bowed their heads. My grandfather and his men had waited nearly two thousand years, for this moment. Would any of them choose death over life?

Heart pounding, I waited. The shimmering receded, and a deafening silence descended. After what seemed like an eternity, one by one they raised their heads and looked about at each other.

A slow smile spread across Terens's face. 'So, I'm still stuck with you all, eh!'

Sam elbowed him as he rose. 'Eternity brother, whether you like it or not.'

I released the breath I'd been holding as relief flooded through me. I was afraid that, just perhaps, one of them—my grandfather, in particular—might have chosen to be released from such a long life. The thought horrified me. I'd lost Luc and Judy, and I didn't want to lose him too. Yet I also knew that after nearly two thousand years, death would've been a blessed release for him. I couldn't blame him if he took that choice because the ending of the curse didn't really change all that much for him. For any of them. Luc had been right to be angry about the whole thing. There really was no gain. If anything, they were losing the precious hours of daylight they'd enjoyed all these months. And now with my blood reverting to back to human, there was no chance any of them would ever enjoy the daylight again.

I blinked back tears.

'Don't be sad, mea neptis.' Marcus approached and touched my cheek. An affectionate smile graced his face when his lips brushed

Sophie's head.

She wriggled and slightly angled her head toward him.

'It's not fair. Nothing changes for you.'

'Except that now I have the choice to die if I so wish.'

'You don't, do you?'

'I have decided to live … as you can see.' He cracked a smile.

'We all did, pet. I like being an uncle, and now I'm one twice over.' Terens gave me a wink, the diamond stud in his ear blinking roguishly at me. 'Who else is going to teach her sword skills?'

'Not for a long time yet,' Alec replied.

'Our turn.' Cal and Sam jostled Terens out of the way to get a look at their new baby niece. 'Hey, cuteness. It's your Uncle Ca-al,' he sing-songed. 'When you're old enough, I'll teach you how to throw a dagger.'

'Which I hope she'll never need to use.' Sophie was no Ingenii, but her father was still princeps of the Brethren, and he had enemies.

'And her Uncle Sam will show her how to destroy her enemies with the click of a finger.'

Who would have thought it? These great and ancient vampire warriors showering gifts on a tiny baby like some kind of fanged fairy godfathers.

There was movement at the entrance. One of Dougal's men ran to him and whispered in his ear. He'd stepped back to lean against the sepulchre's entrance, a beaming smile on his face. That vanished and he turned and disappeared into the night.

Alec noticed it too, for his mouth tightened, and his gaze focused on what was going on outside. He brought the green serpent ring up to his face, and he swallowed. 'Be back in a sec. I need to check something.'

As the guys cooed at Sophie, Alec slid past them to the entrance to look up at the night sky. His shoulders stiffened. That was enough to send warning bells through me. Something was wrong.

Dougal re-appeared, alarm written all over his face. He signalled to

Marcus, who left my side to speak with him.

Even though my vampire hearing was gone, they weren't that far away for me not to overhear.

'Ward's down. It's coming in.'

'Keep it contained. Use the nets. We'll join you.'

The lamia!

Dougal nodded and sped off.

Marcus turned to Alec. 'Get Laura and the baby into the safety of the fortress.' Then he too was gone.

As one, Terens, Cal and Sam left my side and followed Marcus. The whoosh of metal being drawn from hard leather scabbards echoed in the night.

The blood drained from my face.

'Old Stinky's here?' Kari's face froze in an expression of horror before she crouched down and pulled a dagger from her boot. 'Any chance your blood's still toxic, Lolly?'

I shook my head. 'I doubt it.'

Alec turned and our eyes met. We'd discussed the ramifications of me becoming human again. I clutched the blood vial hanging around my neck, and smiled. It was an immortality elixir. A gift from my father, Luc. He knew I'd need it, and I intended taking it.

'Here.' Jake pulled out two swords from under a table and threw one to Alec.

He caught it and strapped it on. 'I half expected this ... but still, I was hoping the green ring wasn't tied to the witch's one.'

'Luc had never been clear on that.' Jake stripped out of his scrubs and into leather pants and a grey long-sleeved T-shirt. 'Kept it to himself.'

Alec helped me rise from my makeshift bed. My legs were wobbly, but I could stand.

'Kari, the baby bag.' I pointed to the rucksack on one of the tables.

We'd trawled scores of baby websites ordering everything online in preparation for the day. Dougal's men had been running relays to collect our deliveries from a post box address in Stirling. Only a few days ago we'd packed the rucksack and left it here in readiness. 'Take out a nappy, blanket and cap. Sophie has to be rugged up before being taken out into the cold. You'll have to do it.'

We'd both spent endless hours practicing on dolls, so we knew how to put on a nappy and bath and dress a baby. She'd taken such pleasure in it and had done it so well that I had absolute confidence placing my baby into her care.

Sophie whimpered, her sweet little face scrunched up in protest when I laid her down between my feet and Kari expertly bundled her up.

Jake and Dominik stood guard at the entrance while Alec helped me dress. Kari placed Sophie back into my arms. Alec scooped me up, kissed my brow, and we stepped into the frigid night air. A light drizzle fell.

'Dom, stay behind me,' Alec said, as the boy whipped ahead to fall in line with Kari and Jake. I knew Dom's behavior annoyed the heck out of her and I couldn't stop an inward smile.

The large timber back doors were ahead. Just a few more metres and we'd be in the warmth of the great hall where a cosy fire awaited.

Shouts came from outside the walls, followed by the whoosh of massive wings. Dougal, Marcus, and the rest of the men ran into the courtyard, throwing nets up high. Kari sniffed the air … and snarled. From the dark, claws descended throwing men violently aside.

The lamia! My stomach dropped. I clutched my baby closer. Only a couple more steps and we'd be safe.

With a sickening thud, the lamia landed in front of us. Massive outstretched leather wings blocked out the light … and our escape. Its yellowy eyes homed in on me and my baby. An evil grin lit up it's ugly face.

My heart pounded. I groped for my dagger with shaking hands. Where was it? I never went anywhere without it. It was always at my waist. But the belt had become too tight as my pregnancy developed. And since we were so protected here, I didn't see the need to wear it. I'd left it hanging in my closet.

Damn it!

'Ya fiend from hell! Go back there,' Dougal shouted and fired off a crossbow. The arrow embedded in the lamia's leathery wing.

The attached net spread out over half the creature's body but not enough to bring it down. Its claws tore it to shreds. Several other pieces of netting clung to its other wing and one of its legs.

'Jake, it's useless!' Alec yelled as Jake stabbed at the lamia with his sword. 'Get back to the tomb.' With me in his arms, Alec turned. Dodging the scrambling men, he made for the relative safety of the sepulchre.

Over Alec's shoulder, I watched horrified as the lamia swept men out of its path like they were mere toys. Some it pierced with its venomous claws, treading on the men as they lay screaming.

Those poor men!

I caught my breath as it narrowly missed Terens, who rolled out of the way.

It rose into the air and landed in front of the tomb entrance just as we reached the steps. It stabbed one wing tip into the ground on our left, the other to our right.

We were hemmed in.

Fear for my baby made my heart race until I was almost nauseous.

With me in his arms, Alec was helpless, his sword swinging unused at his side.

I wanted to scream, and to have the strength to stand on my own so Alec wasn't hampered by me.

But wishing wouldn't make it so.

Grim faced, he took a step back, the creature's incredible stench overpowering, like a thousand rotting corpses left out in the midday sun.

The shouts, yells and screams set off Sophie, who began to cry. 'Ssshhh, it's all right, sweetheart.' I prayed with all my heart while I tried rocking her back to calm, my arms trembling.

How I wished for my blood to still be toxic. I wouldn't have hesitated in slicing open my hand and ramming it into the creature's belly. But to my horror, a thick layer of overlapping scales protected its only vulnerable spot. It had come prepared.

Jake and Kari jumped in front to shield us. Dominik tried his best to look brave. His lip quivered as he clung to Alec's side.

Alec spun around just as Terens ran toward us. 'Take her! Get them out of this! Dom, go with them. That's an order.'

What?

'I love you.' He kissed me, and in the space of a blink I found myself in Terens's arms being carried to the other end of the courtyard and away from danger. Dominik, eyes wide with terror, sprinted at Jake's heels.

'No! Take me back.'

'You and the baby come first, pet.'

My mind went blank at what Alec had done. I knew he was saving us by risking his own life. But I simply couldn't fathom existing in a world without him. And yet, as I looked into our baby's eyes—her father's eyes—the full weight of my responsibility bore down on me. She needed at least one of us alive … or so I tried to convince myself.

'Terens, stop. Please. I can't be away from him now. He's my husband. I need to be here … near him.'

Terens sighed and slowed to a halt. The easy-going and brash, almost lackadaisical, confidence he normally exuded was gone. For the first time, I saw indecision, and a pained expression crossed his face. 'We can't lose you or the baby. That thing' —he jerked his chin in the direction of the battle taking place— 'is unstoppable, and it wants to wipe out Marcus's entire line. I can't … won't let that happen.'

'You stopped it once before.'

'We used Ingenii blood back then. Smeared our swords with it, same as we did with yours. It weakened them enough to capture and cage the smelly devils. It's your blood that kills … used to kill.' He shook his head. 'It's all gone now, pet. Not a drop left anywhere.'

I looked back to where the men fought the beast, my gaze glued to Alec. He and Marcus had just succeeded in throwing another net over it, and another, and another, bagging the lamia within it. But each time, the razor-sharp claws would slice through, and it would be free again.

Please, please, please, let him live. I sent up the silent prayer.

A lone figure broke away from the others.

Kari.

She ran to us. 'They told me you look after you. So here I am. They'll take care of Old Stinky.' Although she sounded confident, the slight tremor in her voice betrayed her fear for Jake, and the way her eyes strayed back to him, I knew I was right.

Dominik sprang to her side, looking up at her like a lost puppy.

So Jake did the same as Alec. He more than cared for Kari.

'I'm glad you're with me, Kari, because—' A strange figure caught my eye. An old man had just appeared, wielding a sword of his own. He took something from his pocket and … inhaled. 'Who is that?'

Terens and Kari looked where I pointed. Terens snarled. 'Pazu!' He tensed and took a step forward, then checked himself. Responsible for me and the baby, he couldn't go anywhere near the battle.

We stood there helplessly and watched as the man entered the skirmish. Then the unthinkable happened. Time slowed till everything appeared in horrendous slow motion.

Alec turned, momentarily distracted by the Pazu's presence.

'Alec, watch out!' I cried out.

The lamia lunged toward him, claws outstretched. Alec turned back and ducked.

But it was too late. The venomous claws tore into him. He dropped his sword, doubled over and fell to the ground.

I screamed.

Startled, Sophie wailed.

Kari yelled something, but all I heard was the sound of my own voice as my world collapsed. 'Take me to him! Take me to him!' I struggled in Terens's arms as my baby cried and kicked in mine. I wanted to be with Alec, even if it meant dragging my body along the ground to be by his side.

Through blurred vision, I saw Jake lift Alec's limp body and carry it from the fray.

With my heart almost torn to pieces, I knew what I had to do. 'Kari, take Sophie. Take her to safety. Please, do it for me. I have to be with Alec.' Before she could protest, I kissed my precious babe. 'Mummy loves you very much.' I handed her into Kari's arms. 'Go now, before I break.'

Mouth trembling and face streaked with tears, Kari hugged my neck. Then with my baby safely tucked to her breast, she sped away, Sophie's cries fading until I could hear no more. I closed my eyes as my heart splintered.

'Dom, go with Kari,' Terens said. 'Protect them both.'

Dominik didn't need to be told twice. His footsteps crunched on gravel as he sprinted after her.

'I'll take you to him.' Terens's voice wavered, his chest rising and falling as he grappled with his own emotions.

As we neared where Jake knelt next to Alec, the lamia broke free from another blanket of nets. The elderly Pazu stood tall before the creature, who backed away from the sword pointed at it. It snapped at the him but continued to back away, as did Dougal's men.

The amazing power of the Pazu sword.

'He's alive … just.' Jake glanced up at us, his face pale, mouth streaked with blood as he tried sucking the venom from Alec's body. But there were too many claw points. 'I'm losing him, and there are no blood vials left.'

'Put me down.' Terens gently lowered me to my husband's side.

Alec's face was deathly white; his eyes were closed. No breath came from him. It was only a matter of time and… I couldn't finish that thought.

With shaking hands, I smoothed the hair from his brow and kissed the smooth skin, his cheeks and his mouth, the memory of our short time together tearing me apart. I brought his hand up to my lips, caressing and kissing each finger as my tears splashed down. The ache in my breast grew and consumed me, spreading through every nerve and fibre of my being, until all I knew was pain.

I clutched my breast. As I squeezed the woolen fabric, my fingers touched something hard beneath.

The blood vial!

How could I have forgotten?

It had the power to bestow life and immortality on any who drank from it. Luc had meant for me to use it if I became human after lifting the curse while Alec remained immortal. But what was immortality to me if the man I loved was dead? To face the ages alone, never to see his beloved face again, to hear his laughter or feel his touch? Immortality at such a price was no better than a living death.

I ripped the vial from around my neck and held it up.

'Take it, and give it to him!'

Understanding dawned on his face. 'That's meant for you.'

'Not without him.'

'Laura, do you know what you're doing? You're giving up your immortality.'

'Wouldn't you do it for someone you love if it meant saving their life?'

Jake studied me for a few seconds. Then his face softened, and he gave me a nod. 'Quickly then.' He tipped Alec's head back, and with my heart racing and my blood thundering in my ears, I unstoppered the tiny bottle and emptied the contents down Alec's throat.

Live, my love, live. Come back to me.

I clutched his hand. Cold, so cold. How long would it be before the blood vial worked? Or had I left it too late?

'Please, Alec, wake up. Don't leave me.' I brought his hand up to my cheek.

Time stopped.

One finger twitched, and my heart flipped.

Then the other twitched, and soon he was squeezing my hand.

A strange combination of relief, joy and laughter bubbled up from within me. And when his eyes opened and he smiled at me, all of those emotions came out at once. Barely able to see through my tears, I dropped my head to his chest and let them take me over.

Alec's arms enveloped me, holding me close to his heart as if he never wanted to let go.

I didn't want him to. Ever.

'You gave me your blood vial; didn't you?'

I nodded.

'Laura, my darling—'

I put my hand over his mouth. 'Don't say it. I don't regret it, and I never will.'

He crushed me to him, but the next instant, he was holding me at arms length, his eyes wide with concern. 'Where's Sophie? Is she—'

'She's fine. I asked Kari to keep her safe.'

From behind us, a shout cut through the night followed by the strangled screams of a creature in pain. Amid the dead and dying Brethren, the old man stood alone, the sword at his side dripping with blood. At his feet lay the lamia's body, it's head some metres away, its cold, lifeless eyes staring into nothingness.

The elderly man started to cough, bent over and fell to his knees.

Marcus tried to go to him, but he doubled over and stumbled backwards.

'Don't know if he means to kill us too. As long as he's holding the Pazu sword, we can't get near him,' Jake said.

'He doesn't look in any condition for another fight.' Alec rose and lifted me as my legs were still too weak.

'Stay here. Don't even think about going near that guy.' Jake grabbed Alec by the upper arm. 'We nearly lost you. I'm not letting that happen again.' Jake glanced at me. 'Laura, keep him here.'

'You bet I will!' I tightened my arms around Alec's neck.

A strange shimmering light appeared and hovered above the witch's tomb. It stopped Jake in his tracks. The light slowly made its way toward us. Within, I could vaguely see a human outline. Oddly, I felt no fear. More curiosity.

The strange apparition neared. It stopped in front of Alec and me and coalesced into a beautiful female form in an ankle-length gown. Her long, flowing hair floated freely about her as if blown by an invisible breeze.

Jake dropped to his knees, as did Terens, then the rest of the men who had rushed to our side when the apparition appeared.

Instinctively, I knew this was Eithne, the witch, who'd cursed Marcus and his men all those centuries ago, and who'd spoken to me when I first stepped inside her sepulchre. It could be no one else.

Smiling, she extended a ghostly hand and touched Alec's face. 'Son of my blood. You've done well, and through you, my curse is now ended. Ask me what you will, and I will grant it.'

Alec sucked in a breath, and his gaze darted to the men, still on their knees before the apparition. 'Please release Marcus and his men, my friends, from vampirism. End their suffering. I've seen the good they've done in the world, spending centuries making restitution. Isn't that enough?'

Eithne turned to the men at her feet. None lifted their heads to look at her. Maybe they didn't dare. I know Luc would have. He'd hated her for having to carry the sin of his father.

'Their suffering could end at any time by choosing death. But they did not.'

Marcus sighed. I was guessing he'd accepted his fate, and perhaps the others too, for they remained silent. Only Terens's fingers clawed deep into the grass as his hands curled into fists.

'Because of you, my son' —she returned her attention to Alec— 'I will grant them and those who they made in their image this boon: no longer shall the sun reject them. They will be free to roam under its light all the days of their lives. They will still need blood to live, but they will also be able to eat all manner of food as they enjoyed before their doom.'

Terens's head popped up first, and a smile that would melt the heart of anyone spread across his face. He turned to Alec with a tearful bob of his head.

My own eyes stung, because it meant that Kari and Dougal, and any they'd transformed, were free of the dark too. I hoped that wherever Kari was with my baby, she'd heard.

'Thank you, my lady.' Marcus rose and bowed, his men following. All glanced at Alec with grateful grins. But what of Alec? Would he remain vampire forever? I wanted to ask her, but she spoke again.

'Because you requested nothing for yourself, my son, I grant you freedom from the darkness. You were never meant to be one of the dark ones, a child of blood like they.' She darted a glance at Marcus. 'That ends this day. To you, I also give all my powers as a child of my blood.' I hoped that didn't mean what I thought it meant. 'Use them wisely, for your life will go on for many ages.'

Eithne extended her hands, palms upward, and tendrils of light flowed from them to Alec until he was covered in a bluish glow, from his arms with which he held me, to the crown of his head. Even his hair glowed and waved about as if caught in static electricity. A second later, the light receded, leaving him with eyes of the same electric blue.

'Alec, your eyes. They're blue.'

His eyebrows shot upwards. He ran his tongue along the top of his mouth. 'They're gone … my fangs. They're gone!' A wide grin curved the corners of his mouth, and he spun me in a circle from sheer joy. And I didn't want to spoil it. For me, it was a bittersweet moment. With her powers transferred to Alec, what did that now make him? A sorcerer or a wizard with an extended lifespan married to a human. Whether I aged slowly, like my mother, Judy, or rapidly now that the curse was lifted, only time would tell. Either way, I would age and die while he would remain young.

My throat dried.

Yet, there was no question about me giving my blood vial to Alec.

I had no choice.

It was either I lose him or he lose me.

That was how it was.

I took a deep breath, kept a smile plastered on my face, determined to make every moment count with him, every second last a lifetime until old age and then death took me.

I laid my head on his shoulder and closed my eyes, breathing in his heady masculine scent, a mix of a forest fresh after a storm and spicy cloves. He was danger and goodness rolled into one beautiful piece of man, and I couldn't get enough of him.

'And you, Laura, child of Rome.' I started when she addressed me. I couldn't see why she should. 'Because you sacrificed your own immortality so my son could live, with the last of my powers, I grant you this gift: so long as one lives so shall the other. Your lives are intertwined. Long shall you both live, love and prosper. And long shall be the lives of your children.'

Her words went through me like an electric shock. Not one that burned and destroyed, but one that energised and infused every cell with new life and with the promise of good things to come.

Deep down, a great welling of happiness rose from my chest. So much so, I thought it would burst from joy. My lips tried to form the words 'thank you', but they simply wouldn't come. I was too overwhelmed. But from the smile she gave me as her apparition faded, I believed she knew.

I gazed at Alec with tears swimming in my eyes.

'Forever, my darling,' he whispered, his lips cool against my brow in a gentle kiss.

'Does that mean I can daywalkee like … always, and eat whatever I want?' Kari's excited voice had me whipping around in Alec's arms. Where had she come from? Cradled in her arms was my peacefully sleeping daughter.

How had she managed to do that?

'Sure does, kiddo.' Jake stood and threw his arm around her shoulder, a beaming smile on his face.

'Me too?' Dominik stepped out from behind Kari.

Alec's smile vanished. 'I'm sorry, Dom. Only those juvy's changed by Sieur Marcus and his men, and Lord Luc and me were given that gift.' He placed a comforting hand on the boy's shoulder.

Dominik's lip quivered. 'It's not fair.' He turned and ran from the courtyard.

Alec's gaze followed him as he disappeared.

'Poor kid,' Kari said, turning sympathetic eyes after him. It wasn't often that she sympathised with the fifteen-year-old who had such a crush on her.

'Kari.' I held out my arms. She passed Sophie to me without waking her. 'You're my angel. Thank you.'

'Nah! That's what aunties are for.'

'I'd say we have an even better incentive for making a daywalking serum. What say you, Jake?'

'Definitely.' Jake tried to shake Alec's hand, which was under my knees. Amid laughter, they somehow succeeded. 'Thank you, brother. I'll never be able to repay you.'

'You owe me nothing.'

Terens, Cal and Sam surrounded us and expressed their thanks as well, clapping Alec on the shoulder and back while making funny comments about his new eye colour.

'Where did you go with her?' I asked Kari while cradling my baby's face against my cheek.

'Up there.' She pointed to the castle keep, a tall cylindrical building crowned with a conical tower. 'I reckoned we'd be safe there for a while, and I could see and hear everything that was going on.' Kari touched Sophie's cheek, her expression warm and tender as she gazed at my baby girl. 'I sang to her, and she fell weepy sleepy. We came down after miss shiny witchy disappeared.'

Marcus stood at a distance. He'd remained silent, studying Alec in a way that had my stomach in a knot. I remembered he'd made a vow to hunt down and kill every witch he could find. If he meant to keep his vow, then Alec was in danger.

I had to dissuade him, but I had no idea how.

Wheezing came from behind us. Alec turned quickly, spinning us around.

The old guy who killed the lamia. We'd forgotten about him, captivated, as it were, by another seismic event. He laid where he'd fallen. Dougal tried approaching him, but the sword prevented him getting near.

'Dougal, stay away from him,' Marcus called out. 'We need to be rid of that sword.'

No Brethren could do it, only a human, and I was the only human around. What the witch had transformed Alec into, I still had no idea, although I didn't care so long as I was with him. Were witches, wizards … whatever … humans?

I wriggled my toes and flexed my calf muscles.

'Don't even think about it, Laura.' Alec shot me a warning look. 'I'll go. And since I'm human again' —he shot me a grin—'he poses no risk to me. Besides, he looks like he needs a doctor.'

A rush of adrenaline tingled through my body. He'd read my mind. Was that a witchy thing? Guess I'd have plenty of time to find out.

Go then. I sent the thought back to him. Perhaps we'd never truly needed the serpent rings. Either that or it'd helped speed the bond that had always been there between us.

I will. He chuckled, kissed my mouth and gently put me down. Jake stood next to me in case I needed support.

Alec strode to the elderly man and crouched down next to him. He took his pulse, helped him sit up, and put his ear to his upper back. The elderly man continued to cough even after Alec placed what looked like a puffer to the man's mouth, the sort I'd often seen my asthmatic students use. But this man's cough was far worse than asthma.

He slumped back against Alec and whispered something to him.

When Alec pulled out his phone, the old man weakly raised his hand and covered the phone, then said something else.

'Can you hear what they're saying?' I asked Jake.

'Yeah. It … concerns you.'

'What? How's that possible? I don't know him.'

'Alec'll tell you.'

Alec had his head right next to the old man's ear. The old man pointed to his sword, whispered something more. Then his head fell back and he stilled.

I swallowed.

Alec looked at us and shook his head. He placed his hand on the man's chest, bowed his head, then laid him down. He reached for the sword and threw it into the air. A bolt of blue shot from his hand. The sword erupted into flame, its ashes blown by the breeze as it floated back to earth.

'Great hounds of hell! Tell me Alec just didn't do that?' Terens's mouth hung open.

As did everyone else's.

My throat dried. I'd only just gotten used to being married to a vampire, and now here he was already showing evidence of becoming a powerful witch … wizard … whatever. And from the skillful way he obliterated the Pazu sword, I took a guess that Alec hadn't only inherited the witch's power but the knowledge of how to use it. No wonder she'd said for him to be wise in applying it. He probably had all her spells and incantations and potions—or whatever witches do—whizzing through his head. I didn't know whether to be excited or concerned. Maybe both. But for the present, I concentrated on the positive.

'He sure did, and he did it for you,' I said.

Jake smiled. He hoisted me and my baby into his arms and moved forward, past the bodies of Dougal's men. I counted three slain by the lamia. Sadness welled in my chest for them and for Dougal. He and those who were left quietly gathered their dead.

Alec rose as we approached. 'Laura, there's something you need to know.' He took me from Jake, and we sat on the sepulchre's steps. 'That old man was Robert Junot, a Pazu. Sommers found him from an address he got from the Pazu youths in Sydney. Same ones who burned down the house. Sommers told old guy where to find us.'

'Oh! The tracker in my phone.' I couldn't believe Matt could sink so low as to have done something like that. But to be fair, perhaps it had been the Pazu in him. That much I was willing to concede.

Alec nodded. 'Junot wanted one kill before he died. So he acted on the information. Being in the last stages of emphysema, he had nothing to lose. He arrived here from Avignon earlier tonight, crossed paths with the lamia and followed it in when the ward collapsed. You saw the rest.'

'That's sad and horrible too. If not for the lamia, he would've tried to kill one of you.'

Again, Alec nodded. 'But he didn't. He's gone and so's the last of the lamiae. How fitting.'

'What is?'

'That they killed each other.'

'Huh! Pity he didn't show up sooner. Those men might not have died.' I looked over to where Dougal had gathered his men's bodies. Among them, surprisingly, he included Junot, a dead Pazu. 'Will he bury them or let the sun burn them?'

'The sun. He'll keep vigil over them the rest of the night, and now that he can daywalk, I reckon he'll stay to see the job done. That's what I'd do.'

'What about the elderly man, Junot? His body won't spontaneously combust.'

'The fire from our Brethren will consume him too. Dougal's awarded him a rare honour.'

The mournful notes of a bagpipe filtered down from one of the towers, where a lone piper stood on the battlements. A lament for fallen comrades. Dougal's remaining men poured petrol over the lamia's remains and set it alight. The sharp-smelling smoke was preferable to the stench that had come from the misshapen, ugly creature. When done, they joined Dougal, and by their comrade's side, fell on one knee and bowed their heads.

This scene would be forever burnt into my memory.

As was another. 'How did you know to burn the sword with magic?'

Alec released a breath—a real breath—which he normally didn't need to do. 'You're breathing!'

He grinned, then inhaled and exhaled again, fully enjoying the sensation. 'I'm completely human, and yet...' His brow creased, and he examined his hands, his fingers, as if seeing them for the first time. 'I feel this power all through me. And ... I know what to say to access it. In here.' He pointed to his temple. 'It's all already there.'

'From vampire to witch, sorcerer, wizard...?'

'Mage. That's the word that's coming to me. She was a mage. So am I.'

'This is going to take some getting used to.'

'That makes two of us.'

I couldn't help it. Maybe it was the euphoria of the moment after everything we'd gone through, but it bubbled out of me. 'Could come in handy if Dominik hacks into another website. You could just zap him!'

He stared at me for a second. Then his face lit up. 'Laura, that's brilliant!'

'What is?'

'I think I may know how to change him back.' He licked his lips, his brow furrowed in concentration. 'Dom's a regular vampire. There is a spell that counters the transformation … but it's not clear. Not sure why. I just know I can't reverse any of Eithne's curses.'

This was exciting. 'It might come to you later.'

'Hope so. The look on his face when I told him…'

'Not your fault.'

Alec sighed and pulled the blanket higher up my shoulders, letting his fingers rest on Sophie's tiny head. 'Junot asked me to destroy the sword.'

So that's why he did it. 'I told Jake you did it for them.'

'I would have still if Junot hadn't asked me to do it.'

I shrugged. 'It's gone anyway. So it doesn't really matter.'

'No, it doesn't.' His gaze turned toward the blaze where the lamia's remains had almost all been consumed by the greedy flames, the smoke of which leapt up to the clouds in a dirty column obscuring the pale autumn moon.

'Our enemies are gone too,' he added.

'So's Matt.' His face sprang to my mind.

We were silent for a moment. Although I hated to place Matt in that category, it was the truth. There was no doubt he would've killed Alec: my stars, he'd almost succeeded. My father, Luc, recognised it long before I did. I just didn't want to believe it. It still hurt when I thought of it. Which prompted another thought: had the Pazu in Matt been drawn to me the day we'd met, or had it all just been a coincidence? Chances are, I'd never know.

It was best left alone.

Exhaustion slammed into me. I leaned into Alec's shoulder, fighting my eyelids' desire to shut. Sophie whimpered and her eyes opened. 'She'll be needing another feed soon.'

'Time to get you both indoors.'

As Alec made a move to stand, Marcus approached. I tensed. Alec stiffened.

'Your vow. Am I now included in it?' For one second, tendrils of blue light illuminated his hands, then died down.

Being human, I had no magic, but if there was a way to prevent Marcus keeping his vow and hurting Alec, I'd find it. It wasn't his fault Alec was now a mage.

'Grandfather—'

Marcus held up his hand. 'Laura, mea neptis, worry not.' He came close, laid his hand on Sophie's head and kissed her. 'I would do no harm to my great-granddaughter's father or my granddaughter's husband.'

Alec relaxed. 'You know I would never—'

Marcus held his hand up again. 'Deus! Let me speak.' He inhaled deeply and folded his arms over his chest. 'The man my son trusted to carry on his legacy who also begged for my freedom ignoring his own, and the man who destroyed the only weapon that could kill me is not the sort of man I need fear as my enemy.'

'I hope never, Marcus.'

Marcus nodded, his smile deepened, and then he laughed. Great peals of booming laughter that had him in tears—real water tears, not blood. He wiped his eyes and studied his hand as if unbelieving. 'Bless you, my boy.'

He and Marcus embraced. They were finally free, no need for an Ingenii anymore. They had the daylight without it. Who would've thought it? The Principate was safe. The only question was, could Alec still remain princeps now that he wasn't a vampire?

No, I wasn't going to think about it now. That was a question for another day.

I looked into my baby's grey eyes and touched her tiny fingers to my lips, utterly content and thankful. 'Well, Sophie, shall we ask your father what he'd like to eat for dinner? He hasn't had a good meal in over a hundred years.'

I couldn't stop the smile that spread across my face.

EPILOGUE

Two Years Later

Alec stepped down from being princeps and passed it onto Marcus. The elders and prefects agreed with the decision, seeing as Alec was no longer a vampire, but they granted him a special status: Mage of the Brethren.

I called him a witch doctor.

Alec had found the spell to reverse Dominik's vampirism. Once again, the fifteen-year-old was fully human and had returned to his family in Prague. He'd also been sworn to secrecy. As far as the Brethren were aware, being adopted into Marcus clan, and underage when transformed, he'd been included in the witch's gift. Alec also gave him a hexed silver ring ensuring no vampire would ever come near him again.

Kari actually hugged him goodbye.

As each day passed, Alec began to understand his magic more, and the reason why he hadn't immediately been sure of the spell to help Dominik. It was that the mage, Eithne herself, hadn't fully explored it. She'd been studying it the week Marcus and his men had ridden into her village. And being pregnant, her magic had been restricted to protect her unborn baby.

Magic, we were quickly learning, had consequences.

We moved back to Sydney, leaving the D'Antonville Chateau to Marcus and the men. He made us promise to come back to celebrate Christmas with them there each year.

Sabine cried when we told her we were leaving. I cried too. But I told her we'd be back for Christmas. And now that the men could eat normal food again, I had no doubt she'd be busy keeping them fed.

The old Residence in Vaucluse had been burned so completely that little could be salvaged. Not even the beautiful old stained-glass window that told the story of Marcus and the witch. It had been sad seeing the wreckage, but as Alec said, it belonged to another age, and that was now past.

We constructed a lovely new house on the site, naming it Dantonville. It contains room enough for family and guests, and unlike the old house, has fire alarms and sprinklers throughout. Sophie happily ran around her new bedroom the day we moved in, chatting and giggling in excitement.

Thankfully, the fire that destroyed the old house hadn't touched the garden. The seat, where Alec and I first kissed was still there. We sit there often, arms around each other, snatching kisses while Sophie plays on the grass.

In three weeks, we celebrate my birthday and the second anniversary of our first meeting in St Andrews Cathedral: when the big, bad, beautiful vampire was waiting for me in that little alcove.

If I had known what awaited me then, would I have consented to it?

Oh yes.

Not having Alec and Sophie in my life was unthinkable, and if going through the darkness was the only way to get to this point, then, yes, I would have done it. But knowing I would also be freeing Marcus, Jake, Terens, Cal, Sam, Kari and Dougal from that dreadful curse was like the frosting on the proverbial cake.

They were my family.

Whispering through my mind, came the words, *Well done, ma petite.*

Warmth spread through my heart, and I snuggled into Alec's embrace. He pressed his lips to my brow and rested his head on mine. Sophie chuckled, chubby little arms upraised to catch the snowy petals that dropped from the Jasmine bushes.

We were home.

The End

Thank you for reading *BloodWish*, the last book in my Dantonville Legacy Series. I loved writing Alec and Laura's story, and sharing their journey with you. It's going to be hard saying goodbye to them. But all good things come to an end – a happy ending.

Keep a lookout for The Dantonville Chronicles: Jake, Terens, Sam and Cal's stories. So, there's more to come.

Until then, happy reading.

Tima Maria Lacoba

Glossary Of Characters, Places And Terms (With Some Extra Information About The Characters)

Alec Munro – Vampire, Princeps and together with Lucien Lebrettan, leader of the 'Brethren', a community of vampires living in Sydney, Australia. Originally a doctor, he had enlisted in the Australian Infantry Forces (AIF) soon after the death of his wife and child. He was later transformed by Lucien while serving in an army medical field hospital in northern France in 1918. He owns and manages a private hospital in Sydney dedicated to blood disease research.

Antonia Pulchra – Daughter of Marcus Antonius Pulcher, twin sister to Lucius. Antonia was the first to carry the Ingenii mutation. She lived for 218 years and was the mother of Paulus, the next Ingenii.

Bloodgifted – Term given to certain members of the Dantonville family who carry the cursed gene, giving them unnatural long life and youthfulness. Their blood alone provides vampires with superior strength and heightened senses, and the ability to daywalk. The Bloodgifted – Ingenii – are much coveted by the Brethren community and were the epicentre of two previous rebellions, the first taking place in the tenth century, resulting in the deaths of two of Luc's men – Galen and Martius – and another in the seventeenth century.

Blood Vault – A secret vault hidden deep beneath the foundations of Chateau D'Antonville in a series of underground caverns in the Rhone Valley. It contains thousands of vials of Ingenii blood collected by Luc through the centuries. Those who drink Ingenii blood experience superhuman strength, enhanced senses and the ability to daywalk.

Cal (Calixtus) – Vampire, former Roman soldier, First Frisian Cavalry Regiment, stationed at Vindobala (Rudchester) on Hadrian's Wall, northern Britain. Part of Marcus' Antonius Pulcher's cohort, he was cursed (along with his comrades) by a Pictish witch into vampire form. Cal is also a widower, having lost his wife in childbirth. Currently, he is bodyguard to the Ingenii, friend to Alec Munro and he owns an Armagnac distillery in France.

Chateau D'Antonville – The ancestral home of the Dantonvilles, and built over the ruins of Marcus Antonius Pulcher's original Roman villa. It is located in the Vaucluse Department of the Provence-Alpes-Cote D'Azur region in southeastern France. The Romans first settled there and produced the earliest wines. The area is littered with Roman ruins, the greatest of which is the Roman Theatre at the town of Orange (pronounced O-ronje), just a ten minute drive from the chateau. The closest cities are Lyon, to the north, and Avignon, to the south.

Constans Thierry, Madame – Human and housekeeper at Chateau D'Antonville, a position of honour in the village of D'Antonville. She is a direct descendant from one of the First Families. Constans Thierry fell in love with Luc when a young woman, and married her husband, Serge, in order to serve in the household and be close to Luc. She betrayed the family in order to have Judith and Laura killed so she could claim Luc and be mistress of D'Antonville.

Dominik – 16 year-old vampire, recently turned by Timur after having been kidnapped by him for the illegal blood-slave racket. Originally from the Czech Republic, Dominik joined the Principate side and becomes Alec's juvenile.

Dougal McTavish – Scottish stonemason transformed by Marcus in the 10th century. Guardian of Drunvela, site of the witch's tomb.

Elders – Group of the world's oldest vampires, who set the rules by which all blood drinkers must abide in order to keep their presence hidden from the human world. They have power over life and death in the Brethren community. They also officiate at every Coming-of-Age ceremony and induct the new princeps. They are among the oldest living creatures on earth.

Eilene Dantonville – Human, wife of John Dantonville. Her first child, a baby named Katie, died of SIDS aged three months. She and John accepted the infant Laura in place of their deceased daughter, in order to help out Lucien and Judith. She loved Laura as her own child.

Eithne – A Pict witch and high priestess of the Caledonian goddess of retribution, Melusine. She cursed Marcus Antonius Pulcher and his men for killing her people in the mid 3rd. century, effectively turning him and his men into vampires. She used kidnapped Roman captives as human sacrifices in bloody religious rites. Ancestress of Alec Munro.

First Families – Humans descended from the original slaves, then servants, at Marcus Antonius Pulcher's villa in Gaul. They make up the bulk of the villagers in D'Antonville, and only they know the secret of the Lords of Chateau D'Antonville.

Grey Bear – Vampire and newest elder, elected to replace the Rebel, Maris. Originally chief of the North American Indian tribe, the Shoshone, he was transformed by a medicine man, during a time of war, to protect his people.

Gilles Bouchard – Mayor of D'Antonville, from one of the First Families.

Ingenii – Latin term for "Bloodgifted".

Jake (Caius Justinius) – Vampire, former Roman soldier and physician to the First Frisian Cavalry Regiment, stationed at Vindobala (Rudchester) on Hadrian's Wall, northern Britain. Along with his comrades, he was cursed by a Pict witch into becoming a vampire. He is a close friend and colleague to Alec Munro, and loves sports cars and racing horses. Currently, he is bodyguard to the Ingenii.

Jean-Philippe Louis Auguste de Reynard – Vampire and 18th century French nobleman who once fought for Napoleon. He was Lucien's illegitimate son and Laura's half-brother. His mother was the Duchess D'Orleans. He was a well-known portrait artist who met Laura in Italy where he fell in love with her unaware he was her half-brother. Jean introduced himself to her by his second name, Philippe. Lucien broke up the relationship. Their romance is the subject of the short story **Laura's Locket.**

Jenny Callen – Human, Laura's best friend and work colleague in a primary school in Balmain. She's had several failed relationships and is currently single, although she is romantically interested in Terens.

John Dantonville – Human, Laura's foster-father and maternal uncle. He is Judith Dantonville's younger brother and Eilene Dantonville's husband. He and Eilene adopted Laura as a favour to Lucien and Judith, but came to love her as his own. His pet name for her is, "baby".

Judith Dantonville Lebrettan – Human, thirty-third Ingenii. Pressured into marrying her first husband, William Allerdyce, by her father, Owen Dantonville, to clear gambling debts. Only meant to be a business arrangement, he raped her on their wedding night. Judith met Lucien some time after and they became lovers. Later she divorced William and secretly married Luc after giving birth to their child, Laura.

Kari (Karelia Anakeinen) – Born in Finland in the late eighteenth century, Kari's family moved to France when her father was offered the position of chief stonemason on the D'Antonville estate in the Rhone Valley. She had been transformed by Jake when the rest of her family died in an epidemic, which swept the region. Kari is Judith Dantonville's best friend, and unofficial bodyguard to the current Ingenii, Laura Dantonville. She is also secretly in love with Jake.

Karl (Karel von Czernin, Count) – Vampire, Czech Prefect and principate spy who befriended Count Timur Szechenyi, the Hungarian Prefect, in order to infiltrate the Rebel ranks and learn of their plans. His easy-going nature hides a sharp mind and decisive character. He is friends with Alec Munro, and secretly in love with the Baroness Milena Flaks.

Kwome – Vampire, and one of the Elders. Originally, Kwome was king of the ancient African kingdom of Benin. He was transformed by his teacher and mentor.

Laura Anne Dantonville – Part human/part vampire, thirty-fourth – and current serving – Ingenii, and Lucien and Judith Dantonville's biological daughter. She is a primary school teacher and former girlfriend of Police Detective Matthew Sommers. Laura was raised by John and Eilene Dantonville, who she believed to be her parents. She was also Jean-Philippe's half-sister.

Lucinda Ortiz – Vampire, and daughter of a minor Spanish nobleman, transformed by Rodriguez, a juvenile sired by Timur. As a result of being turned by a juvenile, Lucinda is slightly mentally disadvantaged. To some, she is known as Loco Lucinda. While a juvenile herself, she found Jean-Philippe dying on the battlefield and turned him. She gifts Laura a beautiful antique dagger as thanks for her kindness. Currently living in hiding in Uruguay.

Maira –Vampire and newly appointed elder. Originally a princess of the Incas, she was transformed by an outcast priest of Supai, the god of death.

Marcus Antonius Pulcher – Vampire, former Roman legionary cavalry commander – Praefectus Equituum – stationed in Vindobala (Rudchester) in the 3rd century AD. It was his actions, which led to him and his men into being cursed by the Pict witch, Eithne. Marcus Antonius is the father of the twins, Lucius and Antonia, and husband to Gallia. He departed Britain after being turned into a vampire and went into hiding at his villa in Gaul (France) – Villa Antonii.

Matthew Sommers – Human, Police Detective Inspector. He was Laura's boyfriend and rival with Alec Munro for Laura's affections. He was attacked and nearly killed by rogue vampires while trying to protect her. Laura broke of their relationship at the end of Book 1 when she learnt of his plans to kill the vampire side of her family in a misguided attempt to protect her. He hates Alec Munro and does not want to let Laura go.

Mea Culpa – Latin for "My fault."

Milena (Baroness Milena Flaks) – Vampire, the Slovakian Prefect and Principate supporter. Her concerns over Count Timur's ambitions – and threat to her territory – lead her to approach Jake into becoming her consort, and thus her protector. Like other aristocrats of her generation (eighteenth century) she believes in the superiority of her noble blood, although Brethren laws discourage class discrimination. Her old-world attitude leads to clashes with more-recently turned Brethren.

O'Toole, Derek – Vampire and Prefect for Hibernia (Ireland) and loyal principate supporter. He was transformed in prison while awaiting execution for leading a rebellion against Cromwell's forces in the mid seventeenth century. His sire, tired of living, walked into the sun three-hundred years later, happy he'd seen Ireland gain its independence from the hated English.

Princeps – Latin term for First Citizen and the origin of the English word, prince.

Principate – The Brethren political system established by Marcus Antonius Pulcher and his son, Lucius (Lucien Lebrettan) to control the Brethren and protect humanity. It is composed of the Elders – Kwome, Zhao, Grey Bear and Maira – as well as Marcus, Luc and Alec. As a result of the death of Maris Quesnel, Grey Bear and Maira were appointed to the office.

Rasputin (Grigory Rasputin) – Vampire and former confidant of the last Russian royal family, the Romanovs. He was transformed in 1917 by the Hungarian noble, Count Timur Szechenyi, the Brethren prefect. Many blame Rasputin for the demise of the Russian monarchy, and his sinister influence over the royal family. Before his execution, he had the ability to mesmerise humans as well as vampires, and he used that to further his master's ambitions to overthrow the Principate.

Sabine Gilbert – New housekeeper at D'Antonville hired by Laura Dantonville to replace the treacherous Madame Thierry. She belongs to the First Families.

Sam (Sempronius) – Vampire, former Roman soldier in the First Frisian Cavalry Regiment stationed at Vindobala (Rudchester) in northern Britain. Along with his comrades, he was cursed by the Pict witch, Eithne, into vampire form. He is also the former lover and sire of Maris Quesnel. Sam is a techno-wiz and responsible for security in the Lebrettan household. Currently, when not hacking into rebel communications, he is one of the bodyguards to the Ingenii.

Serge Thierry – Human and trusted estate manager at the D'Antonville estate. He is a direct descendant of one of the First Families. His family has served as stewards at D'Antonville for over a thousand years. It is regarded as a position of honour among the villagers. One of his ancestors rode to the crusades with Lord Lucien Lebrettan.

Serpent Ring – Ancient artefact created by Marcus Antonius Pulcher on the instructions of the Pict witch, Eithne. It is in the form of a golden serpent with blazing red eyes – symbol of Melusine, the Caledonian goddess of vengeance or retribution. It renders the wearer invisible to vampire senses, as well as burning the fingers of imposters and shooting fire from the serpent's eyes destroying those who physically threaten either princeps or Ingenii. In times of danger, the eyes turn black. Every fifty years the ring is passed down to the next Ingenii.

Sieur/Seigneur – French for "Lord."

Terens (Sextus Terentius) – Vampire, former Tribune attached to the First Frisian Cavalry regiment, stationed at Vindobala (Rudchester), northern Britain. Along with the rest of the cohort, he was cursed by the Pict witch, Eithne, into vampire form. Although he has a reputation as a ladies man, Terens is also a deadly swordsman and is known to have fought off eight armed Rebels in the last rebellion. He has always wanted to try skydiving. Currently, he is one of the bodyguards to the Ingenii.

Timur (Count Timur Szechenyi) – Vampire, Hungarian Prefect and leader of the rebellion to overthrow the Principate by kidnapping the Ingenii, Laura Dantonville, and breed her with a human to produce the next generation of Ingenii. He used his family crest – a snarling wolf's head – to create the outlawed wolf's head rings, which contain a deadly white-oak spike. He is also the head of the illegal blood-slave racket, which traffics in selling underage humans to the Brethren. Timur is Rasputin's sire.

Yves Morrel – Chief of Police at D'Antonville, and one of the First Families.

Zhao – Vampire and one of the Elders. Ancient Chinese warlord turned philosopher. His sire is unknown.

AUTHOR BIO

Tima Maria Lacoba is a former ancient historian and archaeologist who accidently smashed a 3,000 Egyptian vase while on her first dig! Her supervisor made her glue it back together again. It took a week. From there she went on to specialise in late Roman-British archaeology, and the military forts along Hadrian's Wall, because buildings don't smash as easily. Now Ms Lacoba's combined her love of history with another passion—story-telling—to create a dark tale of Roman soldiers cursed by a British witch.

Tima Maria has always been a storyteller, but it wasn't until five years ago that she seriously ventured into writing. The result was *Bloodgifted*. In 2011 it was shortlisted in the Atlas Award and eventually came fourth place. In 2012 it was listed among the top ten in the Choclit Search for an Aussie Star Competition. In 2013, she was offered a publishing contract but declined in favour of going indie, preferring the idea of being in charge of her own creation.

In 2017, *BloodGifted* was nominated for the Golden Stake Award in the International Vampire Film and Arts Festival.

BloodGifted is just the start of a four-part series entitled, *The Dantonville Legacy*. Book 2 - *BloodPledge,* Book 3 - *BloodVault,* and Book 4 - *BloodWish* are available at all online retailers. She also intends to satisfy her fans requests by writing individual books on the other characters in the series. So Terens, Cal Jake and Sam will each have their own story.

Tima Maria currently lives on the Central Coast, an hour's drive north of Sydney in Australia. Her little house is surrounded by bushland, possums and seed-dropping Rosellas on one side, and waterways on the other.

Between bouts of writing, she can be found in the kitchen baking yet another chocolate recipe. This activity is responsible for forming more gothic, urban fantasy stories in her mind for future books.

ALSO BY TIMA MARIA LACOBA

The Dantonville Legacy series:

Laura's Locket: Prequel to the Dantonville Legacy Series (novella)

1. BloodGifted
2. BloodPledge
3. BloodVault
4. BloodWish

www.ingramcontent.com/pod-product-compliance
Lightning Source LLC
Chambersburg PA
CBHW020656110726
47901CB00001B/208